Praise for *Don't Try This At Home*

'Stands out from the rest' *Hello!*

'Funny and heartwarming' *Heat*

'Funny, poignant, life-enhancing – a triumph' Sue Limb

'Hilarious and moving' *Red*

'Witty, honest and upbeat' *Family Circle*

'Very funny and very poignant' *Junior Magazine*

'Witty and upbeat' *Evening Standard*

'Sparkling' *Publishing News*

'Uplifting tale, intriguingly told' *Bookseller*

'Punchy and fast paced . . . If you loved [Alison] Pearson's book
I Don't Know How She Does It, then you'll love this'
U magazine, Dublin

Also by Katie Pearson

Don't Try This At Home

About the author

Katie Pearson worked in television as a producer and director of documentaries. She lives in London with her husband and two daughters.

Katie Pearson

How Long
Have You Got?

HODDER

Copyright © 2005 by Katie Pearson

First published in Great Britain in 2005 by Hodder and Stoughton
A division of Hodder Headline

The right of Katie Pearson to be identified as the Author
of the Work has been asserted by her in accordance with the
Copyright, Designs and Patents Act 1988.

1 3 5 7 9 10 8 6 4 2

A CIP catalogue record for this title
is available from the British Library

ISBN 0 340 82704 1

Typeset in Monotype Sabon by
Palimpsest Book Production Limited, Polmont, Stirlingshire

Printed and bound by
Mackays of Chatham Ltd, Chatham, Kent

Hodder Headline's policy is to use papers that are natural,
renewable and recyclable products and made from wood grown
in sustainable forests. The logging and manufacturing processes
are expected to conform to the environmental regulations
of the country of origin.

Hodder and Stoughton Ltd
A division of Hodder Headline
338 Euston Road
London NW1 3BH

For my mother,
who has always listened to my stories.

Acknowledgements

With thanks to Moira Millar and the residents of Denville Hall, Dr Catherine Waight at the Trinity Hospice, Anne Johnson, Elspet Rix, Tracey Gillham, Evie Garrett, Rona Bourke, Beryl Roberts and all the staff and residents at Cecil Court and my new old friend Kay Hempsall. To Bridget Sneyd, Emma Birkin and Ben Gale who gave me insight into the workings of television today. To all those people who have been sounding boards for this book and provided endless support, especially Claire Harrison, Robert Pearson, Renee Knight, Mandy Richardson, Caro Newling, Rachel Gaunt, Christine Hall, Eric Harwood, Carolyn Ware, Emma and James McCarthy, David Presswell, Gaye Wolfson, Phoebe Fortescue, Anna Ledgard, Helena Kukec, Mark Brighton and Isla Dawes at the Kew Bookshop. To Carolyn Mays for her editing expertise; Helen Campbell, the copyeditor who had a difficult job; Karen Geary, Alex Bonham and the whole team at Hodder. To Clare Conville, my brilliant agent, Maddie and Isabella, my lovely girls but above all to Marcus for just about everything.

'Below my window . . . the blossom is out in full now . . . I see it is the whitest, frothiest, blossomiest blossom that there ever could be, and I can see it. Things are both more trivial than they ever were and more important than they ever were, and the difference between the trivial and the important doesn't seem to matter. But the nowness of everything is absolutely wondrous.'

An extract from Melvyn Bragg's
'An Interview with Dennis Potter',
Channel 4, March 1994

Summer 1997

I can't remember how long we'd all been standing there, at least forty pairs of eyes looking upwards at the sky, but it felt like for ever and my neck was beginning to ache.

'Come on,' muttered Matt under his breath.

'Over there,' cried a hopeful voice. Like rows of sunflowers we all turned towards a thin ray of sunlight peeking round the thick cloud, and the hill in front of me gradually lit up as if a blind was being pulled. I felt the baby squirm in my stomach, still a new sensation for me, and I wondered whether he or she was sharing my excitement at the thought that we might, at last, be able to film.

'Everyone ready,' I shouted.

'Camera running, standby everyone,' called Matt. I could feel the excitement and tension as we all braced ourselves to start. 'At speed . . . and action.'

The incongruous sound of the opening bars of Kylie Minogue's 'I Should Be So Lucky, Lucky, Lucky' reverberated around the Scottish hills and to my horror I realised that it was coming from my mobile phone in my pocket. I wished I'd never changed the ring tone. Someone shouted, 'For God's sake turn the bloody thing off.' I fumbled in my jeans pocket, trying to get hold of the trilling phone, as eager to get rid of it as if it were a ticking bomb. I answered it quickly, turning my back on the crew and walking away, hearing my brother's familiar voice in my ear.

'Molly, I'm sorry to call but . . .'

'Tim, I can't talk now.'

There was silence the other end of the phone and then in a low voice he said, 'I thought you should know Dad's had a stroke, he's in hospital.'

My stomach lurched and the baby inside me lashed out. It took all my strength to speak.

'Will he be all right?'

'They don't know; he's having tests.'

'Should I come immediately?'

'I can't answer that, Molly, it's up to you,' Tim said, his voice breaking with emotion. 'I just thought you should know.'

I turned back to see a row of anxious faces staring at me, waiting for me to get off the phone and get on with my job. It had taken months of planning and research to set up this moment and their frustration was palpable.

'We've got about three more minutes, Molly, until we lose the light,' Matt called, trying hard to hide his irritation. This was the biggest opportunity of my career and all these people depended on me.

'Tim, I've got to go. I'll call you later.'

'Bye, Molly.' His voice sounded small and helpless and I felt terrible as I switched off the phone, knowing that he needed to talk but only too aware that everyone was waiting for me. All eyes were on me and I felt as if they were all, as one, holding their breath in anticipation. I stared up at the sun and the brightness nearly blinded me.

One

Now you see me.
Now you don't.
Now you see me.
Now you don't.

I'm sitting in the reception area, watching my reflection come and go in the automatic doors that swish open and close as regularly as a beating heart. I'm rather enjoying this time to myself, doing nothing except watch everyone as they pass by. It takes me a while to work out what's so different about them all. Then, very slowly, it dawns on me that I'm not used to seeing so many people of this age group together, my life being confined to mums over thirty-five and small children all below the age of seven. As they pass they look vibrant, confident, relaxed, and above all interesting. The girls are beautiful, their clothes suit them perfectly, and they all seem to have an innate sense of style, even if most of them are still wearing jeans. I wasn't like that at their age – I'm certainly not like that now. It took me far too long to decide what to wear this morning and I feel awkward and overdressed in my brown skirt and white Gap shirt, which was the only thing that seemed to look right to my dated eyes. I look down at my jacket sleeve and I'm reminded that the children had baked beans for tea last night.

I begin to be aware of my breathing – in, out, in, out – moving in time to the swish of the doors. And then for a few minutes the reception clears, the doors stay closed and I realise I'm holding my breath. I force myself to take a quick breath but I've lost the rhythm and I start to wonder how to take the next one. I look longingly at the doors and pray that someone will walk in or out

3

– I'm not fussy. What's happening to me? Surely breathing is the most natural thing in the world – I've done it all my life, so why stop now? Immediate diversionary tactics are necessary: I pick up a copy of *Heat* magazine and as I start to look at an unfortunate picture of Julia Roberts' hairy armpits I forget about forcing the breath and my breathing resumes its regular pattern. I look around anxiously, wondering if anybody has noticed, and the thought crosses my mind: how can I expect to go back to work if I can't even remember how to breathe?

I haven't worked for seven years. It didn't feel like not working but that's what people say, isn't it? 'So you've given up work, have you?' I find it hard not to shout back, 'No, I bloody haven't.' Being at home and looking after the children has got to be the hardest work I've ever done in my life. To be honest, most of the time I've enjoyed it, although I do have difficulties sometimes when the words 'I'm a full-time mother' stick in my throat. Before anyone's eyes glaze over I have to point out quickly that I used to be interesting when I worked in television. One man I was sitting next to recently at supper said, 'Did you make children's programmes?' as if that was all I was fit for. Believe it or not, I had quite a successful career making domestic documentaries and was renowned for my intimate portraits of people's lives. I was so proud when one reviewer called me 'the Jane Austen of documentaries'. I should have had the comment framed and placed alongside my husband Aidan's advertising awards displayed in the loft which has just been converted into his study.

'Molly?' a voice murmurs in my ear and I turn quickly to see a tall man peering round my chair to see who I am. Rod Harman always did get too close for comfort.

'Rod!' I say, trying to sound delighted as I struggle to stand up out of the comfy chair.

'All ready for your first day back in an office then?' he says, his patronising tone almost as annoying as the way his attention is immediately diverted by a girl walking by in a tight T-shirt,

4

her tummy button showing. We both stop talking to watch her and my instinct is, 'She'll catch her death in this weather,' whereas Rod's expression can only be described as leery. I suddenly feel my age as I realize that I'm yesterday's woman.

'I'll see you upstairs, Molly,' he says, distracted, and before I get a chance to reply he disappears through the automatic doors in hot pursuit of the bare belly button.

I feel immense relief as I catch sight of Cassie by the lifts and she waves me over.

'Hello Mole.' It's her affectionate name for me. Although I feel comforted by Cassie's familiar face, she does nothing to boost my confidence, as she is further confirmation that I'm definitely wearing the wrong clothes.

Cassie's style is unique. She's never power-dressed or spent a fortune on clothes but she's one of those annoying women who can go into a charity shop and find a fantastic coat for 50 pence, which on her looks great but would make me look like an old bag lady. Today she's wearing a long black full skirt over cowboy boots with a thin, tight-fitting mesh black top, inset with a pattern of dark pink roses, and a thick black leather belt slung over her slender hips.

'I should've worn my jeans,' I say miserably.

'Don't be daft, you look fine.'

An attractive, boyish man with dark curly hair, wearing fashionable thin, horn-rimmed glasses, is waiting by the lifts when we step out. He moves out of the way to let us pass. I smile a thank-you and he looks straight through me, shattering my confidence. I can feel the first cracks starting to appear like in a windscreen that has been hit by a tiny stone.

'How old are these people?' I ask Cassie, and she laughs.

'Robin, whom we just passed, I think he's in his late twenties – it's not that young, Mole.'

Cassie looks much younger than the rest of us; her skin is a tawny gold, even in the depths of winter, and she has a small head with elfin features, which makes her look younger than her thirty-eight years. During the seven years I've been at home Cassie has been consolidating her successful career so that now she is considered one of the best executive producers working in documentaries. I wonder if that's what's kept her looking so young.

'Anyway it's good to work with fresh blood; it keeps you interested and open to new ideas,' she says confidently as she strides along the corridor.

'I suppose so. Doesn't it make you feel old?'

'I don't think about it, I just concentrate on the job. I don't feel any different from anyone else. I know I'm more experienced but I also welcome new influences. You've got to, otherwise you're dead.'

Even from the lifts you can feel the buzz of the office. A film crew overtakes us, having just returned from a shoot with some rushes that are obviously needed urgently. As we follow behind them hurrying along the corridor, the lights are dimmed and we pass a row of makeshift editing suites. In the first cubicle an image of a beautiful actress, whom I recognise from a popular soap opera, is shimmering and flickering, frozen on a screen. She appears to be in a jungle, and sitting very close behind her is a large orang-utan, examining her head like he's searching for nits in her hair. Her expression is an interesting mix of sheer terror and worry about how she looks for the camera. We pass another cubicle and on a small screen a woman has her hands clasped tightly over her eyes and a voice off camera is laughing and saying, 'You can look now, it's not that bad.' Unable to take her hands away from her eyes for fear of what she might see, she moans in a muffled, pained voice, 'I know it's going to be pink, I can feel that it's pink. I hate pink.' I slow down as I really want to see what colour they've painted the poor woman's room but Cassie is striding on ahead, disappearing round a corner, and I don't want to lose her.

As I run to catch her up I hear screaming but Cassie, oblivious, strides on. She passes a final, larger edit suite, which houses a number of screens. Emblazoned across all of them is a close-up of a woman giving birth. This time I stop to watch the baby's head crowning and I feel a pull as if someone has squeezed my ovaries. I must have seen similar scenes many times on television or in films but there is something striking and miraculous about the way it's been shot. The editor leans back in his chair, unmoved by the scene playing out in front of him, which I expect he has seen replayed a thousand times, and says to a young girl, who looks about twelve, but I assume is the director, 'I could murder a latte and a doughnut, how about you?'

She nods her head and carries on writing notes on her shot list while the cries of a baby replace the woman's screams. On the cubicle partition there is a card which says: 'Seven Ages – Episode 1 – Mewling and Puking'.

By now Cassie has disappeared into an open-plan office and I run to catch up with her again, hearing a young researcher shout, 'Fiona, try the dodgy major, he's up for anything at the moment. Failing that there's always the Hamiltons. The person we really need is Gordon fucking Ramsay.' Despite the pressurised atmosphere it feels reassuringly familiar, a microcosm of the BBC where I used to work.

I follow Cassie into her office, which is cordoned off by a glass partition. 'It looks like there's some interesting programmes being made.'

Cassie looks at me and smiles, perhaps a little too patronisingly. 'We're doing well at the moment, but it just creates more of a pressure to keep the ideas flowing to try and get the commissions, which is where you come in.'

'I hope I'm up to it,' I say nervously, looking at all the earnest young faces in the open-plan office.

'Of course you are,' Cassie says, as if the thought has never crossed her mind that I would be anything but capable.

'OK, so where are you going to set up? I'll get Jade, the production secretary, in to talk you through everything – I'm sorry I can't do it myself but I'm due in a sound recording in . . .' she looks at her watch, 'shit, in twenty minutes.' She gathers up everything she needs and then, seeing my face, says, 'Don't worry, Jade will explain all the programmes and help you get set up with a work station. Good luck – give them hell, girl.'

It was only six weeks ago that I first asked Cassie's advice about coming back to work and I was as nervous then as I am today. It was one of those beautiful September days that seem more poignant because you know that summer is coming to an end, and we had decided to make the most of it by having a picnic in Richmond Park. As usual Aidan wasn't with us, I can't even remember what the excuse was this time, so it was just Cassie, Will, her other half, the children and me. As soon as I mentioned to Cassie the idea of coming back to work in television I knew I was in trouble because of the way she started fiddling intently with her digital camera and avoided eye contact.

'I mean, how hard would it be? I haven't worked for seven years but it's not that long, is it?' I said hopefully.

She took a picture of the children as Will patiently tried to explain the rules of baseball. Max looked more interested in hitting Evie than the ball, swiping at the back of her legs and then saying, 'Sorry, didn't mean to.' A golden labrador was standing next to them, his tongue hanging out, ready to leap into action the moment the ball was hit. In the distance his owner was calling but the dog refused to respond.

'You do realise that as far as television's concerned we're talking dog years?' Cassie said, still without looking at me. I knew she was right and that I was being naïve to think that I could just walk back in whenever I felt like it.

'Do you think it's hopeless then?'

'No, of course not,' she said, sounding unconvinced. 'It's just it has changed since your day.'

'You make it sound like I was making programmes with Muffin the Mule, broadcasting live from Allie Pallie.'

'Come on, you know what I mean. Budgets are as tight as the researchers' T-shirts and broadcasters are obsessed with ratings.'

Max was holding the bat in position while Will bowled at him. He took a huge swipe and, to our amazement, made contact. Evie ran after the ball, unaware that the labrador was chasing after her.

'People will see me – right? I mean, I've made some good films in my time – doesn't that count for something?'

'Yeah,' replied Cassie, hesitating.

'What do you really think? Be honest with me, Cass,' I said.

Her neck flushed red but she was a good enough friend to look me straight in the eye as she delivered the bad news.

'I think you might have a problem. I mean, think about the past seven years – don't get me wrong, I'm not belittling what you've been doing with the children, but I know that if it was me I wouldn't trust myself to come back to work. You're out of the loop.'

I felt the blood rush to my cheeks as she continued, 'Also, you know what it's like, they're always after the next big thing and there's plenty of them about. There's this new guy, Robin, who is straight out of advertising and doesn't know how to keep a camera still. It drives me mad but everyone else thinks he's a bloody genius.'

We were interrupted by Evie shrieking and instinctively I leapt to my feet to see her holding the ball above her head while the labrador jumped up, barking loudly and trying to get it. The more Evie cried, the more excited the dog became, thinking it was all part of the game. I ran over to her just as the dog's owner came panting up, grabbed the dog by its collar and dragged it away, apologizing profusely.

I was in shock, not because of the dog, but because of what Cassie had been saying. As I calmed Evie down and walked slowly back to where Cassie was still sitting under the horse-chestnut trees on our tartan picnic blanket, I tried to remind myself of all the skills I'd acquired while being a full-time mother – nurse, coun-sellor, chef, referee, international peace negotiator. Once you've organised successful children's birthday parties for a group of raucous six-year-olds, a film shoot would seem like child's play. Then I realised that of course Cassie has little concept of what my life has been like, of what being a mother entails. She probably thinks I sit around all day baking cakes, shopping and having picnics. But the awful truth is that most of the people who are in a position to hire me will be the same or worse. They're either too young to care, or if they have had children and continued working they may be resentful that I've had the chance to take the time off. You can't have it all – we all know that now. It's official. I made the choice, I gave up work and now I'm paying the price.

I passed Evie a lemon lolly from the ice box and offered one to Cassie who shook her head. Evie sat beside me watching Will and Max play, taking it in turns to hit the ball.

Cassie sighed. 'It's about passion and commitment. You know what the job entails – it's an obsession – but now you have a new obsession, two of them, and that's not a criticism by the way,' she added before I could take offence. Cassie's obsession over the past seven years has been her career and now she is a successful executive producer who can pick and choose her projects. A part of me wonders, if I had carried on working, would I be in her position now? And would I want to be?

'It's what's right – you save your passion for your children, for something more deserving than sixty minutes of programming that eats into your life and then is forgotten in a day, a week if you're lucky. When you had Evie you made the right choice, you really did. Why change it now?'

Evie looked at Cassie when she mentioned her name. 'Change what?' she asked in between licks of her lolly.

'Nothing,' I said quickly, not wanting her to know what we were talking about. 'Just boring grown-up stuff.'

Evie stood up and looked around nervously to check that there were no marauding dogs anywhere, then walked down to where the boys were still playing amongst the long grass. I knew she wanted to show off to Max that she had got a lolly.

Cassie looked at me, uncomprehending. 'Why on earth do you want to come back to work, Molly? I thought you enjoyed being at home?'

I had no option but to tell her. 'Aidan has been made redundant.'

'What?' she said, amazed.

'I know, I can't believe it either.'

'How can he be kicked out of his own company? It's not possible.'

'Believe me, it is. You know he's been keen to move into film production? Well, his partners were all dead against it – they felt it was too risky. It turns out that Aidan committed them financially to a production deal that none of them agreed to. The project collapsed, taking the money with it. Once the partners found out, understandably they were furious – so he's out, no redundancy, nothing, just years of hard work down the drain.' I raised my hands in a gesture of hopelessness.

'Shit. How's he taking it?' Cassie asked.

'I'm not sure. He doesn't talk about it. I think he's trying to wrestle with his conscience.'

'What, Aidan?' said Cassie.

'Don't be like that. I know he can be difficult and sometimes a little opinionated but I think that's what he's finding so hard – there's no one to blame but himself. He knows he was stupid, he pushed things too far, and he was arrogant enough to think he could get away with it.'

'Mum!' Max shouted, his tone full of hurt indignation because he had suddenly realised that Evie had an ice lolly and he didn't.

'There's one here for you when you want it,' I shouted, and turned to Cassie, who was now lying back, resting on one elbow so that she could look at me.

'No one else knows, so don't tell anyone.' My head was throbbing and I could feel a tightness in my chest.

'Molly,' Cassie leant forward and patted my hand reassuringly, 'he'll be fine – it's not as though he's done anything illegal. It won't be long before he'll get another job; he's one of the best in the business.'

'He's decided he wants to write a film script.'

'Right. Of course he does.' Cassie has always found Aidan exasperating. 'But the money has got to come in from somewhere,' she said practically, now fully understanding my position. She looked at me sympathetically. 'The one thing that never changes about television is that it's all about ideas – good, current, fresh, original, exciting ideas. Come up with a good one and it doesn't matter how old you are, you'll get a job.'

So I did what she said and I came up with some ideas, every possible moment when I was ironing, cleaning, tidying up the children's rooms, cooking, walking to school. I carried a small notebook around with me and like an enthusiastic train spotter I wrote down every useful thought. Once the children were in bed I sat at the computer and worked up the ideas and after a few weeks I had what I hoped was a respectable list which would revive my career and our fortunes.

Cassie persuaded Rod Harman to look at them. We had worked together years ago when he was Head of Documentaries and had a formidable reputation for making groundbreaking films. His programmes were contentious but sympathetic, yet in the real world his insensitivity was legendary. No one would even bother to ask Rod for compassionate leave. I used to give him the benefit of the doubt, and perhaps because of that he had a bit of a soft spot for me. So when Cassie mentioned that I was interested in developing some ideas, and particularly when she pretended that quite a few companies were keen to recruit me (all lies as no one had even bothered to reply to my carefully crafted begging letters), he agreed to look at my ideas and eventually made me an offer.

I'm staring at the enormous production board, which is similar to the boards they have in the ER at hospitals, but hopefully these productions won't involve any blood, sutures or broken bones – mind you, if they did, that would probably be good for the ratings. The production secretary, Jade, is also wearing a tight top, which modestly covers her belly button but leaves little to the imagination. There's a glint of gold in her mouth, and trying not to look like I'm staring, I eventually work out that she has a stud in her tongue. She is talking me through the different ideas in a monosyllabic voice.

'We're excited about the new Victoria Beckham programme, *Poth Noth*.'

'Sorry?'

'*Poth Noth*,' she says emphatically, and I look at her blankly. 'Victoria Beckham's new cookery show.'

'Oh, *Posh Nosh* – great idea,' I try to say encouragingly.

She looks at me as if I'm displaying early signs of dementia. 'Victoria'th been in for meetings. She'th got amazing legth.'

I'm watching her lips intently, trying to make sense of what she's saying.

'*Meet the Family* is a genetic programme.' I think she means genealogy but I don't want to stop her in mid-flow. 'People write in and we help trath their family treeth with the help of Michael Woodth – you know, that good-looking bloke who doeth all the hithtory thtuff. Rod's a bit worried that he's a bit too old but he thinkth he might have the Thean Connery factor and he ith an expert.'

'How old is he?' I enquire.

'God, I think he'th well over thirty-five.'

'What about these other programmes?' I ask quickly, changing the subject.

'*I'm a Thelebrity and I Want to Thtay at Home* – a member of the public goes to thtay with a thelebrity and you get to thee how they live. I really want to work on that one. I'm hoping that Rod will thtart letting me do thome retheach but what I really want to do ith prethent.'

I say nothing, but nod as if it's the obvious thing she should be doing. Is it my imagination or is she talking to me more loudly than normal, as if she thinks I might be a bit slow or hard of hearing?

'This one – *Seven Ages* – that looks interesting.'

She lowers her voice. 'Nah, if you athk me it'th a bit boring but it'th Rod'th big commithion. They're following theven different characterth at different thtages in life.'

I think about the woman giving birth whom we saw as we passed by. 'Are they editing the first one already?'

'Yeah – it'th all about the firtht year in a baby'th life.' She wrinkles her nose with disdain. 'I wouldn't mind doing the romantic one but imagine having to do a lot of filming with babieth being thick and all that crying. I wouldn't want to do the old age one either, thpending weeks with thome boring old biddieth – that'th what Robin ith doing. He doethn't theem to mind though. He'th really brilliant.'

She nods in the direction of the young director with the glasses and cool blue eyes who ignored me by the lift. He's sitting at a desk talking on the phone and I overhear him saying, 'She's a dear old bat, reminds me of my gran and she's a real character. She's still working as an actress and she's got more energy than me – mind you, it was one of those nights last night. Look, I can't talk now, I've got so much to do.'

I walk off, trying to find somewhere to set up a base. Jade calls after me, 'Thit anywhere you can find a thpace.'

I put my bag on a desk near the door but it takes me a while to find a free chair. No one speaks to me, everyone is working hard and far too busy for old-fashioned courtesies such as saying hello. The atmosphere is deadly serious, and earnest young faces, entirely focused on their work, surround me. I look at the clock on the wall – 10.35 and I wonder if Max has stopped crying. I take out my mobile to ring the school.

'Lizzie,' I whisper into the phone, so that no one can overhear, 'It's me, Molly – Max's mum. How is he?'

'He's fine – stopped crying the minute you had gone. Don't fuss.'

Dropping Max off at nursery school is usually a simple affair without any trouble – normally he skips into the classroom – but today he was not his usual cheerful self. He was quiet on the way to school and when we walked into the main entrance it was as if he could sense my nervousness. When I took off his coat he burst into tears and threw his arms round my neck. 'Don't go. Don't leave me.'

I had a very different reaction when I said goodbye to Evie outside her classroom. I kissed her goodbye as I do every morning and said nervously, 'Wish me luck.'

'Good luck,' she said obligingly as I hugged her, and when she reached the door of the classroom she turned and said, 'What for?'

'I told you, I'm going back into an office today for the first time since you were born.'

'Oh, right,' and she gave me a thumbs-up sign and disappeared into the classroom.

It was only a few weeks ago that I overheard a conversation Evie had with her friend Scarlet when we were walking back from school. Max was running ahead, hiding in all the driveways and behind the lamp posts, and as we passed by he would jump out at us while I feigned surprise. I could hear snippets of the girls' conversation.

'What does your mum do?' asked Evie.

'She's a lawyer,' Scarlet replied in a matter-of-fact tone. 'What about your mum?'

I strained to hear Evie's response and for a long time she didn't say anything but I knew she was thinking about it. Then I heard her say, 'Nothing, but she talks a lot on the phone.'

I resisted the urge to catch them up to try to explain how hard it is even to attempt to be a domestic goddess, but for the first time since Aidan told me he'd lost his job I felt glad that I might be going back to work.

Since overhearing Evie and Scarlet's conversation I've spent the last few days making the point, 'Now, I won't be here when you get back from school, Evie, as I'm *going to work*.' 'Aidan, will you cook supper tomorrow as *I'm going to be out all day at the office*.' 'You'll have to pick up Max from nursery school on Tuesday as I will be out *working hard*.' While Evie was unaffected by my unsubtle attempts to point out that I was going back to work, it has obviously backfired horribly on Max who has become a bundle of nerves.

Lizzie, the headmistress, hurried along the corridor, saying brightly but firmly in a sing-song voice, 'Come along, Max darling, we've got some lovely things for you to do today. We don't want tears all over Mummy's nice suede jacket, do we?' The state of my jacket was the last thing on Max's mind as he clung on to me.

'This is so unlike him,' I said miserably, as Lizzie began to prise his fingers one by one from around my neck. 'Go,' she mouthed at me over his head.

'Bye, Max. I'll see you later. Daddy will pick you up. That will be a nice treat,' I added lamely, feeling as if my heart was being wrenched from my body in some primitive form of tribal sacrifice. Max howled loudly and held out his hands as if we were being separated for ever.

Outside the school I noticed my own hands were shaking and I strained to hear if Max was still crying. For a brief moment I wondered whether I should cancel going into the office but I knew I couldn't as it would look terrible on my first day and confirm everyone's suspicions that I'm not capable of coming back to work.

I can hear the noise of children in the background as Lizzie talks to me, telling me how happy Max is, and I feel my shoulders drop now that I don't have to worry about him.

'My husband will pick him up . . .'

'Settling in, are you?' I look up and see Rod Harman and immediately switch off the phone as I don't want to give the wrong impression on my first day but I pretend to carry on talking.

'Yes, I'd be very interested in coming to meet you – it sounds an interesting story. Sorry,' I mouth at him, and indicating the phone I say, 'A possible interview for a series I thought might be interesting.'

A corner of his mouth curls upwards in an attempt to smile.

'Monday at ten will be great,' I continue my pretend conversation. 'Until then, bye. Sorry about that,' I say as I put down the phone, trying to look as if I'm being incredibly busy and efficient.

'I just wondered if you're settling in – Jade been showing you round, has she?'

'Yes – very illuminating.'

'I'm afraid we're a bit tight on space but we've got to keep the overheads low. Sorry to start you on a Friday but I wanted to be here on your first day and I've got to go away for a couple of days next week.'

And not just any old Friday, I think to myself, but Halloween, traditionally a busy time in the Taylor household. I managed to finish the pumpkins this morning, having searched for hours for the special pumpkin knife, which I eventually found in Aidan's tool box rather than my knife drawer. Last year I actually made pumpkin soup out of the pulp, but this year it all went straight into the bin. I stared at the vivid orange pulp, the pips like large almonds, and thought a little sadly that now I'm back at work my soup-making days are over.

'So next week you'll be fine using this desk and then we just have to move around as new people come and go. You'll get used to it.'

My heart sinks. Does he think I'm going to come in every day?

'Umm, Rod, to start with I'll only be doing a few days a week, is that OK?'

'Oh, why is that?'

'I'm still trying to sort out childcare,' and I immediately wish I hadn't said anything. I'm tempted to add, 'Not easy to find childcare when you're not being paid any money,' but I think better of it. The truth is that Rod only offered me a chance to come and develop the ideas in the office, and if any get commissioned it's only then that I start getting paid. It seemed a desperate move but at least it's got me back into an office and we've both agreed to a trial period of a month. I won't be able to afford any longer.

'It'll all be fine by next week,' I say as casually as I can.

'Good,' he says, and then he looks at me thoughtfully. 'Molly, do you think you're ready for this? This is quite an opportunity for you and you know I expect commitment. It's incredibly competitive out there and we need more commissions. You've got to be quite tough to make programmes these days.'

I rack my brains trying to think how to prove to him that I'm tough enough to be here and for a brief second I'm tempted to pour my cappuccino over my hand and not flinch to prove how hard I can be. But instead I say, 'Don't worry about me, I'm fine and quite able to deal with being back in an office and developing some great programme ideas. Just give me a little time to get back into the swing of things. I've only been here ten minutes.'

'Mmm.' He looks at me dubiously and then changing the subject, he says, 'I liked your idea about the registry office – *Births, Marriages and Deaths* – it's got it all, hasn't it, especially if you find the right characters and perhaps work out an interactive element. I think it could be a runner. I need some blue-sky thinking, Molly. We should have a meeting once you've got yourself sorted.'

'Great,' I say, trying to sound confident. 'I'll talk to Jade when I've got something to show you.'

'And we must do lunch.'

'Yes, that would be lovely.' Some things never change.

'Anyway, welcome to Pulse Productions.'

I wonder how long it will take me before I stop thinking of split peas and start thinking of 'Fingers on' whenever the name of the company is mentioned. I watch Rod as he walks towards Robin's desk, my smile superglued to my face, masking the panic I am feeling. He stops when he reaches Robin who is blatantly ignoring him.

'Filming starts tomorrow then – are you ready?'

Robin isn't eager to respond, unlike me who jumps to attention any moment that Rod might be nearby, but he leans back in his chair and slowly takes off his glasses, rubbing his eyes.

'We're cool.'

'Who's your DOP?'

'Matt Harvey.'

I have to resist the urge to shout across the office, 'I know him.' Matt and I worked together on the first film I ever directed and we made a great team. Since then we worked on at least five projects together and by the last film I began to wonder whether I could make a film without him. We had a complete under-standing, which went beyond words. I would see something out of the corner of my eye and as I went to whisper in Matt's ear to change his shot I'd discover that he had anticipated what I was going to say and had already made the adjustment. After I stopped working we still kept in touch, but as I became more immersed in childcare we found we had less in common and contact dwindled to Christmas cards. It's a relief to hear a name I recognise at last.

I spend a busy morning on the phone ringing round registry offices trying to gauge the characters that work there and see if it would be possible to make a series. Although I'm enjoying being Molly Mankin again rather than 'Max and Evie's mum', I'm trying to fight off the wave of depression that Rod's comments have induced. I'm sure you don't have to be that tough, for God's sake; surely it depends on what programmes you're making. It's not as if I'm trying to get back into the army. I glance at the clock, 12.30. I wonder if Aidan has remembered to pick up Max; maybe I should give him a quick call. I take out my mobile and start to ring the number and then hang up. It will only infuriate Aidan if he thinks I'm checking up on him. I've got to have more faith in him. But Max will be miserable if he has forgotten. I dial the number and the answerphone kicks in, so I don't leave a message and feel a sense of relief that Aidan must be at the school already. I knew I shouldn't have worried.

The office never clears, as no one seems to break for lunch. Jade does a sandwich run for everyone and I escape into the cloak-rooms to have a moment to collect my thoughts. The sound of my mobile shatters my moment of peace.

'Molly, it's Lizzie at school.' My heart flutters.

'What's happened? Is Max all right?'

'Yes, he's fine, but he's still here. No one has come to pick him up . . . yet,' she adds.

'I'll sort it out. How long are you staying?'

'We've got some clearing up to do so we'll be here for another half an hour.'

Bloody Aidan. Where is he? I ring his mobile and to my relief he answers it immediately, sounding in a very good mood. 'Hello, my love.'

I can hear the sound of people talking in the background. I don't believe it but I think he's in the bloody pub. Hardly able to get my words out, I say tersely, 'Aidan . . . Max.'

'Oh shit.' He immediately remembers where he's supposed to be. 'I completely forgot. I'll go now, it won't take a minute. Bye.' He's gone, leaving me bubbling with fury.

The rest of the day is spent on the phone trying to set up some meetings. I enjoy it despite the fact that I keep glancing at the clock and ringing Aidan to make sure he's remembered to collect Evie, nagging him to remember to take her to a Halloween party. I remind him that the silver glitter is in the kitchen drawer and he'll have to paint her face, oh, and don't forget to put on the pasta for Max's supper as he needs to eat around 5.30 otherwise he'll get grouchy. He tolerates my incessant calls because he knows he made a mistake. I'm still too angry with him to talk civilly and just bark orders over the phone.

It's hard to know when to leave, as everyone else seems to be staying, working late, and I don't want to be the first one to go. Rod is on the phone in his office, Robin is looking at some story boards in preparation for the next day's filming, and even Jade doesn't look like she's going to leave for some time. Other researchers and producers are still working – maybe this is what it's like these days. Six-fifteen and still no signs of departure. I'm fretting that we haven't got enough treats at home for Halloween.

For a few brief minutes I contemplate setting off the fire alarm and using it as a smokescreen to get out of the building. There's no way I'll be home for bathtime now, but I console myself that it's only for one day. I get up to go out to the loo, hoping that the movement will encourage people to think about leaving. I meet Robin on the way and I can't take my eyes off his low-slung jeans with his underpants clearly evident above the belt line. I look up to see him staring at me and as I feel myself redden I try to recover my composure.

'Matt is a great cameraman – he has a good eye,' I say, trying to sound knowledgeable. Robin looks a little surprised that I should have a view on any cameraman's abilities. 'We've worked together in the past,' I say by way of explanation, 'send him my love. Oh, I'm Molly Mankin,' I add with a little laugh. 'I'm here doing a bit of development for Rod,' I explain.

'Oh, OK,' he says, uninterested. I wander off in the direction of the loos feeling even more like a dinosaur, from my age down to the size of my brain. On my return my heart skips a beat when I see Jade picking up her jacket. Thank God, I can go now. I grab my jacket and bag. 'Bye?' I say hopefully.

She picks up her jacket and slips it on to the back of the chair, then sits down again. 'Oh, I'm not going yet – it just fell off.'

Inwardly I groan but it's too late because now I've got my coat on and my bag in hand. I've got to be more independent and not worry so much about what they might all think. It's ridiculous.

'Well, I'm off. See you Monday. Happy Halloween.' No one responds and I leave feeling old and a little foolish.

It's twilight as I walk back from the Tube, the sky a pale inky blue and the street lamps breathing light on to the mini-bite-sized ghosts and ghouls. I stand back, waiting for a group of excited witches to walk up the path and knock on our door. It takes a few seconds before I recognise Evie, wearing her best Hermione Granger expression, which is a mix of trying to look clever and cool.

The door opens and I see Max's little face, excited and worried about what he might see, peer nervously round the door. Aidan is behind him, and standing back on the street I feel distanced from them as if I'm watching a film. 'Trick or treat,' the witches cry. Max grabs the fruit bowl and offers it to them. Suddenly he catches sight of me and thrusts the bowl into Evie's hands, pushes past the witches and runs to me shouting, 'Mummy,' as if he hasn't seen me for weeks. He flings himself into my arms and wraps his legs around my waist. I can't get over what a relief it is to be back home.

Once we're inside Max says mournfully, 'We've run out of treats.'

We all turn to stare at Evie who silently clutches her stash of sweets close to her chest.

'Hand them over then,' says Aidan grumpily, 'for the others when they come.'

'But they're mine,' Evie starts to wail.

Aidan looks at me in frustration. 'I can't do this. It's been a hell of a day. I'm going upstairs to get some work done. See you later,' and without asking me how my day was he disappears upstairs.

'Quick,' I say as I shut the door. 'Let's turn out all the lights and hide.'

'Why don't we just say we've run out of sweets?' says Max innocently.

Evie looks at him. 'Are you mad – who knows what might happen? We could be pummelled with rotten eggs, our bicycle tyres slashed, or decapitated chickens left on the doorstep.' Evie delights in frightening Max with her imagined tricks but is silenced when I switch off the lights, plunging the house into darkness. Max takes my hand and we all jump as we hear a loud knock on the front door. 'Shh,' I whisper, and we sit down on the stairs huddled together as if in fear for our lives. The knocking gets louder, we do nothing, and after a few seconds we hear the sound of retreating footsteps. Out of the darkness very quietly Max begins to sing 'Happy Birthday to me' and I remember the last time we turned out all the lights in the house was on Max's birthday when it was time for the cake. There's something soothing about sitting on the stairs in the darkness holding on to my children and I want to stay here for ever.

Two

I pass my mother a brass object and watch her as she turns it over and writes a price code on the base. 'A miner's watch stand,' she says by way of explanation. 'They'd take the watches off their chains and hang them up when they were working, protected in their cases from the coal dust. They were very common but nowadays you don't see many of them around.' My mother has been spending her Saturdays dealing in small collectible antiques on the Portobello Road since I was a teenager. She nods over to Cynthia, sitting opposite, who, to be honest, looks the oldest antique in the arcade. 'Thanks for this – I'll share the profit with you.' Cynthia waves her hand as if money is not important.

'I'm glad you're here, Molly. Do you think you can rearrange some of my stock at the front?' she asks. 'You always do it so much better than me.' I get to work setting out the Victorian travelling inkwells, card cases, strange animal pin-cushions and thimble sets into an appealing arrangement.

'You need Aidan for this sort of work.'

'Oh, I don't think so, darling – far too modern for my little stall. He'd do better higher up the road. How is he?' she asks anxiously.

'I'm not sure.'

She has been a steady presence in my life. Every day I'd come home from school bursting with stories or grievances about the day's affairs and she would always listen to me, passing pertinent comments and making me think that I'd handled everything brilliantly. But when my father had his stroke it was as if a transparent plastic curtain dropped between us, which I still find impossible to penetrate.

For a few minutes we're silent, my mother engrossed in marking up her stock and me in rearranging the table in front of her stall. When I've finished I squeeze through the gap that divides her stall from her neighbour's and sit down on the empty stool beside her. We have to time our movements like a couple performing a carefully choreographed dance routine, so as not to knock into each other or, worse, into the stock.

'Have you rung Tim recently?' my mother asks, always keen for us to stay close as a family.

'No, I'm sorry, it's been a bit difficult. Mind you,' I add as an afterthought, 'he never rings me.'

'They've set a date in March for the wedding.'

Tim, my older brother, has decided to get married, very late in life, to Helen. I don't say anything and I wonder why I don't feel happier for him. Helen is inoffensive and friendly but she has the irritating habit of nervously repeating herself and she's much too eager to please. She reminds me of a tiny chihuahua dog that quivers when you look at it.

'She's a nice girl,' says my mother, reading my thoughts. 'You'll be able to make it, won't you?'

'Of course.'

Neither of us says anything but I know what she's thinking. She smiles at me. 'Now that you're working.'

'Not that I'm getting paid. I've given myself a month to see how things work out but pretty soon I'm going to have to get some money from somewhere.'

'Do you have to do this, Molly?' she says, reaching across to pick up the duster. 'It's just I thought after . . . everything you'd decided to stop work and be with the children.'

'Yes I did, and it was the right decision then, but I've got no option. I need to earn some money.'

'Or Aidan could get another job,' my mother says defiantly.

'Aidan married a career woman who was earning a good salary and suddenly I gave it all up and became an old-fashioned house-wife.'

My mother looks at me.

'Not that there's anything wrong with that,' I add quickly, not wanting to criticise the way she has lived much of her life. 'He was so supportive when I followed my heart and decided to give up work and be with the children. Now it's only fair that I should support him while he writes this script. It's very important to him.'

'Is this the story about the hooligans in America who have to break in wild ponies?'

'It's a good idea, and they're not hooligans, they're deprived children who've never had a decent chance in life. It's an amazing reform programme and more constructive than flinging them all into jail,' I say defensively. 'They match the personality of the boy to the horse and by working together they reach an understanding and lives can be changed. I think it could be very inspiring and Aidan has wanted to write it for years. Now is his chance and I can't deny him that.'

'Well you could, not everyone would react like you.'

I'm not sure whether this is a compliment or a criticism.

'What are you doing about childcare?' my mother asks innocently, and then she stops polishing the inkwell and looks at me.

'Ah well . . . yes. . . .' I shift uncomfortably on my stool.

She puts down the duster and I feel that she's bracing herself, anticipating what's coming.

'I know it's a lot to ask but I was wondering whether you might be able to come and help look after the children?' I say it quickly, hoping that speed might make it sound more appealing.

My mother takes off her glasses, rubs her eyes and sighs. 'Oh Molly, you know I love the children, but I don't know – the business takes up a lot of time and energy.'

'You could still do that on Saturdays.'

'Well, I do have fairs sometimes during the week.'

'How often – once a month?'

'Something like that.'

'Aidan could cover on those days.'

'. . . and what with the wedding coming up . . .'

I immediately retract. 'No, it was silly of me, I know it's

26

difficult – I just wondered, that's all. You're the only one I trust really.'

My mother doesn't look at me. 'Let me think about it.' She gives my hand a reassuring pat. 'I'm sure something will come up.' She picks up the watch stand and starts to dust the base and I know that the subject is closed. The arcade is filling up with potential customers, most of whom are crowding round Cynthia's stall opposite.

'Off you go. I can't keep chatting and you're affecting the trade.' I give her an awkward kiss, the shelves rattle behind her, and we both put out our hands to catch any falling objects.

Our house is within walking distance of my mother's stall in the Portobello Road and as I make my way back I wonder why we don't visit her more often. I suppose it's not easy taking small children anywhere near antiques, as they want to touch everything and invariably end up breaking exquisite objects, which their pocket money wouldn't cover even if they saved up for the rest of their young lives.

Saturdays are special in Notting Hill, with the market breathing new life into the streets. Even on a grey November day like today I feel invigorated. I stop to buy some tulips from the flower stall on the corner of the road, and it's only when I reach the end of our road, in what used to be the unfashionable part of Notting Hill when Aidan first bought the house over fifteen years ago, that I wonder what we're going to have for lunch and why I didn't buy anything other than flowers. Already my domestic halo is beginning to slip.

The house is remarkably quiet as I open the front door. I notice that there is a crack in the plaster along the short corridor which opens into the main living area.

Aidan is sitting at the granite breakfast bar calmly reading an *Interiors* magazine. He looks up as I come in and switch on the kettle. 'What did she say?' he asks, making no attempt to mask his eagerness.

'Did you find it that hard yesterday?' I say as I throw my coat on to the hard cream Italian sofa. I see Aidan twitch with irritation. 'Sorry, I'll hang it up in a minute.'

I start opening cupboards trying to find a vase or a jug for the tulips while Aidan follows me, closing each cupboard door as I move on to the next.

'I'm sorry, Moll. Maybe there's something wrong with me but I don't know how you've done it all these years. Just one day was enough for me. You know I love the kids but I haven't got the patience.'

'It wasn't even a whole day,' I say, filling up a white ceramic jug for the flowers.

'Don't you think the glass one would be better?' Aidan suggests.

'This will be fine.'

He says nothing but I feel his disapproval because in our household he is the grand master of style. Any aesthetic decision and we have to bow to Aidan. But lately I've been feeling a childish surge of defiance. Sometimes I dig out my old crockery from the days when I shared a flat with Cassie and Jo. The thin line of blue round the white plate offends Aidan's aesthetic sensibilities. I don't know how he survived growing up in Croydon, or maybe it's what made him the man he is today. Our house interior is an adman's dream and a housewife's nightmare. Before I met Aidan I never knew there were so many shades of white – quiet white, chalk white, new white, old white, not quite white – the list is endless. Aidan reassures me that he really cares about colour even if it is just white. As well as white he loves clean, clear spaces with no clutter. I, on the other hand, love clutter, and sometimes I create little illicit piles of it – even if it's stashed away in a cupboard I feel better just knowing it's there.

Now he's watching me as I arrange the flowers and my heart sinks because it won't be as he wants it. He sighs, 'They're so demanding and everything has to be planned.'

I laugh. 'I did most of the planning; all you had to do was follow instructions.'

'I know, you don't have to say it . . . I'm sorry . . . I screwed up . . . it's just I'm not that sort of dad.'

'What, the reliable sort?' I feel guilty as soon as I've said it and I look up and see his face. 'I'm sorry – that was mean of me.'

I walk over to him and put my arms around him. 'Are you all right?'

'I don't know what I am. I feel lost.' He buries his head in my shoulder and I stroke his hair. 'I'm sorry about yesterday. I don't know what's wrong with me, I can't concentrate on anything except for the script and then I sort of lose myself. I know it's tough on you.'

'I can cope. I only wish I was bringing some money in.'

'We'll be all right for a while. Look, I don't know what you think about this, but I rang round a few agencies on Friday.'

'Ad agencies?' I say, feeling relief that he might be thinking about working again.

'No, nanny agencies.'

'Oh, right.' I let him go and move back to the jug of tulips, trying to keep the disappointment out of my voice.

'I didn't realize it was so bloody expensive and you have to pay them a search fee as well. I know you're not keen on the idea but it was just a thought.'

'It seems crazy if I'm not even earning. We can't afford it.'

'I know.'

Neither of us says anything for a few minutes, both lost in our own thoughts.

'Where are the children?' I break the silence.

'Playing upstairs. I don't suppose Jo could help out?'

Jo is my oldest friend, our fathers were at college together and I've known her all my life. I shake my head. 'It's not a good idea. Let's face it, she has enough trouble with her own children; they run riot. And apart from that it's not practical – she lives too far away and she's still acting when she gets the chance. I wouldn't want to ask her.'

Happy with the tulip arrangement, I put the jug on the side table by the sofa. Aidan stares at it and I know he's desperate to start rearranging the flowers. Resisting temptation, he sits on the sofa looking despondent, and I wonder if it's because of what's happened to him over the past few weeks or because of my flower-arranging skills.

'Let's wait and see what happens. You never know, maybe Mum will come round. She did say she would think about it. In the meantime I'll see if I can organise some play dates for the children so they'll be out of your hair this week, and maybe I could put a card in the local shop for some part-time help.'

Aidan smiles. 'I do love you,' he says, and just hearing the words makes me feel better until he continues. 'Listen, Moll darlin', do you mind if I bow out today and do some work? I can make up for yesterday.' Before I have time to answer him he's halfway up the stairs.

'You haven't forgotten I'm going out with the girls tonight?' I shout after him.

'No, of course not,' he shouts back, and although I can't see his expression I know that he had. We never seem to do things together as a family at weekends, but today I suppose I don't mind as it also gives me a chance to make up for yesterday.

'Mummeee!' Max interrupts my thoughts by screaming down the stairs, 'I can't find my car.'

'Have you looked for it?'

I run up the stairs and expect it to be right in front of Max's eyes as these things usually are. Is it because their eyes are smaller that they can't see the bigger picture and find it impossible to see things that are staring them in the face? I rummage round Max's room but the car he's looking for is almost too big for even him to miss. It's a blue plastic Early Learning Centre car, which is too babyish for him but he still loves playing with it.

'When did you last have it?'

'I can't remember but I need it now.'

I run upstairs to Aidan's study and see his back hunched over his white laptop.

'Sorry to interrupt the creative flow, but have you seen Max's car?'

'What?' Aidan turns round as if coming out of a trance.

'You know, the blue plastic one with the yellow go-faster stripe?'

'Oh yeah – I took it to the dump.'

I hear Max's footsteps as he runs up the stairs.

'Aidan, you didn't – you know how much he loves it!'

'I didn't realise.' He looks panicked. 'Honest, I thought he was far too big for it now.'

Max arrives to hear Aidan's last few words. 'No, I'm not too big for it – have you seen it, Dad?'

Aidan looks at me.

'You tell him,' I say, and I leave them, feeling angry with Aidan for his insensitivity.

I find Evie practising her dance moves to S Club's 'Don't Stop Moving' on her dance mat in her bedroom. I'm waiting to hear Max's scream of fury when he hears about his beloved blue car but nothing happens.

'Look at this move Rachel taught me yesterday at school.' Evie wriggles her bottom from side to side and I wonder what else Rachel is teaching her.

'She's so lucky to have such a fantastic name,' says Evie breathlessly.

'What's so great about the name Rachel?' I ask, still waiting to hear Max's cry.

'It's the same name as Rachel Stevens in S Club – why didn't you call me a cool name?'

'Evie is a lovely name,' I say, thinking of the endless discussions Aidan and I had about names. It was a distraction from thinking about my father – a way of focusing on the future. 'You could have been called something much worse.'

'Like what?'

'Well, I seem to remember your father was keen on "Summer".'

'Eugh.'

Max comes into the room looking composed.

'All right?' I ask him, trying not to sound worried.

'Yeah – Dad's promised to buy me a proper toy car that you can get in and drive – a silver one with alloy wheels like James Bond's.'

Ah, I think to myself, I wonder who'll be paying for that.

It's early evening. I put my numb fingers in my pockets because I've forgotten to bring any gloves, unprepared for the cold autumnal nights.

'So any idea where we might be going?' asks Cassie again, looking at her watch. Our girls' nights out together have become a regular monthly excursion and something we all look forward to.

'Nope, but you know how Jo likes to be inventive.'

'Do you remember the paint-ball evening she organised?'

'It was bloody painful and it took me weeks to get the dye out of my hair.'

'Psychologically interesting though – seeing how aggressive people become.' She stares pointedly at me.

'I wasn't aggressive, I was just entering into the spirit,' I say defensively.

'Maybe competitive is a better word – I was glad you were on my side.'

'Maybe we should have stuck to the book club idea.'

'But we never got round to talking about the bloody books.'

Never happy to stand around doing nothing, Cassie picks up a newspaper that has been chucked into a bin and starts reading the headline 'Cure For Old Age'.

'I know a cure for old age,' she says as she opens the paper. 'It's called death.'

She was reading a newspaper when I first saw her in a long queue of wannabe researchers for a job that had been advertised in the Media section of the *Guardian*. There seemed to be thousands of applicants for the one job of interviewing the great, the good, the seriously mentally disturbed, aka celebrities. She was standing next to me calmly reading her paper while I tried to stop my hands shaking, and she stood out because of her dark hair, cut very short. There was something exotic about her, possibly because she smelt of oranges which, as I later discovered, was because she had spilt a bottle of freshly squeezed orange juice down her skirt. What was incongruous was that when she opened her mouth she had a broad Liverpudlian accent.

She got the job but I was taken on as a trainee and we worked in the Specials Department, which made us feel superior, like we were members of an elite force – the SAS of television light entertainment. Who dares wins an interview with Rod Hull and Emu. After a few years of interviewing we both branched out – Cassie choosing to make hard-hitting documentaries tackling the big subjects while I concentrated on quirkier human-interest stories. When I gave up working I never thought my career was over, merely 'on hold', but in the meantime Cassie went on to be part of Pulse Productions and since then has produced countless successful documentaries.

'OK, I'm here.' We both swing round to see someone who looks like Jo but with spiky hair about six inches shorter than we're used to.

'Jo?' I say tentatively.

'What do you think?'

'It's very short.'

She looks disappointed and pats the back of her head. 'It's such a strange feeling – I feel like I'm floating not walking, it's so much lighter not being weighed down by all that hair. Do you think it looks terrible?'

'I need a few minutes to get used to it.'

'It makes me look younger, don't you think?'

'Yes, I suppose it does – no, it's good, really good,' I say encouragingly.

Jo has always used her hair as a way to define the various stages of her life – she's been a Bay City Roller fan, a pink punk, but that didn't last long, as she looked uncannily like a badger. My personal favourite was the Meg Ryan period but for the last five years or so it's been straight and its natural colour, except for the odd highlight here and there. She's the only girl I've ever met whose hair is the same colour as her eyes – 'marmalade eyes', her husband Finn calls them. I'm much more boring as I've had the same long wavy dark brown hair all my life, only occasionally when I'm feeling particularly daring have I added a hint of henna. I'm a wash 'n' go sort of girl and I hate fussing over the way I look as it seems such a waste of time. I've always found that the more trouble I take with my appearance, the worse I look.

It always surprised me that Jo and Cassie got on so well, Jo being what Cassie would call a 'posh tart'. When Jo and I got the chance to rent a three-bedroom flat in Tooting, Cassie was keen to move in, and to my surprise we all got on very well. That was long before any of us was married.

'Where are we going? I'm starving,' says Cassie.

'Follow me,' says Jo, as if she's leading a group of primary school children.

'I hate bowling,' Cassie says gloomily, 'my fingers always get stuck in the bloody ball.'

Jo looks disappointed by our obvious lack of enthusiasm. 'I thought you'd enjoy it – we can talk, eat, drink and have a bit of exercise all rolled into one. I thought it was inspired.'

'Well, yes,' I say, trying to sound keen.

'Did you know that those boys who gunned down all those children in Columbine High School in America – well, they went bowling first,' says Cassie, looking at me knowingly as if to say, who knows what we'll want to do after a few hours bowling?

Jo, visibly irritated, says, 'Well, if you don't like this idea we could always go skating, there's a rink just over there.'

'Remember the Washington sniper?' I say to Cassie, and she nods her head. 'Apparently he went skating before he went on the rampage.' Cassie laughs and then tries to look serious as Jo flushes with frustration.

'No, bowling is great,' I say quickly. 'Don't we have to change our shoes?'

'Over here.' Cassie is already at a counter unzipping her black boots. 'Size four,' she says to the man behind the counter who looks at her as if she should be accompanied by a responsible adult. We struggle out of our boots and shoes, all except Jo.

'Aren't you playing?' I ask her.

'I've got my own,' she says a little smugly, pointing at her compact leather bag.

'That's why you're so keen – you're a bloody expert.'

She looks a little embarrassed. 'No, of course I'm not. Don't you remember that short film when I played the drug addict? It was set in a bowling alley and I kept the shoes. I can't bear the thought of other people's feet.' She wrinkles her nose in disgust as the man behind the counter thrusts two pairs of bowling shoes in front of us.

'These are almost cool,' says Cassie about her suede brown and cream bowling shoes, 'and they're really comfortable.' She stands up straight having tied the laces. 'I'm never taking these off.' Only Cassie can make a pair of rented bowling shoes look good. Mine are a nasty purple plastic with green velcro that look terrible with my short red skirt.

Jo has already found her way to our lane and has typed our initials on to the screen. The balls look impossibly big and the lane stretches for miles. I decide to get the first round of drinks in and as I come back Jo is in position at the head of the lane, looking stylish in black jeans with matching black and cream bowling shoes. She's holding the ball up high in front of her, concentrating on the skittles standing firm and straight at the end of the lane like infantry about to engage in battle.

'She's been practising,' I say to Cassie.

'I have not,' Jo shouts back at me indignantly. 'Stop trying to ruin my concentration.'

She takes a little run and flings the ball in the direction of the skittles and it rolls along the lane before veering off to the right and running into the aisle. 'You deliberately put me off,' she says, looking grumpy.

'I didn't mean to, but you looked so professional.'

'There's a definite slope on the lane; maybe we should move.' For a second she looks upset and then grins. 'Whose stupid idea was this anyway?' She looks at the drinks. 'Oh sorry, Molly, I should have said – I'm off the booze – strictly a water girl – I'm detoxing.'

'Are you feeling all right?' asks Cassie, amazed.

'I need to clear my pores. I got offered a job the other day.'

'That's fantastic. What is it?' I ask enthusiastically.

Jo's face falls. 'It's an advert. I've taken the golden shilling.'

'I wish I could,' I say sincerely.

Cassie is standing by the place where the balls are regurgitated, watching them emerge like solid bubbles in the bath. She scrutinises each one until eventually she picks a small purple ball. She runs her fingers over it as she walks up to the front of the lane, pulls back her arm and throws the ball straight and strong. It never deviates off its path and heads straight into all the skittles, sending them flying. The screen flashes 'Strike', and without acknowledging what seems to me to be her tremendous achievement she takes a sip of beer and says to Jo, 'What's the advert for?'

We're all standing staring at the gap at the end of the lane in amazement. 'That was really good Cassie,' says Jo with admiration.

'Yeah, well, I had a boyfriend who was keen and he taught me a thing or two.'

'And where did you learn about the bowling?' I ask, and they both groan.

'You've got another go,' Jo says.

'Go on then,' says Cassie, picking up another ball.

'What's the job?'

'It's an advert for one of those miracle-working skin products for the mature woman – L'Oréal.'

'Because you're worth it,' we all say together in cod American accents.

'Well, what's wrong with that?'

'I'm the "before" face for this anti-wrinkle cream. Can you

believe it? Do I look that old? I told Jean, my agent, that I'm not going to do it – it's just too humiliating.'

'What did she say?'

'She told me how much money they were offering.'

'When do you start?'

'Thursday. It's thirty thousand pounds and I get a repeat fee and more when it gets sold abroad. They want to buy me out for a year.'

'Jo, my heart bleeds for you. What does Finn think?'

'Oh, Finn,' says Jo dismissively. 'You know what he's like. There are times I think it's more like arm-wrestling than a marriage. We're always fighting. Sometimes it's in subtle ways, like who reads the most stories to the children in a week, but mostly we just throw things at each other. At first I think we both thrived off the drama of it all.'

'Like Burton and Taylor,' says Cassie.

'Please – more Patsy and Liam,' Jo replies, watching Cassie's ball as it strikes all but one of the skittles.

'Whose turn is it now?'

'Mine,' I say reluctantly, and Jo continues in full flow, 'I'm fed up with him always criticising the way I bring up the boys.'

I move to choose my ball, still listening to what she's saying, but neither Cassie nor I say anything. I think we all agree with Finn when it comes to their children.

'How are your two?' Cassie asks me.

'Fine,' I say briskly, trying to change the subject. Children are the one contentious area between all of us.

The balls are huddled together like eggs in a nest and I choose a dark blue ball with a marbled effect. Jo continues, 'Things are difficult. He hasn't had an acting job for over a year now. It really is a ridiculous way for grown-ups to make a living.'

I roll my ball, trying to remember what I was told to do all those many years ago. I think I was about ten the last time I went bowling. The ball hits the lane so slowly I almost lose the will to live watching it crawl its way up to the skittles. I put my hands over my eyes, embarrassed by the ball's slow progress, and as I turn away I look across at the neighbouring aisle and see a group of elderly women. Two of them are puzzling over the scoring system while another in a lilac cardigan is picking up her ball and approaching the lane. She looks supremely confident and apart from the grey hair remarkably agile for her age. The ball travels straight down the lane and she scores an easy strike. The other ladies stop chatting to say well done but they act as though her success was expected. They're obviously veterans of the bowling alley.

'How old do you think they are?' I ask Jo.

'Sixty-five, seventy.'

'Really? Do you think they're that old?'

'Maybe even older – that one with the cardigan could be in her late seventies.'

'Not really?'

'That's not so old when you think about it – the average life expectancy has risen to eighty,' Cassie says knowledgeably.

'But it's just that you don't expect to see them being so active.'

'They can't all go to bingo.'

I laugh. 'Well, it's less taxing.' I look back to see my ball still making its stately progress along the lane.

'You can hardly call bowling an aerobic sport,' says Jo, smiling at the group of women.

'That'll be us before you know it,' says Cassie.

'I can't imagine it – they look like a different species to me,' I say.

'I know it's a terrible thing to say but I don't like old people,' says Jo, 'all those wrinkles and the smell.'

'Don't be daft – they're no different from the rest of us.'

'I feel the same way about old people as some people feel about children. I don't really know how to talk to them,' I say, and Cassie looks at me as if I'm disappointing her.

'I know it's silly.' I sigh. 'I can't get the tone right and I always end up sounding patronising.'

'They're only people like you and me. Honestly, I don't believe you two.'

'I don't intend to ever be old, but just say we don't defy the laws of nature, then I think we should grow old together and set up a sort of geriatric commune.'

'It's called an old people's home,' I say.

'No, it wouldn't be like that, with us it would be different.'

'What about the men?'

'I can't imagine Aidan in a commune – he's a man who likes his space and he'd get in a state about the way the flowers were arranged.' We all laugh.

'God, none of you would want to grow old with Finn; if he's difficult now he'll be impossible by then. Anyway, we won't have to worry about the men as they'll die off before us – they always do,' says Jo with relish.

'Will would be all right with his archaeological expertise. He knows a thing or two about old ruins.'

'Will won't be around,' Cassie says, looking down at her drink.

'No, probably not his sort of thing,' I say.

'No, we've split up.'

We all turn to look at her in amazement. The screen flashes 'Strike' and we turn back to see the clear space where there should be skittles.

'That's incredible,' I gasp.

'Unbelievable,' says Jo.

'How could something so slow and pathetic bring down all those skittles?' I ask in shock.

'Must have been perfect positioning,' says Cassie, now our resident bowling expert. We watch as she writes down the score, feeling awkward, not knowing what to say.

'Why didn't you say anything earlier?' I ask, feeling guilty that I've been immersed in my own problems.

'What's there to say?' She shrugs her shoulders.

'Are you all right?' I ask.

'Yes. I suppose so.' She looks round at our stunned faces. 'This was exactly the reason I didn't say anything earlier. I'm sorry I mentioned it – I don't want to ruin the evening. Come on, let's get some food, I'm starving.'

We look at each other, not quite sure what to do.

'I'm going to order some food – are you happy with the most disgusting-looking fish and chips?' Cassie says, sounding quite normal.

'I'll come with you,' I volunteer, leaving Jo alone to practise her technique. 'I'm so sorry, Cassie. When did it happen?'

'We decided a couple of nights ago. We're both so bloody miserable we had to do something, so he's going to move out of the flat.' She's walking quickly and I'm having trouble keeping up with her. I'm finding it impossible to know what to say. It's been years since anyone I've known has split up and I'm searching to find the words. All I seem able to talk about these days are minor emotional problems, children's schools and the price of organic vegetables. I give her arm a reassuring but inadequate squeeze as she heads off to order the food. I go back to Jo who is sitting on the side and drinking her mineral water.

'Unbelievable, isn't it?' she says.

'I never thought it would happen to them.'

'If Will and Cassie have split up there's not much hope for the rest of us.'

'Don't be silly.'

'Makes you think though. They've been together the longest and they always seemed strong.'

'It's been tough recently, since the IVF and everything. That must have put a lot of pressure on the relationship.'

'I didn't think Will wanted kids?'

'But you know what it's like – if you can't have something then you find you really want it.'

'Do you think she'll be all right?' I ask. I try to imagine what it would be like living on my own.

'She'll cope – she's a strong, independent girl – look at her.'

We both watch Cassie walking towards us looking like she's ready to take on the world.

'Don't look at me like that, you two – I wish I hadn't bloody told you.'

Cassie tries to make a joke of it but I know her too well and

40

her smudged eye-liner has not passed unnoticed. Jo tries to change the subject.

'So we're still on for lunch tomorrow?'

'Definitely – the children are looking forward to it,' I lie.

'Cassie, do you fancy coming over? It's only the two families.'

'No, I don't think I will . . . I'm a bit . . .' She doesn't finish her sentence.

'Are you sure?' I say, trying to sound encouraging. 'We'd all love to see you.' I'm hoping that she will detect the pleading tone of my voice and read my eyes which are trying to flash desperate messages to her – 'Please come, I need your help' – without alerting Jo to my lack of enthusiasm.

She ignores me and shakes her head. 'Sorry, guys, I'm just not in the mood – you understand?'

'Yes, of course,' Jo and I say together.

As we get up to go I look over to see the old lady with the lilac cardigan sitting on her own. Her friends seem to have gone and I wonder if she has someone to go home to or if she comes bowling for the company. She is staring into the distance and I try to imagine what she is thinking and what it would be like to be alone. Gradually she focuses on me and before I have the chance to look away, very slowly she lifts her hand in a small gesture of acknowledgement and I find myself lifting mine back in return, feeling a connection through the years.

Three

'Are we supposed to know?' Jo hisses at me as she takes my jacket and flings it over the banister. Aidan is walking ahead along the narrow dark corridor that leads into the kitchen. I look at her blankly.

'About his job, is it all right that we know he's lost it?'

'Oh God, I don't know,' I say, feeling slightly panicked. When it all happened Aidan was insistent that I didn't tell anyone and of course I didn't tell a soul except for Cassie, Jo, my mother – oh, and my brother Tim. His pride was at stake and he hates the thought of anyone talking about him, which is understandable. Now that he's writing I would have thought it's OK for people to know, but I'm not sure. I pause in the corridor, looking at the pictures of Jo and Finn's family, stretching back a couple of generations, which line the walls.

'Nice pictures,' I say, buying some thinking time.

'Thank you. We've just finished getting them all framed.'

I stare at a 1930s black and white wedding photo. The bride is staring unsmiling at the camera and something about the shape of her eyes and her long nose looks vaguely familiar.

'My grandmother,' explains Jo. 'They divorced later and it caused a great scandal when she ran off with the chauffeur.' She peers at the picture. 'She doesn't look very happy, does she?'

I can hear Finn offering Aidan a beer in the kitchen.

'I wouldn't say anything about the job unless he brings it up.'

'Shit, I need to tell Finn.' She rushes ahead into the kitchen just in time to hear Finn saying, 'Heard about the job, mate, that's a bit of a bummer, isn't it? How are you coping?'

Aidan tenses up and glances over at me, making me feel like a Judas. Finn hands him a bottle of beer.

'Now you know how I feel – I haven't worked for over a year.'

'Aidan's writing a screenplay,' I say, trying to make amends for my betrayal.

'Fantastic – is there a part for me in it?'

'Finn.' Jo tries to silence him.

'What?' says Finn, looking hurt. 'I wasn't being serious.'

Evie and Max either side of me are clinging on to my arms. Sunday lunch with Jo and Finn is not one of their favourite activities.

'Evie, look at you – I love your braid,' says Jo. She turns to look at Max. 'The boys are around somewhere – I'll go and give them a shout.' Max flinches and looks around nervously as if he'd much rather she didn't.

'We've put the dog outside because I know he bothers you, Evie,' Finn says, trying to be kind.

'She's much better about dogs these days,' I say protectively. Loud barking and the sound of trainers pounding down the stairs stop me saying anything more. The dog, a bearded collie, comes tearing into the kitchen, quickly followed by the eleven-year-old twins hollering at him, 'Hey, Big Bum, come here, you mongrel.'

Jo puts up her hands, hoping to slow them down. 'How many times do I have to say it – he's called Nigel.'

'Come off it, Mum, that's a ridiculous name for a dog. Anyway, he only comes when you call him Big Bum,' shouts Jake, the bigger of the two boys, as he slows down, watching his brother chase after the dog. Evie flinches and squeezes my hand so tightly that I gasp.

'I thought I told you to put the bloody dog outside,' Finn shouts. 'Boys, come back here and say h—'

Before he can finish his sentence both Jake and Ben have run out into the hall.

'Don't shout at them, Finn, they're just letting off a little steam,' Jo says, opening the oven door to do the same to the roast chicken. Smoke wafts into the cramped kitchen. Finn takes Evie's other hand and looks at Max. 'Come on, guys – Evie, I need you to help me sort out those big boys and Max, if you like tanks, Jake has got a great one with two armoured vehicles upstairs.'

The children follow him tentatively. Evie glances back at me, trying not to look as worried as I know she feels.

'Do you want a hand?' I say to Jo.

'Yes, always,' she says gratefully. 'Can you take over the gravy? It tastes disgusting and needs rescuing.' She moves out of the way, handing over the wooden spoon to let me taste the gravy, and starts getting the plates out of the cupboard. Aidan sits down at the table but he's not really with us. I can see he's thinking about the words in his head, working out his next scene, riding across an American plain on a sturdy horse with the wind tugging at his hair, far away from the cluttered kitchen of a cramped terraced house in South London.

The boys seem to have grown out of Jo's house. There are piles of papers on every surface, football boots with mud wedged into the soles spreading over the kitchen floor, children's artwork hanging off the walls, and a general feeling of chaos. Aidan sticks down one of the flapping corners of a huge picture with a piece of dried-out Blu Tack, which is still attached to it. It's a bold picture of a beach with a rough sea, figures sunbathing and playing ball; real shells and rocks have been stuck on to pieces of sand-paper.

'You should have some of these framed – I think they're really good,' Aidan says, standing up to get a better look at some of the pictures. Finn is carving the chicken and the children have sat down at the table, the boys, incapable of sitting still, either nudging each other or stealing cutlery.

Jo smiles. 'They are quite good, aren't they?' she says, trying to hide her obvious pride. 'They might be monsters but at least they're artistic monsters.'

'Do you like art, boys?' Aidan asks.

'It's all right,' says Jake disinterestedly, wiping his hands on his 'Darkness' T-shirt. Ben is polishing his knife on his T-shirt which has a skull with a dagger protruding from its forehead.

44

'It doesn't have to be boring old pictures, you know – have you heard of Damien Hirst?'

The boys shake their heads.

'He pickles dead cows in formaldehyde.'

'Cool,' says Jake.

'Another artist is planning to make a video of David Beckham sleeping.'

'That's something I'd like to see. Leg or breast?' asks Jo.

'David Beckham doesn't have breasts,' says Jake in disgust.

'I was talking about the chicken, duh,' says Jo.

'I'm happy with anything,' I say, trying to be helpful.

Ben and Jake are listening intently to everything Aidan is saying, while pretending not to be interested.

'Then there's this girl who uses her unmade bed and calls that art.'

'I bet she never got any pocket money,' says Finn as he finishes carving the chicken.

'Well, it's paid off – she's made a fortune now,' says Aidan, smiling at Jo as she hands him a plate.

'Mum . . .' says Ben.

'Don't even think about it, Ben. Pass the vegetables round,' Jo says as she puts a plate of food in front of him.

Jake is looking excited. 'I always thought we were making an artistic statement in our bedroom by not clearing up. I know . . . this whole house could be a work of art – we could make millions!'

Aidan laughs. 'Brilliant idea, and there's no reason why not, but it's not as easy as it looks – there is a little bit of work involved.' By now he has a captive audience and he starts talking to the two boys about exploding sheds and growing grass over sculptures, feeding their imaginations.

'How's school, Evie?' Jo asks down at our end of the table.

'Fine,' says Evie unhelpfully.

'What do you want for Christmas, Max?'

'A gun or a tank,' replies Max, taking one mouthful. Then, without looking at me, he says in a monotone, 'Thank you for a lovely lunch. Can I get down now?'

'Max, you've only just started.'

Resigned, he starts to push his chicken about his plate, thinking that if he rearranges the food it will look like he's eating it. I see him looking at the dog hovering by the door hoping for some titbits.

Jo looks benignly at Max. 'He can get down – I don't mind,' and Max, with a huge grin of relief, pushes his chair back and goes to pat the dog. The bigger boys seize their moment and leave the table and within seconds we can hear the sound of the television blaring out from the front room.

'Boys, what are you doing?' shouts Jo. 'Oh, I give up,' and I think how tired she looks.

'Oh, let them watch it, we don't mind.'

'I'll just go and see what they're watching. I think the football's on,' says Finn a little too eagerly as he scrapes his plate clean of gravy. He looks at Aidan who says, 'Yeah, good idea, I'll come too.'

'Can I go?' asks Evie eagerly.

Jo looks at me and says, 'What can you do? I've made apple crumble for pudding.'

'That's fine. We can have it later. I'll help you clear up, then why don't we go to the park and make the most of it?'

I pick up a chestnut-brown conker and even though Max isn't with me I put it into my pocket to give to him later. A few leaves are still resolutely clinging to the trees but as we leave the main path we start wading through the rough sea of leaves on the ground.

'Evie always tells me to watch out for hedgehogs – apparently they hide under the leaves.'

'Not in Battersea Park, I think,' says Jo as she watches the dog bounce through the leaves like Tigger, barking loudly, excited to be outside. The park is busy with children on tricycles, toddlers insisting on pushing their buggies looking like their milk has been laced with brandy as they lurch across the paths. Skate-boarders sway from side to side and couples walk welded together as if they're in training for a three-legged race. A jogger runs past us, her ponytail swinging; the dog runs after her and Jo shouts, 'Hey, Big Bum.' The runner turns and glares at her, as do an elderly couple and a young mother pushing a pram.

Jo looks apologetic. 'Sorry, I didn't mean . . . I was just calling my dog,' she splutters as she rushes past them and tries to grab the dog who is getting over-friendly with a Jack Russell terrier.

As we walk together, savouring our independence, she asks me, 'So how's work going?'

'I'm not sure really. I've only been there a day and it's good being me again, but it is still a little daunting. I think it's going to take me a while to get back into the swing and it would help if everything was sorted out at home. I still haven't got any child-care and after just one day Aidan is already finding it difficult. How do you two manage?'

Jo kicks a stray ball back to some boys who are playing football. 'The children are older and it makes it much easier because they're at school for most of the day. This year Finn hasn't worked and he's good with them, better than I am if I'm honest, so it's not so difficult. Have you tried the Working Mums' nursery for Max? It's supposed to be fantastic.'

'Yes, I've tried, but there's a waiting list. He'll be ready to go to university by the time he gets in.'

Jo hesitates. 'I think it'll be good for Aidan to have to spend some more time with them both.'

'Do you?'

'Yes – you're so over-protective of him – you do everything in that house.'

'I know, but—'

'Come on, Molly, you're always making excuses for him. He's not so much of a genius that he can't help out, especially as he's the one that's put you into this position.'

I don't like her criticising him but I know she has a point.

'You spoil him.'

'I don't.'

47

She ignores me. 'And I bet he hasn't asked you anything about your first day back at work.'

I think about Friday night and how Aidan disappeared up into the study without asking me anything and didn't come down again until I was fast asleep.

'It's not an easy time for him at the moment.'

Jo gives a derisory laugh.

'Aidan doesn't ask questions – he makes statements about things so that the focus switches back to himself.'

'Why this attack on Aidan?'

'I'm sorry, Molly – I just think you need more support.'

'So criticising Aidan is you being supportive?'

'From him, I meant.'

We've both stopped walking and she links her arm with mine. 'I'm a bit worried about you – that's all. I'm giving you a gentle nudge.'

'It feels more like a big dig in the ribs. I knew what the deal would be when I married him. He's not like other men and he never pretended that he would be an involved father. When I decided to give up work he didn't try to dissuade me, and it's worked up until now but you can't expect him to change overnight.'

'I don't,' says Jo.

We walk down a thin pathway that leads to a large pond. The smell of toast and tea wafts from the nearby café and a young couple walk by holding hands, the girl's head resting on her boyfriend's shoulder.

'How about you and Finn?'

She doesn't say anything but looks down at her feet. 'Oh, I don't know, it seems so churlish to complain, especially when I think about Will and Cassie, but it's not great.'

'Why?'

'Oh, everything and nothing. We've been together fourteen years. I'm feeling so old.'

I laugh. 'Thirty-eight isn't old – don't be ridiculous.'

'Well, I don't feel good about myself, and he doesn't do

anything to boost my confidence. We bicker constantly about petty, silly things and I hate the way he treats me. I know he's only teasing but I don't want him to call me "old girl", and don't ask me about the sex.'

'How's the sex?' I know my role in these conversations after all these years.

'Terrible. He's only interested first thing in the morning when the children are wandering in and out of the bedroom, and call me strange but I don't find that relaxing. We've stopped touching each other – we don't even hug these days. The sad thing is I don't *want* him to touch me. I hate him kissing me. We don't talk about it – what can you say? "Sorry, darling, I find you physically repellent"? That would be the end of the marriage.' She pauses, letting her words sink in. 'Maybe I should read some books: *How to Reignite the Passion in Your Marriage*. God, just thinking about it makes me feel sick. Is there something wrong with me?'

'Of course not. It's probably just a stage.'

We walk on in silence until Jo says, 'I still can't get over Will and Cassie.'

'I know, I can't believe it. They've been together longer than Aidan and me. Can you imagine how painful it would be to split up and be alone again?'

'We'd never be alone because even if we separated there would still be the children,' says Jo.

'Does that make it better or worse?' I ask, but she doesn't reply.

'It seems such a shame after all those months of wondering whether to go down the IVF route with all that worrying, waiting and pain, for it not to work, and now this.'

We stop at the play area and watch the children playing on the swings and clambering over the wooden train.

'I can't imagine what she must be feeling,' I say.

'Do you ever think what it would be like not to be with Aidan?' Jo asks me earnestly.

I don't answer her but instead say, 'Do you wonder the same about Finn?'

'Yes, and sometimes it's terrible and then other times it's exciting, especially if there was someone new.'

I think about meeting someone different and feel nothing but fear and worry. When I was younger I relished change, but now it's unsettling, especially because of the children. I feel that, despite our problems, Aidan and I are a unit, a team. He's definitely the captain and I've always been a team player.

The fading November sunshine reflects off the silver bar of the climbing frame in the playground and I remember the first time I saw him. I had to interview him for a programme I was researching. I'd read countless articles about him, seen him on late-night art shows talking about the latest trends in advertising in a direct and unpretentious way. The first thing I noticed when I was ushered into his minimalist office by his inscrutable Japanese assistant, was his hair. The press cuttings called it 'grey' but that didn't begin to describe the colour that crowned his head. It was silver and seemed to shimmer as if glowing with all the bright ideas that were formulating inside his head. I was relieved that he didn't shake my hand as I thought I might get an electric shock. He didn't say hello but as soon as he saw me he launched into a long but fascinating explanation about the power of advertising. He then leapt up and said, 'I've got to do a presentation – do you want to sit in?'

I sat and watched him, dazzled by his energy and his originality with which he impressed everyone. When he'd finished they all applauded, and when I asked his secretary, 'Does this normally happen?' she replied, 'Only with Aidan.'

That night we had dinner and went to bed and that was it. I never slept with another man.

When Jo and I get back nothing has changed. Everyone is still sitting in front of the television, the children on the floor with their backs to the sofa, Finn snoring quietly, his mouth slightly open. Aidan is slumped in an armchair and when I look at him I realise that his hair is no longer silver but a dull grey.

Four

Breakfast in our house is usually a mad rush, to which the Benny Hill soundtrack would be an ideal background, with us all working at double speed. I have to concentrate on every detail. It is like juggling, and if I drop one ball, say if Max decides he wants Coco Pops instead of Ready Brek, I lose my rhythm. I make myself a cup of tea and when I turn round Max is surrounded by little crumb mountains and is pointing what remains of his toast at me.

'Max, what are you doing?'

'I've made a gun,' he says, immensely pleased with himself.

It's hard to reconcile the shape in his hand with anything remotely resembling a gun but I can see that despite all my attempts to be politically correct I will soon have to give in to his demands for at least one weapon of mass destruction.

Aidan wanders sleepily into the kitchen, wearing an old pair of tracksuit bottoms. I hear the intake of breath as he sees the mess, and as he opens the fridge door he grumbles, 'Is there any more milk?'

I resist the urge to shout directions to the local shop at him but try to stay calm as I grab a school reading folder, a packed lunch, water bottle, coat, hat and scarf and eldest child. 'You need to do a big supermarket shop today. I've left the list by the phone.'

Aidan doesn't say anything.

'Aidan, did you hear me?'

'Yes, yes, of course,' he says, and I walk out of the house, slamming the front door as hard as I can. It's been three weeks since I started working and still it doesn't occur to him to think about helping me in the mornings, even if it was just offering to unload the dishwasher or take the children to school. I hope Aidan notices that I've left Max with him.

As Evie and I walk to school I think to myself that it is my duty to train Max to be a domestic animal as well as a hunter-gatherer, so that some woman in the future will be so grateful to me. Later, I don't so much take Max to school as frogmarch him there to make sure that I get to work on time. Max asks breathlessly as he tries to keep up with me, 'Who am I going to play with today?', resigned to the fact that these days he rarely comes straight home from school.

'Thomas.'

He groans, 'Not again.' His expression is similar to the one Thomas's mother Jenny made when I asked her if they could come over. Luckily she was too polite to say anything but 'Yes, of course' through gritted teeth.

'I know it's a dreadful imposition but it won't be for much longer,' I said, but I could see Jenny was not convinced and who can blame her? I have no reason for saying this, as I'm not actually progressing in my search for suitable childcare. Only one woman responded to the advert in the shop and she couldn't speak a word of English. That's not strictly true: she could speak five words, which were 'three hundred pounds a week'. I terminated the phone call as quickly as I could considering she didn't seem to understand the word 'goodbye'.

I couldn't have got through the last few weeks if it hadn't been for Jenny but it's cost me a fortune in Marks and Sparks goodies and flowers which I present regularly as peace offerings.

'I miss our Starbucks sessions,' Jenny said when I asked her about Max coming to play.

'Me too – how is everything?'

'Not so much fun without you. I've started doing yoga on a Friday morning – oh, and I meant to tell you I've signed us up to do the wreath stall for the Christmas fair. Is that OK? I'll need your help.'

'Yes, of course.' I feel it's the least I can do. This year our

Christmas will be coming from a catalogue.

'Stay and have a drink when you pick Max up tonight,' she says hopefully.

'OK, see you tonight, and Jenny . . . thank you.'

The beauty of Max going to play with Thomas is that his older sister Rachel is Evie's favourite friend at the moment: ever since she introduced Evie to 'Busted' they spend most of their time devising dance routines. I have tried to return the favour by asking Rachel and Thomas over at weekends but Jenny looked as if I'd said something sacrilegious. 'That's kind of you, Molly, but for us weekends are the one time we can all spend together. You know how it is.'

I only wish I did.   .

As soon as I walk into the office I realise something is up. Jade is on the phone, Rod is pacing up and down his office like a marauding lion. I'm surprised to see Robin, as I was under the impression that he would be away filming for at least three weeks.

'Shouldn't you be—' I say innocently to him and he glowers at me, cutting me off mid-sentence. 'Zip it,' he says quietly and I feel like I've been slapped.

Around his desk are boxes of camera equipment, and an assistant cameraman is sullenly checking the lenses and marking up tapes.

'When did you start working here?' says a voice I recognise almost as well as my own brother's. I turn to see the familiar boyish face.

'Hello, Matt.'

He smiles, showing the lines and creases that he's acquired over the years since I last saw him. We hug and I suddenly feel more confident.

'I thought you'd stopped working,' he says, drawing back and looking a little embarrassed by his obvious delight at seeing me.

'Well, I've sort of started again – I'm only developing a few ideas at the moment, but who knows what may come of it?'

'Good to see you.'

'You too, Matt.'

He's part of my former life – who I used to be.

'How's it going? The filming, I mean.'

Matt glances at Robin and then says under his breath, 'Fancy a coffee?'

'Have you time?'

'Yes, all the time in the world if things keep on going like this. Come on, I can't talk here, let's go upstairs.'

We sit opposite each other nursing our cappuccinos conspiratorially.

'How are you?' I ask, relieved to be with a friendly face at last.

'All right.'

'Still with Ann?'

'Hanging on in there.' He grins.

'So how's the filming?' I ask, bracing myself for his enthusiastic response as everyone keeps telling me that Robin is a genius.

'God, it's been awful.'

For some inexplicable reason I find myself smiling. So Robin isn't so bloody marvellous after all. 'Why, what's so bad?' I try to keep the eagerness out of my voice.

'Well, you know what the premise of the series is – the Seven Ages of Man.' I nod my head. 'Each film follows a central character who is representative of that stage. Well, we're doing the final one – old age "sans teeth, sans everything", only Robin,' he practically spits the name, 'wants to present a more positive side of old age. I think what he wanted was a skate-boarding granny, and to be honest Florence is a gem – not that she's easy. I don't know whether it's because she was, sorry, *is* an actress – she gets very cross if you talk about her career in the past tense – but something happens when she's on camera and her face is amazing to light. It's not that she's a beauty but she's very . . .' he flounders trying to find the right word, 'alive, and that's wonderful to see in someone of her age.'

'So what happened?' I say eagerly, thinking how little time it takes to get into the swing of office gossip.

'The first few days have been going well, filming her at the retirement home for actors where she lives; believe me that's quite a set-up. She's still pretty active so we've been following her routine, getting to know the staff and the other people who live there. Thursday afternoon she's always out but she won't let us come with her so we have a few hours to kill. My assistant Nick is always keen to get some hands-on experience so I let him go with Robin to do some general shots.' He stops and takes a sip of his coffee. 'I shouldn't have done it but he was eager and I thought they'd be fine together.'

'Well, what happened?' I'm dying with curiosity.

'There was this old guy who was lying on his bed . . . according to Nick the room looked amazing because of the way the light was shining through the window and they thought he was sleeping.'

'But he wasn't sleeping?'

'No, he wasn't . . . he was . . . well, you know. It had only just happened and his daughters had left the room for a break – I think they'd been there for days at his bedside.'

My palms go sweaty as he speaks. I imagine hands clawing the air, holding on to life, gasping for breath. I close my eyes to try to get rid of the image as Matt continues, 'The family came back as they were filming and the staff, who have been very co-operative up to now, were really angry, especially the home administrator. She was livid with Robin and started giving him a real earful. "What do you think you were doing? Did you get permission to film other residents like that – what were you thinking of?" Robin, who hates being told off, just snapped, "How could I get permission if he was dead for Chrissake?"'

'He didn't say that?' I say, shocked. 'Oh my God, that's awful!' but I find I'm close to laughter. 'So what's happening now?' I ask.

'Well, Florence had a fit when she heard – turns out that Arthur, the man we'd been filming, was a good friend of hers and now she's trying to decide whether she wants to continue. The thing is, we've been filming for two weeks, I get on really well with her, and we've got some good footage which will all go to waste if we stop now. It's going to be difficult starting from scratch because we're running out of time. Robin was a bad choice. They all think he's a brilliant director but all he cares about are his shots and his career. He's not very sympathetic. It needs someone with sensitivity.' He pauses and looks up at me. 'I wish you were doing it, Molly.'

'I'd love to do it, not least for the money, but they'd never let me.' I smile at him, grateful for his confidence in me. 'Apparently I'm out of the loop. No one thinks I'm up to making another film. They're probably right.'

Matt shakes his head. 'Bollocks – you'd like Florence and you'd make this film brilliantly – they don't know anything, that lot.'

'There is another problem. I'm just not very good with old people – I don't know how to deal with them. Silly, isn't it?'

He smiles. 'Florence isn't your typical old woman. I think you'd get on.'

Jade, who has obviously been sent by Rod to find me, interrupts us. 'Rod ith looking for you, Molly, you're thuppothed to be having lunch,' she says in her lisping, monotone voice.

'Better get back or else they'll think I'm skiving,' I say to Matt.

'Think about it, Molly,' he says.

'No. Absolutely not. No way,' says Rod emphatically.

'But won't you at least think about it?' I plead with him.

I had waited for at least forty-five minutes before broaching the subject of me taking over from Robin and directing the film, and I can see by his reaction that it was a wise move.

'Molly, you haven't directed for seven years – that's a hell of a long time. Things have moved on.'

'I'd noticed,' I say defiantly. 'And maybe not for the best. Why can't I do it? I've made a career out of these sorts of documentaries – I'm good with people. I can draw them out of themselves without being too intrusive and people like talking to me. Why

56

don't you let me give it a go? At least let me go and meet Florence. After all, what have you got to lose? She's refusing to continue with Robin, and how easy is it going to be to find another director,' I correct myself, 'I mean a good director to take over and work well with her?'

I'm aware that the restaurant tablecloths are white linen and beautifully ironed as Rod sits in silence staring at me. It's suddenly become the most important thing in the world for me to do this film, and not only because at last I'd be getting a proper salary for the three or four months it would take to make it.

I continue to press Rod. 'Apparently Florence gets on with Matt. I've made at least five films with him and we work extremely well together; we have a shorthand. You know what it's like. That could save you a lot of time and money.'

If there's one way to get to Rod it's to mention cutting costs, but he doesn't react and just sits there shaking his head. 'I don't know, I just don't know.'

For a few seconds I feel sorry for him but it doesn't last long. 'What is your problem with me doing it?'

'I just don't think you're ready to commit to a project like this. It's my baby, Molly, and I'd have to be sure you could give it a hundred per cent.'

For a minute I falter. Maybe he's right, but I feel so sure that this is the right project for me. I just know it.

The remaining hours of the day are ticking by agonisingly slowly. I watch different people traipse into Rod's office, see him on the phone ringing round all the excellent directors he knows, and all the time I'm praying that they're unavailable. I can't bear it any longer – I haven't been able to concentrate on anything else all day, not even my favourite registry office programme. I get my coat with one final glance in Rod's direction, to see him talking animatedly on the phone. As I walk past Jade's desk Rod opens the door and I look hopefully in his direction. He stares blankly at me and then says to Jade, 'Get Matt on the phone' and retreats back into his office, leaving me no wiser.

As I travel down in the lift I think, 'Why can't it be me?' I walk through the reception and out of the automatic doors, taking a deep breath and bracing myself for the cold air that greets me. It's beginning to rain and a few drops trickle down the back of my collar. The thought of the children makes me walk quickly. Today of all days I feel in need of a hug.

'Molly!'

I hear a shout and turn to see Rod without a coat running towards me. He reaches me, puffing, and says, 'OK – you can go and meet her but I'm not making any promises. We'll just see how you get on and take it from there.'

'Thank you.' I feel overwhelmingly grateful and I'm tempted to say, 'You won't regret it,' but I don't want to push my luck. My hair is dripping wet and Rod hands me a huge file – the ink on the label has run, making it illegible.

'Here are some research notes that you can look at tonight and we'll talk after you've met her.' He is having trouble getting the words out, still puffed from running, his thinning hair hanging in wet streaks down the side of his face. 'You'd better not screw this one up.'

'I won't.' I'm so pleased I move forward to give him a hug and then think better of it, as it's not very professional. People hurry past us, heads bent against the rain, some struggling with umbrellas in the cold wind, all rushing to get to the Tube station. It occurs to me that they may think we're having a romantic moment together but I don't care as my heart is soaring and I'm ridiculously pleased – this is better than romance.

As I open the door I hear 'Bang bang bang . . . dddddd' and I can see Max peering round the staircase pretending to shoot me with something that I vaguely recognise. Nowadays if he's not Spiderman he's constantly under assault from unknown forces, but at this precise moment it's me that he's attacking.

I put my hands up, immediately surrendering. 'Max, what have you got in your hand?'

'A gun,' he says as if stating the obvious but it doesn't look like a gun to me.

'Max, put it down,' I say sharply.

'No. Don't want to!'

'What is it in its normal life? Can I have a look?'

Reluctantly he hands it to me and as soon as I hold it I recognise it as my father's old super 8 camera which I haven't seen for years, and lying on the stairs is its battered leather case. I stroke it, surprised at how emotional I feel. I used to think the camera was physically attached to my father, an extension of his arm, as he always had it with him. Images of hot beaches, being buried in the sand, picnics in the shade, all captured on grainy film, my father's long shadow occasionally caught when the sun moved unexpectedly, but usually an invisible presence. He was only an amateur, but he loved filming, and I suppose it was because of his enthusiasm that I went into television.

'Can I have it back now?' demands Max.

'Where did you find it?'

'Dad found it in those old boxes he was clearing out in the loft to make space to do his writing. Please can I have it back now?' he says, tired of having to explain things.

'Max, you might break it and I'd be very cross – it's special – it belonged to your grandpa many years ago.'

Max is not interested in the details. All he wants is his newly acquired gun back.

'Let's see if we can find something else that you could use,' I say, trying to be helpful.

'No, that was a really good gun.' He starts to howl and I realise that I'm not handling the situation very well. I'm surprised at myself. Before I was working I knew exactly how to diffuse a situation like this, but tonight I haven't got the energy or the imagination so I resort to bribery.

'Would you like some chocolate?'

He nods his head, his eyes fixed on the camera in my hand, and like a sniffer dog hot on the trail of chocolate, Evie comes into the kitchen demanding, 'Can I have one?'

'How was your day, Evie?'

'Fine,' she replies, enjoying the chocolate. 'Guess what?'

'You've had a row with Scarlet?'

'No, nothing like that.'

'S Club have split up.'

'That happened ages ago – don't be silly.'

'I give up.' I wipe Max's nose but he's stopped crying, soothed by the chocolate.

'I'm playing the sleepy shepherd in the Christmas play.'

'That's fantastic.'

I think back to this time last year when I had time to enjoy planning for Christmas. Even then it seemed unbelievably busy, but I think I'd managed to buy nearly all the presents by the beginning of December. This year it's going to be a little different.

'It's the main part,' Evie says proudly.

'Well done. What do you have to do?'

'Sleep a lot I should imagine, sounds good to me,' says Aidan, walking into the kitchen.

'I've got some news too,' I say, and then think, how do you explain that going to meet an old woman in a retirement home is exciting? I try my best but then Max says, 'But you said you'd take me to judo tomorrow. I haven't been for weeks. You promised.' I have a vague memory of making this promise and immediately feel guilty.

Aidan looks blankly at me. 'I can't – I've promised to meet Terry – it's to do with the script. He thinks he might know someone who would be interested in investing. I've got to go.'

'Mum, I'm sorry to do this, but is there any way you could look after the children tomorrow? It's just for the day. If this meeting works out I might have got myself a job and it's an exciting one.'

I can hear the disapproval seeping along the telephone line.

'It'll only be for tomorrow.'

'And then what will you do?' she says.

'I don't know, I'll have to work something out.'

Something in my voice makes her relent. 'Well, all right,' she says stoically.

'Thank you, you're the best mother I've ever had, as Max would say.'

She laughs.

'Guess what Max just found?'

'I give up,' she says.

'Dad's old super 8 camera – I haven't been to check the box but I should imagine all the old super 8 films will be there and the projector. I'd love to see them again.'

'Yes,' she says quietly.

I press the phone tight to my ear, 'Mum?'

'I've got to go – my supper is spoiling. See you tomorrow, Molly.' She puts the phone down and I feel lost.

'Mummee,' Evie calls down the stairs, 'there's no loo paper.'

I hang up and go upstairs to discover she's right – there isn't a single scrap of loo paper or tissue as I used the last one wiping Max's nose.

'Aidan!' I shout up the stairs, 'Did you go to the supermarket?'

I hear a quiet, 'Oh shit,' followed by a pause. Then, 'I'll go now,' and before I get a chance to remind him about all the other things we might need, he's out of the door, leaving me to put the children to bed and wonder what we can have for supper.

'Matt – it's Molly.'

'Hi'. He sounds surprised to hear me.

'I wasn't sure I had the right number still – but I wanted to tell you that Rod has agreed, eventually, to let me go and see Florence tomorrow. If it works out then I think he'll let me direct the film.' I feel excited just saying it.

'That's fantastic.' He sounds genuinely pleased.

'Look, I'm sorry to ring you at home but I thought it would be good to speak to you before meeting Florence. Is there anything I should know about her? Obviously I've got the research notes that Rod gave me but I thought there might be things that you've picked up over the past few weeks filming with her?'

'Don't worry about it. The main thing is not to patronise her or treat her any differently from anyone else. She's bright and she's all there but she doesn't suffer fools gladly. What does annoy her is any dithering and people being pretentious. I think you'll get on really well – she'll love you.'

When I come off the phone I can hear Aidan downstairs unpacking the shopping and as I walk into the kitchen he holds up a packet of processed frankfurters and says, 'Where do these go?'

'In the bin?' I suggest, moving to unpack the rest of the bags.

'Don't be like that, I love them.'

'Good – well, you put them where you can find them,' I say peremptorily.

'Look, I'm sorry about the shopping, but Molly, it's been three weeks of this – I can't do it any more. I had an inspired day today, it was flowing out of me, and I can't think about super-markets, school runs or judo lessons. Don't you understand?'

'I'm trying, Aidan, but we've got to eat, the house has to be cleaned, and the children should be able to carry on with their lives, doing the things they enjoy doing, as long as we can afford it.'

'We can't go on like this,' says Aidan, taking out a bag of crisps and opening it.

'What do you want me to do?'

'Get us some help.' Aidan is cramming crisps into his mouth. 'I didn't have lunch today,' he says as he wipes away the crumbs from his mouth and picks up another huge handful.

'Mum can come tomorrow.'

'Good old Elizabeth – I knew she'd save the day. I don't know why she's not leaping at the chance to help us out. You'd have thought it would have been something for her to do.'

'It's not that easy for her, you know. You know how exhausting it can be looking after the kids, and she's got a lot on, what with the wedding and her business.'

'Well, we've got to sort something out.'

'I know, but after tomorrow I'll know more where I stand. If the meeting is a success then we will have some money coming in and I can start to look around seriously for someone to help us.'

'This meeting tomorrow – what's that all about then?'

I stop taking the apples out of their plastic bag and stare at Aidan, making the most of the moment. I resist the temptation to ring Jo and say, 'You're wrong – he asked a question, he is interested after all.' Instead I start telling him about the project.

'What's good about it is that it's a film, part of a prestigious series and not just a make-over programme or a magazine show, and if I can do it it would be a great kick-start to my career.'

'Have you discussed money with Rod yet?' Aidan holds up two packets of Hobnobs as if asking where he should put them.

'In the cupboard by the fridge,' I say, marvelling that we could have lived here for so many years and he still doesn't know where anything is kept. 'No, there's no point. First I've got to persuade Florence to carry on with the filming and then I can discuss money.'

'You need an agent.'

'This isn't Hollywood, Aidan.'

'It's bloody slave labour what you're doing at the moment. If you're not careful Rod will be asking you to pay him for the privilege of directing this film.'

I feel worried, and Aidan comes to me and puts his arms around me. It feels awkward, his chest firm and unforgiving, and I don't know whether to drop my head on his shoulder or to look at him.

'Don't worry – I'll do your negotiating if you like, if you give me ten per cent.'

'I'm not worried about that at the moment, but what does worry me is if it does work out I'll be working even harder. I'll need your help in other ways.'

Now it's Aidan's turn to look worried. He lets me go and picks up as many bottles of beer as he can carry and walks over to the fridge. 'Of course, I understand,' he says, but as I look at him using all the available space in the fridge stacking his bottles of beer while the children's yoghurts sit abandoned on the side, I wonder if he really does.

I work late into the night reading all the research notes on Florence Bird and by the time I've finished the house is dark, save for the reflection of the street lamp shining through the windows, and glancing at my watch I'm surprised to see how late it is. I go to check Evie and Max, something I do every night before I go to sleep. As I walk into Evie's room I'm suddenly aware that someone else is in there crouching by the wooden shelves. For a second my heart beats faster.

'Who is it?' I whisper.

'Who do you think?' replies Aidan sarcastically, and I resist the desire to laugh with relief. Who did I think it would be?

'What are you doing?' I whisper.

'Nothing,' he says guiltily, and as if he can make out my sceptical expression in the dark he reluctantly adds, 'All right then, I've just been rearranging her shelves.'

Peering through the darkness, I can see rows of china dolls evenly spaced, the perfume bottles that she was given by her grandmother carefully placed for maximum effect. He's holding up her coloured pencils in his hand.

'I'm just going to reorder her colours so that they're colour-co-ordinated – it will make it much easier for her when she's doing her drawing.'

I wonder whether losing his job has made him more obsessed than usual or if he's always been like this.

'She won't be pleased that you've been fiddling around with her things,' I say to him.

'But it looks better, doesn't it?' he says with a strange glint in his eye.

'I'm going to bed.' And I leave him to start rearranging the beanie toys to satisfy his well-tuned aesthetic sensibilities.

Five

I switch on the wipers but it's not raining hard enough, so they soon start squeaking on the dry windscreen. 'It will only take you forty minutes from where you are,' Matt said last night but he failed to mention the queues of traffic stretching both ways along the dual carriageway. My head is full of Florence Bird, character actress and comedienne, and I know more about her than I do about my mother's life – her Lancashire roots, father a vicar, mother the typical vicar's wife, and Florence an only child. I know that she upset the family when she announced she wanted to become an actress, 'like I'd announced I was going on the streets'. I read about her early days as a comedienne and even how a jealous comic drew moustaches on all her posters because she was getting more laughs than he was. I'm up to date with all the friends she met and kept throughout her career and how she joined ENSA during the war, later touring with the regional repertory companies, married, had a child, appeared in countless television series in supporting roles but fame was always elusive. She's one of those actresses whose face everyone knows but who still remains anonymous. All I hope for from today is that we get on and I can persuade her to let me finish making the film.

I dressed carefully this morning, determined to make a good impression, and after much deliberation chose an inoffensive plain skirt, cardigan and sensible earrings, as I don't want to intimidate Florence. Should I call her Mrs Bird, which sounds so formal, or Florence, which could be too familiar? So much rests on this first meeting, I must get it right. 'Just be yourself,' my mother always says, but what if that isn't good enough?

*

There's nothing theatrical about the sign for Russell Court, the retirement home for actors where Florence/Mrs Bird lives, but what was I expecting? Searchlights on the driveway like a big opening night in Leicester Square or a dancing troupe to welcome each new visitor? My journey, however, is getting increasingly dramatic as I make my way along the long winding drive. I have to slow down as I peer through the windscreen, my wipers groaning at double speed, straining to keep it clear. Then suddenly, through a little gap that remains clear for an instant, Russell Court looms in front of me. I park the car and notice that my hands feel clammy, even though it's cold outside, and I wipe them on my jacket as I make my way up the stone steps into the stately late-Victorian mansion.

The entrance hall is equally impressive, with a grand staircase and a number of oil portraits in large gilt frames. I walk to the bottom of the stairs and peer up at the pictures of Sarah Bernhardt, Ellen Terry, Laurence Olivier, Vivian Leigh – they're all here. Three men are pushing a large Christmas tree back into an alcove beside the stairs to leave enough room for people to pass. On the right are some lifts and opposite a few chairs placed for visitors. I've arranged to meet Eleanor Garnett, RGN, the home administrator, here, so I sit down and acclimatise. On the small table to my right are more pictures. The biggest photograph shows a portly Edwardian man surrounded by a group of elegant elderly men and women, dressed in their Sunday best, standing almost exactly where I'm sitting. The inscription reads, 'Gerald Russell welcomes Queen Mary to Russell Court'. I study the faces in the photograph, fascinated by the individual expressions, until a voice drags me back to the present.

'Can I help you?'

'Yes, I'm here to see Eleanor Garnett.'

The woman gives a little nod and sits down beside me. Eleanor Garnett is exactly as I imagined her to be, if not a little older than I expected, and there's no trace of the slight Scottish accent I thought I'd heard when we spoke on the phone. Although called a home administrator, she's central casting for an old-fashioned matron, from the tip of her immaculately permed hair to her carefully polished, sensible shoes.

I introduce myself and she says, 'Yes, we were expecting you. I must say we're all surprised that Florence has agreed to see you, but we've said we'll meet you and then decide whether we want to continue participating in this project.' She pronounces the final word with a slight curl in her lip as if it is distasteful.

Putting on my politest voice I say, 'I'm very grateful that you've let me come today.'

She looks at me with a curious expression and I try to lighten the atmosphere by smiling at her. For a few seconds we sit in silence, listening to the sound of an old grandfather clock, and I struggle to adjust to the more sedate pace of life, resisting the urge to try to speed things up. The lift doors open and two elderly women step out, one wearing a long dark velvet coat and hat, walking slowly with a stick; the other, doing up the buttons on her bright red mac, appears to be more sprightly. She takes the arm of her companion, who protests loudly. 'Dora darling, I really think I should take the wheelchair – we won't get anywhere at this rate.'

'No, Elspeth, they said you should try to walk more. I don't mind going slowly.'

'You'll be handing out stars next, silver if you can get to the gate and gold if you make it to the village.'

She has a wonderful deep voice that could only have evolved through years of acting and smoking. They look at us with curiosity and Eleanor quickly introduces me. 'This is the new one they've sent us – I'm sorry, dear, what was your name?'

'Molly,' I say.

They look at me with interest, taking in every little detail, and I feel awkward.

'We'd better be going, if we want to be back by lunchtime,' says the more agile of the two.

'Fish and chips and peach melba today,' says Eleanor encouragingly.

'Come on, I'll race you,' Elspeth says drolly as she leans on her stick and with supreme effort forces her left foot forward. As they disappear slowly out of the front door I look expectantly at Eleanor, but she just remains in her seat and when I catch her eye she only smiles at me but does nothing. I look at my watch and hope that she'll notice, and when I catch her eye a second time she smiles again and looks away down the corridor so that I think we must be waiting for someone.

I break the silence. 'How many residents do you have here?'

'Around forty when we're full – there's quite a waiting list, you know – but not everyone comes in permanently. Dora, whom you just met, is on a mini-break, a short stay while her daughter has to go away and she can't cope on her own. We like these transitory visitors – it keeps us on our toes.'

A woman in her late fifties, with short hair and an efficient manner, walks past. She nods at my companion and looks anxiously towards the front door. She hovers at the bottom of the staircase.

'Waiting for someone, are you?' asks Eleanor.

'That bloody woman from the television company. She said she'd be here about ten minutes ago. I should have expected it – they're never on time and always in a hurry. I don't know why we're even seeing them again.'

I feel my face turn scarlet but I jump to my feet and say, 'I'm Molly Mankin from Pulse Productions – I'm sorry I've been talking to Eleanor here – I didn't realise I was supposed to be meeting you as well.'

She looks acutely embarrassed, but not being the sort of woman who would ever apologise she introduces herself. 'I'm Eleanor Garnett, the home administrator.'

'Oh, but I thought . . .' I say, turning back to my elderly companion still sitting beside me.

'I can never remember who I am,' she says, grinning happily.

'This is Margery,' the real Eleanor Garnett says, and now I can detect the Scottish lilt to her voice that I had heard previously on the phone. We're both feeling a little stupid and very awkward.

68

'Florence is waiting for you. Come with me,' she says, and as I follow her along the corridor I glance back at Margery who gives me a little wave.

Eleanor leads me along the wide, well-carpeted corridors, which remind me of a plush Bournemouth hotel. A large black nurse swings her way along the corridor towards us, humming under her breath as she pushes a trolley with tea and biscuits.

'Good morning, Comfort.'

'Morning, Eleanor.'

'Oh, watch out, here's trouble.' Comfort laughs amiably as a well-dressed man in a jacket and tie with his thick white-grey hair slicked down approaches, a copy of *The Times* newspaper folded under his arm. There's something about his face that I recognise and I wonder if it was from some drama series from my childhood or an old advert. He stands flat against the corridor wall but he doesn't make it easy for us to pass.

'Morning, ladies,' he says, slowly enunciating every syllable.

'Morning, Maurice,' Eleanor replies briskly as she walks past as quickly as possible.

'Marvellous breasts,' he says, clearly enunciating each syllable. I'm not sure whether he's referring to me or to Eleanor.

Comfort, clearly used to such comments, says, 'A biscuit, Maurice?'

I glance back and he smiles at me mischievously, his eyes glinting under his thick grey twirly eyebrows that turn up at the ends like question marks. His expression reminds me of Max when he knows he's being naughty. Eleanor pays absolutely no attention and we continue in silence while I try to read the names on the doors as they flash by: 'Miss Violet Cartwright', 'Mrs Elspeth Todd', 'Miss Dora George'. I imagine the excitement these women must have felt when they first saw their names written on a dressing-room door, and think that perhaps in those days their names would have been accompanied by a star. I try not to look too closely into the rooms where the doors are left ajar, worried I might see something distressing. I realise that I've blocked my nose and I'm breathing through my mouth, expecting an unpleasant smell of cabbage and urine, but to my surprise when I eventually breathe normally, Russell Court smells of pot pourri and polish.

I make conversation with Eleanor, trying to discover useful information, but she's reluctant to talk, not wanting to waste her breath on me. Along the corridor walls are black and white photographs, taken from scenes in films, and costume design drawings from landmark theatrical productions.

'Are all the residents actors?' I ask, persisting, determined to prise some useful information out of her before our journey's end. She stops abruptly to make way for a balding man wearing a battered black leather jacket and leaning on a shiny black stick, walking slowly towards us like an injured insect.

'Morning, Bernard.'

'Morning, Mrs Garnett,' he says gruffly, concentrating on his journey without registering my presence.

As we turn a corner Eleanor says grudgingly, 'Bernard, whom we just passed in the corridor, was an eminent film and theatre director, but we have had stage managers, producers, designers – there has to be some connection with the theatre. Actors get priority but we also have been known to have the odd ballet dancer, though only from the Royal Ballet.'

Encouraged by her response, I keep probing. 'And what about you, do you have a connection with the theatre?'

'I used to be an agent but I qualified as a nurse as well.' She looks annoyed with herself, as if she's divulged too much information.

I follow Eleanor into a large room with tall windows overlooking the gardens. A small false Christmas tree stands on an oak sideboard; paper chains and sparkly decorations are balanced precariously along the picture rail. There are a few elderly people dozing in chairs, one man with his mouth wide open, and the ones who are awake watch me expectantly. A woman in pink smiles at me and as I smile back I notice the grey hairs flowing from her chin. Eleanor is leading me towards a woman sitting in the corner by a window reading a book with a magnifying glass and I immediately recognise her from the newspaper cuttings. As soon as Eleanor introduces us she seems to disappear, she leaves so quickly.

Florence looks elegant in black slacks, polo neck and red lipstick, and with one glance I realise that I've worn completely the wrong clothes as I'd imagined her being more twin-set and perm. I hover until Florence indicates to the chair to her left. 'Do you want to sit down? You might find it more relaxing.'

I smile nervously as I sit down. 'Thank you. This is a lovely spot.'

My voice booms out in the silent room. We have a view of each other and of the lawns and the trees blurred by the rain.

'Awful weather and it's so chilly, isn't it?' I say, trying to make conversation. My voice sounds false, too keen.

'The weather – not exactly an original start to a conversation but a useful ice-breaker. I think it's boiling in here as they always have the heating on full blast to keep our old bones warm I suppose.' She runs her fingers along the rim of her polo-neck sweater as if letting in air to cool her neck.

'Would you like some tea?' She's being guarded and cordial but there is no warmth in her tone and her pale green eyes are fixed on my face.

'That would be lovely.' I smile at her but get nothing in return. She stares at me, and to avoid her scrutiny I look away out of the window and catch sight of a solitary magpie circling round the far end of the building. I crane my neck to see if his mate is nearby, but he's alone and I wonder if it's a bad omen.

'So you're the Boy Wonder's replacement?' Her intonation gives away her Lancastrian roots, her voice, deep and gravelly, rumbling from her chest.

'I'm sorry?' I ask, my voice sounding squeaky, lightweight in comparison.

'The Boy Wonder.' She makes a tutting sound. 'He thought he was so clever but I'm sorry, I find it very difficult to trust a man who walks around with his underpants showing. I was never sure about him, sometimes you just know with people don't you?'

I feel uncomfortable – does she know with me? I feel my face flush red and wish I could take off my cardigan but I've only got an old T-shirt on underneath that has gone off-white in one of Aidan's mixed washes. As we've got on to the topic of Robin remarkably quickly I think I should apologize for him.

'I'm sorry about Robin – I don't really know him – I've only just joined the company but I think what they did was unforgivable really. Was the man . . .' I hesitate, trying to put it delicately, but in the end I finish lamely with, 'a good friend of yours?'

She raises her hand and gently pats her carefully coiffed hair, making sure everything is in its proper place, and I notice she's wearing a gold bracelet packed full of different charms.

'Do you mean Arthur, the one they filmed?'

'Yes.'

She runs her fingers over the charms without looking at them, first a tiny gold key, next a sea horse and finally three monkeys all hanging together, depicting 'Hear no evil, see no evil, speak no evil'.

'We're all friends in here, this is our home, and we all get along pretty well. I worked with Arthur over fifty years ago in a revue at the Brighton Alhambra.'

She leans forward and looks around to check that no one can hear us. 'To tell the honest truth, I couldn't stand the bugger but still, there was no need to do that to him. You can't go round filming people like that. The Boy Wonder was a bloody idiot and Arthur's family were very upset and I don't blame them.'

She pauses for a minute. 'Mind you, for an actor who could never stop mugging it was probably one of the stillest performances he ever gave.'

She sits back in her chair and looks at me to see what I make of this. I smile, but as I notice that she is completely deadpan I wonder if I'm supposed to. She starts to pour out the tea, her hand remarkably steady for an eighty-three-year-old, her charm bracelet knocking against the tea pot. Noticing me watching her, she says, 'I like to pour it myself. They indulge me with proper cups and saucers. I've never got accustomed to mugs. Milk, sugar?'

'Just milk, thank you.'

She passes me my cup and saucer which rattles as soon as I take it from her. I put it down quickly on the table in front of us. Florence continues, 'I think the Boy Wonder thought we were going to be like a geriatric Fame Academy springing about on our Zimmer frames in the canteen. I always felt we were a disappointment.'

She stirs her tea, never taking her eyes off me. 'What did you expect – Gloria Swanson?'

I laugh again. 'I was looking forward to meeting you – I've only read the research notes but it seems as if you've led an interesting life.'

She guffaws. 'Interesting life.' She imitates my accent. 'Some might say that.'

'Would you say that?'

She looks straight at me, those eyes startlingly direct, her white hair carefully brushed off her face, softening her features. She has a small mole on her chin and her face is a mass of lines, wrinkles and creases, and I survey them, hoping they might provide a clue to her character, like a sailor studying his navigation charts.

'I can't complain.'

She's not saying much; her silence is theatrical. She takes a sip of her tea and I notice the pronounced veins on her hands, the liver spots like large freckles, and a big knuckle-duster of a gold ring with one large topaz nestling in between two smaller stones. She has long, well-kept nails painted red and I close my fists hoping that she won't notice my own badly chewed nails. As she puts the cup down she stares at me again.

'So what were you doing before you decided to come and bully an old lady into making a film?'

She's trying to get a reaction, so I smile at her, attempting to hide the fact that I'm finding her hard to gauge. I'm not sure I'm the bully round here.

'Nothing . . . well, it wasn't nothing . . . I haven't been working the past few years . . . well, I have . . .'

She looks at me impatiently. I try to collect my thoughts, remembering Matt's warning that she hates any dithering.

'What I mean to say is I used to work and made lots of films but I gave it up when I had my children, so I've been looking after them for the past few years.'

'How many?'

'Seven,' I mumble, hoping she can't hear me.

'Seven children – like the old woman in the shoe.'

'No, not seven children, seven years and only two children.'

She looks unimpressed by this information and I realise that she's auditioning me. I feel that any minute she will shout 'Next' and make it clear that I must leave.

'Why did you give up work?'

I don't want to tell her my reasons and anyway, I thought I was supposed to be doing the interviewing. She's interrogating me like a prosecuting lawyer and I wonder if she's drawing on a previous performance in a legal drama series.

'It was because of family concerns.' I try to sound circumspect.

'And that interfered with your work?'

'I just wanted to be with my children.'

'Ah.'

Once again I can't tell if she approves or disapproves and I realise that she is looking over my shoulder. I turn, following her gaze, to see a woman with thin hair dyed pale brown, walking slowly towards us humming happily to herself.

'Oh no, not now,' Florence mutters under her breath, but the woman takes no notice of Florence's expression and holds out her grubby white paper bag, the sort you'd find in an old-fashioned sweet shop.

'Toffee?' she offers, and to my surprise she bends down and kisses my cheek.

'Thank you, Violet,' Florence says, irritated by the interruption.

'Do you want one?' Violet holds out a toffee to Florence.

'No, I don't,' she says tetchily. 'Now, please leave us alone – we're talking.'

As she hobbles off Florence leans forward. 'Sorry about that. It's very sad. She's on the turn, if you know what I mean. Perfectly harmless but she's always doing that, and you can imagine the toffees play havoc with all the false teeth round here. Thankfully that's not a problem I have.' She grins a Cheshire cat grin and knocks her front teeth with her knuckles.

The atmosphere between us seems to be lightening and I think we're beginning to get on quite well. I look around the room. Florence seems out of place – it seems too soon for her to be here.

'Why did you decide to come here?' I ask.

'That's none of your business,' she snaps, and I'm stung by her tone. 'I feel very lucky to be here. You do realise that this is no ordinary retirement home where you turn up like an anonymous old bat and no one has a clue who you are or what your life was like? Can you imagine how depressing that would be? In here we're all from the same world and the bar is an extension of the green room. We don't just talk about the old days but about friends we have in common and the work some of us are still doing. It keeps the old grey cells ticking over and I like a good gossip. Funnily enough, I've spent a lot of my life trying to avoid actors *en masse* but they're a good bunch in here. You wouldn't believe how difficult it is to get into this place – harder than Eton. Do they have retirement homes for documentary directors?' she asks me.

For a few minutes we sit in silence, and my mind races trying to think of something to say that won't offend her, but before I can she interrupts my thoughts.

'So why did you decide to come back to work?'

I'd be a useless politician as I'm one of those people who have to answer a question if asked. So I find myself telling her about Aidan losing his job, but trying not to sound as if I'm too desperate, I talk about my desire to make a good film.

'So you think a film about me would be good?'

'Yes – I think the whole series is interesting, following the different stages in life and focusing on individuals. It's not a fashionable idea but it will make a change from makeover and reality shows.'

'*Wife Swap*'s one of my favourites.'

'Really?' I say, surprised.

'Yes, I find it fascinating.'

'Well, I think this series could be fascinating if we can pull it off.'

'Do you think you can pull it off?'

'Yes, I think so, especially with Matt. We've made so many films together that we trust and understand each other.' I pause, watching her reaction. 'Well, that is if you're happy to continue making the film with Matt after everything that's happened?'

'Matt's a nice boy.'

It's the first time I've heard her voice soften and I imagine that Florence may be one of those women who get on better with men.

'It wasn't Matt who was irresponsible,' Florence says.

'Matt would never have done anything like that,' I agree with her.

'I don't trust his assistant – he won't be allowed back into Russell Court if I know Eleanor. In fact I'm amazed she's let any of you back.' She leans forward and says conspiratorially, 'I insisted, you know.'

'I'm glad,' I reply, 'but I'm curious – why did you insist? I would have thought you'd be pleased to see the back of us.'

For the first time since we've met she looks flustered. Her thumb nervously strokes the topaz ring which slides from side to side on her finger.

'Call it professional pride.'

'Florence,' I say her name cautiously as it's the first time I've addressed her directly but she doesn't seem to mind, 'why did you want to be in the film?'

'Why, do you think I shouldn't do the film?'

'Well, no . . . obviously I think you should do it but I'm curious to know why.'

'Would you do it? Or let's put it like this, is your mother alive?'

'Yes.' Again the conversation is getting a bit too close to home for me.

'Well, would you want her to do something like this?'

And before I can stop myself I answer honestly, 'No.'

'Why not?' She looks surprised.

'Well, she's a different personality to you.' It would be my mother's idea of hell. 'Also, I know what a dreadful imposition it is to be constantly filmed. Not only would I not wish it on my mother, I wouldn't do it myself.' What am I saying? Is this the way to go about persuading her to let us continue filming?

'So you've met me for, how long, for half an hour, and you think you know me so well already?' I can't tell whether she's getting cross or if she's teasing me.

'My mother would hate all the attention, she just wants to get on with life quietly and independently.'

'And I'm just an old notice box, is that what you're saying?' she says, watching my reaction like a bird of prey waiting to make its move.

Cross at her probing questions, I decide attack is the best method of defence. 'You still haven't answered my question – why do you want to do this film?'

'I don't think I do,' she says flatly, leaning her head back against the chair, and I feel an acute pang of disappointment. 'I'm tired. I think you'd better go.'

There's nothing more I can do. I had my chance and I blew it. Why was I so honest? A bit of fudging and I probably could have persuaded her. I stand up, straightening my sensible skirt, and feel at a loss for words. 'Well, goodbye.'

She doesn't respond.

'Thank you for the tea anyway.'

She still doesn't say anything.

'Please take some time to think about it.'

She doesn't even look at me, and after pausing for a few seconds I turn to go. As I walk out of the room Violet waves at me with a toffee still in her hand and I can hear loud snores coming from the man with the open mouth. The woman I met in reception and mistook for Eleanor, the home administrator, is sitting near the door reading a newspaper and doing the crossword. As I walk past her she looks up over her reading-glasses and says amiably, 'See you again, my dear.'

'I hope so,' I say, thinking that it's extremely unlikely. I find myself thinking that when I get to the door I'll turn round, and if Florence is watching me then I may still be in with a chance. Once I reach the door I glance back quickly but Florence is in her own world, sitting in the same position staring out of the window, watching the rain dripping from the trees.

I don't want to go home immediately and it's too late to go to work, so I drive to the supermarket to buy all the essentials that Aidan forgot yesterday. As I wander aimlessly pushing my trolley between the aisles, I run the conversation I had with Florence over in my mind. Why was I so honest? How could I be so stupid? Maybe Rod is right and I'm not ready for all of this. The thought of Rod makes me feel worse. I can't even begin to think how furious he is going to be now that I've put his precious project in jeopardy.

Back home, my mother is all smiles. 'You're back earlier than I expected. How was the meeting?'

'Not good.'

'I'm sure it went better than you think.'

'I don't think so, Mum, but thanks. Everything all right here?'

'Evie has gone to play with her friend Rachel and I've just dropped Max off at judo. Aidan called to say that he won't be back until later because he's having supper with Terry – he sounded quite happy.'

'Good. Listen, thanks, Mum – you can go if you want.'

'You sure you'll be all right?' she asks, concerned.

'I'm fine.'

*

After she's gone I sit on a bar stool nursing a herbal cup of tea, feeling useless. I look around at the empty, clean kitchen that my mother has tidied up, the surfaces gleaming as shiny as a Flash advert. The bags of shopping lie slumped by my feet on the floor. After gazing at them for a few minutes I finish my tea and start to unpack the shopping, putting aside tonight's supper from the mountains of food I bought to freeze. I put on my apron, wash my hands, pull down the chopping board, take my sharpest knife and start chopping onions. It takes only a few minutes before my eyes start to water, but instead of being irritating it feels cathartic. For the rest of the evening I chop, stir, mix, beat, whisk and fry in a frenzy, punctuated only by collecting the children and putting them to bed. This is my domain, this is what I can do, this is all I'm fit for. Here in my kitchen I feel confident, secure, comforted and, by the time I hear Aidan's key in the door, exhausted by my orgy of cooking.

He walks into the kitchen where the work surfaces are straining under carefully labelled freezer bags full of bolognese sauce, leek and potato soup, chocolate brownies, flapjacks, biscuits and fairy cakes, not an inch of granite to be seen. He looks slowly around, taking in the mountains of food, before he focuses on me.

'The meeting?'

'Don't ask.'

He walks over and strokes my arm sympathetically. 'At least we won't starve.'

I try to smile.

'I'm sorry,' he says, shrugging his shoulders.

'So am I.'

I undo my apron and hang it over the bar of the oven before switching off the lights, and we walk up the stairs to bed, both of us silent in the darkness.

Six

I'm dreading going into the office as I know Rod is going to have his 'I told you so' expression and I'm going to find it hard looking anyone in the eye since I've failed so miserably. I travel up in the lift feeling that people are staring at me, and I wonder if I've got toothpaste on my top, mascara in my hair or a sign saying 'loser' stamped on my forehead.

Walking down the corridor, I hear a familiar voice shout at me, 'So how did it go?'

Cassie runs to catch up with me and just as I start to tell her about yesterday's disastrous meeting, Rod Harman comes out of his office and barks, 'Molly, in here . . . now.'

'He always did have a way with words,' says Cassie. 'Don't worry, what's the worst that can happen?'

'I don't want to think about it . . .' I say, following after Rod, '. . . but I want to be buried in my suede jacket with photos of my children in my pockets.'

'OK, I'll make a note,' says Cassie, and as I walk into Rod's office I quickly put my head back around the door and say, '. . . or do you think that's bad luck?'

'Molly,' Rod growls, and I go back in and shut the door behind me. He is shuffling papers round his desk, ignoring me as I stand near to the door ready to make a quick exit.

'Listen, I'm sorry . . .' I hesitate, not sure what to say except, 'Sorry I was useless, and you were right, I'm not fit to do anything but wipe my children's bottoms,' but somehow I don't think that would be appropriate.

'I've just had Russell Court on the phone.' His forehead wrinkles with worry. 'I don't know what you did or said . . .' He pauses, looking at my anxious face.

'I can explain,' I struggle to interrupt, but he doesn't let me finish.

'. . but she's on board again.'

'I'm sorry?' I say, not understanding what he's telling me.

'The old lady, Florence Bird, has said she wants to carry on filming and she'll only do it if you're involved.' He speaks as if he's explaining it to a small child with learning difficulties.

'That's amazing,' I say, stunned.

'Something about you being an "honest lass".' Rod says the word as if honesty is an alien concept to him. 'I'd like you to start filming as soon as possible – would Friday be too soon?'

'I'm sure that's fine,' I say quickly, worried that he might change his mind.

'That's less than a week and you've got a lot of work to do before then.'

I stand up, dazed, and as I get to the door he adds, 'Oh, and Molly, you had better make this work. I've put my neck out on this one – any hiccups and you're off the project.'

Still stunned by the news, I walk out of the office.

'What happened?' asks Cassie gently.

'Well . . .' I pretend to look like I'm about to burst into tears. 'I think . . .'

'Oh, Molly,' she says, trying to be supportive.

'I think I'm going to be very busy.' I allow a broad smile to cross my face while Cassie looks bemused. 'The old woman said yes and what's more she said she'd only do it with me.'

'That's bloody amazing.'

'I know.' I give Cassie a hug. 'She must be bloody bonkers but I don't care. What a relief. At last we'll have some money coming in.'

As the news settles a runner pulls a trolley piled high with boxes in front of me. He heaves the first box on to the desk and it towers above me like a cardboard Everest. I peer inside to see files bulging with research notes, mini-mountains of video tapes stacked high – presumably the rushes that Robin has filmed – recordings of old TV programmes and films that Florence must have appeared in, and sheets of shot lists explaining all the contents.

Cassie comes round to my side of the desk and picks up the first video that is perched on top of the precarious pile.

'*The Good Old Days*,' she reads out loud and then picks up another tape.

'What's this, *Worzel Gummidge*? Your Florence has had an interesting career,' she says drily, and then, seeing my expression, says kindly, 'Do you want a hand?'

I couldn't be more grateful if Sherpa Tensing had offered to carry me on his back to the summit point. 'Would you?'

'I can help you with a bit of research. I'm not too grand for that and the police series is signed off so I'm in between projects at the moment. We've got a lot to get through. I'll book a viewing room and you start reading these. Oh look, there's another one,' and with that she heaves another box on to my desk, groaning with the effort.

'And I wonder why I can't have children,' she says as she puts her hand to her back and staggers back to her office.

Thursday lunchtime and my phone rings.

'Hi, I'm in reception,' says a cheery voice.

'Jo? Sorry, were we supposed to be meeting?' I ask, dazed, my mind half on the image of Florence dressed as a ventriloquist's dummy sitting on Terry Scott's knee in the 1960s.

'No, I've just finished filming my advert, darling.' She's pretending to be actressy; she doesn't usually speak like this. 'I was in Dean Street – so I thought I'd drop in and whisk you off for some lunch. If Cassie is around it would be great if she could make it. Do you have a window?'

I look at the other boxes that I haven't even opened. 'Not exactly.'

'Oh, come on – even if it's only for half an hour – a girl's got to eat. Come and share a packet of Philadelphia with me – it will be lovely,' she says, putting on a silly voice. 'Please,' she pleads.

'OK. Cassie is helping me out at the moment so I'll just check with her, but only half an hour. I'm just weighed under with research – I start filming tomorrow.'

'You're filming?' she says, amazement in her voice. 'How did that happen so quickly?'

'I'll tell you over a sandwich and a smoothie in Soho Square. You buy for both of us and I'll pay you back. I'll have a tuna and sweetcorn on brown.'

'Come on, Molly, this is Soho. You'll have to do better than that. How about chicken tikka with roasted vegetables in a seeded bap with some beetroot crisps and a mango and bilberry smoothie?'

'If I must,' I say, distracted.

'Remember, image is everything,' says Jo.

I put the phone down, look at my watch, and glance back at a magazine profile of Florence that was written in the 1970s. There's a close-up picture of her leaning towards the camera. She looks confident and in control, a more refined, sharper image of the woman I met a few days ago.

Jo looks fantastic – the best I've seen her look in ages – but that might be because she's covered in makeup which makes her appear very glamorous.

'You should have seen my "before" face.'

'"Before" what?' I ask, finding it hard to drag myself back into the real world.

'Before I've supposedly used the miracle anti-ageing cream. God, they made me look terrible. What was a little depressing was the amount of time it took to make me look this good.'

'Is the cream any use?' asks Cassie.

'I haven't a clue.'

'Probably just haemorrhoid cream,' says Cassie. 'Do they give you free samples?'

'You must be joking. Each pot costs about a thousand pounds.'

We're having trouble keeping up with her as she's speeding along the pavement towards Soho Square.

'What's the hurry?'

'You said you only had a few minutes and I want to make sure we get a space to sit down.'

We pass an attractive blonde girl in a biker jacket and jeans.

'Kate Winslet,' Jo mutters under her breath.

'Where?' says Cassie, looking round frantically to see if she can spot her.

'On your left, Gwyneth Paltrow,' I reply.

'You're kidding?' Cassie says desperately, swinging round to see her. I step on to the road to avoid bumping into a tall, lanky, dark-haired man in black leather, browsing at the outdoor stand by the international newsagents.

'Jarvis Cocker.' I check his face as we walk past.

'Good one,' says Jo.

'Oh God, you're playing that stupid look-alike game.'

'It is interesting though, that when you look at people carefully they do look like someone famous, even if it's just in the clothes or the way they walk.'

Two schoolboys cross the road in front of us.

'Ant and Dec?' Cassie grins.

We sit on a bench in the middle of Soho Square, silently eating our baps. We're the only ones mad enough to be sitting outside as there's a sharp wind and it's bitterly cold. Jo pauses between bites, trying to work out how to wedge the sandwich in her mouth without smudging her expertly applied lipstick.

'So filming tomorrow and you two are working together.' She raises her eyebrows at Cassie.

'I'm just giving her a helping hand. She's got me hard at it, day and night.' She's teasing me. 'I'd forgotten how nervous she can be.'

'I'm not nervous,' I protest. 'Well, maybe a little.'

'She'll be OK as long as she's wearing her lucky knickers,' says Jo to Cassie, who snorts with laughter.

'I do not have lucky knickers, I've never had a pair of lucky knickers in my life,' I say indignantly. None of us talks, we're all concentrating on chewing our baps. Cassie catches a stray piece of red pepper before it drops into her lap.

'It was a lucky bra,' I mutter, and they smile at each other. 'It seemed to work in my interviewing days and the one day I didn't wear it Charlton Heston threatened to pull out of the show at the last minute – do you remember?'

'Yeah, but didn't that have more to do with the fact his wife was ill than because you weren't wearing your lucky bra?' says Cassie logically.

'How do you know?'

Jo changes the subject. 'Cass,' she says, her mouth full, 'how are things with you?'

Cassie looks uncomfortable. 'Not great,' and when I glance at her I can see how miserable she looks and I feel terrible that I've been too busy and preoccupied to find out how she's feeling.

'You need to get out there and have a fling – move on,' Jo advises Cassie. Despite the smudged lipstick she is glowing – working again obviously agrees with her and I wonder if it's having the same effect on me but doubt it somehow.

'I can't begin to think about it at the moment – it's too soon, it's not even a month since he moved out,' Cassie says miserably. 'I just want to go away, not for work but to have some thinking time.'

'Well, Finn and I have been asked to house-sit an old manor house in Devon over Christmas and New Year. Some friends of his are going to Australia and they've got chickens, ponies and dogs that need looking after. So you're all invited for New Year – I think it could be fun. Come and do some thinking then, Cassie.'

'I can't think about tomorrow, let alone Christmas, but it does sound tempting,' says Cassie.

I look at Jo's glowing face and ask, 'So it's all going well, Jo?'

'Yes – it's great, really good.' She smiles enigmatically and I notice her blush as she takes a sip from her smoothie. To distract me, she looks over my shoulder and says, 'Across the road with the Puerto Rican model type – Mick Jagger.'

We all three stop and look to the other side of the road.

'It *is* Mick Jagger, you daft divvies,' says Cassie, and we all start giggling, the laughter bubbling up inside.

*

It's way past the children's bedtime by the time I get home but as I close the front door a voice calls out, 'Hello, who's that?'

Evie is waiting up for me and I go straight upstairs to find her looking sleepy but determined to stay awake, her Harry Potter and S Club posters competing on opposite walls of her bedroom. I'm amazed Aidan has allowed them to remain intact.

'Look at this.' She opens her mouth and wiggles her wobbly front tooth, then scratches her head sleepily and slips down under the duvet.

'Big money for that one,' I say.

'How much?'

'A pound, I should imagine.'

She smiles happily. 'Enough for a kitten?'

'Perhaps not.'

'Mum, you will come to the Christmas show, won't you?'

'Of course. Now, you must go to sleep, it's very late, and I'll see you in the morning.'

Downstairs Aidan is cooking a Jamie Oliver recipe – a prawn, pea and mint risotto. It's the only thing he knows how to cook but he does it meticulously, the individual bowls of chopped mint, prawns and peas all neatly laid out in the order in which they will be required. He pours a large ladle of stock into the saucepan and stirs it with a wooden spoon, then looks up as I sit down at the table.

'Year Two are doing Santa's Grotto this year.'

'Oh God, the school Christmas fair – I've promised to help Jenny out on the wreath stall.'

'They've asked me to be Father Christmas,' Aidan says gloomily, still stirring. The idea makes me laugh.

'You're the wrong shape.'

'They're desperate.'

'What did you say?'

'No way, I'm not doing it. That American woman, Scarlet's mother, what's her name?'

'Sandra, Sandy.'

'She treats me like I'm a house husband.'

I get up and go over and kiss his cheek. 'Where are my slippers, darling?'

'Get off, you're going to spoil the supper.'

'Did you manage to get any Christmas cards?'

'Nope.'

'What about the squeezy yoghurts for Evie's lunch box, oh, and the music book she needs for her cello lesson? Did I mention Max's swimming goggles broke last week and he can't swim without them, he keeps getting eye infections?'

Aidan slams down the ladle. 'For God's sake,' he says, irritated, 'stop – I can't concentrate on cooking this properly with you wittering on.'

Hurt, I silently open the fridge and drink some orange juice out of the carton, as I know this irritates Aidan. He glances sideways and notices what I'm doing but says nothing. I don't offer to help as I know he won't welcome it but I watch him as he meticulously counts out the prawns and divides the peas, putting half of them into a bowl to be whizzed up into a vivid green purée. He adds the peas and the prawns to the risotto.

'It's nearly ready.' Chopping the mint he glances at me. 'Are you all set for tomorrow?'

I'm surprised he's remembered I start filming, he seems so lost in his own world. I make a note to mention to Jo that her appraisal of Aidan was wrong. It's his third question in three weeks, not that I'm counting.

'I haven't really had enough time to prepare. I just hope I'm up to it.'

'Of course you are. Get the plates out.'

We have two crockery cupboards in the kitchen, one for the children's easy plastic Ikea cups and bowls, another for the huge white plates and bowls that Aidan insisted were included on our wedding list. I resist using them because even though they look wonderful they don't fit into the dishwasher and my life is too short, particularly at the moment, to handwash crockery. Tonight, as Aidan has made the effort to cook, I take out two white plates one at a time because they're so heavy.

'Did you get much writing done today?'

'I only had two hours this morning; it's hardly enough time to write my name. My main problem is that I still need to do more research.' He hands me a plate of steaming risotto, which smells delicious, and I sit down at the kitchen table. Just as I take my first mouthful Aidan says, 'I was wondering, what would you think of me going on a research trip to America?'

He times it perfectly as I have a mouth full of risotto and I'm powerless to respond.

'Terry is going out there to do a big pitch and he wants me to come with him as a consultant. He'll pay for the flights and I only need to do a couple of days' work with him and then I could use the rest of the time to do some research. It's a good opportunity, also it's some extra cash.'

I knew there had to be a reason why he cooked supper. I finish my mouthful, pierce a prawn with my fork and look at him. 'I start filming tomorrow, I'm incredibly nervous, and I think your timing sucks.'

Aidan says nothing and we both continue eating in silence. I break first because I always break first.

'I'm sorry, I know it's important to you, but can't we talk about it another time? I presume you're not planning to go before Christmas, are you?'

He looks uncomfortable. 'It's the week leading up to Christmas and I'd be back by Christmas Eve,' he says, as though that makes it better.

'A week – are you mad? Aidan, you can't. Who's going to look after the children? And I was relying on you coming to Evie's play and Max is playing the tambourine in his concert. I promised Evie I'd be there but you know how things can change. I wanted you as backup. If everyone is coming to us for Christmas there's so much to organise and I think I've got to film right up to Christmas Eve. Can't you wait until the New Year?'

'They'll pay for my flights – it's a fantastic opportunity, Molly. I might not get another chance like this next year.'

I feel the tears prick my eyes and the panic swell in my chest. I've suddenly lost my appetite. 'Please let's talk about it later.'

'I'm sorry, I know it's not a good time, but Terry needs an answer as soon as possible. You know a week is not that long,' he says, taking a sip of beer.

'But who's going to look after the children while I'm filming?' I ask, wondering how he can be oblivious to my panic.

'What if your mother comes to stay?'

'I don't know, she wasn't very keen to do Tuesday; I can't imagine what she would say if I asked her to come for a whole week. It's quite a lot to expect.'

'I need a week to make it worth my while and to be honest, Molly, we need the money.'

We finish the meal in silence, feeling awkward. When he's not looking I glance up at him. In only a few months the balance in our relationship has completely changed. We can't communicate at all these days, we're so lost in our own private worlds. I don't think I can cope without him, but it's a practical not an emotional response. I feel myself detaching as I force myself to think of the filming tomorrow. I wonder what Florence is doing now. Is she excited or nervous about the prospect of our filming? I can't imagine Florence being nervous about anything.

Seven

It's twelve o'clock in the morning and Matt is running on the spot in the middle of Florence's room while we all watch.

'Running,' shouts Gerry the sound man.

'You're very close,' Matt says, and Florence scowls at him and says crossly, 'You're not supposed to say anything.'

'Sorry,' Matt says apologetically and then adds, 'Sorry for saying sorry.' He grins, and looking at Gerry he puts his hands close together to indicate 'smaller'.

'Runner,' says Florence, and Matt puts his finger on his nose and points at her.

'*Blade Runner*,' she says.

'Absolutely right,' says Matt, impressed by the speed with which she's guessed it.

'Told you I was good,' Florence says, pleased with herself.

'Molly, it's your turn.'

'I think we should start filming – we're just wasting time,' I say impatiently. Florence stares at me and I begin to wonder whether the same principle applies to names as to owners looking like their dogs. The name 'Bird' suits her perfectly as I feel her pecking away at my confidence.

'Go on, this is a great ice-breaker – it will help you to relax a little.'

'Relax!' I want to scream at her, 'What makes you think I'm not relaxed, for God's sake?' but I don't want to upset her on our first day of filming.

'Some of the best directors I've ever worked with do games like this. I remember doing a small role in Mike Leigh's first film and we all had to dress up in character for days before filming started, which was difficult for me as I was playing an ageing prostitute. Tommy, my husband, wasn't too pleased.'

Trying to hide my irritation, and determined to get this over and done with as quickly as possible, I draw a box with my hands and then point at the television set on the table by the window.

'Television,' Matt says.

I follow his example and make the sign to make the word smaller. 'Tele,' says Gerry, looking pleased with himself. Again I put my finger to my nose and wonder what Rod Harman would make of this if he could see us. I then pretend that I've got a huge stomach.

'Tellystomach,' Gerry says, and then shakes his head, realising what a ridiculous suggestion it is.

'Teletummy,' says Matt slowly.

'Teletubbies!' shouts Gerry, taking his headphones off to check that he's got it right.

'Very revealing,' says Florence, smiling broadly, and I wonder what on earth made me choose that. Florence stands up slowly, massaging her hip, and very efficiently, as if she's speaking a language in which she is fluent, she goes through all the opening motions so that very quickly we know it's a film and it's two words. She's wearing her charm bracelet on one wrist and on the other a collection of silver bracelets, of differing widths, which jangle together and make quite a noise when she holds up her hands.

She mimes putting on what appear to be a coat and hat, picks something up and, looking very cross, points at the wall with whatever she is pretending to hold in her hand. Then she puts up two fingers to indicate the second word and points at Matt and Gerry, then looks like she's rearranging something down the front of her pants. We all look at her blankly and a little embarrassed. She looks exasperated and makes a big circle with her hands. I look questioningly at Matt.

'The whole concept,' he whispers back, and Florence glowers at him. Then, very slowly, she starts to waltz around the room with an imaginary partner.

'I don't know what you're doing,' I say, my patience beginning to run out, 'but it looks like ballroom dancing to me.' She stops and turns, pointing at me.

'Ballroom?' I say, and then the answer becomes obvious. '*Strictly Ballroom*!' I shout, for a minute carried away by the game.

Florence smiles her approval. 'Very good.'

'Strictly what?' says Gerry, looking totally confused.

'*Strictly Ballroom* — great film by Baz Luhrmann — the guy who did *Moulin Rouge*. One of my favourite films,' I say, surprised that Florence should have thought of it.

Florence eases herself down carefully into her favourite chair. 'I'm exhausted.'

'What was that bit when you were fumbling around inside your . . . ?'

'Ballroom, Gerry — think about it?' says Matt. Gerry looks unsure and then turns a livid red. Florence seems out of breath and I am worried that she'll be too tired for us to film today.

'Let's get started,' I say briskly. 'Why don't you give us a quick tour round the room, Florence?' I suggest.

'If you think it would be interesting,' she says, leaving me in no doubt about what she thinks of my suggestion.

I look at Matt to see if he's happy and with one eye he nods back at me. He balances the camera on his shoulder, looks across at Gerry, who gives him a thumbs-up, and says to me, 'I'm at speed,' and we're filming at last, the adrenalin pumping. I can hardly believe that it has been seven years since I last did this.

'It's not a big room but I spend a lot of my time in here.' Her bracelets are jangling and I can see Gerry wince every time Florence moves but I don't want to interrupt her. She walks over to the wooden chest of drawers on top of which are rows of photographs in an assortment of frames. She picks up the one nearest to her, of a boy dressed in school uniform.

'This is Bill. He's my son.' Florence is talking to camera in a way that makes me expect her to say any minute, 'Today, children, we're going to look through the round window.' Seeing my expression, she reverts to her normal tone. 'He lives in Canada and comes over whenever he can. He's going through a hard time at the moment. He married a Canadian girl.' She makes a face. 'She's all right but so earnest and definitely not right for Bill. They parted a couple of years ago but he feels he's got to stay out there to be close to the two children.'

She runs her fingers over the frames and pauses at a 1940s studio photograph of a woman in uniform. 'Is that you?' I ask.

'No, she was a very dear friend of mine,' she says, but doesn't elaborate.

Surprisingly enough for an actress, there aren't many photos of Florence, but there is one of her standing in a porch in front of a white door that must have been taken at least forty years ago. She stands next to a man; their arms are linked and they look happy and relaxed. It's hard to relate the old woman with carefully coiffed white hair swept back from her face, lined with soft loose skin, to the one in the picture.

As if she follows my thoughts Florence says, 'The funny thing is that I don't feel any different now from how I felt then. The shock comes when I look at myself in the mirror.' She looks at me. 'Nothing can prepare you for it.'

'Like childbirth,' I say.

'No, much worse,' she replies.

'Do you like to watch your old films? Is it strange seeing yourself as a young woman again?'

'It doesn't bother me, but I feel for some of the others in here. The other night they were showing an old movie of Elspeth's on television made when she was only twenty years old and exquisitely beautiful. It seemed so cruel to remind her of how she once was.'

'Did she mind?'

'I didn't ask her because she fell asleep in the middle of it. I don't blame her as it wasn't a very good film.'

A mobile phone rings and I realise it's coming from my bag which I've left by the door. I grab the bag and leave the room, indicating to Matt to carry on without me. 'Hello,' I hiss into the phone.

'Molly, is it all right for Max to go round to Thomas's this afternoon? His mother just rang and I said I'd check it out with you.'

'It's up to you, Aidan,' I reply, trying to contain my irritation, 'but yes, of course, if it means you'll be able to get on with some work. Oh, and by the way his fleece which he'll need is upstairs in Evie's room. I must go – speak later, bye.'

I go back into the room and Florence is showing the camera a black and white photo of her husband Tommy who is holding a trumpet.

'He was a professional trumpet player; he played at the Café de Paris after the war. I was getting on for those days but I wasn't keen to settle down, I was having far too good a time. I don't want you to think I didn't have lots of offers but they were never quite right and I never trusted the good-looking ones. Tommy was a brilliant trumpet player – the way he could play those notes, it would squeeze your heart and give you goosebumps.'

A tap on the door behind me makes me jump.

'Anyone in? Am I too early?' It's an apologetic voice, which belongs to a small, plump woman, her wispy hair tied back in a bun, half of which has collapsed. I recognise her from my first visit to Russell Court when she was helping her elegant companion in the long velvet coat. She's wearing sturdy shoes and a cardigan, a size too small, the buttons straining to do their job. She looks startled when she peers round the door and sees us all but Florence welcomes her as if she's a late addition to her audience. 'Dora, come in, come in.'

I try to move away from the camera to avoid being in shot but space is limited. Matt continues filming and Dora grins at us all, running her tongue over her bottom lip. Then she smacks her lips together and sits down in the large green armchair near the window.

'I'm showing them round my room.'

'Why?' asks Dora.

'She thinks it's interesting.'

Dora looks at me as though I'm the one who is senile.

'Your usual, Dora?' asks Florence.

'Let me get it,' Dora replies, anxious to help, but Florence is already up and silences her with a gesture. She goes into the bathroom, and I peer round the door and see her filling a glass with sherry, and craning my neck further I can see that the whole of one wall is a unit stacked full of bottles of drink.

'The bar downstairs is only open for an hour twice a day, so I stock up here. I don't want you to get the wrong idea but this is a special occasion, an excuse to celebrate. Dora always has a dry sherry; it's whisky for Maurice, the old boy at the end of the corridor.' She pours herself a G and T. 'Would you like one, any of you?' She looks from Matt to me to Gerry.

'Bit early for us, Florence, but maybe later on.'

'Cheers then.' She and Dora sip their drinks.

'I'll be glad when I've had enough,' Florence says, smiling. I feel convinced that this is a performance she's putting on for our benefit and not part of her normal routine.

'You've hardly enough room for any medicines in the bathroom,' I say.

'This,' she replies, indicating her glass, 'is the best medicine there is. I keep all the pills in here.' Beside her bed there is a cabinet. She opens the door, which reveals rows of pill bottles and a plastic dispenser, clearly labelled with the days of the week.

'It's exhausting just looking at them all. Sometimes I wonder if they're trying to keep me sedated, controllable. I feel like Jack Nicholson.'

There's another knock on the door and Gerry, who is standing in front of it, turns and opens it with one hand.

'Am I indecently early?' says a husky voice.

'Elspeth dear, we were just talking about you – I think you can squeeze in.'

An elegant woman, whom I recognize as Dora's walking companion, wearing a purple velvet turban and a long silk kaftan lying in folds around her legs, is being pushed in her wheelchair through the door. Just as she looks like she's made it into the room, the wheel of the chair jams against the door frame and she clings on to the arms to prevent herself from falling out of the chair. Her turban slips forward as she's pulled backwards through the door, disappearing from sight, and as she retreats we hear her say gruffly, 'For God's sake, Bernard, can't you be more careful?'

'It's not very easy, you stupid woman. Trying to push a wheelchair on this carpet is like trying to drive it through snow.'

Elspeth appears again and she corrects her expression, trying to smile graciously for her audience. This time Bernard has over-compensated: the other wheel catches on the door handle and she's catapulted out of the chair, landing face down on the bed. She manages to recover remarkably quickly, using the arms of the wheelchair to help her sit back. Her turban has slipped right down over one eye and as she rearranges herself she says as calmly as she can and as if her driver can't hear, 'He's being impossible.'

Bernard looks less than happy, his bald head pink with exertion. 'That's the last time I offer to push you.'

'Sit down, Bernard. Are you all right? Would you like something to drink?' asks Florence, concerned.

'Just water, thank you.'

Dora passes him a glass of water as he sits down on the arm of the chair nearest to me and I notice his hands are shaking as he drinks. Elspeth smiles, then puts her hands up to her turban and pushes it back into its proper place. Her exquisite blue eyes and refined cheekbones are a clue to her former beauty, but her skin is so taut from cosmetic surgery that when she speaks she gives the impression that she's talking through clenched teeth like a ventriloquist.

'Dora won't mind taking me back later,' she says.

'Of course, Elspeth,' says Dora obligingly, looking nervously at Bernard to gauge his reaction, worried that he may feel she has usurped his role. Bernard doesn't seem to care but stares morosely at the carpet, saying nothing, trying to recover from his exertions.

'We're being a bit naughty; we've started drinking already – what do you fancy, Elspeth?' Florence asks.

'A whisky and soda, darling, my usual.'

Matt looks at me as if to say what on earth is going on, and the room feels even smaller than before. Another knock on the door and Matt swears softly under his breath, 'Jesus Christ.'

Bernard glances across at me and the crew and says, 'Small unit, aren't you? I used to work with hundreds but that was film of course.' I remember that Eleanor, the home administrator, told me he was a director.

'Did you work only in film or theatre as well?' I ask politely.

'Both, but I loved film best. Especially the edit where everything was controllable.'

'We worked together a couple of times, didn't we, darling?' Elspeth says. 'He was very strict, but I always felt safe with him in those days,' she adds pointedly. Her turban is slipping again and a stray strand of grey hair has fallen loose. Bernard still doesn't say anything and I notice that he's broken out in a sweat.

Another tap on the door announces the dapper man with white hair and a lecherous manner whom I passed in the corridor when I first came to meet Florence. He squeezes past Elspeth's wheelchair, nods to Bernard and manoeuvres his way into the centre of the room. I notice he gives a quick glance at the camera to check which way it's pointing.

'Maurice, how lovely,' says Florence, as if she's hosting a cocktail party, which I suppose she is. Gerry looks at me and raises his eyes to the ceiling.

'Gather you've got an audition next week, Florence?' Maurice says, looking at the camera.

'Yes, for a comedy drama – they say that Judi Dench is going to be in it but they always say that, don't they? Drink, Maurice?'

Maurice looks preoccupied. 'Do you think I should change my agent?'

Nobody says anything, but I notice that Dora gives another nervous glance in Bernard's direction as if she's worried about him. Matt is now hemmed in and unable to move. A phone rings again and the sound surprises me as I thought I'd switched it off. Irritation ripples across Gerry's face.

'Let's stop for a moment,' I say to Matt as I make my way gingerly through the crowd, stepping over walking sticks and round Elspeth's wheelchair to grab my bag and get out into the corridor. It's Aidan again, sounding fed up.

'Max says he doesn't want to go and play with Thomas – I don't know what to do. I'm going mad here, Molly, and where did you say his fleece was?'

'Aidan,' I say through gritted teeth, 'don't ring me unless it's an emergency, and I'll see you later.' I can hear Max saying, 'Can I speak to her – is that Mummy? Please can I speak to her?' and then there's a rustly sound as the phone is passed over to him and a little voice that makes my stomach lurch says, 'Hello, Mummy. When are you coming back?'

Before I can answer him I hear a shriek from inside Florence's room and Matt shouts, 'MOLLY!'

I run into the room to see Bernard lying on the floor where he has fallen from the arm of the chair. He looks pale and is clutching his left arm, unable to speak. An alarm bell is ringing and Florence is bending over Bernard's pale face, saying remarkably calmly, 'It's all right, Bernard, you're going to be all right.' The sight of his ashen face contorted in pain makes me want to retch. Matt is loosening Bernard's shirt and Maurice, looking flustered, says, 'I'll go and check someone is coming.' Elspeth sits helplessly, anxiously twisting the end of her turban round her fingers, while Dora sobs quietly in the corner.

It takes me a while to recover from the sick sensation in my stomach that Bernard's stroke has induced and I feel ashamed of myself.

'That wasn't exactly the best morning's filming,' Matt says, trying to sound cheerful, as though it was just a minor blip.

'Do you think he'll be all right?'

'Eleanor seemed to think he had a chance,' he replies. 'I suppose we have to view this as an occupational hazard. It's going to be one of the problems of filming in a residential home.'

I smile weakly at him.

'Are you all right? You seem very shaken.'

'My father . . . he had a stroke,' I say, struggling to find the words.

'I remember,' he says gently and I remember how sympathetic Matt was when I told him that my father had been taken into hospital.

'Matt, I don't think I can do this.'

He looks startled. 'Of course you can.'

'But even before Bernard collapsed this morning was a disaster.'

'Well, you need to control it more and switch that bloody phone off; that's one lesson I would have thought you'd have learnt.'

'Maybe Rod was right – I'm not ready.'

'Yes you are – don't be so hard on yourself – come on, Molly, we can do this. This is just your first day, for Chrissake. Florence is playing with you – she never "entertained" when we were filming before, she's just testing you.'

His brow wrinkles and he looks very serious. 'It's about focus when you're filming; that's got to be all you think about. I know it's hard but you've got to forget about everything else.'

'Live it and breathe it.' I'm remembering what we used to say to each other when we worked together.

He nods his head and repeats it like a mantra. 'Live it and breathe it.'

Eight

I blow hard, feeling light-headed as the red balloon grows tauter. I pinch the end tightly so that no air can escape, taking the balloon away from my mouth to see how big it is.

'That's got to be enough, Jenny,' I say, my head spinning pleasantly from the lack of oxygen.

'How many have you done?' she asks, unpacking a big cardboard box full of Christmas wreaths. I count the balloons as they try to escape across the school gym.

'About twenty.'

There's a loud bang, one of them pops, and we all jump as if we've been shot.

'Nineteen,' I say.

'Tie them in bunches of four and we'll fix them to the front of the stall.'

Another balloon pops and I feel guilty, thinking it might be something to do with the way I've blown them up. Jenny frowns and I know she's cross with me because I forgot all about decorating the wreaths until last night at nine o'clock when the phone rang and I could hear her usually friendly voice straining to control her temper.

'Are you coming over?' she demanded.

I dropped everything and ran round to her house to find her single-handedly winding fake red berries into a wreath, her hands raw. We worked long into the night but my attempts were not inspiring.

'Great, well done,' says Jenny, trying to be encouraging as she struggles to tie a wreath to the bars on the wall in the school gymnasium.

'I'm so sorry, Jenny,' I say.

'Oh, don't worry about it – it's only the Christmas fair. It's not the end of the world,' but I know it is important for her, as it was for me this time last year.

'What time do the doors open?'

'We've got about ten minutes to get all of these wreaths displayed.' I think about last year and the rush once the doors were opened, with marauding old-age pensioners elbowing bumptious schoolchildren, everyone desperate for a Christmas bargain.

'Can you pass the next one up to me?'

I pick up a rather sparsely decorated pine wreath with a few fake presents dangling along the sides, a motley pine cone and a tartan bow hanging limply off-centre. I recognise it as one of the wreaths I decorated late last night and I feel embarrassed as I pass it up to Jenny.

'Shall I add a few more things to it?'

'No, we haven't got time – don't worry, I'm sure someone will like it,' she says hopefully. She's trying to be kind to me, which only makes me feel worse.

I pass her a glorious wreath decorated with berries, slices of dried orange, cinnamon sticks and cherubs peeping from behind a flowing red satin ribbon.

'One of yours?' I ask her as she takes it and she looks embarrassed.

'I've had more time than you.'

'Is it me or is Christmas early this year?'

Jenny laughs as she winds the garden wire round the wreath, securing it on to the bars. 'How's it been going anyway?'

'Mm, OK – it's been a difficult first week as the woman we're filming, Florence, is unpredictable, and that's putting it kindly.'

'Why is she being difficult?'

Jenny climbs down the steps and moves them along to the next set of bars, holding the wire clenched between her teeth.

'I don't know. She wants to be in control and sometimes it's just not possible. I wonder if she might be scared.'

'Of you?' Jenny looks surprised, pointing at another wreath for me to pass to her.

'No, of something else, but I'm not sure what. One second she's all smiles and the next she wants us to stop filming.'

'Did you say she was an actress?'

'Still is.'

'How old did you say she was?'

'Eighty-three.'

Jenny climbs down the steps and stands back to admire her work. 'That's impressive.'

'Yes, they look great,' I agree with her.

'No,' she laughs, 'I meant still working at eighty-three. I stopped working when I was thirty-two.'

She moves the steps along to the next rack of bars and climbs up. I pass her another wreath with brash purple and red balls and two My Little Ponies tied on with cheap silver ribbon.

'I thought it might be a bit different,' I say defensively, wondering whether I had too many glasses of wine when I was decorating the wreaths.

'Hello, stranger,' shouts Sandra, Evie's friend Scarlet's mother, across the school hall. She's sorting through a huge cardboard box of books and videos beside another stall selling delicate jewellery designed by two of the school mothers. As I look across at her I wonder whether I should buy Helen, my brother's fiancée (such a strange, pretentious word), a necklace, but I don't really know what she likes. It occurs to me that I don't know very much about her at all considering she's about to become part of the family.

'How are you?' Sandra's voice booms across the hall.

I smile and wave back. 'Listen, thanks for having Evie over for tea so much recently.'

'Don't mention it, I'm getting quite used to seeing her every time I come home from work. She's almost one of the family.'

I'm not sure this isn't a barbed comment but maybe I'm being over-sensitive. She walks over to our stall, picks up one of my wreaths and looks unimpressed.

'Are you enjoying being a working girl again?'

'Yes,' I say, determined to sound convincing. Sandra glances at Jenny and I know they have been talking about my chaotic circumstances. We're interrupted by Mr Harper, the caretaker, switching on the Christmas tree lights, and the strains of 'Jingle Bells' begin to echo around the hall, reverberating off the gym bars.

'I am opening the doors,' he says grandly, and Jenny hisses at me, 'Quick, we've got to get the rest up.'

'I'll give you a hand,' volunteers Sandra and we pass the wreaths between us, as efficiently as old-fashioned firemen passing buckets of water to quench a raging fire.

The hall fills quickly and it isn't long before I spot my mother with Evie and Max heading for the cake stall and filling their paper bags with mince pies, ginger biscuits and cakes decorated with thick, brightly coloured icing which contain enough E-additives to keep them bouncing off the walls right up to Christmas Day. My mother waves at me, pays for the cakes and herds the children over.

'Choose a wreath quickly before they go,' I say to the children, and I watch their faces as they survey the display of wreaths.

'I like the one with angels,' says Evie.

'I want that one with the ponies,' says Max.

'Oh no, that's awful, don't you think, Mum?' Evie appeals to me.

'I like it,' Max says.

'You can't – it's horrid, isn't it, Mum?'

I make the mistake of pausing for a second while I look at the wreath, wondering what Aidan would say about one My Little Pony, let alone two, hanging off his front door.

Max bursts into tears. 'You hate it.'

'No I don't – it's one of mine.'

Evie looks at me as if she's having to reassess me in light of this breach of taste. As Max sobs dramatically I get disapproving looks from the other parents as they wander past full of Christmas cheer.

'Max, give this to Granny,' I say, handing over a plastic bag to him, hoping that will make him feel better. Still sniffing, he pushes it in my mother's direction.

'What's this?' she says, surprised.

'It's an early Christmas present to say thank you for agreeing to come and help when Aidan goes away.'

She opens the bag and pulls out a tea towel covered with children's self-portraits.

'I'll show you which one is me,' says Evie, grabbing the tea towel.

'Thank you, darling.' My mother catches my eye. 'You shouldn't have. Where is Aidan?'

'I made a deal with him that he could go to America only if he agreed to be Santa Claus for two hours.'

My mother smiles. 'Was that altogether fair?'

'I don't see why not. He never does anything for the school and I think it's about time he mucked in a bit more, especially as I haven't been contributing much recently. I'll just clear with Jenny that we can go and have a wander and see how he's getting on.'

My mother and I make our way through the seething crowds of parents and children while Evie loiters behind us, still trying to find her self-portrait on the tea towel, and Max skips on ahead.

'Aidan as Santa is something I'd like to see,' says my mother as we fight our way towards the reception classroom, alias Santa's Grotto. The sense of excitement builds as we approach the long queue of children and adults waiting to see Santa. Squeals of laughter rise from the homemade grotto constructed out of old army groundsheets and crushed milk-bottle tops draped over an Ikea tent. Two small elves, Hannah and Lucy from Year One, are busy taking money from the children, although they have to keep asking the grown-ups to work out how much change they're owed. They take it in turns to peek into the tent, their faces shining with delight at what they're witnessing. A small boy, his cheeks pink with pleasure, comes out of the grotto, clutching his present and saying to his mother, 'That's the best Father Christmas I've ever seen.'

Peering round the corner, I see my husband, Santa framed by flashing pink-flowered fairy lights, half of which are broken. Sitting on his knee is a pretty, moonfaced girl with bunches and the two of them are giggling happily together. I turn back to my mother, stunned by what I'm seeing. This is not the Aidan I know, and I feel guilty that I've obviously underestimated him all these years. He looked appalled when I mooted the idea about agreeing to him going to America as long as he promised to help out in Santa's Grotto. Of course he tried to talk me out of it but I was determined not to concede, thinking that it would be good for him, but I never realised how good it would be for all the children at Evie's school as well. At first he moaned about doing it but he soon stopped as he became reconciled to the idea. Now, looking at him doing such a good job, I'm so pleased to see him entering into the spirit of it all.

My mother stares at me in amazement. 'Well I never.'

I feel flushed with ridiculous pride at seeing this new side of my husband, and I'm tempted to rush back and tell Jenny to come and see for herself because I know they all think Aidan is cool and aloof.

Evie is standing beside me. 'Do I have to join the queue?' she asks, hoping that as Santa's daughter she might get preferential treatment.

'Afraid so. Where's Max?' We all look around but Max is nowhere to be seen. Leaving my mother and Evie to queue, I go back into the hall to find him. I pass Sandra. 'Go and see Aidan as Santa – he's doing a great job,' I say to her, full of enthusiasm. I want to shout it throughout the hall, especially when Sandra raises her eyebrow to indicate she finds it hard to believe.

My happiness is slightly marred by the fact that I can't find Max anywhere and I start to get a little worried. I try to battle back through the seething queues of people, some waiting for lunch, others for the pantomime performance to begin. The recorder group has started playing on the platform and I duck out of a side door, relieved to be outside, away from the cacophony of carols, and make my way towards reception. As I pass by the staff-room door I hear a voice.

'Max, is that you?' I call.

The voice continues, 'If you set up the meeting for the Thursday, Terry, I'll be over the jetlag and I'll do a better job of pitching.'

I walk round the fixed wooden picnic bench and sitting on the ground with his back leaning against the staff-room door is Aidan, talking on his mobile phone. He looks up at me and does a double take and for a second he stops talking. Looking slightly shamefaced, he struggles to his feet, lowers his voice as if he imagines that I won't be able to hear him and says, 'Got to go, Terry mate, sorry, I'll call you back later.' He puts the phone into his back pocket and just stands there staring at me, trying not to look guilty.

'I don't understand,' I say, bemused. 'I just saw you in Santa's Grotto . . . so how did you get changed so quickly . . . ?'

I know by his expression that he has been nowhere near Santa's Grotto all morning.

'It's not you, is it?'

'No,' he says.

'Who is it then?'

'Roy Chudleigh – he's one of the best – did Bloomingdales in '99 and he's a backup for Harrods this year.'

'You promised me.'

I feel so disappointed. He stares at me, his impatience evident in every gesture.

'I fixed it up through Terry's agency. I thought it was an inspired idea and you can't say that it hasn't been a great success. The children are having a fantastic time and it's all because of me. Just think about it, it wouldn't have been possible if I hadn't organised it.'

'Have you paid for him to do it?'

'It's a busy time for him; he wasn't going to do it for love.'

'I don't believe you, Aidan Taylor – this is cheating. I don't think you should go to America.'

'Don't be like that – I would have been crap at it, you know

I would. I've got to go, I've booked the flights, and Terry's expecting me to be there so I can't pull out now.'

I turn away, surprised by how angry I feel.

'Oh, come on, it's not that bad, not like that Santa last year that was arrested for downloading pornographic photos,' Aidan appeals to me.

Speechless, I stride off in the direction of Santa's Grotto where I find Evie at the head of the queue and Max beside her.

'Where have you been?' I say grumpily to Max. 'You mustn't run off like that.'

'I didn't, I walked.'

I look at Max and Aidan's blue eyes stare back at me.

'I saw Thomas and we went into the big hall to the art stall and I made you this.'

My anger evaporates as he hands me a silver card covered with Christmas stickers, drawings of huge misshapen hearts and his wobbly signature inside.

'Thanks, Max.'

I give him a kiss and we're interrupted by one of Santa's little helpers shouting, 'Who's next to come and see the best Santa we've ever had?' and Max and Evie smile proudly at me and I haven't the heart to tell them that Santa is not who they think he is.

It's the start of a new week at Russell Court. Gerry is quietly whistling to himself as he fixes the radio microphone on to Florence's cardigan.

'Time for our little game then?' Florence looks at me.

I've given in gracefully and even schedule our game of charades into the filming timetable, as it seems to be so important to her. I've learnt to choose my battles and charades is one I'm prepared to lose. Some days she forgets about it but not today.

A knock on the door rescues me from making a complete fool of myself once again. Gerry stops whistling and when I look at his face his mouth is slightly open and he's staring gormlessly over my shoulder. I turn round to see a girl in her early twenties with indecently long legs and bottle-blonde hair, heavily made up, her eyelashes drooping from the weight of the mascara.

'Morning everyone,' she says in a husky voice. Gerry watches her as she walks across the room, and suddenly I feel like I'm in a cocktail bar rather than a residential home.

'Can I get you anything – cup of tea, biscuit?' she says suggestively.

'No thank you, Wendy – have you met the crew?' says Florence politely.

Wendy flashes us all a seductive smile. 'Hiya.'

She turns back to Florence. 'I've booked your hair appointment with Sharon – so it'll look lovely for your Bill when he comes over.'

'Thank you, dear,' Florence says as she watches Wendy turn on her heels like a model at the end of a catwalk and leave the room.

'Who was that?' says Gerry, gazing at the door.

Florence chuckles. 'That's Wendy, but I call her Wendy Wannabe – no guesses what she really wants to be.'

'She's an actress?' Matt says, trying to look as if he hardly noticed her.

'Yes, but she helps out as a relief carer when someone goes on holiday. She's pretty harmless but I think she views the job as a way of furthering her career. She's always around when the agents come visiting, so you can imagine how excited she was when she heard you were going to be filming. You'll be seeing a lot more of her I should imagine.'

Gerry looks as if the idea appeals.

'And your son Bill is coming over?' I ask Florence.

Her face brightens and she looks excited. 'Yes, for Christmas, you'll meet him then. We're not allowed family on the actual day,' she says a little sadly.

'That's terrible,' I say, shocked. 'Why ever not?'

'So that nobody feels left out. Obviously if you want to be with the family you can go out and visit relatives but none are allowed in. Christmas can be a difficult time when you're old and have no one – a lot of actors never establish roots because we can be a peripatetic lot and that gets tougher when you get older and all your friends have gone. So here we celebrate it together and this year you'll be here.'

I realise that she is presuming that we'll be filming on Christmas Day, which is something I hadn't even considered.

'Ronnie Corbett might be popping in to say hello,' she says to tempt me. I am silent.

'It could be my last, you know?' she says, piling on the emotional blackmail.

'Oh, come on, Florence.' I try and joke with her. 'You've got plenty more Christmases left in you.'

She goes quiet and I'm surprised by her sudden change in mood.

'I haven't decided about the days we're going to film over Christmas,' I say quickly, wondering how the children would react if I told them I wasn't going to be with them on Christmas Day.

'Breathe, Molly,' Florence says.

'I'm sorry?'

'You don't breathe properly – it's very important. With you it all comes from up here.' She pats her chest. 'You'd feel so much better if you breathed from down here.' She holds her diaphragm. 'It's what they taught us at drama school. Hold on to this part and feel it move up and down – that's right – that's much better. Now, don't you feel calmer?'

I do as she says, taking deep breaths, filling my lungs with air, and I feel better until I catch sight of Matt and Gerry watching me. Feeling more than a little foolish, I pick up my notes and say as efficiently as I can, 'OK, today I thought we'd film you at lunch.'

'I don't think so,' Florence says, and I'm caught unawares by her vehemence.

'Oh, why not?'

'Well, it's not very interesting.'

Both Matt and Gerry look at me as if they think Florence could have a point.

'I just want to get a feel of your routine.'

'I don't feel up to it today.'

'Couldn't we just try?'

'If you're so keen, go and film the others. I think I'll have a sandwich in my room.'

Matt looks at me in a way I find hard to decipher and I don't know what he's thinking. Filming over the past week has been going relatively smoothly and we've found ourselves slotting back into the familiar pattern of working together, but I know he has picked up on the fragile power struggle between Florence and me.

Later he corners me. 'Are you OK?' he says, concern in his voice.

'Yes, I'm fine. She's not easy. Sometimes I wish we were filming some gentle old biddy who does what she's told.'

'It wouldn't be so interesting.'

'You think so? Sometimes I think I'll be the one going to an early grave.'

'So what about Christmas Day?'

'What do you and Gerry want to do?' I ask.

'Well, if we have to work we will. How important is it for the film?'

'I don't know. I'm not sure, I need to have a think about it.'

'So what are we going to do now?'

'Let's go and film some of the other residents in the restaurant and then come back and film some more with Florence this afternoon.'

'Are we allowed any lunch?' Matt asks.

'Lunch – you must be joking, no time for lunch,' I tease him.

'Sometimes I wonder whether I was wise to encourage you to do this film.'

He turns away and for a few seconds I wonder if he's being serious, but when he turns back and sees my troubled face Matt quickly says, 'Come on, Molly, let's go and tell Gerry the good news about lunch – he will be pleased.'

Nine

'Now, Granny, you mustn't worry if you get killed,' Evie explains patiently as she watches my mother trying to work out how to use the GameBoy Advance. 'Just keep pushing that button – no, not that one – this one.'

They are both huddled together and Max is climbing on to one of the kitchen chairs, desperate to join in. Aidan is in America despite my disapproval but it would have been churlish of me to make him cancel everything at such late notice. I still can't get over the feeling that I've been duped, as if Aidan has cheated on me. The only advantage was that he tried very hard to make it up to me in the week leading up to his trip. It makes all the difference that my mother is in charge, in fact if I'm honest everything is running much more smoothly than it does when Aidan is at home.

'Children – teeth, and you'd better get a move on or you'll be late for school.'

I chase Max in the direction of the stairs but he rushes into the living area, singing at the top of his voice, 'When Santa got stuck up the chimney he began to shout – BLAST OFF.' And he hurls himself like a human rocket on to the hard white sofa.

'Mum, it's really difficult brushing my teeth – look,' says Evie, sticking her tongue behind her front tooth and making it stick out at a 45-degree angle.

'Don't, Evie, it makes me feel sick,' I say. 'Just brush around it, but you've got to get a move on or you'll be very late.'

'Leave it to us,' my mother interrupts. 'You get off or you're going to be the one that's late. Have you brushed your teeth?'

I smile as I pick up my bag and shooting schedule and make my way towards the front door while my mother takes Evie and Max upstairs.

'Oh, and Molly, I've been thinking, why don't you all come to me for Christmas this year as it's too much for you at the moment? It might be a tight squeeze but I think we'll manage.'

An overwhelming sense of relief floods through me and I think I'm going to cry. 'Really, are you sure? Thank you so much.'

I go to give her a hug but it's slightly awkward, as we don't do it that often. She laughs, embarrassed by my public display of affection.

'See you later at the play,' I shout up to Evie. 'Break a leg.'

'Why should I want to do that?' she shouts back down the stairs, her mouth full of toothpaste.

'It's just an expression that actors use,' I explain.

'But it's silly.'

'Well yes, I suppose it is – they think saying "Good luck" is unlucky.'

'Why?'

'I haven't a clue – I'll ask Florence.'

'Go.' My mother hurries me towards the front door as if she's shooing out a cat.

'Abraham Lincoln comes to mind for some reason – something to do with his assassin breaking a leg in the theatre when he was trying to get away, but why that should be lucky I've absolutely no idea. Theatre is full of ridiculous superstitions,' Florence says in answer to my question as she settles back in her seat. She seems to be enjoying the journey to London in the car that the production company have provided to take her to the audition. I'm crouched on the floor so that I don't get in shot, Gerry is wedged beside me, so indecently close that I can smell his hair gel, and Matt is in the front so that he can film both the driver and Florence.

'Mmm, lovely interior – I love the smell of leather in the morning,' Florence comments, leaning back and stroking the seat. She plays with the electric buttons, opening and closing the back windows.

'Would you have gone to the audition if they hadn't sent a car for you?' I'm trying to get my elbows in a comfortable position.

'Difficult to tell – it would have depended on how good the script was and how easy the journey. It does get harder at my age. I'm not so fond of the travelling; it tires me.' She looks at Gerry and me crouched at her feet. 'Are you sure you're all right down there?'

I nod my head but say nothing, hoping she'll continue talking to camera. Intuitively she carries on, 'Cars make me feel special – dressing rooms with my name on the door, that's good too, and people I don't know knowing who I am – all perks of the job. As if it's all meant something, but then at other times you become painfully aware that you're just another face. Sometimes I feel different, special even, and then other days I'm a nobody. I mean, who has heard of Florence Bird?'

She chuckles. 'It even rhymes. "Who has heard of Florence Bird?"' she repeats to herself.

'Do you want people to know who you are?'

'It's sort of part of the job because if you're successful people will have heard of you. But I'm not grumbling. I've worked all my life and earned a good living. There's been such variety of work as well, and how many eighty-three-year-olds do you know who can still do the job? I've always tried to resist the limitations that other people try to impose on me. Who says you should stop working at sixty-five? It's ridiculous. I did a job the other day when they sent a car for me at eight in the morning. I didn't need makeup or costume, I just wore my old mac which they thought was perfect. I had one line to say, pretending to talk to myself, which I do all the time so that was easy, and then I had to take a dog out for a walk and I was back at the bar in Russell Court by twelve-thirty. And for that I got paid five hundred pounds, and do you know, I felt like a footballer, call me David Beckham. Not that it often happens like that.'

'Do you have to work?'

'Well, let's just say every little helps, but I think it keeps my brain active and most of the time I enjoy it. If I didn't work I might as well be dead.'

'Do you mean that?'

'I can't imagine not working. It means there's always something different to look forward to.' She pauses. 'It's one of the things I like about Russell Court – all the comings and goings, actors coming to visit, people like Dora staying for a few weeks – I think that keeps us all going.' She stares out of the window.

'How's Bernard?' I ask tentatively.

'He's doing well considering it was less than a month ago he had his stroke. He's back at Russell Court; he's a resilient bugger.'

'Did you find it upsetting?'

'What do you think?' she replies sarcastically, and I realise that it was a stupid question.

We're in a huge hall with a wooden floor and neon strip lights. A group of actors are rehearsing and the atmosphere is tense. A tall, gangly man with floppy blond hair, holding a script in one hand and a pencil in the other, is shouting, 'Where the bloody hell is he? What time was his call? Vicks, why isn't Malcolm here? He knew we were going to rehearse this scene today.'

Vicks, a young, boyish girl in jeans with short, shocking-pink, spiky hair, pulls her mobile out of what looks like a holster. 'Don't worry I'll call him,' and within seconds she's on the phone.

'Tell him if he doesn't get his arse over here immediately he's out of a job.'

In frustration the director throws the script on the floor and snaps the pencil in two. Florence, unperturbed, sits herself down on one of the plastic chairs that have been placed around the edge of the room, where she's quickly noticed by a friendly-faced woman in her mid-forties who bustles over and greets us all.

'Florence – thank you for coming in. Did you get the script?'

'Lovely to see you again. Very interesting, isn't it?'

'Are you up for it?' the woman asks.

'I don't see why not – if they want me to do it. It's better than that advert I did where I had to dress up as a belly dancer – not attractive at my time of life,' she says, looking at the director who's having his pencil stuck back together again with gaffer tape.

Looking from Matt to me to Gerry, the friendly woman nudges Florence: 'You're a bit of a star then.'

'It's taken you this long to realise it? Call yourself a casting director?' Florence teases her.

The director comes over to Florence and just as he's about to kiss her suddenly shouts, 'Vicks, I'm going to need a steadycam as well.'

Vicks, on her mobile phone, nods her head to indicate that she's heard what he said and he turns back to Florence and kisses her on both cheeks. 'Thanks for coming in. How are you?'

Florence immediately stands up to show that she's fit and able. 'Bearing up for a geriatric.'

'You're looking splendid. Come over here and meet Paul, the writer, and we can have a little chat.'

He leads Florence over to where the writer is sitting looking miserable and anxious. He nods a shy hello.

'What did you think of the character?' the director asks, getting a chair for Florence to sit down in and seating himself opposite her, beside the writer.

'I get the feeling she's a bit of an old cow,' says Florence directly. The writer winces but he laughs.

'I think you may be right but her heart's in the right place. Do you mind reading for us?'

'My eyesight isn't great and I've always been terrible at reading but I could get the gist of it for you if you talk me through it.'

'OK, I'll set up the scene and you do what you can improvising. Happy?' He looks anxiously at the writer, who shrugs his shoulders.

Florence metamorphoses in front of my eyes. She rounds her shoulders, shuffles along as if she's wearing slippers, and in a strong Mancunian accent she says, 'Where the fuck have you been, you little tosser?'

The string of expletives that follow amazes me but the director seems delighted by her performance. At the end of the scene he says enthusiastically, 'That was great, Florence.'

She smiles and sits down quickly. I think she looks pale but she's determined not to show them any weakness.

'Are you happy about the later scene? We'll shoot it carefully but I'm afraid it has to be you, because it needs to look realistic.' I don't know what he's talking about as Florence refused to discuss the script with me when we filmed her reading it. All she would say enigmatically was, 'Wait and see.'

She coughs and says, 'You won't make it too grim, will you?'

He smiles reassuringly. 'We'll do our best.'

Once we're back at Russell Court Matt takes me to one side.

'Have you decided about Christmas yet? It's just that Ann is giving me a hard time about it and I need to tell her one way or the other. No pressure, mind.'

I feel flustered because I haven't given Christmas much thought. 'I'll tell you tomorrow, Matt.' I look at my watch. 'Shit, is that the time? I have to go.'

'So we've finished for today?'

'Yes – it's Thursday afternoon and you know Florence never lets us film. I'll see you in the morning.'

'Molly, I just want to ask you something about filming Florence at the hairdresser's – I've had an idea about how we could shoot it.'

'Great,' I say, backing out of the room. 'I'll call you tonight about it.'

'I need to show you really – can't you stay for a few minutes? It won't take long.'

'No, I can't, I'm going to be so late and I promised . . .' I stop not wanting to admit where I'm going.

'Where are you going?' he asks accusingly. I look at him, weighing up whether or not to tell him, and for a second I think of inventing a more dramatic excuse. Instead I confess, 'It's Evie's school play – she's the sleepy shepherd. I can't miss it, Matt. Aidan is away so I've got to be there.' I feel guilty, unprofessional. 'Show me tomorrow. I'm sorry. Bye, Gerry,' and I rush out of Russell Court without giving Matt a chance to say anything.

The blast of cold air makes me shiver and as I run to the car I realise that a few thin flakes of snow are floating down from the sky. For a second I'm tempted to stop and stare, then I pull myself together, look at my watch and realise that if I drive quickly I should be able to make it.

'Sorry, sorry, oh sorry, thanks, sorry . . .' I whisper as I try to manoeuvre my way through the row of knees to get to the seat that Jenny has saved for me, which has a great view but is right in the middle of the row. Nobody says anything but I sense their irritation as I brush past knees and trip over feet until eventually I collapse into the empty seat.

'Thanks,' I whisper to Jenny who flashes a tense smile at me.

Max and my mother are sitting the other side of Jenny and as soon as Max sees me he shouts, 'Hello, Mummy.'

'Shh,' says a man in front of me who is holding up a video camera and recording the whole proceedings. My mother passes Aidan's video camera via Jenny. Surprisingly enough, he insisted that I take it to film Evie in her first major role, but he doesn't fool me – I know that his feigned interest is a pathetic attempt to make amends for the Christmas fair incident.

My mother leans forward. 'I tried to start it but I couldn't make it work, sorry,' she whispers.

I look at the stage and I can't see Evie anywhere. Jenny points at what looks like a pile of clothes lying on the floor. 'She's sleeping.'

'Have I missed much?' I ask Jenny.

'Only about five minutes and I don't think Evie would have noticed. She's had her eyes closed. She's very good,' she whispers back.

It takes some time before my heart beat returns to its regular pattern and I settle into my seat and begin to concentrate on the performance. It's not what you'd call a lavish production but the backdrop of an enormous palm tree is effective and there's something reassuringly familiar about the costumes, recycled every year, the only variation being the assortment of tea towels the shepherds are wearing on their heads. This year most of them are wearing simple striped tea towels and I pan along the row of bored shepherds, one picking his nose and staring intently at his bogie while another waves at his mother while mouthing, 'I'm not allowed to wave.' I focus on a plump girl, her round cheeks pink with embarrassment, who is wearing a floral tea towel decorated with vivid blue cornflowers and forget-me-nots. Judging by the look on her face, I imagine that this school play is one that she'll never forget. She's watching the man with the video camera in front of me who is going through a range of gestures which he's obviously been rehearsing for months with his daughter and she's trying to copy him.

I prod Jenny. 'Who's that?' I ask, nodding my head in the direction of the man.

'Alan Harker – you know, Poppy's dad – her mum works in the City and he looks after the two girls. Watch out, I think Evie's on the move.'

I switch on the camera, take the lens cap off, and focus on the bundle of clothes on the stage out of which Evie emerges wearing a suede waistcoat with a fake fur lining (borrowed from Jo), and a fetching bandanna tied around her head. She slowly raises her arms, yawns loudly as she gets to her feet, and starts to sing a song, supported by the other shepherds. My view is partially blocked by Mr Harker who is still gesturing, albeit more subtly, to Poppy, who can't take her eyes off him. As he signals to her I keep getting flashes of fingers and arms through my viewfinder. The music teacher, Mrs Crossly, conducts from beside the piano, her wide mouth silently singing the words, her eyes bulging with enthusiasm or an overactive thyroid complaint, I'm not sure which, her facial expressions so large that she would definitely win a local gurning competition. With the professional instinct of a documentary maker I find myself focusing on her, and then I pan over to the piano player, Mrs Bagley, who ends the song with a

Mrs Mills flourish, turning to the audience with a smile that's all eyes and teeth.

Now it's time for the reception children to make an appearance dressed as angels, a moment usually high on the 'Ahh factor'. They walk down the aisle, their hands clasped together in prayer, their tinsel haloes waving above their heads, robes made out of sheets dragging along the floor. I swivel in my seat to film the parents' reaction – mothers' eyes filling with tears, the loving glances they flash at their husbands, the flash bulbs making the children blink like mini-stars in front of the paparazzi, giving them an early taste for celebrity. I notice that Mr Harker has left his seat with his video camera and moved into the aisles to get a better view. The children are crammed on to the stage and the ones at the back have to stand on tiptoe to be seen – even then it's just the top of a tea towel, a halo above a pair of wide eyes desperately scanning the audience. Evie is saying her lines in a monotone, but at least it's a loud monotone, whereas we're all struggling to hear the rest of the cast. Poppy rattles through her lines and every time she finishes one she casts an anxious look at her father who is now climbing the gym bars, which last weekend were covered in Christmas wreaths, to get a better view. Part of me feels guilty that I'm not as desperate as Mr Harker is to film my darling daughter.

The play continues predictably, but I concentrate on filming the audience, finding them far more fascinating than the action on stage. On most of the parents' faces is a look of blind ador-ation; it's as if they've left their critical faculties at the entrance to the school hall and entered a wonderland of parental devo-tion. Their faces betray no trace of how tedious the play really is. The younger members of the audience, who are still at nursery school, are better critics and give up trying to spot their siblings on stage and instead start rifling through their mother's hand-bags, tipping them up and sifting through the contents as they search for old sweets while smearing their faces with lipstick.

The headmistress, dressed in a red trouser suit, her eyes glazed over, is staring at the Christmas tree by the door far away from the stage where the main action is taking place. I notice that Mr Harker, keen to film the big finale, has climbed even higher and is hanging with one hand like a baboon from the bars while his other hand fumbles in his bag for a new tape.

The orchestra start playing the traditional 'Oh Come all Ye Faithful', their squeaky recorders squawking like turkeys about to be slaughtered. Mrs Crossly is waving her arms enthusiastically, willing the children to make it through to the end. 'Oh come let us adore him,' they sing haphazardly while Mrs Crossly wipes the sweat from her forehead with her arm and continues to conduct more emphatically than ever. Mr Harker, dangling from the bars, leans out precariously, scanning the stage and then focusing on his daughter who is looking from side to side to check that she's still doing the right thing. Evie stands centre-stage, and I remember that I should be concentrating on her. As I whip round to focus on the stage, the music builds to a mighty crescendo, the recorders screeching loudly, 'Oh come let us adore him . . . Christ the Lord.'

There is a scream followed by an almighty thud and the whole of the gymnasium floor shudders as Mr Harker plummets to the floor. There is a collective gasp and a moment's silence as everyone sits shocked into stillness. It lasts only a few seconds and very soon he is surrounded by a gaggle of anxious people who help him to hobble out of the hall into the reception area, still clutching his precious video camera. The head teacher whispers something to Mrs Crossly who nods at Mrs Bagley at the piano and the recorders to play an encore.

The applause at the end of the show is louder than usual, with everyone trying to compensate for the dramatic interruption. While the whole of Key Stage One take a bow on stage I'm suddenly aware of Mr Harker's face peering through the small glass window of the door leading to the school reception. One eye is bandaged and he is holding the camera up to his other eye, determined to film to the bitter end. This side of the door at the end of a row of chairs a small boy is desperate to go to the loo and I watch him tug at his mother's arm, pleading with her. She picks him up and rushes headlong for the door. I look away, bracing myself for the inevitable crash which follows.

'Well, that was quite an experience,' my mother says, looking visibly relieved that the whole ordeal is over. 'I don't remember coming to see any of your Nativities, Molly – I think they spared us that.'

'It was much easier to be a parent in those days,' I say, trying to make a joke of it.

'It's all much more hands on these days – so exhausting for everyone,' says my mother, yawning.

'Sorry it's a bit stuffy in here.'

Max sits on my lap while we wait for Evie to come and find us.

'Well, that was an interesting Nativity – Evie did well,' Jenny says. 'Did you manage to get it all on tape?'

'Oh yes, I'm sure I did,' I say, feeling a pang of guilt and worrying that perhaps I might have got a little carried away with the peripheral action.

We don't have to wait long before Evie, Rachel and Scarlet come back into the hall and make their way to our seats looking a little self-conscious.

'Well done, Evie, you did very well,' I say.

Everyone murmurs in agreement while she looks embarrassed by the compliments.

'Mum, you were so embarrassing filming like that.'

'Me?' I say, taken aback. 'What did I do? It wasn't me who was embarrassing. I just wanted to get it all for your father to see. Look, I've bought you something to say "Well done".' I give her a purple sugar whistle, one of Evie and Max's favourite sweets.

'Can I have one?' whines Max.

'If you ask nicely,' I say, giving it to him anyway. I feel guilty that I didn't think to bring any more for Scarlet and Rachel. We say our goodbyes and as we walk towards the headmistress who is waiting by the door ready to receive us as if we were late guests at a wedding, I hear Rachel pleading with her mother, 'Can I have a sweet?'

'I told you I haven't got anything.' Jenny is trying not to raise her voice.

'Evie's mother brought her sweets,' Rachel says sulkily, and I hear Jenny reply, 'That's because she feels guilty because she's working.'

I feel like I've been stung but I don't look round, pretending that I haven't heard. We make our way out through the doors, filing past the headmistress standing by the Christmas tree, and she congratulates Evie on her magnificent performance. I see Jenny chatting to some of the other mothers and no one invites me over or makes me feel welcome. I realise sadly that now I'm working I've passed over to the other side. I'm no longer one of them and Jenny and I are no longer the friends we once were.

'How was Evie's play?' Aidan is on the phone from America.

'Very Christmassy – she remembered all her lines and didn't bump into any of the sheep.'

'I think Florence is beginning to have an effect on you – you're becoming a bit of an old comedy thesp,' he teases me.

'What do you mean?'

'You're talking like Noël Coward.' Aidan is chuckling the other end of the phone and I imagine him in his bright hotel room at the start of the day while here it's already dark and although it's still early in the evening I'm ready for bed.

'I had a bit of a strange reaction from the other mums, even Jenny.' I tell him what she said but I can hear he's not listening to me and I imagine him watching the television with the sound turned down.

'Mmm,' he says again. I know he hasn't been listening to a word I've said.

'Aidan, I'm leaving you for a twenty-year-old toy boy.'

'All right, love, I'd better go too or I'll be late for the meeting.'

Bastard. It's all right for him being a thousand miles away with nothing to worry about except his script and what to order from room service.

'Is that Dadda, can I speak to him?' interrupts Evie as she walks into the bedroom, still in her school uniform.

'Aidan, have you got time to talk to Evie?'

'Of course,' he replies, and I wonder what happened to the important meeting. I pass the phone to her and start trying to undress her as she talks, as it's already past her bedtime. I imagine his side of the conversation as I hear her monosyllabic responses: 'Fine. Yes. No.'

Then she moves on to more serious matters. 'My tooth is really wobbly and Granny taught me a song, "All I want for Christmas is my two front teeth,"' and she sings to him across the Atlantic. 'It's not exactly cool but I like it,' she adds. 'Everyone thinks it's going to snow tonight,' she says, and Max, having been alerted by the song, wanders into the bedroom.

'Is that my dad?' he asks possessively. I nod my head.

'Can I talk to him?'

'Evie, it's Max's turn – give him the phone. Go on.'

Reluctantly she hands over the phone and Max gets straight to the point: 'Are you going to bring me back a present?'

I can hear Aidan laughing at the other end of the phone. Absentmindedly I pull Evie's school sweatshirt over her head. It's a snug fit round her head and gets stuck so I give it a quick tug and she yells. Irritated that she's making such a fuss, I bend down saying, 'Don't be so silly, Evie,' but as I look at her face I see blood spurting out of her mouth.

'Oh my God,' I shriek, realising with horror that her tooth must have got caught on the sweatshirt and I have yanked it out.

She's holding her hand up to her mouth, shocked. 'My toof,' she wails and her cries intensify when she sees her hand covered in blood. Max has turned pale and I can hear Aidan saying, 'Max, what's happened? Pass me back to your mother – MAX.'

I guide Evie out of the bedroom into the bathroom, grabbing a flannel and running it under the cold tap. 'Hold this, Evie. Don't worry, you'll be all right. I'm so sorry, my darling.' I feel terrible.

'My toof – where is my toof?'

Evie can't speak properly because of the gap in the front of her mouth but I can see she is beginning to be more worried about her money from the tooth fairy than the blood, which is a good sign. I run downstairs to get some ice, cursing myself for my carelessness, and Max follows, excited by the drama. I rush upstairs again, Max close behind me, swiping at imaginary assailants on the way up.

Back upstairs I hand Evie the ice wrapped in one of Max's muslins and before he can protest Evie holds it to the gaping hole in the front of her mouth and gradually her sobs subside.

'Have we lost the tooth?' she says mournfully.

'I'll go and check,' and as I walk back into the bedroom I see the phone lying on the bed and I can hear a faint voice shouting, 'Hello – what's happening – can anyone hear me – Molly, for God's sake, what's going on?'

'It's me, it's OK – I just pulled Evie's tooth out.'

'You did what?' he says.

'It was a mistake but I've got to go. She's fine now, so no need to worry. Must go,' and without giving him a chance to berate me I hang up. Max has followed me to the bedroom in search of more excitement. I pick up Evie's sweatshirt and a tiny tooth drops to the floor. Max leaps forward and picks it up.

'Here's the tooth,' he says, brandishing it delightedly as if he's found the hidden treasure, and he runs down the corridor to restore the tooth to its rightful owner.

'It's a beauty, isn't it?' I say, trying to cheer Evie up, and her face brightens.

'Do you think the fairies will give me more money because it's a big one and because of all the blood?' she says thickly, trying to talk and dab at the same time.

'You'll have to wait and see – you poor thing.' I stroke her head. 'I'm so sorry, Evie – I'm a terrible mother,' I joke.

'No you're not,' Max says, climbing on to my lap, but Evie doesn't look like she agrees with him.

Ten

I can see by the expression on Florence's face that she has something she needs to tell me, and having filmed with her for some time I pride myself that I've begun to understand her changing moods and can anticipate what she's going to do or say.

'I don't want to do it any more,' she says.

OK, maybe I don't know her that well, I think as the feeling of panic surges in my stomach. I never expected this.

'What do you mean, Florence?' I ask as calmly as I can. She twists the large topaz ring on her finger nervously backwards and forwards, and the monkeys on her charm bracelet seem to stare defiantly at me, mocking and taunting me, except for the one who can't bear to look at me.

'I never wanted to do this film but you made me,' she says, staring at me, her eyes filling with tears. I can hardly see her lips, they are so thin, but the skin above her top lip is puckered and her chin is beginning to wobble like a child's. I can't believe what she is saying.

'Oh Florence, I didn't.' My voice sounds petulant like a seven-year-old child's. For a minute I wonder if we're going to start shouting at each other, 'Did,' 'Didn't,' 'Did.' But I refrain from resorting to childish behaviour and say calmly, 'I certainly didn't make you – in fact, if you remember, I tried to talk you out of doing it . . .'

As I try to explain, I see big tears begin to fall from her eyes. She looks so miserable and I feel terrible for putting her into this position. She turns her head as if she doesn't want me to see her cry. Matt and Gerry look at me as if I've committed the worst crime known to mankind. I try to appeal to them, 'I didn't do anything,' but my words are drowned by the sound of Florence's sobs.

I wake with a start but the crying continues. It's not Florence, it's Evie, I realise as I stumble out of bed and blindly make my way to her bedroom, my eyes swollen with sleep. She looks distraught, her pillow is on the floor, and her Harry Potter duvet cover is dishevelled as if she has been searching for something. Clutched tightly in the palm of her hand is her tooth, which she holds out to show me.

'Fairy Floss didn't come.'

The feeling of guilt is so strong that I feel like I'm in a Tom and Jerry cartoon and I've just been hit over the head with a frying pan. It's still quite dark outside and as I pull the curtains open I can see that it's been snowing. I sit down and hug Evie who is still crying although she's trying to control herself.

'Why didn't she come? She always comes.'

Thinking quickly, I say, 'Well, you've been lucky in the past, maybe it's something to do with the snow.'

She looks at me, unsure where I'm going on this train of thought, but desperate for a reasonable explanation.

'I expect the Snow Queen had to call a state of emergency last night. All the fairies had to help out with wishes to be granted and people to be saved, especially with these icy conditions – I should imagine that your tooth was the last thing on their minds. It doesn't mean that it's not important to them, but just put it back under your pillow and I bet they'll come tonight.'

She seems a little reassured by my explanation and gets out of bed and looks out of the window at the snow. By now Max has come to see what is the matter and he stands by the bed in his Spiderman suit, his hair dishevelled from a long night's sleep.

'Don't worry, Evie – just wait and see, it will be all right. Now we've got to get dressed or we'll be late for school.'

I hear the door opening downstairs and realise my mother has arrived. She comes upstairs and Evie explains the horror of last night and the fairies' neglect. As I go back to my bedroom my mother catches me up.

'I feel terrible,' I say to her, tears welling up in my eyes.

'Don't be so silly – it's only the tooth fairy – just give her more money tonight and she'll be fine about it. Don't give yourself a hard time about this, and Molly?'

'Yes?' I feel miserable.

'I've been thinking.' She pauses and then takes a deep breath. 'I've enjoyed spending more time with the children. If you want, I can look after them for you until you finish the job.'

Relief floods through me. 'Do you mean it . . . I mean, are you sure . . . Oh God, thank you.'

I want to hug her but her smile is fading and she says very seriously, 'This is not a long-term solution. I can't do it for ever, so when this job is finished, if you're going to carry on working like this then you and Aidan have to think seriously about who is going to look after the children. Is that clear?'

'Perfectly, and thank you so much.'

'Sit down, Molly,' Rod says gravely, and I can tell by his tone that it's going to be bad. I thought it was ominous when he called me yesterday to say he was coming to see 'how we were getting on', but I convinced myself I was just being paranoid. Now that we're alone in a small sitting room in Russell Court, our knees practically touching, I brace myself because I think my instincts were right. Rod leans forward.

'The rushes are looking OK.'

I've never liked 'OK', it's just not good enough. 'Fine' is another word that reeks of mediocrity.

'What do you mean by OK?' I say, hoping my voice sounds more confident than I feel.

'Well, when I say "OK" I mean it's been well shot. The old woman is looking good, Matt has captured the atmosphere of this place, and I'm basically happy with the camera work but . . .'

'What's the problem?' I'm clutching my pen.

'There's no other way of saying it, Molly.' Rod shifts uneasily in his institutional chair. 'It's boring.'

'Boring,' I repeat after him.

'Yes, boring,' he says, irritated.

'Rod, if you don't mind me saying – what did you expect?'

He looks uncomfortable. 'I don't know, it's difficult to say – you need to interview her more, I want to know more about her life and what she feels about ageing. You need to draw her out. I don't care about how many hip replacements she's had or about her little excursions, and nor does the viewing public. You need to get under her skin and I want details – that's what's interesting. Insight. I'm not learning anything.'

'We haven't been filming that long. I wanted to build up her trust after the Robin incident,' I say, searching for an excuse.

Rod looks exasperated. 'You've been filming for over two weeks and that's long enough. Look, there isn't the time or the money, so you'd better get a move on or else . . .' He stops himself.

'You're not thinking of getting another director – you can't.'

Now I feel sick and Rod just looks at me without saying a word. 'OK, I'll start doing more probing interviews,' I say.

'Maybe you should e-mail me your questions beforehand and I could give you a few pointers,' he says.

This is becoming insulting. 'If you think it's necessary you can e-mail me the areas you want me to cover,' I say, trying to control my anger. How dare he talk to me like this? I can see by the expression on his face that he's regretting his decision to let me do this film.

'Rod – I'll get what you want but there are different approaches and maybe my softly softly approach could be perceived as being old-fashioned but it's worked in the past and I think it will work here. Constructive advice is welcome but anything negative is just not useful.'

His whole body tenses, his eyes narrow and he raises his voice. 'Don't be so fucking naïve, Molly – don't talk to me about "softly softly" and "old-fashioned approaches". I don't want to hear it.

I took a risk with you and you'd better start delivering.' He tries to check his anger and drops his voice, which makes him sound even more threatening. 'Listen to me, Molly, the bottom line is that things had better start changing and if the rushes don't improve . . . well, I'm sorry.'

He doesn't need to finish his sentence as I understand what he's saying. I want this conversation to finish immediately and I can feel the tears pricking my eyes but I'm determined not to cry in front of him as that would add to my humiliation.

I stand up proudly, trying to control my hands which are shaking. 'I have to go. Florence is waiting for us to start.'

'I'll come along then and say hello and watch for a bit if you don't mind,' he says frostily. Of course I mind but there's nothing I can do about it.

Florence is very gracious when she is introduced to Rod. She becomes almost regal, puffed up with her own importance. She just loves all the fuss and Rod is very good at making her feel special.

'When is your hair appointment, Florence?' I say, interrupting their social niceties.

'In ten minutes – have we got time for our game?'

'Not today, Florence,' I say hopefully as I look from her determined grey-green eyes to Rod's grim expression. She ignores me completely.

'Your turn to start, Molly – make it a good one as the boss is here.' I'm tempted to throttle her but instead I smile in what I hope is an unthreatening manner. I hold up my fingers to denote three words while avoiding eye contact with Rod. I pretend to hold up an old-fashioned film camera, turning the handle to indicate that I'm doing a film. First word and I point at myself.

'Me,' says Florence.

'Mine,' suggests Matt.

I pretend to wrestle with an imaginary thief and make out that it's my bag. I can feel Rod's amazement and I avoid looking at him.

'My,' says Florence. I nod my head: please can I get this over with as quickly as possible? I don't have to look at Rod to imagine his expression of disapproval at this time-wasting exercise and I feel my humiliation is complete. I pretend to drive a car and then pull my ear to indicate 'sounds like', and touch my ear again.

'Car – ear?' Matt says.

'*My Brilliant Career*,' I falter, bitterly avoiding Rod's gaze. 'OK, let's go or we'll be late,' I say, walking briskly out of the room and along the corridor to where the hairdresser sets up her makeshift salon.

Rod catches up with me and grabs my arm. 'What do you think you're playing at?'

'It's called charades or in Florence's day, "The Game",' I reply grimly while carrying on walking.

'But it's a complete waste of time.'

I stop walking and turn to him. 'I know, but to be honest it doesn't take up that much time and it keeps Florence happy, which is more than the Boy Wonder was capable of doing.'

'Who?' says Rod, looking at me as if I am deranged.

'It's Florence's name for Robin,' I mumble, wondering how much longer I'm going to be allowed to stay on this project.

The sound of an automated buggy cart interrupts us and I turn to see Bernard in his trademark shiny black leather jacket determinedly driving towards us with Dora running behind him fussing noisily, 'Not inside, Bernard . . . Bernard, no . . . Bernard – you're not allowed to drive it inside.'

It's the first time I've seen him since his stroke and although he's slumped to one side in the seat he looks just the same as before. He slows down when he sees us and comes to a halt beside Rod. One side of his body appears to be partially paralysed due to the stroke, but with his good hand he beckons me to come closer and I lean towards him.

'I hope . . .' his voice is slurred from the stroke and he struggles to speak the words, '. . . you've done a wide shot.'

I smile at him and say, 'Good to see you back, Bernard.'

Dora fusses her way along the corridor. 'Come on, Bernard,

we've got to park that outside,' and with a look at me as if to say, 'Men, what can you do?' she guides him back to the front hall.

Rod looks at me and says, 'Well, have you?'

'Have I what?'

'Done a wide shot?'

'Don't be ridiculous, of course we have,' I say, making a mental note to check with Matt about wide shots, and before Rod has a chance to say anything else I push past him to catch up with the others.

We film Florence having her hair washed. As her hair is being towelled dry she suddenly seems vulnerable and much older than I have ever seen her look before. Her prominent cheekbones look skeletal without the softness of her hair. In front of the mirror she scrutinises her face, while Sharon, the hairdresser, puts in the rollers.

'I've had to look at myself so often making up before a show – you learn to detach.'

'How do you mean?' I ask her.

'Well, you view yourself dispassionately. I mean, I know my forehead is too short, but my eyes have always been one of my best features although they looked better when they stood on their own without this supporting cast of wrinkles and bags.' She pulls at the loose skin on her eyelids and then places both hands on either side of her eyes, pulling the skin taut and making them look Chinese.

'Did you worry about ageing?' I ask her, hoping that I'm not being too blunt.

'I don't think anyone likes growing old but there's not much you can do about it. It's the physical deterioration that makes it so difficult. Everything is fading. It's like I've been wrapped in muslin. You can't see or hear clearly so you have to retreat into yourself. I think ageing is a real test of character.'

'How do you think you're shaping up?'

She looks at me thoughtfully. 'I give myself tests, passages to learn to make sure my brain is still functioning. I force myself to remember names of people I met when I was twelve. There was one man, Edmund Danes, whom I really liked, and I've always remembered him although I only met him once. I know when I can't remember his name that it's over.'

She pauses. 'I'll tell you what it's like. Do you remember when your children were very small, not that long ago for you, but every day something new would happen, a step, a new word, holding a spoon? Getting old is like that in reverse, every day a name, a thought, an action – something as silly as opening a jar of olives – and your hands just can't do it and what's frightening is that you will never be able to do it again. It's another skill that's lost. You forget the names of close friends, sometimes they re-emerge but often they are forgotten for ever. It's like living in a fog that occasionally clears but you know it's only going to deepen.'

We're all silent except for the whirring of the camera.

'But apart from that it's fine.' She smiles at Sharon who with nimble fingers is winding the final roller into her hair.

'Did you always want to act?'

'Always. My mother was horrified. It wasn't considered a suitable career and when I told them I'd got into drama school it was as if I'd said I was going on the streets. My father was a vicar but although he kicked up a fuss I think he understood because what he loved about his job was the performance. He had a good turn of phrase, did my dad. All my mother expected of me was to settle down near to the family and have children. Lucky for me everything changed with the war.'

'Were you ambitious?'

'Oh yes – you had to be. I always loved performing, making up plays and singing. It used to drive my mother mad. I'd sing all the time. Her greatest fear was that I would be big-headed, so she put me down at every opportunity. When I was about ten a friend of my parents, Harry Wakefield, worked in radio, which was very new in those days. He'd heard me singing and got me on to one of the earliest variety shows. I'll never forget it. I sang a song called "Lucky Star".'

She coughs, clears her throat and starts to sing in a fragile voice,

> 'You are my lucky star. I saw you from afar.
> Two lovely eyes at me, they were beaming, gleaming.
> I was star struck.'

Florence pauses to see if I recognise it. 'Do you know it?'

I say, 'I think I do, I didn't realise it was quite so old.'

'Thank you,' she says, staring at me.

'I didn't mean . . . sorry.' I feel ashamed of my insensitivity. Sharon stretches a plastic cap over all the curlers to keep them firmly in place.

'They made such a fuss of me, and having grown up in a household where I was never praised it had a big effect on me.' Florence glances up at me. 'Just a terrible notice box.'

She raises her lightly pencilled eyebrows at me and Sharon helps Florence out of the chair and into another in the corner where the drier is set up. Other residents are arriving, sitting down in the chairs that have been placed in the corridor so they can wait their turn.

'Let's do a shot of the queue here,' I say to Matt and he nods.

'I've just got to change tapes.'

Wendy Wannabe is helping to settle the other residents as they wait for their turn at the hairdresser's. Matt and Gerry are being very slow changing tapes and I realise that they're being distracted every time Wendy bends over to help one of the residents.

'Come on, guys, get a move on,' I say sharply, and they look like a couple of guilty schoolboys. I see Rod is also mesmerised by Wendy's obvious charms and as I look back at Florence I can see she's watching everything that's going on with a smile. Feeling strangely disgruntled, I go to check whether any of the other residents mind us filming them while they wait their turn.

I recognise Margery immediately as the woman I mistook for Eleanor, the home administrator, on my first trip to Russell

Court. She looks worried as she sits down waiting her turn for the hairdresser, and mutters to herself, 'Don't want to be a nuisance, sorry.' She stares blankly at me until her eyes focus and sounding a little confused she says, 'I know you, don't I – how silly of me. I'm sure I know you.'

'We met a few weeks ago and had a little chat,' I say. 'We were never properly introduced – I'm Molly and we're making a television documentary.'

'I'm . . .' For a moment she looks worried and then she says happily, 'I can never remember who I am. I'm probably terribly famous.'

Elspeth, who is sitting next to her, leans across and says, 'Margery – she's called Margery.'

'That's it, funny old name, sounds more like something you spread on your toast,' says Margery, her face lighting up.

'No wheelchair today, Elspeth?' I ask her.

'No darling, they're trying to make me walk more but it takes me all day just to get from my room to the bar. Imagine my frustration when I arrive just as it closes. I'm a bit quicker if Dora helps but at the moment she spends most of her time with Bernard and he's very demanding since his stroke.'

She stares at me and gives a little cough. 'Remind me what your programme is about, darling?'

'Old age,' I mumble, wondering if Matt has finished changing tapes.

'I wonder if you could tell me, just out of interest, why you chose Florence for your film?' She looks at me.

'It wasn't my decision. I sort of inherited her,' I say, trying tactfully to extricate myself.

'It's just that she's not so old.'

'Really?'

She beckons me closer. 'That is, in comparison with the rest of us. I'm ninety-two, Maurice turned ninety a few months ago and Margery here is eighty-seven.'

'Am I?' says Margery, sounding surprised. 'That's awfully good, isn't it?'

'Are you both still working?' I ask them both.

'Unofficially,' Elspeth replies, 'but I've more or less retired; I just haven't got the energy. Maurice hasn't done anything for a while. He used to do a good line in Nazi generals but even that's dried up recently, which bothers him. He, of course, blames his agent. Margery is doing very well. Aren't you?'

'Doing what?' says Margery.

'You're doing well. She's the radio queen – she's been in *The Archers* for years.'

'I do enjoy it,' Margery says, experiencing a moment of clarity.

'Florence has had a late flowering – since she's been here she's been working a lot. I think now that she doesn't have to cook for herself or run a home she can conserve her energies for work.'

'Do you ever do shows here at Russell Court?'

'What, perform them ourselves?' Elspeth looks horrified at the thought. 'Oh no, too much like work.'

She looks over my shoulder and I'm aware that Rod is hovering behind me, impatient for me to start filming again. I feel flustered and for a minute I forget what I'm supposed to be doing.

Elspeth looks back at me. 'Was there anything else, darling?'

'Oh yes . . . do you mind if we film you now?' I ask, worried for a moment that she might object.

'Go on, film away to your heart's content. I don't mind.' She shifts in her chair to the left. 'This is definitely my best side,' then she pauses and says, 'But I won't strip off, you know.'

I'm aware Rod is watching me as I talk to Matt about the way we're going to film the queue. As he sets up the camera Rod imperiously calls me over. 'Molly, a word.'

For a minute I feel tempted to resort to his tactics and start swearing, 'Fuck off and leave me alone.' Maybe he'd respect me more if I did but after our little chat I haven't got the confidence. Like a teenager who's behaving badly in class, I stand sulkily while he talks to me.

'That interview with Florence is a classic example of what I'm talking about,' he says.

'What do you mean? I thought that was interesting.'

'Yes, but you didn't go far enough – when she was talking about her eyes you should have asked whether she'd ever thought about plastic surgery – about getting old and what it feels like.'

'I asked her about ageing,' I retort.

'Yes, but you didn't probe. It was the perfect opportunity to talk about death or whether she's thought about her funeral and any regrets she may have. You're just not digging deep enough, Molly.'

To me what he's suggesting is like being involved in a hit-and-run incident where everyone is left bruised and battered. The people being interviewed feel abused and ultimately the interviewer becomes manipulative and uncaring. I think back to the sequence we've just filmed. Wouldn't it have been crass to ask her about death when she's having her hair done with so many people around? But maybe I'm being over-sensitive about it all.

'I get the point,' I say quietly.

'Good,' he says, his tone peremptory, and I want to slap his smug face.

'Now can you leave us to get on with it? I find it very difficult to concentrate with someone breathing down my neck.'

For a second he looks surprised. 'I've got to go anyway – I've got a meeting with the controller of BBC One at three o'clock. But remember what I said.' As if I could forget.

I try to smile at him but I find it hard as I watch him gather up his things. He taps Matt on the shoulder and says, 'I'm off – keep up the good work.'

He walks over to Florence, who is under the drier, and shouts at her, 'Bye, Florence – lovely to meet you – see you again soon.' He picks up her hand and kisses it. She smiles graciously and as he walks past the queue of elderly ladies she waves regally at him. She catches my eye and I wonder if she suspects what's been happening.

Elspeth beckons me over and I bend down to hear what she has to say. 'Did I tell you about my second husband? He couldn't cope when I fell in love with Juliette, the French help – such a pretty little thing. I said to him, "I love you too, my darling," but Englishmen are so funny about things like that. My third husband was much more understanding.' She is in full flow and I glance over at Matt, hoping he'll rescue me.

'Molly, come and look at this – I think it's working well.'

'I'm sorry, I can't talk now,' I say apologetically to Elspeth.

'That's all right, you go and do what you have to do. Margery and I can play "I spy".'

'I'm useless at that game – I can never remember what I've chosen in the first place.'

'I change it all the time anyway,' says Elspeth, and they both laugh like schoolgirls.

I walk over to Matt who stands back from the camera so that I can look through the eye-piece.

'Is everything OK? What did the Rottweiler have to say for himself?' Matt asks me, looking worried.

'The rushes are looking good – he was pleased with what you're doing.'

Matt looks relieved. 'But?'

'What do you mean?'

'There's always a "but",' he replies.

I don't know whether I should tell him but I need his support. 'He thinks I'm not probing deeply enough.'

Matt doesn't say anything and I'm aware that he probably agrees with Rod. I can't bring myself to tell him that he also thinks what we've shot so far is boring.

'I think it is time to change gear,' he says diplomatically, and seeing my worried expression he adds, 'Don't worry about it.'

I laugh.

'You're doing fine, Molly – she's not the easiest person. I think you've just got to be a bit pushier and don't let her run the show. It's like dealing with children – they'll respect you more if you show them who's the boss. You know?'

I watch Florence reading her two-years-out-of-date *Hello!* magazine under the drier and think to myself 'Right. I'm in charge and we're going to do things my way from now on – No more Mrs Nice Guy.'

Eleven

We're all standing shivering in the parking area round the back of Russell Court, staring at a machine which looks like a golf cart.

'Do you need a licence for this thing?' Florence demands, leaning heavily on the arm of her son Bill who arrived at lunchtime. He is looking anxiously at his mother, unsure whether she approves of his present.

'No, nothing like that – look, it's got different speeds and it's very easy to operate. All you have to remember is to charge it up after you've ridden it but it only needs a service once a year – it's one of the best models on the market.'

His voice is low and rises at the end of his sentence, turning it into a hesitant question. The years living in Canada have left their mark.

He pauses to see if her reaction is improving and then adds, 'It's easy to drive and I thought it would give you some independence.'

'It's very generous of you,' she says, attempting to be polite, and I can see the look of disappointment cross his face. He's not what I expected from all the photos of the major events in his life that I've seen. I feel as if I know him well because of all the things Florence has told me about him. I could tell you about his graduation, marred by the news that his girlfriend was pregnant; his wedding day, uncomfortable because the bride didn't want her parents to know that she was four months pregnant despite the voluminous dress, and the drama surrounding the birth of his first boy, Charlie. This was Florence's favourite story and she relished telling me how Bill had to deliver the baby on their bathroom floor because his wife, refusing to believe she was in labour and having a phobia about doctors, left it too late to go into the hospital. The paramedics told him what to do on the telephone. Bill said it was like being on a plane with no experience of flying when the pilot is suddenly struck down with food poisoning from the in-flight meal and you have to land the plane single-handedly while being talked down by ground control. When Florence told me this, I thought it was a typically male response and wondered what his wife thought of being compared with a 747.

Bill's not like his mother except for the green colour of his eyes, magnified by a pair of round, thin-rimmed glasses. He runs his hands through his long light brown hair which curls over his shirt collar. Florence, repentant about her lack of enthusiasm, gives him a kiss.

'I just have to get used to the fact that I'm an old lady – it's not that easy,' she smiles at him, 'but this will be useful – I'll be able to ride to the shops and up along the river. It is very thoughtful of you. I suppose I'd better have a go.'

She climbs into the seat and Bill shows her how to start it. 'Where's my crash helmet? I'm going to ruin my lovely hair,' she jokes.

Matt is filming and I'm trying to keep out of the way. Within minutes Florence has mastered the simple controls and she's whizzing round the car park, swerving around the parked cars. When she drives up beside us she says, 'It's rather fun. I could get used to this. Want a go, Molly?'

I shake my head.

'Go on.'

I can see Bill watching me with his mother's bird-like intensity. I get on the machine and Florence puts it on to the slowest speed. 'Don't want you to hurt yourself,' she says patronisingly.

I meander around the car park feeling a little self-conscious and foolish, especially when Eleanor, the home manager, comes out with a sheet of paper which looks like a fax. She starts to walk towards me and then, with an impatient sigh as if she can't be bothered to walk across the courtyard, turns round and hands the fax to the nearest person, who happens to be Bill. He looks at the piece of paper and then at me as Eleanor says loudly and impatiently, 'It's a fax for you from Mr Harman. Next time, will you ask him to contact you direct – I am not a message boy and we need to keep our fax clear in case of an emergency.'

Without another word she walks back into the house, her whole manner exuding efficiency. I drive the machine back to Florence and quickly get off it. Bill hands me the fax while Florence is chattering away: 'I'll call it my dream machine and pretend it's a motor bike. I've always fancied one of those. Thank you, Bill – maybe I could organise races with Bernard. He's got an enormous black one, very vulgar.' She hooks her arm through her son's and they start to make their way slowly back inside.

I glance at the fax from Rod.

INTERVIEW SUGGESTIONS

1. Ageing – how does she feel about getting old? Has she ever considered plastic surgery? What's the worst thing about it?
2. Career – details about famous people she's worked with. No boring theatrical anecdotes about obsolete stage actors, rep experiences or landladies, please.
3. Sex – when did she lose her virginity – what was it like? Does ageing affect your libido? Many lovers? Contraception? When did she last have sex – what was it like?
4. Marriage – was she always faithful and was he? Any skeletons?
5. Second childhood – remember the programme within the context of the series – concentrate on frustrations, childish sense of humour, tantrums, incontinence and dependency.
6. Death – what does she think about it? How do they all react in the home when someone dies? Ever contemplated suicide? Has she planned her own funeral? Is she frightened of dying?

It looks like he has scribbled these ideas down in between meetings. As I go through the list I feel horrified that Bill might have read them. Of course there are areas I've considered and plan to cover, but put so baldly they look crass and salacious. Not for the first time today I feel furious with Rod.

When filming is finished for the day Bill comes up to me and, making sure Florence is out of earshot, he says, 'I need to have a word.'

My heart plummets. Florence is chatting to Gerry as he takes off her radio mic and Matt is busy marking up rushes and clearing camera equipment out of Florence's room. We walk together silently to the small sitting room I was in earlier with Rod. It feels like one of those consulting rooms in hospitals where they take you aside to tell you in private that you have inoperable cancer and only a few months to live. I can see by his face that he's read the list and he's very worried.

Rather than sit and be talked at, I take the initiative. 'It's very good to meet you at last – we've heard so much about you – obviously.'

'I wish I could say the same about you.'

'What do you mean?'

'I had no idea that you were filming my mother and that you were covering such intimate areas.'

I sit in a stunned silence. It never occurred to me to ask whether Florence's relatives had been contacted as I assumed that Robin and Rod had sorted all that out long before I took over the film.

'I'm sorry, I thought you knew . . . and that list, well, you mustn't worry about it – it came from my boss Rod Harman who is a very well-respected documentary maker but he can be a bit . . . insensitive sometimes and obviously I won't be asking your mother about her sex life or the intimate details of her marriage to your father . . .'

I'm in full flow, and as I look at his shocked face I suddenly realise that he had no idea what was on that list, and I shut up immediately but it's too late.

'I don't make a habit of reading other people's mail,' he says, simply implying that as a guttersnipe journalist I would be rifling through people's dustbins in order to find a grubby story. 'I'm going to insist that the filming stops. I don't want my mother put through this at this time in her life.'

I can't believe what he is saying and I find myself wondering how well he knows his mother.

'I think she really wants to do this,' I say, struggling to keep calm.

'And I don't think she does – I think she's found herself in a difficult position and doesn't know how to get herself out of it. My mother has always found it hard to say no.' He takes his glasses off and rubs his eyes before putting them back on again.

'Have you talked to her about this?' I ask.

'I don't have to – I can see it. I have talked to Eleanor, the administrator, and she agrees with me. She says it's been very unsettling for the other residents but my main concern is for my mother. Why should she do this – what possible good can it do her?'

I am floundering and I can't answer his questions. I don't know why Florence should do this except for the simple fact that I feel sure she wants to.

'Look, I think you need to talk to her about this. But also you should spend some time with us. Watch us working with her and then if you disapprove we'll talk again.'

'No, I don't think so.'

'Why not?'

'Because I think you're taking advantage of her.'

'But that's just not true.'

We're both getting angry, talking across each other, and I can feel my neck has flushed red.

'I insist that you stop filming immediately.'

'You insist?' I say incredulously. 'And what gives you the authority to insist?'

'I'm her son and if you don't stop I'll . . . I'll sue.'

The sound of a loud laugh makes us both turn to the door and there is Florence standing in the doorway.

'I'm impressed – I didn't know you both cared so much.'

Bill springs to his feet and goes to help her as she walks slowly towards us and today I notice that she's using a stick. Is it my imagination or does she seem less robust than she did a week ago?

'I came to tell you that I got the job. I thought you might want to film me hearing the news.'

'It's a bit late for that if you've already heard,' I say, irritated.

'Oh, you don't need to worry about that, I can just pretend – that's what I've spent most of my life doing. Meg Ryan does orgasms, I do phone acting.' She gives me a demonstration of speaking on an imaginary phone. 'Hello, yes, speaking, yes, really, well that's marvellous news, I'm delighted.' She looks at us both and I can see that she's trying to alleviate the palpable tension in the room.

'That's not the way I work,' I say irritably, but she ignores me and continues to talk. 'They need me for two days in January – so it could be an interesting sequence for your film, that is, if Bill approves.'

She eases herself into the chair that only a few seconds ago Bill was sitting in. I can see that he is trying very hard not to lose his temper, digging his nails into the palm of his hand. His mother continues, 'I'm very touched by your concerns, Bill, but we need to sit down quietly, you and I, because you've forgotten one thing.'

'What's that?'

'You've forgotten to ask me what I think . . . what I want.'

Bill looks uncomfortable and doesn't say anything but turns away and walks over to the small window which looks over the car park.

'This isn't the way to discuss this,' she insists.

'Do you really know what you're doing?' he asks without looking at her.

'I'm not gaga yet – I know exactly what I'm doing.'

Bill comes back to her side. 'Well, I don't think you do – I don't think you understand the implications. Do you want to be out there with people knowing everything about you? It's going to get personal, very personal, and they'll want to film everything, and I mean everything.'

'Bill, I'm not stupid – I have thought about this. This isn't just a whim.'

'But Florence . . .'

'Be quiet for a minute. I want to do this and I want to do it with Molly.'

For a second I feel elated. I never knew she felt like that, and she's certainly never let me know it, but Bill looks furious, upset and exhausted all at the same time.

'You're still jetlagged, Bill, let's talk about it in the morning.'

He says nothing and then glances at me, uncomfortable that his authority is being undermined in front of me.

'Look, I'll leave you two – we can finish for today,' I say quickly.

'Yes, that's a good idea, Molly dear.' She smiles at me warmly and for the first time since I've met her I feel like giving her a kiss. I step towards her, but one look at Bill's solemn expression tells me that it's definitely not the moment. As I leave them Florence puts her hand out to touch Bill's arm but he moves away, out of her reach.

Matt is waiting for me in Florence's room. He looks worried.

'What's going on?' His brown eyes are awash with concern.

'Well, I think you could say it's been one of those days.'

'What's up with him? I thought he didn't look happy.'

'That's an understatement. He doesn't like us doing the film – no one consulted him about it and he's worried.'

'Do you think it will be all right?'

I smile at him. 'Yes, I do, I really do.'

'Have we finished for the day? Because I can tell Gerry to start packing up.' He picks up the camera.

'Yes, we're done. Matt, what I don't understand is why does she want to do this film?'

'She's an actress, for Chrissake. Listen, I could do with a drink. Gerry, are you coming? Molly, how about it?'

'We could always raid Florence's bar,' I say, giggling. I'm feeling light-headed already.

Gerry pretends to look horrified. 'I wouldn't dare – anyway I've got to get out of here – I feel like I'm becoming institutionalised. Beer and a smoke, that's what I need. There's a pub in the next village – last one there is paying.'

As we walk through the hall, united like the three amigos, we pass residents many of whose faces are now familiar. I see Maurice at the top of the stairs and he waves at me. I wave back and walk a little faster – the front door is in sight. Elspeth, the wheelchair beauty, passes on her way to dinner pushed by Dora, who stops when she sees me.

'I just wanted to say goodbye as I'm going home tomorrow.'

'Oh, that's good,' I say encouragingly.

'Is it? I don't really want to go; I rather like being here. I feel useful.'

'Can you stay if you want?'

'They don't think I'm ready,' she sighs. We hear the sound of the gong ringing for supper.

'I must go – maybe see you again,' I say as Matt and Gerry open the front door. We hear the distant wail of an ambulance and as I turn back I see a look cross their faces as if they're wondering, 'Is it for me?' I pause for a second and then, realising I'd better be quick now that Maurice has made it to the bottom of the stairs, and feeling a little guilty, I wave again and quickly close the door before he gets the chance to reach me. Matt and Gerry are waiting in the crew car, all the gear loaded, and we speed down the driveway making our getaway.

The boys made sure I was the last one into the pub and I'm standing at the bar paying for the first round of drinks. Elvis is singing about how lonely he's going to be this Christmas while the heaving throng of people unwinding after a day at work compete for the barman's attention. I'm feeling guilty about not driving home immediately but somehow the thought of avoiding bathtime tensions is a relief.

'Molly, have you thought any more about working Christmas Day?' Matt asks as he tries to open a packet of salted peanuts at the same time as carrying two pints of Guinness.

'I've tried not to think about it but I have a nagging feeling that we should do it. What do you two think?'

'Told you – you owe me a fiver,' says Gerry, grinning at Matt who looks a little embarrassed as if he wishes Gerry would keep quiet.

'What's this?' I ask, looking from one to the other.

'Well, Matt thought you wouldn't dream of filming on Christmas Day because of family stuff.'

I look at Matt, who is staring intently at his pint, and I can just imagine how the conversation went between them.

Gerry: 'Do you think we'll have to work on Christmas Day?'

Matt: 'Don't be soft – Molly would never leave her family – God, she's finding it hard enough on normal days. Don't worry about it.'

My mind is made up. 'Sorry, boys, I think we will have to.'

'Bollock brain,' Matt says under his breath, scowling at Gerry.

'New Year's Eve as well?' asks Gerry, grimacing.

'Yes – I think filming New Year with Florence could have a poignancy.'

Matt looks disgruntled. 'Ann will kill me.'

'Matt, the last time we were working together I thought she gave you an ultimatum – marriage or else . . .'

'Yes,' he says quickly, looking very uncomfortable.

'So what happened?' I'm enjoying watching him squirm.

'Nothing, I'm still thinking about it.'

'Do you think you've had enough time to think about this one?'

'It hasn't been that long.'

'No, silly me, only seven years – it's not that long. Don't you think it's a bit unfair on her, keeping her hanging on all this time?'

Matt glances at Gerry, obviously uncomfortable talking about this in front of him. 'I just can't quite do it. Some days I think, "Yes I'm ready – let's do it" but something always happens to make me change my mind.'

'Why aren't you sure?'

'I don't think it's her; she's great, we get on very well, but it's been so long now there's no spark. It's all too normal and there's no more surprises. I know if we did do it it wouldn't be that special and it shouldn't feel like that, should it?' He appeals to me as if I'm the expert on marriage. I think about my marriage, about Aidan who'll be home in a few days, and I'm surprised how unemotional I feel about his return. We've settled into a comfortable routine while he's been away, thanks to my mother, and I've got used to his absence. Even at night I guiltily look forward to stretching out over both sides of the bed. I reassure myself it's a natural response, a survival mechanism to deal with his absence. Did I always feel like this when he went away? I do remember it would always take time to readjust to having him home again, however pleased I was to see him.

Matt takes a sip of beer and nurses his pint glass.

'Maybe you should spend some time apart and then it might help you decide one way or the other,' I try to suggest helpfully.

'I don't want to think about it. Are you sure you want us to work Christmas Day?' he says, changing the subject, and I haven't the heart to pursue it.

'Yes,' I say emphatically. 'We could do a half day on Christmas Eve so you're back early and then another half day on Christmas Day. Don't look so gloomy, it might be fun.'

He finishes his pint. 'Well, I think we deserve another drink – same again please, Molly?' he grins.

'You'd better start thinking about the presents you're going to get us,' Gerry says as he pushes his empty pint glass towards me.

'Presents – you sound like my children.' I push the empty glass back towards Gerry. 'Your round, I think.'

'I'll give you a hand,' says Matt and I can just imagine what he's saying to Gerry as they walk to the bar.

As I'm waiting for my drink I start thinking about what I still need to do before Christmas. I've ordered wrapping paper, ribbon and tags from the school and most of the stocking presents are from a catalogue. I only hope they come before Christmas and the children don't get suspicious about the number of packages arriving through the post. There are still a few presents I need to get although Aidan and I have agreed to buy something together this year. Whenever I buy him a present it's inevitably wrong, so now he likes to choose it himself. I've ordered a book for Tim, a pair of gardening boots for my mother, and I bought a necklace at the school fair for Helen. I'd like to get something for Florence, but what could it be and when am I going to have the time?

I watch Gerry and Matt walking back to the table trying not to spill the drinks. The music has changed and now Bill Nighy is feeling Christmas in his fingers and toes and I have my brainwave.

'I've got a great idea for the perfect present for Florence.'

'Typical – got her sorted – what about us?' says Gerry.

'Sorry, excuse me while I make a phone call.'

Cassie answers immediately.

'How are you doing?'

'Surviving,' she says brightly.

'Look, I can't really talk.'

'Now there's a surprise.'

I choose to ignore her sarcastic tone. 'Cassie, I'm sorry, but I need you to do some research for me.'

Silence on the other end of the phone.

'Please?'

'Oh Molly – it's nearly Christmas – I've got so much to do.'

'Remember Michael Caine?'

She groans. 'You're not still going on about that? It was years ago. We've got to be square by now.'

*

She's right. It was eighteen years ago and we had just started working together when the Svengali figure who ran the department, called Bob Beaumont, walked into our office and clicked his fingers.

'Cassie – Michael Caine interview in two days' time – all right?' We both sat gaping at him.

'Well, get on with it, and you . . .' for a minute he couldn't remember my name, '. . . Holly . . . you give her all the help she needs. Good luck.'

I couldn't believe it and neither could she. I watched her prepare for the interview; my job was to discover amusing anecdotes and interesting facts that people didn't know about Caine, which was hard as he was possibly one of the most popular chat-show guests on the circuit.

The night before the interview Cassie stayed late to work on her questions and I could see she was nervous.

'Where are you meeting him?' I asked.

'Langan's,' she replied tensely. 'God, I need a fag. I hate posh restaurants. Why couldn't we meet in the local fish and chippie or round at his place but not in a posh restaurant?'

'Listen,' I replied, trying to be helpful, 'my friend Jo is going out with Richard Shepherd, the chef and Caine's business partner. Shall I ring her and get her to put in a good word for you?'

For the first time in the weeks we'd worked together she looked impressed by something I had to offer. 'Would you?'

I immediately rang Jo, knowing that she'd help.

'No problem – I'm seeing him tonight. Consider it sorted.'

The next day Richard Shepherd arranged for Cassie to come half an hour earlier to Langan's and plied her with champagne cocktails. Caine joined them at the bar chatting happily, thinking she was a friend of Richard's.

At the allotted time of their interview Caine got up and said, 'Sorry, I've got to go and meet a bloody researcher – I hate these things.'

'I'm afraid that's me,' said Cassie nervously.

Caine looked at her and then started to laugh. 'Thank God for that. You're all right, I can talk to you. Come on then, let's get started.'

She had the best hour of her life – they got on brilliantly and she was eternally grateful for the kick-start to her talk-show career. After that, if ever I needed anything I just had to say the magic words 'Michael Caine' to get her to agree.

'This is the last time I'll do it, I promise.'

'That's what you said last time,' she says, her voice mellowing. 'OK – fire away and I'll see what I can do, but no promises.'

'Cassie – thank you and now I owe you one – big time.'

'Just hold that thought,' she laughs. 'Now, what do you want me to do?'

'Now let me get this straight. You want me and the kids to come with you on Christmas Day and hang around while you film?'

The line crackles with his anger and the phone feels hot against my ear.

'Well . . . yes,' I reply.

'That's going to be a lot of fun. I don't believe you, Molly. I think you're getting obsessed with this woman. It's as if she's got some kind of hold over you.'

'I'm not obsessed and it's not as sinister as you make it sound. Our time is limited and I don't seem to be getting the best footage, so Christmas will be an event. I need it for the film and it will impress Rod that I'm really committed. And you never know, you might find it interesting. It's not like a normal old people's home, it's very beautiful, and they'd love to see the children.'

Aidan is silent on the other side of the world.

'I'm sorry, I know it's not ideal, but it's only for one day.' I don't think now is the time to mention New Year's Eve as well.

'It just happens to be quite an important day, a family day.'

I seem to remember Aidan and me having the same conversation only a few months ago, but then our roles were reversed and now he's the one reminding me of the importance of family time. It would be funny if only I didn't feel so miserable.

'It's too late now – it's all settled. Florence is expecting us and I've worked out a deal with the crew. Look, we can have some family time afterwards down in Devon when we go and stay with Jo and Finn. Cassie has decided to come as well; it's going to be good.'

Aidan is not convinced. 'That's hardly family, Molly.'

'Don't worry, it will be fine.' My voice sounds small, unconvinced and unsure whether once again I have made the wrong decision.

Twelve

'Ho, ho, ho,' says Aidan, standing on the doorstep wearing a Father Christmas hat, the red of which matches his bloodshot eyes. I'm impressed, however, that he's attempting to get into the spirit.

'Have you got me a present?' says Max eagerly two seconds after Aidan has stepped through the front door.

'Presents, presents and more presents,' says Evie, gleefully rummaging through Aidan's plastic bags. 'I love Christmas.'

'Stop,' he says, for a minute looking hurt, worrying that perhaps presents are all they care about.

I only got home half an hour ago myself, relieving my mother who was trying not to panic about everything she had to do before tomorrow. I try quickly to tidy up the mess we've made of Aidan's perfect space in the ten days since he's been away. I stuff the toys into cupboards, putting the yellow plastic garage – that Max rediscovered in the cellar to which Aidan had banished it months ago – into the garden. I manage to wedge Max's pirate ship into one cupboard but as I walk away I hear the door burst open and the ship topple on to the floor. I decide to leave it and go to give Aidan a kiss but he's more intent on making sure the children don't find their presents.

'You're both going to have to wait until tomorrow. It's Christmas Eve, guys,' he says, appealing to them both. He stares at the huge tree standing proudly in the window.

'What do you think?' I ask him.

'Well, it's great, but call me old-fashioned – I thought people usually put balls, lights and decorations on their tree.'

'There hasn't been enough time and you know how much you love to do it, so I thought I'd save it for you.'

'Thanks,' he says unenthusiastically.

'Cup of tea or a drink?' I look at my watch and think we're in the no-man's-land of the afternoon.

'Not now. Let me take my stuff upstairs and then I'll start on the tree.'

'I brought all the boxes down from the attic,' I say.

'Well, that's something. I suppose we should count ourselves lucky that you're here.'

His tone is sarcastic but I'm distracted by Max and Evie as they begin to unwrap Aidan's delicate glass snowflakes that he bought in Venice. They fling the bits of newspaper at each other and I wait to hear a crunch as they step on one of his precious decorations.

'Stop!' Aidan roars so that both children freeze, and he tries to recover his composure. 'Sorry to shout,' he says as calmly as he can, 'but these decorations are precious and I don't want you to break them.'

Evie, suddenly remembering something, rushes upstairs to find her school bag. She comes downstairs holding out a home-made papier-mâché star which she has painted purple with silver glitter sprinkled over the top. Aidan's reaction is not exactly enthusiastic. Every year we have the same decorations, everything is white or silver from the star to the lights, and Aidan takes her star barely hiding his disgust. I long for him to be enthusiastic and give Evie some praise but the look on her face reminds me of Bill's expression when he gave Florence her 'geriatric cart' as she later called it.

I put my arms round Evie and take the star from Aidan. 'It's lovely, such a cool colour, and it works so well with the glitter.' I know I'm over-compensating for Aidan's initial response and he tries to make amends.

'Well done, Evie, where shall we put it?' he says, moving round to the side of the tree where it will be less visible. Evie points to the centre of the tree and when Aidan tries to put it deep into the branches she says, 'We made them with holes in the top so they can be hung with thread.'

'Great,' says Aidan, and putting aside the star he sets about unwrapping all the other decorations and unwinding the first of five sets of fairy lights, while I try to keep Max amused by screwing up the bits of newspaper which I then feed to him to kick into a cardboard box goal.

By the time Aidan's finished the tree looks pretty in a pristine, controlled and calculated way, a designer tree, Aidan's tree. For a moment I wish I had bought the gaudiest, brightest bauble which I could place in a prominent position so that everyone can see it. Even the gingerbread men and star biscuits made by the children have to be decorated with white icing. Forget it, Bing, I'm not dreaming of a white Christmas, I want a red, gold or even a purple one. I'm so bored of white; in fact if I'm honest I'm so bored of Christmas.

I put on *Home Alone* to occupy the children and as they settle in front of the screen I go upstairs, grabbing the opportunity to wrap some presents. Just as I start to unroll the wrapping paper the doorbell rings. I hear the children rush to the door as if it might be Father Christmas himself taking a more orthodox approach to delivering his presents this year. The door opens and Cassie's laugh heralds the first stirrings of Christmas spirit in me which is soon quashed when I hear Aidan saying, 'I'm sure we've got Christmas cake somewhere, Molly always makes one.'

I feel rage surge through me. Does he think I've got time to make cake?

I run down the stairs and into the kitchen. 'Didn't manage to do it this year – can't imagine why,' I say, giving him a look as I hug Cassie. 'I'm sorry I haven't got any cake,' I tell her. 'How about a digestive biscuit or one of Sainsbury's excellent mince pies?'

'I've got what you ordered,' Cassie says, and for a minute I don't know what she's talking about.

'Florence's present.'

'You have? That's fantastic.'

She rummages through her bag and hands me a small parcel. 'What's it like?'

'It's not great quality, as you can imagine, but I think she'll like it.'

'Cassie, you're a star – thanks so much. I think we can say categorically that Michael Caine is finally a thing of the past.'

'You said that last time,' she laughs.

'No, I really mean it.'

'You said that and all.'

'Was it hard to find?'

'You don't know the half of it. I've never had so much trouble finding anything in my life – you wouldn't believe the amount of research I had to do.'

'Really?' I say, feeling very guilty as I know she has enough to do without me creating more work for her.

'Don't look so worried – you know me, I enjoyed the challenge and I was determined to find it. I was like a little ferret – you would have been proud of me.'

Aidan is curiously eyeing the package. 'What's this?'

'Wait and see – you'll find out tomorrow. I think I'm going to have a beer to celebrate, anyone else?'

'So Christmas Day – usual stuff – your mum, Tim and his girlfriend here for lunch, is it?' asks Cassie, and Aidan, who's getting me a beer, grimaces.

'Hasn't she told you?' he says.

'We're working,' I say quickly.

'What do you mean? Actually I will have one of those,' she says, watching me take a sip of cold beer.

'I've got to film tomorrow so we're all going to go.'

'You're kidding.' Cassie is staring at me in astonishment.

'Don't you start. It's probably not one of the best decisions I've ever made but I want to be with the family and we've got to film so it seemed the only solution. Actually Florence is looking forward to meeting them all and it may not be such a bad thing.' I look at Aidan's exhausted face. 'You never know, it might be fun; at least it's something different.' He refuses to look at me so I continue, 'We'll then drive on to Mum's for an early Christmas dinner, which will be a first as we've traditionally always had a Christmas lunch.'

'Will Tim be there?'

'Yup, and Helen.' I can't help myself but I pull a face.

'Is that good or bad?' asks Cassie.

'Well, it's something that we've got to get used to as they're getting married. She's fine, isn't she?' I appeal to Aidan.

'She's very nice,' he says, 'and that's the problem – she tries too hard. Always keen to impress Molly.'

'Do you really think so?' I ask, amazed as he's never mentioned that before. I look at Cassie's tired face and feel a pang of guilt that until now it never occurred to me to think what she might be doing her first Christmas without Will. How could I have been so insensitive?

As if reading my mind, Cassie says, 'I'm off up to Liverpool to see my cousins. It's going to be a strange one. I used to always spend Christmas with Will's family.'

'Have you spoken to him or seen him?'

'Last week, but neither of us knows what to say any more. I don't see the point, it only upsets us both. Do you know what I find hard? It's not having anyone to consult. We used to discuss everything and he'd help me with the tiniest decisions. Maybe I was too dependent on him but the other thing that's hard . . .' She hesitates, and we both look at her. 'It's the sympathetic looks.' She stares back at us. 'Like you two are doing now. I don't want people to feel sorry for me. Don't,' she warns as I move to give her a hug.

'I've got to go and do some wrapping,' Aidan says, not wanting to get drawn into a conversation that verges on the emotional, and as he gets up he says, trying to joke, 'To be honest, you're not getting any sympathy from me – I was relieved when you two split up; he was so intense and worried all the time. I never liked him.'

Cassie grins. 'You never like anyone,' she says.

'True, but that has its advantages. Happy Christmas anyway, and now I've got to decide whether I should wrap or write.'

'Definitely wrap,' I say emphatically. 'Please,' I add hopefully to his retreating back.

I hear the children laughing and realise that they've reached the climax of *Home Alone*, which explains their absence. 'You driving up tonight?' I ask Cassie.

'I'm going straight on from here.'

'Are things OK?'

'Don't get me all weepy. It's this time of year, I don't see the point of Christmas without children. I'm so bored of thinking about myself all the time, I want someone else to think about, to build my life around.'

'Have you ever thought about adopting?'

'Will and I did talk about it but it's such a big step. Anyway, he still could have children, I'm the one who can't.'

'But lots of people do adopt.'

'I don't even have a partner and I don't know if I could do it on my own. I haven't got the confidence – the thought terrifies me.'

'But you're brilliant with my two.'

'That's easy, and I can hand them back.'

We're interrupted by a shriek from the front of the house. 'Evie has eaten the last bit of my gingerbread man – I was saving the good bit till last.' Max is beside himself.

'Look what you're missing,' I try to joke to Cassie, but it sounds shallow and I immediately regret saying it.

'What are you doing eating the tree decorations anyway?' I shout at them, and they both look sheepish.

'We were hungry – we haven't had any tea,' says Evie accusingly.

'Oh God, I'm sorry, is pasta OK?' I ask her.

'Pasta, pasta, pasta,' chants Max, jumping up from the floor and doing a food version of a rain dance.

'But no vegeterribles,' warns Evie.

'Come on, Evie – they're good for you.'

'It is Christmas – please just ham and cheese – I'll even eat those little round cabbagey things that make you fart tomorrow if we don't have to have vegeterribles tonight.'

'Evie!'

Cassie is laughing at my expression.

'All right, but then we've got to get upstairs for bath and stories otherwise you'll still be awake for Father Christmas.'

In his excitement Max's rain dance becomes more like a whirling dervish. He rushes round the house, stopping to get his breath, wiggling his hips and pointing an imaginary gun. Evie chases him and when she catches him hugs him until he can't breathe and they collapse on to the floor giggling, until Max starts to cry because Evie's elbow has gone into his eye.

'I've bought them both something; can I give it to them now?' Cassie asks me.

'Go on then.'

She goes out to her car and the children say anxiously, 'Is Cassie going?' and peer out of the window trying to see where she's gone. She comes back inside carrying a large box, which she gives to Evie, and a smaller, squidgy parcel, which she hands to Max. I see him look at Evie's parcel and I know what he's thinking. When you're four, size really matters. Evie is ripping the paper off in an excited frenzy and I help Max with his present, trying to encourage his enthusiasm. His present is a soft beanie dog. I read the label on his red collar: 'He's called Muddy.' Max smiles, acclimatising himself to his new present.

'Oh my God.' Evie is staring at a picture on the box of a disco light ball. 'Thank you so much.' She flings her arms around Cassie and kisses her. 'Quick, I need some scissors to open it up.'

Once the box has been ripped apart and we've plugged in the disco ball, Evie puts on her S Club CD and turns the lights off and she dances while Max tries to jump over and through the revolving lights.

'That's very generous of you – you shouldn't have.'

'Don't be silly – I like buying for them. Look, I should be going.'

'Oh, don't go, you can stay while I cook their tea and we can chat – we've only just started.'

She looks at her watch. 'The traffic will be awful and I won't be there until midnight if I don't get going now – I'm sorry.'

'It's lovely to see you, Cassie – New Year's resolution that we spend more time together?'

She smiles at me as if she's thinking, 'That'll never happen.'

'I'm looking forward to going to Devon – Jo said it was a lovely old house with chickens and geese. Fresh eggs for breakfast – I can't wait.'

'I've got a bit of a problem,' I say nervously, looking to see if Aidan is in earshot. 'I'm going to have to work on New Year's Eve.' I lower my voice. 'I haven't dared mention it yet to Aidan.'

'Molly, is it entirely necessary?' Cassie looks at me. 'Don't you think you're overdoing it a bit?'

'It's too late now. I've booked the crew and told Florence.' I concentrate on draining the pasta for the children's tea, but I'm aware that Cassie is watching me.

'Supper's ready,' I shout, and the children come running into the kitchen.

Cassie looks at her watch. 'I'd better go,' she says, and we all follow her into the hallway where she takes a bright red lipstick out of her bag. She looks at her reflection in the hall mirror and expertly applies the lipstick while we all watch, mesmerised.

'Can you do your kiss thing?' Evie asks, and Cassie gives them each a huge kiss, leaving the mark from her lipstick on their foreheads. They both giggle and go up on tiptoes to admire themselves in the mirror. She gives me a hug and leaves the scarlet imprint of her kiss on my cheek, and the children shriek with laughter as I admire myself in the mirror.

'I won't wash for days.'

'Happy Christmas, you lot – hope you get everything you want.'

The children open the door and she walks down the path.

'Cassie!' I shout after her.

'What?' she says, turning, thinking she must have left something.

'Thanks.'

'For what?'

'For getting the tape and you know . . .'

She turns and walks down the street and part of me wishes I could go too.

Thirteen

'Why do we have to have Christmas with a load of boring old people?' whines Evie. I slow down as I drive over the sleeping policemen in the street, trying not to bang the children's heads on the roof of the car, although if Evie continues to moan like this it might be just what she needs. Max is pushing the button that operates the window so that he can stick his new sword out and brandish it in a threatening manner at everyone as we drive past.

Despite my guilt at making them do this, I try to be optimistic. 'How do you know they're boring if you haven't even met them?'

Evie sulks.

'One day you'll be a boring old person too.'

She looks at me sceptically and I notice that she's beginning to hone her ability to raise an eyebrow in a disconcerting manner.

'I know it's unbelievable but one day you'll be an old lady.'

'What, as old as you?' she says, her eyebrow dropping, unable to keep the amazement out of her voice.

'Maybe even older – it is possible.'

I turn to look at Aidan who is having difficulty keeping his eyes open. We had a restless night, both of us unaccustomed to having another body in the bed. I'm just not sure how this is going to work today. I've come armed with colours, a GameBoy, numerous presents from Father Christmas, magazines and a secret stash of sweets as backup, and Evie insisted on bringing her disco ball.

'It's not for long and then we go to Granny's for a lovely Christmas dinner. Besides, I think you'll cheer them all up – they love seeing young faces.' I look at Evie's sulky expression and wonder whether this is entirely true.

As we turn into the big sweeping drive the children fall silent, surprised by the grandeur of the place. Walking up the steps they look amazed and inside the entrance hall they are practically open-mouthed as they take in the huge staircase with the portraits staring dramatically from the walls. 'You never said it was like Hogwarts,' Evie says in reverent tones.

The crew are waiting for me, looking smarter than usual because of the occasion. They grin when they see me and I feel self-conscious just helping the children out of the car.

'Matt, Gerry, meet Evie, Max, and this is Aidan.' I mumble Aidan's name, longing for this to be over. I feel awkward introducing them all, my two worlds colliding. I rather like the thought of having separate lives and a separate identity for each life.

I can see Matt looking at Aidan with interest and I can't stop myself making excuses for him. 'Poor Aidan, he's terribly jetlagged as he only came back from America yesterday.'

I can tell instantly that Matt is not impressed, and even though I know it's silly it bothers me. I take Aidan aside. 'Try and keep the children out of my way. You can watch for a bit but they'll probably get bored – you know what it's like. Eleanor, the woman who runs the home, said that you could go into the gardens and have a look around. There's a small sitting room over there where the children can draw or read. They've got cocktails at eleven and then lunch but we don't have to stay until the bitter end. I'll come and find you when we've finished.' I look at his exhausted face. 'I'm so sorry about this.'

With what looks like a supreme amount of effort he smiles and leans forward to kiss me. I automatically lean away from him before looking around to check that no one can see us before I present a cheek. It just doesn't feel right when I'm at work to be kissing anyone, even if he is my husband.

'See you later,' I say, eager to get started.

'Happy filming,' he replies miserably.

When I walk into Florence's room I'm surprised to see Bill standing beside her because of the Russell Court rules that don't allow family on Christmas Day. Over the past few days' filming leading up to Christmas he made sure that we never had to exchange more than a few words, and tended to leave as soon as we arrived. Today I'm relieved that he doesn't immediately scowl at me, but he avoids eye contact. Florence is looking elegant in a 1950s Dior skirt and white shirt with a wide black belt and black shoes with kitten heels.

'Happy Christmas, Molly, don't you scrub up nicely?'

'I was just thinking the same about you. Happy Christmas, Florence.'

'I haven't seen you in a skirt since that ghastly plain thing you wore when you first came to meet me.'

That was a lifetime ago.

'A bit of a mistake. I wasn't sure you'd noticed.'

'I know I have problems but I'm not that blind. This is lovely – red really suits you.'

I had made an effort this morning, particularly as we were going on to my mother's, but I find it embarrassing talking like this as I don't want to be the centre of attention.

'And are these your lovely children?'

Evie and Max have followed me into the room, while Aidan hovers in the doorway.

'Well I don't know about lovely,' I joke, putting my arms protectively around them both.

'Are you having a good Christmas?' she asks them, playing the role of kindly grandmother. They both nod their heads.

'What's your name?'

'He's called Max,' says Evie because Max is too shy to speak for himself.

'What did Father Christmas bring you? He did come this year, didn't he?'

Max points his sword at her.

'Now, that is what I call a sword.' Florence waves her arm in

164

Bill's direction. 'He's my boy – I know he's big now but when he was little all he really wanted was a gun.'

Max looks accusingly at me as if to say, 'See, that's what normal people get.'

Bill crouches down so that he's head to head with Max. 'My favourite was a holster, do you know what that is?' Max nods his head. 'Well, I had a holster with two guns that were shiny and silver and had bucking bronco horses engraved on the wooden handles and you could use caps in them. They made a terrible noise but I thought they were great.'

Max is spellbound, even if he is finding it difficult to imagine Bill as a small boy. He looks at Florence. 'Did you get anything from Father Christmas?' he asks her shyly and Florence points at Bill.

'Him – he was an early present from Father Christmas.' Max stares at Bill who grins back. It's the first time I've seen him smile and it changes his face dramatically.

Max is trying to work out how Bill would have fitted on to Father Christmas's sleigh. 'Did he come wrapped up?' he asks slowly.

'Don't ever let anyone wrap you up – the sellotape is agony,' Bill says seriously.

'No worse than a leg wax, you great baby,' Florence teases her son. She turns to look at Evie, bringing her into the conversation. 'What about you, young lady?'

'I've never had a leg wax,' says Evie, and Florence chuckles.

'And what's your name?'

'Evie.'

'Ah, now that's a great name . . . see that picture over there? Yes, you can bring it to me. She was one of my closest friends. I knew her for years. She's lovely, isn't she?' she says, showing Evie the black and white picture of a handsome woman wearing uniform, her hair neatly permed in the fashion of the day. She has her back to the photographer but she's looking over her shoulder, staring enigmatically at something beyond the camera. Despite the film-star pose she manages to look approachable.

'What happened to her?' asks Evie, staring at the picture.

'She died,' says Florence sadly, 'a long time ago . . . do you know, I still miss her. Anyway, she had the same name as you. Her proper name was Evelyn but I called her Evie.' She leans forward and tucks a strand of Evie's hair back behind her ears. Evie scratches her head and lets the strand fall back again.

'Tell me, what did you get for Christmas?'

'Cassie bought me a disco ball.'

'That sounds energetic.'

'It's brilliant,' says Evie.

'Well, I'd love to see it.'

'And I got these.' Evie shows her some walkie-talkies that Aidan brought back from America.

'That's marvellous – shall we see if they work? You go down the corridor and I'll wait for you to contact me.'

Evie is delighted with this idea and disappears out into the corridor while Matt and I discuss the first setup.

'Can you read me, can you read me?' The sound of Evie's voice reverberates around the room and Florence delightedly picks up her walkie-talkie.

'Reading you loud and clear. Any activity to report, number one?'

'Nothing interesting, just a load of old people going down the stairs. Over and out.'

Florence laughs. 'She's a bit more direct than you, Molly.'

'I think they're going down to the sitting room for drinks. We'd better get a move on before they run out of whisky.'

Aidan has been loitering by the door, unsure whether to come in or stay in the corridor. He nods at me to come over.

'What's happening?' he asks me as quietly as he can to avoid drawing attention to himself.

'It's the Christmas drinks party – can you take the children as we need to get started?'

'Aren't you going to introduce us, Molly?' says Florence flirtatiously.

'Florence – Aidan, Aidan – Florence,' I say ungraciously. I'm finding this very awkward.

'A delight. Are you coming to have a drink? Do you mind if I lean on your arm and we can chat on the way down?'

This is a terrible idea because if we're going to film, the last thing I want is Aidan in shot. Matt looks at me as if to say, 'Well, go on, do something.'

'Florence, I'm sorry, but Aidan can't be in the film.'

'Why ever not? He's very presentable,' she says, looking at him admiringly.

'Because he's not part of the story.'

'Oh, do you think so?' she says.

'It would be better if you were with Bill.'

'Bill's not supposed to be here on Christmas Day – we smuggled him in through the back.' She sees my expression and sighs. 'All right, we got a special dispensation as he's come such a long way, and he's allowed down for a drink. Eleanor made an exception for him but he can't stay for lunch.'

'You can take your mother downstairs on your way out,' I say, not in the mood to banter.

'Well, you're the boss,' Florence says, and we both know she's lying.

The bar of Russell Court is transformed into a genteel version of Santa's Grotto and is already packed with residents. Maurice is holding court in front of the fireplace as though he is the host of the party. Some of the other residents are sitting in attendance. A wisp of a woman dressed in floating powder-blue chiffon, almost the same colour as her hair, wafts past, looking down her nose at us with narrowing eyes. I almost expect her to start waving as if she's travelling in a state carriage.

Florence whispers to me, 'Have you seen Phyllis before? She doesn't like to mingle much – a bit grand for the likes of us. She was a big star in the thirties and has never quite recovered. She's very snooty about the rep actors and she hates television – thinks it quite vulgar. She'll expect to be waited on hand and foot as she can't do a thing for herself. She's like a big baby. Phyllis, how lovely to see you.'

167

Phyllis graciously inclines her head and slowly glides past, continuing to work the room.

Elspeth, wearing a dark green velvet turban dramatically woven round her head, is being pushed in her wheelchair by Margery, who is wearing a tinsel crown in an attempt to be festive. Elspeth smiles up at Bill who is standing beside his mother. 'Such a lovely boy,' she sighs, and Florence smiles proudly.

'Stop me if I've told you this before but when I played Cinderella in panto at Birmingham rep – it's the only time I've done panto,' she adds quickly for my benefit, 'well, my Buttons was being played by a beautiful—'

'Darling Elspeth, you have told me this quite a few times,' says Florence patiently, but Elspeth ignores her and launches into the story about her beautiful Buttons.

I see Comfort attend to a hunched figure in a wheelchair sitting near the window and I realise that it's Bernard. She takes a glass of wine from the table beside him and holds it to his lips. I steel myself to go over and as I get close to him I'm aware he's watching me.

'How are you feeling, Bernard?'

'Fantastic,' he says ironically. His voice is still slurred but better than it was when I last saw him when we were filming outside the hairdresser's. The left side of his body appears to be paralysed but his eyes are blazing with anger. 'Can you think of anything worse – Christmas with a bunch of bloody actors?' he mutters.

'Shh,' says Comfort, 'they might hear you.'

'Good,' he says slowly, and although it's hard to tell I wonder if he's trying to smile.

I find Matt filming individual residents, and when he sees me Gerry anxiously removes his headphones.

'I'm having difficulty getting individual conversations – I can hear Florence because she's wearing a radio mic but I can't do them all and it's difficult getting in there because there are so many people. I keep tripping over wheelchairs and sticks – it's like a bloody obstacle course.'

'I'll let you know in advance who we're filming and give you a chance to get close to them – don't worry, Gerry, I understand the problems.'

He looks at me gratefully. I go back to Florence who is standing alone.

'Hasn't Elspeth any family?'

'Married four times, no children of her own, but some stepchildren who never visit. I'm glad I wasn't a beauty.'

'I wouldn't say that,' I say.

'You know what I mean,' she replies.

I see a little girl walking around the outside perimeter of the party and it's a shock when I realise that it's Evie, with Max following close behind. For a minute I had forgotten that my children are here and I look around for Aidan to check that he is keeping an eye on them. He's standing at the door, his arms crossed like a bodyguard, keeping an eye on the residents and the children. Evie is talking to Maurice now, Max is standing beside her and they both seem to be concentrating. Maurice puts his hand up to Evie's ear and produces a coin. She puts her hands to her ears to see if there are any more and giggles. 'Do it again,' I hear her say.

'Will you do it to me?' asks Max.

I'm searching for good characters and interesting shots. I bend down and whisper into Matt's ear, 'When you're ready there are a couple of women by the bookcase.' I wave at Gerry, who is standing behind Maurice. They both wave back at me. I point at the two women to let Gerry know what we're doing. Maurice looks at the women and mouths back at me, 'Too old for me,' and I find it hard not to giggle.

Matt finishes his shot and moves the camera. 'Well spotted, Molly – they're extraordinary. Do you think they're twins?'

They both have straight white blonde hair that flicks up at the edges and pale faces thick with powder, blue eye shadow and bright red lipstick. They look grotesquely pretty and are wearing matching cream skirts and jackets and white stockings. We watch as they giggle together like excited schoolchildren, fingering their pearl necklaces like rosaries.

Eleanor, the home manager, is looking very neat and precise sipping her sherry, her eyes surveying the room, always on duty and never quite relaxed. I watch Bill walk over and talk to her. There is an informality about him which is appealing and I can see that she finds him charming. He is concentrating intently on everything she says, giving her his full attention.

'Go on, you know you want to,' a voice beside me startles me.

'Sorry?'

'Toffee?' she says, holding out a small, well-fingered white paper bag full of old-fashioned toffees in their wrappers.

'Oh, no thanks, Violet.'

'Are you sure?' she says, staring at me as if I'm mad, and then wanders off looking like she's about to burst into tears. Bill kisses his mother goodbye and glances across the room at me. He raises his hand slightly as if to say goodbye and I nod at him, watching his retreating back.

The sound of a gong being rung silences the room and people slowly start to make their way to the library, which today has been set up as an alternative dining room. Others, such as Maurice, who are having Christmas lunch with their families at nearby restaurants or in private homes say their goodbyes, leaving only the hard core behind. Matt and I follow Florence, filming her as she walks slowly through the hall arm in arm with Elspeth, Bernard bringing up the rear in a wheelchair, pushed by Comfort. There's a round of applause at the first sight of the splendid long mahogany table centre-stage, heaving under the weight of silver candlesticks, lines of glittering cutlery, sparkling glasses cut from the finest crystal, red and gold Christmas crackers, and in the centre a huge flower arrangement of berries and dark red roses.

'Is it always like this?' I ask Florence.

'Yes, marvellous isn't it and all that,' she waves her arm at the cutlery and glasses, 'legacies from dead actors. The candlesticks were Gielgud's, the glasses Noël Coward's, apparently the gravy boat belonged to Peggy Ashcroft – they're always kept for occasions like this. I found it a bit overwhelming when I first came – a bit like Miss Havisham's wedding feast, without all the cobwebs and dust.'

I move out of the way as food is being served. The carers are impressively attempting to include everyone and although some of the residents are incapable of feeding themselves and conversation is limited, the atmosphere is the liveliest I've seen since I started filming at Russell Court. I keep catching snatches of conversation: Elspeth saying, 'Did I tell you about the time I played Cinderella? Buttons was so . . .' Margery is talking about her mother: 'We used to help her make the Christmas pudding and we always had goose for Christmas lunch.' Out of the corner of my eye I see the children staring greedily at the food, and when Comfort gives them both a mince pie, Max screws up his nose in disgust as he takes a bite. He spits it out into Evie's hand, making Comfort roar with laughter. She hands him a satsuma instead, which he grabs and runs off to find Aidan to peel it for him.

As the meal is coming to a close I say to Matt, 'I'm just going to get Florence's present from the car – carry on without me; I'll be back in a few minutes.'

I meet Aidan in the hall, holding satsuma peel in his fist, and I'm struck by how exhausted he looks.

'How much longer?' he asks.

'Soon, I promise. I've just got to give Florence her present and then we can leave. You poor thing, you look terrible.'

'That's probably because I feel terrible,' he says, stifling a yawn.

'I know this isn't an ideal way of spending Christmas Day . . . but it could have been worse.'

Aidan doesn't say anything and just looks at me.

*

Outside the day is dull and unremarkable and as I open the boot of the car, which is stuffed with wrapped presents, I hear the sound of gravel crunching behind me. I turn to see Evie running towards me.

'Mama, are you going to get my disco ball?'

'No, I'm getting Florence's present.'

'Can I show her the ball?'

'Not at the moment.'

'But she said she wanted to see it.'

I sigh, not prepared to have a battle with her. 'OK, whatever,' I say, irritated, and then, feeling guilty, I add, 'Evie, you've been really good, well done. I've nearly finished.'

She takes out her disco ball, carefully winding the flex round the stand, while I pick up Florence's present and a large portable tape machine – I've even bought some spare batteries just in case. We walk back inside, Evie holding her ball proudly like one of the Three Kings bearing gifts to the baby Jesus. When we are indoors she disappears off to the main sitting room. I see her pass the huge tree in the hallway and once inside she sits down, carefully unwinding the flex, looking around for a socket to plug it in. I look around for Aidan, worried that she shouldn't be playing with sockets on her own, but I'm not quick enough and soon beams of disco lights stream out of the sitting room. They reach into the hall, accompanied by Evie singing quietly to herself the all too familiar sound of S Club's 'Don't Stop Moving'. The fairy lights on the Christmas tree flicker in a pathetic attempt to compete with the revolving rays of bright light shining from the disco ball. Evie jumps up and starts practising her best moves and Max runs past me to join her. 'Don't run, Max, and be careful,' I warn him as I make my way back to the library.

When I walk back into the room there is a lull in the conversation. Elspeth is trying to stop herself from falling asleep as her head drops slowly on to her chest but I notice one of her feet seems to be moving in time with Evie's singing. I shut the door behind me and see Violet stuffing her paper bag with the remains of her Christmas dinner. Margery is smiling her fixed, polite smile with a slightly panicked expression as if she's not sure what she should be doing, her tinsel crown slightly skewed. Bernard is concentrating on trying to steady his shaking hand, determined to hold on to his spoon.

I put the tape machine in front of Florence on the table amidst the debris and she looks surprised when I give her the small parcel.

'Happy Christmas, Florence.'

'Oh my dear – you shouldn't have.'

She looks intrigued as she tears the paper to reveal an audio cassette tape. 'Thank you, it's what I've always wanted.'

I smile. 'Put it on,' I urge her.

Gerry leans forward and pushes the button to open the compartment so that Florence knows where to insert the tape. It slips neatly into place and she clicks the compartment shut. There is an expectant silence in the room apart from the constant rumbling of deep breathing punctuated by the occasional snore. All eyes that are open are now watching Florence as she pushes the button to make the tape play. There is a moment's pause and I worry that the batteries aren't fitted properly or that the machine is not working, but then a crackling sound like the beginning of an old record fills the room and very faintly an orchestra starts to play.

As the first chords fill the room suddenly all the lights go out. Matt swears softly and I hear Violet give a little shriek. I can just make out Comfort moving swiftly towards the door and I hear her flick the light switch to see if the main lights are working. Nothing happens. Gerry moves a candle closer to Florence to help Matt continue filming. Florence looks round, curious as to what's happening, but she quickly turns back to the tape machine that continues to play in the semi-darkness. She is listening hard and I can see her struggling to recognise the music. A high and slightly quivery voice starts to sing; at first it's faint and distant and hard to hear, but once our ears have grown accustomed, like eyes adjusting to the dark, the voice begins to sound clearer, confident but above all very, very young. The voice on the tape sings,

> 'In my imagination I touched the starlit sky so bright
> In my imagination there I saw you in the night.'

Florence leans her head and moves closer to the tape machine to hear better as the little voice continues singing.

> 'And then one day I found you, how could I help but realise
> My lucky star was smiling, right there before my very eyes.'

Her eyes widen and for a minute she looks amazed and shocked, smacked by the memory. A ghost of a smile flickers across her face. She nods her head in recognition and glances at Margery, who says, 'What is this?'

'Shh – just listen,' Florence rebukes her, drinking in the sound of her own childish voice singing through the years, her head swaying gently, moved by the memories and the music.

> 'You are my lucky star, I saw you from afar
> Two lovely eyes at me, they were beaming, gleaming
> I was star struck.'

Some of the other residents sleep on, oblivious to the drama playing out before them. Comfort is checking that everyone stays calm in the darkness and Eleanor comes in and whispers something to her. They both look over in my direction while Florence's girlish voice sings on,

> 'You've opened heaven's portal here on earth for this poor mortal
> You are my lucky star.'

When the music finishes Florence sits very still, looking down at her wrinkled hands dotted with liver spots, the veins prominent. No one says a word and very slowly she turns to me, her eyes brimming with tears and says simply, 'Thank you.'

Eleanor interrupts the moment by expertly pulling me away

from Florence so that we can't be overheard. She looks disgruntled.

'I think you should go now.'

I'm surprised by the abruptness of her manner. 'We were planning on leaving but can we do anything to help?'

'I think you've done enough already.'

'What do you mean?' I ask, puzzled, but she doesn't need to answer me as over her shoulder I see Aidan holding on to Evie's disco ball, the flex frayed and charred.

Fourteen

Evie sits in the back seat of the car cradling her broken disco ball like a mother nursing a baby.

'So why was she crying?' she asks, looking like she wants to do the same. She is bemused at seeing a grown-up old woman in tears, because in Evie's world crying is for children. 'Was it because my disco ball upset all the lights?'

'No, nothing to do with your disco ball, it was the tape she was listening to. She had never heard that recording of her voice before and the amazing thing was that she was only ten years old when she sang the song – that's only three years older than you.'

Evie goes quiet taking this in. Aidan is driving but I'm wondering if I should have offered as I watch his eyelids drooping.

'Aidan!' I say sharply and he wakes himself up with a start.

I look at the children sitting together in the back seats and continue, 'She sang it seventy-three years ago – that's a very long time ago.'

I'm feeling pleased with Florence's response; Cassie and the BBC Sound Archives came up trumps. It must have been one of the earliest recordings ever made, but I knew that if such a tape existed Cassie would be the person to find it.

The roads are deserted, everyone having done their travelling earlier in the day, and it's only forty minutes before we are turning into the narrow gravel drive in front of my mother's cottage. Always thinking ahead, my parents had moved here when my father retired, choosing it because it was equidistant between London, where I lived, and Warwick, my brother's university. They only had a year there together before my father had his stroke but it was long enough to make all the changes they needed and to feel settled. Now I think of it as my mother's cottage, with only a few reminders that my father ever lived there. I lean across Aidan and hoot the horn to announce our arrival and the small white front door opens and my mother waves at us from the porch. The children bounce up and down on the back seat, excited that at last Christmas can begin. As we unload our bags and the presents Tim comes out to give us a hand.

'Hello, youngest,' he says, using his affectionate name for me. He gives me a kiss and then looks at the overflowing boot. 'How long are you staying?'

'I know, I think I've over-compensated this year for working so hard. Everyone is going to be spoilt.'

'Sounds like my sort of Christmas,' he says, groaning as he takes the first big holdall out of the boot. I grab two bags of presents and follow him into the cottage. The front door opens straight into the sitting room and as always, except during hot summer days, there is a well-established log fire burning. The children run excitedly to look at the tree to spot their all-time favourite baubles and to count their presents. My mother's tree is very different from Aidan's, decorated with coloured lights and covered with glittery angel hair draped over the branches, which the children adore. I sink into a chair by the fire, exhausted but relieved to be able to hand over all responsibility.

'Tea or champagne?' my mother asks me.

'Silly question,' I reply, and she hands me a champagne flute full of bubbles. Aidan is shaking my brother Tim's hand, while Evie hangs off Tim's other arm trying to grab all the attention. Like a pesky monkey she clings on to him, refusing to let go, and everywhere he walks he has to drag Evie along with him. It's good to see him.

'It's been ages, Tim.'

'Too long.'

Hovering behind him is Helen, his longstanding girlfriend and soon-to-be wife. Why do I feel such a sense of disappointment to see her? She has mouse-brown hair and an intelligent face entirely free of makeup and although she's no beauty there's no denying that she's attractive. To be honest I find her dull, and when I look at my dazzlingly brilliant brother she doesn't seem good enough for him, but then what do I know?

'Hello,' she says hesitantly.

I summon up the goodwill to give her a warm welcome. 'How are you, Helen, lovely to see you.' I'm trying too hard and my words sound hollow to me but I hope no one else notices my over-enthusiastic tones.

As we sit down to Christmas dinner Tim taps his knife against his wine glass and announces, 'I,' he stops himself and looks at Helen, 'I mean *we* have a special announcement to make.' We all look at him expectantly. Oh God, I think to myself, and I glance surreptitiously at Helen's stomach to see if there's a bump. As I look up our eyes meet and I immediately feel guilty.

'We would love Evie to be a bridesmaid and Max, if he can bear it, to be a page boy?'

'A bridesmaid,' Evie squeals. 'I'd love it,' she says, looking delighted. Max hasn't a clue what being a page boy involves and neither do I.

Tim continues, 'You have my solemn word that you won't have to wear black velvet knickerbockers or any frilly shirts.'

Max smiles, although he has no idea what his uncle is talking about.

'It's OK, I'll wear my Spiderman suit,' he reassures us.

Tim throws another log on the fire and sparks fly up the chimney. It's now just the two of us alone together, the others having all gone to bed. I'm beyond tiredness, still unwinding from the filming and Florence's reaction to the tape.

'So are you enjoying being back at work?' he asks, settling back into the armchair that our father loved to sit in.

'I'm not sure "enjoy" is the right word. It's stimulating, challenging and exhausting.'

'Is it what you expected? I mean, has it changed much since you were last working?'

'Everyone at the office is about ten years younger than me.'

'That isn't necessarily a bad thing.'

'I suppose.'

'Do you regret giving it up?'

'I don't think so – no, it was the right thing to do at the time. It seemed so awful what happened with Dad ...' I find I can never bring myself to say it. 'After that I felt the balance of my life was wrong.'

'It wasn't your fault, Molly.'

'I know.'

'He understood.'

'Did he really? I'm not sure I do.'

'Do you need to talk about it? It might help, you never know?' he says, trying to help.

'No, not now,' I say quickly and I sip my hot chocolate, which is instantly soothing and reminds me of my childhood. The log on the fire that has been burning gently suddenly ignites, making the room brighter. Tim takes a sip of whisky from the glass that he's cradling in his hands. I decide to change the subject.

'How are the wedding plans coming on? I imagine Helen is really organised.'

'She is, but everything has been a bit tough for her recently.'

'Why is that?'

'Didn't Mum tell you?' he asks, surprised that I don't seem to know what he's talking about.

'Tell me what?'

'Her mother died a few months ago.'

'Oh my God, I'm sorry – I didn't know. How awful.'

We both stare at the fire in silence.

'Were you there?'

'Yes, for Helen's sake – I didn't know her mother that well. I must say this is a cheery subject for Christmas Day,' Tim says, taking another large sip of his whisky.

'I'm sorry. It's so terrible.'

'Terrible and inevitable.'

'Anyway, how are things with you – work still good?' I say, trying to break my mood.

Tim laughs. 'On a lighter note.'

'Well, go on – how are things in the world of academia? Are you enjoying being head of your department?'

'I spend more time than I would like on the admin side but the teaching is good and the students still seem enthusiastic – well, some of them anyway.'

'Any chance to do any more writing?'

'I'm thinking about it – there seems to be an appetite for history at the moment so I've got a few ideas I'm mulling over.'

'And everything's OK with you and Helen? No pre-wedding nerves?' I say, trying to keep the hope out of my voice. When did I become this unpleasant or have I always been like this?

'We're fine,' he says as if to reassure me and I wonder if he has any idea what I feel about her.

'You will be there?' he says, suddenly looking anxious.

'I wouldn't miss it for the world,' I reply as I scrape the bottom of the mug for the best bits of chocolate that never quite dissolve into the milk.

Fifteen

The back door crashes open letting in a cold blast of air as Evie runs into the enormous kitchen kept warm by the Aga. She's still wearing her muddy boots and carrying something very carefully in her hand.

'Evie, what about your boots?' I cry in exasperation.

She looks down at her feet and then back at the trail of mud behind her leading from the back door and then at Jo who looks unperturbed.

'Don't worry about it. We're in the country. No one minds a bit of mud. Did you find any?'

'There were lots,' she says breathlessly, and then very slowly she opens her hand to reveal a pale brown speckled egg.

'It's still warm,' she says with awe in her voice. 'Max is bringing the others.'

There is a shriek outside followed by a thud and then a few seconds of silence broken by Max's cries echoing around the Devon valley. I rush outside, thinking to myself that if he's making that much noise he can't be too badly hurt. He's lying flat on his stomach with his hand outstretched, surrounded by broken eggs. I hear Jake, one of the twins, laughing. 'I told him not to carry too many,' he says unhelpfully as I pick Max up, trying to avoid getting covered with yolk and bits of sticky egg shell. I wonder whether Jake had anything to do with him falling over, but I banish the thought from my mind as Max sobs in my arms and I wipe away his tears with my hand.

'I wanted you to have one for breakfast,' he says between sobs. Jake looks away, embarrassed by the emotion. I kiss Max's wet cheek.

'Tell you a secret – I really want Jo's homemade muesli,' I say quietly to him, unaware that she is standing behind me.

'You'll be lucky then – it's Sainsbury's best.'

'Oh, I thought that while you're staying down here you'd be playing the role of self-sufficient housewife. I've always seen you as a Felicity Kendall type and the dungarees would suit you.'

'You can laugh, you with your fancy London ways,' Jo says in a broad Devon accent, 'but actually I think I could adapt to country life – I've really enjoyed being down here. Here, Big Bum, come and clean up for us.' She calls to the dog who is sitting in his basket by the Aga refusing to move. We all follow Jo into the kitchen and the dog reluctantly gets up, stretches and yawns and slowly makes his way outside to where the eggs lay shattered.

'He hasn't taken to country life – I have trouble getting him to go outside. I think he's frightened of the rabbits.' Jo gives the dog a pat and Evie tentatively puts out a hand to stroke him as he walks by. Jo and the family have been housesitting since Boxing Day and after a couple of days relaxing at my mother's we drove down, arriving last night in the dark.

'How long are you staying here?'

'Until the second of January – school starts on the fourth and we need to get ourselves sorted out – you know how it is. Finn's friends have been in South Africa for Christmas but they wanted someone to keep an eye on things.'

Another blast of cold air signals Finn and Aidan's arrival into the kitchen. They're usually wary of each other, friends through circumstance rather than choice as neither of them would choose to spend time together if it wasn't for Jo and me. But down here they seem to be getting on better than ever before.

'Have you had a good look round, Molly? It's a fantastic place they've got here. It's not just the house – they've got stables, outhouses, an enormous barn, their own woods.'

Red-cheeked, Aidan sits down beside me and I shiver because I'm still only wearing my pyjamas with a sweater pulled over the top. He puts his arm around me but it feels heavy on my shoulders and I have to resist the urge to shrug it off.

'They've got this enormous vegetable patch and Finn says it's full of carrots, marrows and even artichokes. Imagine eating your own artichokes.'

Now fully recovered from his jetlag, he is more animated than I've seen him in months. His trip to America seems to have energised him and in comparison I feel jaded.

'Imagine,' I say, wishing I could feel more enthusiasm.

The path up through the fields to the woods is steep and slippery but I'm enjoying the challenge. It's invigorating being out in the open and we're striding out, not worrying about pacing ourselves for small moaning children who seem to be exhausted only a few yards beyond the back door of the house. Cassie, Jo and I have escaped, leaving the men to keep an eye on the children for an hour. Cassie, her short dark hair tucked into a woollen hat, is leading the way along the muddy track that runs beside the farmhouse.

'So how's work, Molly?' Jo asks, and I find myself telling them about Florence and how tricky she is. They both laugh when I describe the game of charades and Rod's reaction.

'But are you enjoying it?' Jo asks.

'Yes and no – as you can tell, I'm a bit confused about it all at the moment. I enjoy working with the crew, but I don't like the pressure and the responsibility and I worry about the children and the effect it's having on them.'

I'm getting puffed talking and walking.

'The children seem really well,' says Jo, stepping round a large puddle in the track.

'It's hard to tell sometimes,' I say.

'What, you mean they'll be in therapy years down the line – well, it was when my mum went back to work that it all started to go terribly wrong – these feelings of neglect and abandonment have ruined my life,' Jo teases me.

'Well, you never know,' I say and they both laugh at me.

'I feel like I've got two jobs and I'm not doing either of them well. I'm being a second-rate mother and a mediocre director.' I glance at Cassie. 'Don't breathe a word of this to Rod.'

'As if I would,' she says, hurt that I could think such a thing.

'How much longer have you got to film?' asks Jo.

'It's not fixed and I think a lot depends on how the other programmes in the series are doing. I've probably got a month or two and then I have to start editing.'

'Well, the great thing is that you've got your mother. You should trust her and just concentrate on the job,' she says pragmatically and I switch the attention back on to her.

'So tell us about you – what's been happening?'

'Nothing much, but I have got another job off the back of the advert. This time it's a drama for TV – a small part, but it's something.'

'That sounds good.'

I look at Jo as she walks beside me looking content.

'How are you and Finn?'

'We're good – really good,' she smiles at me and I'm taken aback as it's not what I expect.

'What's up, Jo?'

'Nothing.' But she can't resist an enigmatic smile.

Cassie tries to prise information out of her but uncharacteristically for Jo we can't get another word out of her. We stop to climb over a stile and her parka hood catches on a hawthorn bush.

'Save me, somebody – I can't reach.'

'Only if you tell us what's been happening,' I say, putting on my best Nazi interrogator voice that even Maurice would have been proud of.

'I shall never reveal my secret however much you torture me,' Jo says.

'Ah, so there is a secret?'

'Not really.'

Both Cassie and I stare at her as if to say, we're not moving an inch unless you tell us what is going on. Jo laughs and then concedes, 'All right, I'll tell you.'

We move closer to Jo and she leans forward and whispers, 'I don't know quite how to say this . . .' she tails off mid-sentence, teasing us.

'Go on,' Cassie urges her.

'Well . . .' She's looking first at Cassie and then at me as if she can't decide whether to tell us or not, and then, as if she's made the monumental decision to confide in us, she says solemnly, 'I've given up caffeine.'

'Is that it?' I say.

She nods her head and adds, 'It's done wonders for my skin.'

'Shall we leave her here?' I say to Cassie.

'No, she'd frighten the locals.'

'Very funny. Get on with it.'

I carefully untangle her coat from the bush and we both run to catch up with Cassie who has walked ahead, keen to get to the shelter of the woods as it looks like it's going to pour down with rain.

'Was Christmas as bad as you expected?' I ask Cassie.

'No.'

'Oh good,' I say, relieved.

'It was worse.'

'Oh Cassie, I'm sorry.'

'Don't be. It's not your fault. It's nobody's fault.'

'Do you miss Will?' Jo asks her.

'The strange thing is I don't feel anything at the moment. I'm numb.'

'That could have its advantages,' I say, thinking of my own emotional state.

'I'm not sure it's very healthy,' Jo says, looking at Cassie with concern.

'Come on before it starts to pour,' says Cassie, and as she walks ahead Jo and I look at each other before running to catch her up.

The path narrows as we enter the woods and we walk in silence until we come out on the top of the hill with the fields and woods stretching out before us. We stand looking out across the valley over the top of the wood and down at the house below that looks like a Legoland model. The thick grey clouds are moving fast across the sky and it's hard to distinguish between them as they all merge into one dark ominous sky, and I wonder why nothing ever stays the same.

Aidan is sitting up in bed, reading a copy of *Country Living* of which there are a stash in our room.

'Look at this.' He points to the property page. 'A beautiful Queen Anne rectory in Dorset for almost half what we'd get for our urban box. Think of all that space we could have.'

'Are you thinking of moving down here?' I say, half joking.

'Well, why not?'

I look at him in amazement. 'You don't do country. You need pavements, traffic lights, noise.'

'You get noise in the country.'

'Not the right sort of noise. What about the urban edge you keep talking about? It's lovely to visit the country but you don't want to live in it. Think of all the mud sullying your white carpets. You would go mad or else expect me to spend all my time on my hands and knees scrubbing.'

'We could have another colour,' he says, still flicking through the magazine.

'Are you serious?' I'm tempted to touch his forehead to feel if he's got a temperature.

'Maybe it would be good for me?' he suggests.

'What would I do about work? More to the point, what would you do about work?'

'Well, I can write anywhere.'

For the first time I realise that Aidan doesn't intend to go back into advertising. I don't know what I thought was going to happen, perhaps that this was just a temporary blip while he wrote his script and then came to his senses. The full weight of what he's saying makes my stomach cramp. This is it now – this is going to be my life, scrabbling to find work in television, permanently exhausted and worrying about childcare and more importantly my relationship with my children. I feel too tired to pursue the conversation. I switch my bedside light off and plump up the pillows before I collapse into them. I've drunk too much Rioja and I'm thinking about Florence and trying to plan the next few sequences we need to shoot.

'Why don't we go into a few local estate agents and maybe we can view some houses as we're here for a few days?' says Aidan, full of enthusiasm.

'I've got to work,' I say sleepily as I turn away from him.

'Not on Friday? It's New Year's Eve.'

'Mmm?' The bed feels soft and the sheets smell like they've been freshly laundered. There's a hint of lavender in the room and I'm beginning to drop off to sleep until Aidan nudges me.

'Molly, what are you talking about – you're not working on New Year's Eve, are you?'

I sit up dozily. 'Well yes, I am actually.'

Looking at his expression I feel guilty that I hadn't told him earlier.

'Why didn't you mention it before?'

I rub my eyes. 'I'm sorry – there just never seemed enough time.'

'What, a four-hour car journey didn't give you the opportunity to drop it into conversation?'

'Don't give me a hard time. You were the one who wanted this.'

'I don't want you to work so hard that you don't spend any time with us. First Christmas Day and now this.' He looks like he's having trouble understanding.

'You don't have to change your plans – you can stay down here with the children. There's no need for you to come back to London with me. It would be pointless as I'll be at Russell Court anyway.'

Aidan doesn't reply.

'I'm sorry, I should have told you about it, but I've got to be there.'

'Are you planning to come back down?'

'I'm not sure there's much point. It would only be for a day and then everyone has to leave.'

'Have you mentioned this to the children?'

'No,' I say guiltily, 'I didn't want to worry them.'

'I don't understand what's happening, Molly.'

'It's only work – it's not a big deal but I should have told you before. I'm sorry.'

'This is getting ridiculous,' he mutters, almost to himself, as he throws the magazines on to the floor. 'Do you know, you haven't asked me one question about what happened in America?'

'I did when we spoke on the phone.'

'Hardly, and there was usually some domestic crisis going on in the background.'

'You don't ask me any questions about my work. What do you expect, Aidan? I can't do everything and still be interested.' I'm trying not to raise my voice. 'You wanted me to go back to work and it's not the sort of work you can clock on and clock off. That's why I gave it up all those years ago.'

'You gave it up because of your father.'

'Yes, and now here I am back where I was before, making the same mistakes and all because of you.'

'I don't think you're handling it very well, Molly.'

'Thanks for pointing that out, Aidan,' I say, feeling the tears close to the surface. 'And of course you're being so helpful and accommodating.' I am becoming inarticulate with anger. 'Oh, just turn the bloody light out.'

He turns out the light and we lie side by side, silent in the darkness.

Through the window I watch Evie, my white-faced city kid, running from the field where the chickens are kept towards the back door.

'Evie is looking pale this morning – have you told her you're leaving?' asks Jo, concerned.

'Yes, she's not very pleased with me.'

'She's not the only one,' Jo says peremptorily. 'I wish you'd told me earlier, Molly.'

'Would it have made any difference?' I say.

'I would have been prepared, that's all.' She comes over and sits beside me. 'I never get to see you these days. I was looking forward to us spending this time together.'

'It won't be like this for long.' I try to sound convinced but Evie running into the kitchen interrupts me.

'No eggs this morning?' Jo asks her as she fills the kettle, and Evie bursts into tears.

'What's the matter?'

'The chickens . . .' she says between heaving sobs. 'It's terrible . . .'

We drop everything and run round the house past the boys who are playing commandos on the makeshift wooden swing and through the gate to the chicken coop, unprepared for the sight that greets us. It looks like the morning after a fierce battle – the field is littered with chicken carcasses, their heads hanging from a thread, feathers everywhere. Buckets of feed and water bowls are overturned, the ground stained with blood. Evie sobs quietly beside me and I turn her away from the gory sight.

'Was it a fox?' I ask incredulously.

'Either that or an Exocet missile,' says Finn.

'But we didn't hear anything in the night.'

'I suppose it must have been quick – maybe there were two of them,' suggests Aidan.

'I thought it was unusually quiet this morning,' says Jo, looking shocked as she walks across the field, picking her way through the carcasses. 'What are we going to tell them when they come home? They'll be so upset. That's why we're staying here, to try and stop this sort of thing happening.'

She starts trying to clear up the mess by picking up a container used for chicken feed.

'I'm taking Evie back to the house,' I say, guiding her out of the field. Max is running towards us and I catch him and turn him round before he sees the carnage.

'What is it – what's happening?' he asks excitedly.

'A fox got into the chicken coop last night.'

Jake makes a gurgling noise as he drags his finger across his throat as if slitting it with a knife. His brother Ben laughs and Jo flashes them a look. 'Stop it, boys, you're upsetting the younger ones.'

Max tries to push past me. 'Can I have a look?' he says eagerly. I manage to pick him up and turn Evie away from the field, trying to protect my children from the brutal realities of country life and Jo's reprobate sons.

Back in the kitchen I make hot chocolate and as I boil the milk Evie looks at me.

'Why do you have to go? I don't understand.'

'It's work and it's only for a few days.'

'But even when we come back you'll still be working.'

I nod my head, the guilt breaking through me in waves.

'Can I come with you? I won't get in the way, I promise,' she pleads with me.

'Oh Evie, I'm sorry but you can't. I tell you what, we'll catch the pony today and you can have a ride on him later before I go. There's so much for you to do down here – tomorrow I think Jo is planning to have a winter picnic on the beach.'

'It's no fun without you,' she says, frowning.

'Oh Evie, that's not true, you know how much you love being with Cassie, and Daddy wants to spend some time with you after being away.' She looks at me sceptically.

'I'm sorry but I can't do anything about it. Please try and enjoy the next few days and I'll see you back in London. When this is all over we'll have plenty of time together.'

'Mum,' she says earnestly, 'you do still love us?'

I'm shocked by the question and I look at her solemn face.

'Of course I love you, Evie. If I could I'd spend all my time with you but I can't at the moment and we've just got to make the best of it.'

I pull her close and she clings on to me. I glance up to see Aidan standing in the doorway watching us.

The pinched expression on Evie's face when we said goodbye is imprinted on my mind as Aidan drives me to the station. When he stops the car by the station entrance I turn to him and say, 'I'm sorry but I have to go – it's all been arranged.'

He shrugs his shoulders.

'You will keep an eye on her, won't you – I think she's really upset. About the chickens I mean.'

'Yes,' he replies curtly. As I take my bag out of the boot of the car he doesn't get out. I go round to his side of the car and lean into the window.

'I'll call you.'

'I can't wait,' he replies.

I look at my watch – I've only got a few minutes until the train goes.

'Happy New Year then.'

'Happy New Year.' He can hardly bring himself to look at me he's so angry. This is a terrible end to a turbulent year.

'Aidan, I'm sorry.'

'Me too.' And for the first time since we argued last night he stares at me, his eyes holding mine, until the sound of the announcer over the tannoy announcing the train to London gives me an excuse to look away.

Sixteen

Florence looks more fragile when I first see her but maybe it's because she's smiling at me and I'm not used to her being so benign. Her elegant hair is slightly more dishevelled and she looks less immaculate than usual and worn out, but I'm touched by how pleased she is to see me.

'That was really a very lovely thought, that tape recording. It made me quite emotional.' Her voice is huskier and her breath more laboured than usual.

'It was my pleasure,' I say, meaning it.

'Bill and I have been out shopping for your little ones.'

'But you didn't need . . .'

She doesn't let me finish. Bill is carrying a plastic bag which he hands over to Florence and she passes on to me. I look inside and see nestling on the bottom a gun holster with two small guns.

'Do you disapprove?' Florence asks.

'They're like the ones I had when I was a kid,' Bill adds. 'I don't think they did me too much harm but you might not agree.'

He's grinning at me, his face framed by soft curls. His eyes really are like his mother's – full of life and penetrating.

'It's really kind of you, he'll love them.'

Underneath the holster there is a compact purple camera which I take out.

'For Evie?'

Florence nods. 'Thought it might be a start – she might follow in your footsteps. She's a bright little one, your Evie, but I didn't want to wrap the presents until I'd shown them to you . . . just in case. You know, I did enjoy meeting them both.'

I remember Evie's shocked face as she saw the chicken carcasses and I feel a pang of guilt that I'm not with her.

'Thank you very much – they'll love them.'

'Now, I hope you don't mind, Molly, but I was thinking we should go out to the local pub to celebrate the New Year.'

'Really?' I ask, amazed. I don't have to turn and look at Matt and Gerry as I can feel the smiles on their faces at her suggestion.

'I've had enough of it in here and as I start my filming job next week I might as well get used to getting out and about a bit more to build up my stamina.' She looks exhausted.

'Oh right, um . . . I'll need to get permission from the landlord, he might be a bit worried about a film crew turning up on his doorstep with no notice on the busiest night of the year.'

'Bill had a little word with him yesterday as he's got to know him quite well over the past few weeks. He was delighted about you coming. He enjoys putting on a party.'

Bill hands me a card showing a picturesque pub which I recognise as the place where the crew and I went and had a drink before Christmas.

'Sorry, have we thrown you?' he says.

'I just wasn't expecting this. Let me have a few minutes to think about it.'

I leave the room, worried that I'm being railroaded into a decision. I have to consider what would be best for the film. Having filmed the Christmas party it would be a bit repetitive to do another sequence at Russell Court. Gerry and Matt materialise at my side as if they've been beamed in.

'What do you think?' I ask Matt.

'It's a good idea – we need more sequences outside the home. It will make the film more interesting.'

'You just want to have a pint while you work.'

'Do you know, that thought hadn't even crossed my mind.' Matt grins at me and continues, 'No, I'm serious. I think it would make a good sequence, a refreshing change.'

'Refreshing,' says Gerry like an echo.

'What about equipment – are we geared up to film in a large, dark, busy pub?'

'It's not much different from filming here. We'll manage.'

They both look at me expectantly and for a minute I can imagine exactly what they were like as small boys.

'OK,' I say slowly. 'We'll do it.'

Florence is pleased with my reaction. 'Just give me half an hour to myself to have a rest and make myself look presentable. Bill, you go as well. I'll see you later.'

Bill and I stand outside her door, lost for what to say to each other.

'I'm sorry,' he says, looking a little embarrassed.

'For what?' I say.

'The pub, it was my idea. I hope you don't mind?'

'No, not at all,' I say genuinely. 'I was wondering how we could make it different from Christmas, so you've made my life easier in a way.'

'I'll take you to the pub now so you can do a recce and I can introduce you to Jed, the landlord, and Rachel, his wife. We can come back and pick up Florence afterwards.'

I look at my watch and see that it's eight o'clock already. 'We haven't got long to get set up. Matt and Gerry can follow us in the crew car.'

Bill and I haven't been alone together since our fight and I think we're both feeling a little awkward. I try to make polite conversation as we walk along the corridors, my hand skimming along the rail provided to help the residents.

'Have you had a good Christmas?'

He laughs. 'Well, it's good to see my mother but I have to confess that I can think of better ways to spend Christmas than being in an old people's home full of actors.'

'Well, at least it's better than being in a home full of accountants,' I say.

'I'm an accountant.'

'Oh God, sorry – well, it's not that accountants are boring or anything, it's just they have a bad reputation and it's probably completely unfounded and actually some of the accountants I've met are really quite interesting . . .' I tail off and when I pluck up the courage to look at him I see that he's smiling.

'You're not an accountant, are you?'

'No.'

'So what are you?'

'I'm an astronaut.'

'I thought Canadians weren't supposed to have a sense of humour,' I say.

His face gives away little but his eyes are very expressive. 'They don't, but I'm not really Canadian – I've just lived there for fifteen years.'

'Ah.'

We pass Maurice, as always looking dapper.

'Going to the party tonight, sir?' says Bill.

'Are you going to be there?' Maurice asks, looking directly at me.

'No, not tonight, Maurice.'

'Well, I don't know if I can face it. Actually I've got one of my old films showing on the box tonight – I might just curl up with a glass of champagne and watch myself. I could think of worse ways of spending an evening.'

'Happy New Year,' I say kindly, and before I can stop him he leans forward and kisses me on the lips. I'm so taken aback that I don't know what to do.

'We must be on our way,' says Bill, putting his hand on my back and skilfully guiding me away from Maurice into the hall. Once outside we both laugh like rebellious teenagers caught smoking behind the bike sheds.

'The old bugger,' Bill laughs.

'I just didn't see it coming.' I still can't quite believe that he actually kissed me.

'Do you make a habit of kissing people in corridors?'

'Do you mind? I'm a respectable married woman.'

'You've gone red,' he teases me.

'So would you if Maurice kissed you.'

'Fair point.'

I'm surprised at how relaxed I feel with him because of his easy manner. He seems so different from the man who challenged me about filming his mother.

As we crunch along the gravel towards the car park Bill chuckles, 'I was just thinking about Maurice. Maybe when you get older it's liberating, nothing matters any more and you can do whatever you want. If you feel like kissing an attractive woman then just go ahead and do it.' He looks at me. 'Do you know, old age might not be such a bad thing.'

'This place is quite a good advertisement for old age,' I say, flattered that he called me attractive. I'm pleasantly aware that we're flirting with each other, something I haven't done for years.

'Actually it has been interesting getting to know everyone here. There are some great characters. You know Bernard, the director?'

I nod. 'The one who had the stroke. He's always giving me advice.'

'Well, I think there's a little romance developing between him and Dora.' Bill is proud of his inside knowledge.

'Florence's friend who went home last week?' I say, surprised.

'That's right. I call her the dormouse; she's always so nervous and people keep finding her dozing in the strangest of places. Once she was found asleep in the linen cupboard.'

'You're making it up,' I laugh, and then, thinking about Dora and Bernard, I say, 'But Bernard hates actors.'

'Ah, but you see, Dora was a stage manager most of her life – she knows how to serve a director. It's a match made in heaven and it all started when Bernard was banned from using his buggy – the geri carts I call them – because his eyesight has got so bad. Dora started reading to him and one thing has led to another.' He grins at me. 'I think it's charming – gives us all hope.'

'Do you think they . . . ?' I ask, wondering why the thought should be so unappealing.

'Now, that I don't know, but he's dreadfully upset she's gone home and Elspeth tells me that Dora may be back soon.'

'How do you know all this?'

'This place is a hotbed of gossip – after all, they haven't got much else to think about. Elspeth is my main source but she's not been very well the past few days,' he adds. 'Chest infection. They're all a bit worried.'

We've reached the car park and I can see Matt and Gerry waiting in the crew car. Matt holds up his arm and points emphatically at his watch and I nod an apology.

Bill gets into his hired car and from the inside he opens my side door for me. 'Come on, it's getting late.'

As we drive along the narrow country roads I take sneaky glances at him, watching his profile as he concentrates on driving.

'Are you really?'

'What?'

'An astronaut.'

'What do you think?'

I look at him closely, wondering what astronauts look like.

'Does it matter what I do?'

'Well, I suppose not. I'm just curious.'

He makes no attempt to satisfy my curiosity.

'Not too far to go now,' he says, checking in the mirror to see that the crew car is still behind us. 'Your kids are great,' he adds.

'Thank you.' I never know how to respond when people pay me compliments about my children. 'Your two boys – do you get to see them much?' I'm trying to sound suitably vague, as if Florence hasn't told me about his personal situation.

'This is the longest I haven't seen them.'

'Oh, that must be hard.'

'It is.' He pauses and then glances across at me and adds, 'I don't live with them any more but I see them at weekends and during the week in the evenings.'

'I can't imagine what that's like.'

'I wouldn't recommend it.'

'I hated it when my father went away,' I say, and then wonder whether I'm being insensitive, rubbing his nose in it.

'Was he away a lot?'

So many questions. I'm not used to someone showing such interest in me.

'Not too much – he was a teacher but he had progressive ideas about education and was always being asked to speak at conferences.'

'It seemed as if my dad was always on tour.'

For a minute I'd forgotten that Bill was Florence's son. 'Of course, Tommy Bird – trumpeter. So he was away a lot?'

'Yeah – it was quite hard on all of us.'

'What was he like?' I'm genuinely interested, as Florence hasn't talked about him much.

'He was a quiet man – I think that's why he loved the trumpet because on stage he could make all the noise that he never could in his normal life. Florence was the loud one.'

'They seemed to have a good marriage?'

'Yes, I think they did, but how much do you really know about your parents' marriage? She was devastated when he died.'

'We're there,' I say, trying not to sound relieved, as I don't want to talk about his father's death. 'Thanks for the lift,' I add as I open the door.

'Don't mention it – I think we had to make up for some lost time.' He smiles at me and I think how wrong first impressions can be.

The recce is straightforward and everyone at the pub seems delighted that we're going to film. I leave the crew to set up a few key lights while Bill and I go back to collect Florence. I enjoy the journey back with Bill playing me his favourite compilation tape, and we sing along to Van Morrison, Louis Armstrong and some cheesy songs from Elton John, but at least it makes a change from S Club.

As we drive up to the main entrance to Russell Court Frank Sinatra is playing in the main dining room. The opening lines of 'You Make Me Feel So Young' float out through the windows and I can see Violet and Margery sitting on chairs around the perimeter of the room, like faded wallflowers at a party waiting for someone to ask them to dance. 'You make me feel as though spring has sprung.' Some of the residents are wearing party hats perched on their heads. My heart sinks, and I'm glad that we're not filming here tonight. I've always hated New Year's Eve because of the intense pressure to have a good time. Frank croons on, 'And every time I see you grin I'm such a happy individual.'

I look at Violet still clutching a small white paper bag and imagine that she has a stash of toffees in her room salvaged from the days when she used to run a sweet shop to supplement her acting career. Her hand shakes as she sips her drink. I wonder what sort of year she has had and what the next one will be like. Does she think about the future or does it become too frightening once you reach a certain age? I make a mental note to ask Florence about this tonight when we film. Even at my age I can't see my way through another year – all I know is that we can't go on like this. I think of Aidan and the others in Devon sitting down to supper and I wonder if they'll drink a toast to me and if Evie and Max are still up or sleeping peacefully and not dreaming of scavenging foxes.

Bill has gone ahead to see if Florence is ready and I slowly make my way up the stairs.

'Molly!' I hear him call my name and there's something in his tone of voice which makes my stomach lurch. I speed up so that I'm running up the last level of stairs and along the corridor to Florence's bedroom. The door is slightly ajar and as I push it open my heart is pounding, terrified at the thought of what I'm about to see. Florence is lying on the bed, very pale, her mouth slightly open. I gasp, horrified.

'No,' Bill says beside me, 'it's all right, it's not what you think. I thought the same at first . . .' I look at him, uncomprehending. 'But she's just sleeping,' he says, his voice breaking.

He looks devastated. 'A dress rehearsal,' he says, his voice sounding weary.

I step forward and touch her forehead. I've never touched her before. 'She's OK.'

Bill says nothing but all the time looking at his mother he takes hold of my hand and very gently pulls me to him. Unsure what to do, I put my arms around him and hold him. It seems an entirely natural gesture, devoid of sexuality, full of human compassion, I reassure myself. After what seems like minutes I pull away and Bill looks embarrassed, as if he's suddenly realised what he's been doing.

'I'm sorry.'

'Don't be.' I drop my voice, trying not to wake her. 'Let's leave her to sleep.'

We close the door and silently turn to face each other. He takes a step closer to me and I can feel his breath on my face; he is very close. He bends his head towards me and unexpectedly, without touching me with his arms, kisses me very gently on the lips. It's as if an electric current has passed between us. His lips feel soft, but I pull back to look at him and then I find myself turning my head to be kissed again. I feel I have no control over my actions, that this is something that is inevitable, as essential as breathing. As Bill strokes my face with his finger I come to my senses and force myself to turn away from him. I sit down on the top of the staircase, the sound of Dean Martin slurring 'That's Amore' echoes up from the living room, and Bill sits down beside me, too close.

'I suppose I can't use the excuse of old age – not quite yet.' He tries to break the awkwardness.

'I'd better get back and tell the others that we won't be filming after all,' I say, my voice sounding strange, as if someone else is speaking. 'I don't think she's going to wake up now. What do you think?' The more I speak, the more I feel my sanity returning.

'Molly, I didn't mean . . .' He doesn't finish his sentence.

There is an awkward silence. I know I must go.

'This is my mobile number. Call me if she wakes up in the next hour but I must go and find the crew; they'll be wondering what's happened.'

'What will you do?' He stares at the carpet on the stairs.

'I don't know.' I feel confused. 'There's no point filming without Florence. I suppose we'll have a drink and go home.'

'Is that what you want?' he asks without looking at me.

I stand up and he looks up at me, and I have to fight the desire to stay with him. 'I have to go,' I say as if by saying it I'll make myself do it, and without another word I force myself to walk down the stairs without looking back.

I can't remember the last time I was in the house on my own – maybe it's never happened. I'm not sure I like it. The rooms seem very empty and the house lifeless without hearing the children shouting, the phone ringing or the sound of Aidan tapping away on his computer. I also can't remember the last time I spent New Year's Day on my own. We didn't film last night – I stayed in the pub with the crew, half expecting Bill to join us but he never did, and when I think about what happened between us I wonder if I imagined it. I know rationally it was an instinctive response to our fear about Florence – he probably would have kissed anybody, even Eleanor the home administrator. I was just lucky that I happened to be there with him . . . well, I don't mean lucky, it's just that I was there. It felt so easy and comforting, but passionate too . . . my heart is racing like it used to when I had teenage romances. I never expected to feel like this again . . . this is ridiculous, I must pull myself together, but his lips were so soft . . . STOP thinking about it. Although it's still early I get out of bed quickly, not wanting to be alone with my thoughts.

As I make myself a cup of tea I wonder what it would be like to live on my own, something I've never had to do except for a few months in between flatmates years ago. Does this make me a weak person? Do you have to spend time on your own to have any self-knowledge?

I go upstairs to the loft, which has been converted into Aidan's office, and I sit down in his chair at his desk, which he had made out of a couple of oak railway sleepers. The surface is clear apart from a photo of the children and me taken at

Somerset House ice rink last Christmas. We're standing by an enormous Christmas tree where the baubles are about twice the size of Max's head.

To my left there is a wafer-thin metal tray with a few documents neatly stored in clear plastic folders and clearly labelled. On the top sits what can only be Aidan's script. I pick it up and weigh it in my hands, impressed by the number of words on the pages and surprised by how professional it looks, but guilty that I know so little about its content. This script is Aidan's other life, the other woman, and I feel a pang of jealousy that it contains so many thoughts and emotions that he hasn't shared with me. Obviously we've talked about various scenes but we've had so little time together lately and I've been too involved in planning my film and too exhausted to do more than grunt a few answers and collapse into bed. He's right, I don't ask him any questions any more. And I feel terrible that I left Devon for nothing. I'm not sure I can even tell Aidan that Florence fell asleep and that we didn't film anything last night. I must make it up to him and to the children, start the New Year as I mean to go on. I look again at his script – he has never given it to me to read but I've never asked to see it. Maybe it would be a good thing to read it and show my interest. I open the first page and then close it again.

I go downstairs to the bedroom and lie down on the bed but I can't go back to sleep; my brain is chattering. Aidan's script is part of my future: isn't it only right that I should read it to see if my future is secure? I walk upstairs again to check that the script is still there. I know it's a ridiculous thought. What did I think would happen? Did I imagine it might have spontaneously combusted in the last ten minutes? He need never know . . . but shouldn't I ask him first? The memory of last night weighs as heavy as Aidan's script. I pick it up gingerly, and feeling guiltier than ever I turn over the first two pages and read the title:

'TRUST'
by
Aidan Taylor.

The irony is not lost on me but I start reading the first few lines and soon it's too late to stop.

It takes me two hours of intense concentration to finish the script. It's obvious that it is a work in progress and the end is unresolved. I put it back where I found it, worrying that Aidan will notice that it's been moved. I suppose I could pretend that I'd been dusting his desk but I know that's one excuse he'd never believe. I sit still, staring out of the window, wondering what I'm going to do. Because it's not that the script is bad. It's terrible.

Seventeen

A quick glance at the kitchen clock tells me we've only got five minutes to get shoes and socks on, brush teeth, fix hair, finish doing the packed lunch and find the holiday spellings that we're meant to have learnt. It's taking me a while to get back into the morning routine after the Christmas break. I spoon-feed Evie's Weetabix in an attempt to speed up breakfast.

'Mum, I'm not a baby, stop it,' she says in disgust.

'Feed me, please feed me,' pleads Max.

I shove an enormous spoonful of soggy cereal into his mouth and wonder what's happened to my mother who is already five minutes late. An early riser, she generally manages to avoid the queues of traffic on the motorway. Evie scratches her head, which is something she's been doing a lot since the massacre of the chickens. I've been looking out for any signs of worrying behaviour and I wonder if she's developing a nervous tic.

Aidan pours himself a cup of coffee and stirs it nervously with a teaspoon although he hasn't put in any sugar or milk. He is going to a breakfast meeting with a producer who might be interested in investing some money in the script. I resist the urge to say, 'Don't get your hopes up too much.' I haven't said anything to him about the script since they came back from Devon; after all what could I say? And maybe, please God, just maybe I'm wrong and it's a work of genius which I'm too stupid to recognise. He's still furious with me about leaving Devon although it sounded as if they all had a good time. We've managed to avoid each other but I've resolved that tonight when I come home I'm going to make a big effort and try to talk to him before things get any worse.

*

I hear the front door open and I shout out, 'Morning, Mum.'

'Sorry I'm late – the traffic was terrible. You off somewhere, Aidan?'

Aidan kisses the children and pulls his case off the kitchen table. He waves at me over their heads.

'Good luck,' I say, trying to be encouraging.

'Thanks.'

The children rush to the door to give him a send-off.

'Is it a meeting about his script?' my mother asks, filling the kettle.

'Yes.'

'Have you read it?'

I nod my head miserably and lower my voice. 'But Aidan doesn't know that I've read it.'

'Oh dear. What's wrong with it?'

'I've been trying to work out what is so bad about it. Apart from the story being unconvincing, the main character unsympathetic, the action gratuitously violent and the sex boring . . . I check myself, realising that I'm talking to my mother, but she doesn't react as she pours the boiling water into her coffee, so I continue, 'What really shocked me was how angry it was. After reading it I felt how little I really know Aidan.'

My mother looks at me sympathetically. 'That doesn't sound good,' she says, and she takes a sip of coffee and then looks at the clock. 'Aren't you going to be late?'

'Oh my God,' and I follow Aidan outside, the children trailing after me without wearing their shoes, slipping on the frosty pavement, Max shouting, 'Mum, it's a dragon-breath day.' He stops and blows, his breath circling above his head like smoke.

Florence is in Makeup, wearing a purple towelling dressing-gown that has seen better days, and Matt is filming her as she's being made up.

'What do you think?' she says, pulling at the dressing-gown.

I'm not sure what to say and she chortles at my discomfort. 'Let's just say I won't be asking to buy this one off production when we've finished. Do you know, when I was doing revue shows years ago just after the war we had so much time in between acts that I used to do my own sewing. I'd sew all my own underwear with perfect French seams – I made some lovely nightdresses – Marks and Spencer's, eat your heart out.'

She's very chatty and I suspect a little nervous about filming today.

'Sometimes the men would cobble their own shoes or do a bit of woodwork.'

'Like Harrison Ford,' I say. 'He built his own house in the Hollywood hills.'

'What, in between takes of *Raiders of the Lost Ark*? He must have been bored!' she says, laughing. 'Can you imagine some of the other stars around today making their own shoes? Might help curb Russell Crowe's temper,' she goes on, enjoying herself.

'Tom Cruise could build in his own platform wedges,' I add, and we're both giggling. Matt is smiling and I notice that the pretty makeup girl, Susie, is laughing and keeps looking up at him.

'Don't point that thing at me,' she flirts.

'Why ever not?' he says, flirting back. What is it about a film shoot that makes us behave like this? Maybe it's because of the nerves and the fact that actors feel vulnerable exposing them-selves for the camera, or maybe it's just that everyone usually involved in filming is so often young and good-looking.

'Big scene today, Florence?' I ask, watching Susie expertly dabbing some foundation on her cheeks.

'A bit of flashy dialogue. That's always worrying because I have trouble remembering the name of my own son let alone twelve lines of dialogue.'

The mention of Bill brings a flush to my cheek and I hope no one notices. I haven't seen him yet and I presume he's keeping a low profile either to avoid me or just to keep out of the way. It's only been four days since that night but it feels more like four years and more unbelievable as the days pass by. Every time my mobile rings I wonder if it might be him, but he hasn't called and I think it's for the best.

I recognise a teenage boy from the audition, sitting beside Florence, flicking through a magazine.

'Are you all right?' I ask him, concerned because he looks terrible, with sallow skin, one eye all puffy and red, with dark shadows under the other.

'Yeah I'm fine,' he grins.

I sit down next to Florence and whisper, 'Makeup has got their work cut out with him.'

Florence says coolly, 'Molly, he's just finished being made up. Have you been to many drama sets?'

Matt is doing some shots outside the makeup trailer, which is lined up alongside a number of other trailers in the drab South London car park. Steam rises from the plastic cups of tea and coffee. It's very cold and everyone is wearing thick padded anoraks, warm gloves, scarves and hats. A small queue of extras are waiting for tea and coffee and the smell of the bacon butties makes my stomach rumble, reminding me that I was so busy trying to force Ready Brek down my children's mouths this morning, I forgot to eat my own breakfast. Frost glistens like icing sugar on the neat fences of the terraced houses and I'm so hungry that I have to resist the temptation to drag my finger along the fence and lick it, hoping for a sugar rush. Instead I join the queue and shout over to Matt and Gerry, 'Fancy a cuppa?' They do a thumbs-up sign and quickly move out of the way of an electrician carrying some lights to join the others that are being set up round one of the tiny terraced houses. When I get to the head of the queue the woman with greasy hair behind the counter looks at me suspiciously.

'Haven't seen you before, love,' she says accusingly. She's staring down at me and makes me feel about twelve years old.

'We're filming a documentary about one of the actresses in the film,' I explain in a small voice.

'Well, I'm sorry, if you're not part of the unit you have to go elsewhere for your tea – we're not running a charity here and we're stretched enough as it is. Bloody cheek.'

'It's all right, Janice, she's a friend of mine – could you waive the rules just this once and give us some teas?'

I turn to see Jo standing behind me wearing a striped woolly hat pulled low over her ears.

'I wondered how long it would take you to notice,' she giggles.

'What are you doing here?' I ask, confused.

'Working – how about you? Thanks, Janice, you're a star.' Janice grudgingly hands her the teas. 'I've been on a few shoots with Janice over the years – bark worse than her bite – you know the type.' She hands me a tea.

'I'm here with Florence.'

'Is she playing the granny?' Jo asks. 'From what you've said about her that's not how I imagine her at all.'

'Have you got a part in the comedy drama?'

'No, I just like hanging around film sets – makes me feel comfortable – yes, of course I'm in it. I'm playing a nosy neighbour – it's nothing much but at least it's a job.' She smiles. 'Small world.'

I look around, wondering where Bill is.

'Are you all right, Molly? You seem a bit nervous.'

'Filming – I can never quite relax.'

'Looking for us?' Matt and Gerry join us and I introduce them to Jo. I try to be nonchalant but the truth is I'm hoping to see Bill at any moment and I'm nervous at the prospect.

'Can I meet her?' Jo asks.

'Who?' I say, still distracted.

'Now let me see, Nicole Kidman, Chlóe Sevigny, Julia Roberts – the famous Florence, you idiot, who do you think?'

I look at Matt to check his reaction. 'When do you think they'll start filming?'

He looks around at the busy technicians still setting up. 'I think we've got a while.'

'All right then,' I say to Jo, 'come and meet Florence,' and we walk towards Makeup together.

I pause outside the makeup trailer. 'But remember, no terrible tales of me growing up or things we used to do together. This is a professional relationship.'

She looks very serious and says, 'Of course, what did you expect?'

'What happened then?' Florence is desperate to know the details.

'Well, she was so intent on flirting with him she put her head forward to do a Farrah Fawcett Majors type of flick with her hair and hit her forehead on the back of the chair. When she looked up her hair looked great but there was blood pouring from her forehead and the rest of the evening, our first big night out with grown-up boys, was spent in casualty waiting for her to have stitches.' Florence and Jo are laughing conspiratorially and I'm thinking I must have been mad to introduce them.

'Thanks, Jo,' I say.

'So you've known each other for years?' Florence asks, looking from Jo to me.

'Our fathers were good friends.'

'Jo, haven't you got to go and get changed or something?' I say, anxious to stop her launching into more anecdotes.

'No, it's all right, we're not doing my scene until after Florence's.'

The door of the trailer opens and Gabriel, the director, peers in anxiously as if he's looking for someone. He sees Jo and Florence and says, 'Morning, girls. All ready, are we?'

Jo smiles at him coolly, Florence watching her before she turns to Gabriel and says, 'How are you – all prepared?'

'As much as I'll ever be.' He has a nervous laugh. 'We'll call you in a minute, Florence – Jo, we won't need you until later.'

'That's fine,' she says, hardly looking at him. Gabriel's appearance has changed the mood in the trailer and I'm relieved that it's brought a stop to the girlish reminiscences. As soon as he leaves Jo gets up and says, 'I'd better go and tell Wardrobe I'm here. Hope your scene goes well, Florence, I've really enjoyed meeting you.'

'You too,' says Florence and she holds Jo's hands as they kiss on either cheek.

'Look after yourself,' she says intently, and Jo, looking slightly puzzled, replies, 'Don't worry, I will. See you later, Molly.'

Once the door to the trailer closes Florence sighs. 'Is your friend married?'

'Yes, why?' I reply,

'I think she's got to be careful,' Florence says enigmatically, taking off her rings and putting them carefully into a little Chinese silken pouch that she's brought with her.

'What do you mean?' I ask, watching as she has trouble pulling the last big topaz ring off her index finger.

'Couldn't you see?'

'See what?' I say, not understanding what she could possibly be referring to.

'Jo and Gabriel.'

It takes a few seconds for her meaning to register, the time it takes for the rumblings of a volcano to register on the Richter scale.

'You don't think that they're . . .'

Florence looks up at me. 'I'd put money on it.'

'But she was so cool with him.'

'That's what was so suspicious – she was trying very hard in front of you not to give anything away, and did you see how quickly she left after he went?'

It makes sense, especially when I think about how buoyant Jo has been whenever I've seen her, and I thought it was all because of her going back to work. Florence is watching me and I say slowly, 'Are you always this perceptive?' I wonder if she has an inkling of anything that has passed between Bill and me.

She smiles at me and I smile back at her, hoping that my face betrays nothing, and then I quickly say, 'I'll just go and check on the crew.'

Outside the trailer I take a deep breath, aware that I am over-reacting. A girl I recognise from Florence's audition strides past me on her way to the makeup trailer. She has bright orange spiky hair and she's clutching her walkie-talkie.

'Yeah, Gabriel, I'm on my way to get Florence now.'

I can see Matt and Gerry chatting to Susie the makeup girl but as soon as they register me they come straight over.

'I think she's about to start filming. Let's see what we can get.'

The trailer door opens and Florence, in her grubby purple towelling dressing-gown and slippers, walks gingerly down the steps, holding on to the makeup girl's hand. She looks up and smiles at us regally as she makes her way down. When she sees the girl with the spiky hair she greets her: 'We've met before, haven't we? You must forgive me but I've forgotten your name. Don't take it personally, I'm the same with everyone – I'm a bit like a goldfish in a bowl. Mind you, it means I never get bored because everything seems new and interesting.'

She stops for a minute – just talking seems to exhaust her. I look around anxiously for Bill, worried that she's not going to be able to do this. I find myself in an impossible position today because Florence is not my responsibility and the production company have only given us permission to film if we remain as unobtrusive as possible and don't get in the way. The woman with spiky hair is very patient and gives Florence time to recover before she replies to her question.

'We met at the audition – I'm Vicks, the first AD.'

'I've always thought that sounds like a date rather than a job title,' cracks Florence, finding her voice again. 'But something is different – I know, it's the hair, wasn't it pink last time?'

Vicks smiles. 'I don't think there's anything wrong with your memory, Florence,' she says as she takes Florence's other arm and between them they start to walk slowly towards the hub of activity.

'Do you mind me saying, dear, I think pink is more your colour – orange is very draining.'

It is obvious that Vicks is not interested in talking about colour with Florence and with quiet determination she manages to point her towards the terraced house, nodding encouragingly and not listening to a word she is saying. We follow her in to the camera position we've been allocated inside the house but it's a tiny location, crammed full of technicians and equipment. It's boiling hot due to the combination of the big lights and the central heating.

'Thermostat's packed up,' an electrician says to me as he pulls his sweatshirt over his head. 'It's all or nothing and it's too bloody cold out there not to have it on.' Condensation is dripping down the inside of the windows and the atmosphere is much tenser than I expected, considering they're filming a comedy drama.

Under her makeup Florence is looking very pale and as soon as she gets inside the room she slumps down at the kitchen table. For a minute I wonder whether she's just getting into the character she's playing. The young boy is brought in and I'm squashed against a wall at the back of the room, leaving Matt more or less to film on his own. I squat down on the floor and find a gap between the rows of human and inanimate legs from where I can just about see Florence's head. Gabriel the director is sitting by the monitor checking the shot and chewing his fingernails thoughtfully. He leaps up and goes to talk to Florence and the boy. They huddle for a few seconds and I'm reminded of a rugby scrum, then Gabriel bounces back to the monitor and Vicks shouts for silence. 'Let's walk it through,' she cries. Florence does the whole scene sitting at the table, and judging from Gabriel's reaction he's not happy with her performance. I can't stop staring at him, trying to work out if Florence's suspicions about him and Jo are justified.

'Don't you want to move around a bit, Florence?'

'I think it has more impact if I'm sitting.'

I'm intrigued to see how Gabriel will deal with Florence's strength of character. He stares at her. 'OK, let's try it your way.'

A props man leaps forward and lights the cigarette Florence has to smoke. 'Quiet, everybody,' screams Vicks. 'We're going for a take . . . ready, turnover . . .' The assistant cameraman puts a board in front of the camera and shouts out the scene number and as he leaps to the side Vicks shouts, 'And action.'

Florence takes her first puff of the cigarette. The young boy comes into the room, switches on the light, sees her at the table and looks shocked, surprised to find her there. Florence does her speech fluently, the swear words ringing round the tiny kitchen, her Mancunian accent perfect. The scene ends with the boy walking out of the kitchen and slamming the door shut as she stubs out the cigarette in a saucer already overflowing with butts.

'Cut.'

Gabriel leaps to his feet. 'Very good, guys, but can we do it again? This time, Florence, I want you to do it standing up by the sink and at the end chuck the cigarette into the sink.'

Florence looks worried but being the true professional she gets up slowly and walks to the sink. As they change the camera position slightly to accommodate the new action, she grips the side of the sink. She still looks deathly pale but there's nothing I can do as I'm so far back, removed from the action.

'Ready, everyone, we're going for a second take,' shouts Vicks. 'We'll do an end board, so straight into the scene everyone . . . turnover and ACTION.'

This time Florence is less fluent and she gets some of the lines muddled – not that it makes much difference to the sense of the piece – but she seems rattled and when they've finished Gabriel moves forward to reassure her but he doesn't look happy. I overhear a conversation he has with Vicks: 'It's a bit of a bore but we'll have to do close-ups with her sitting and standing and then I can make the choice in the edit.'

Florence is sitting down again and I wish someone would get her a glass of water. 'We're going to run the scene again doing close-ups on Florence; just give us a few minutes to relight and set up,' shouts Vicks, the fount of all knowledge.

For a brief moment there is a gap between Florence and me as the legs clear and I quickly make my way to the sink and grab a glass from the cupboard and fill it from the tap.

'Florence, drink this.'

She smiles faintly at me.

'Don't fuss,' she says, but she can barely speak. I look around, wondering whether I should have a word with Gabriel, but he's having an intense conversation with the cameraman and Vicks is nowhere to be seen. In only a few minutes the lights are set and they're ready to do the whole scene in close-up.

Florence is slumped in her chair but I see her try to sit up. She takes another quick sip of water, puts the cigarette in her mouth and again someone lights it for her. Vicks is back in prime position. She looks at Gabriel, he nods at her and she shouts clearly, 'And action.'

They run through the scene and Florence is word perfect this time.

'Thank you, Florence, that was great,' shouts Vicks and then her face drops in horror. 'Wait a minute, who put that glass of water there – it wasn't there before.'

Everyone goes quiet. The heat in the room suddenly becomes unbearable. Matt glances over at me and I duck down even lower, my heart thudding.

'Let's look at play-back on the monitor – we might be in close enough not to see it,' says the director of photography.

Florence stands up to get into her position by the sink. One minute I see her standing and the next I see drops of water in the air as if someone has let off a small sprinkler. There's a crash as the glass hits the floor, followed by a recognisable thud that makes me want to retch. I stand up immediately to try to see what's happening. Vicks, shouting, as usual, says, 'Stand back everyone – clear the room.'

Gerry is opening as many windows as he can find. There's a group of people huddled round Florence as she lies immobile on the floor and I can do nothing. Someone shouts, 'She's still breathing.'

I look across at Matt, who has just stopped filming, and I make my way over to him. 'What can we do?'

'Nothing – they're getting a stretcher. Let's get out of here.'

Outside we gulp in the cold air, a relief after the oppressive heat and stale air circulating inside the room. Florence is carried past us, lying flat on the stretcher, blood pouring from her forehead where she must have clipped the table as she fell, a wet stain on her towelling dressing-gown from the glass of water. We follow the stretcher at a distance as they take her to a trailer beside makeup where a medical officer is waiting, and we watch as the stretcher is taken inside and the door closes, leaving us standing outside in the cold.

Matt looks at me. 'Molly, you look terrible. Sit down.'

I feel angry with myself for being so feeble. I look up to see Jo hurrying over.

'What's happened? Are you all right, Molly?' She drops down beside me.

'I'm fine but Florence just passed out.'

'No, I don't believe it – she was so . . . perky earlier on.'

Within minutes the door to the trailer opens and we all turn expectantly to see the medical officer.

'Are you family?' he asks me.

'Well no, but we're with Florence – we're making a documentary about her. How is she?'

'She's all right – we're just running some checks to make sure.'

'Is she awake?'

'Yes – I'll tell her you're here; she's a bit confused. What did you say your name is?'

'Molly . . . and Matt and Gerry,' I say, indicating the others – after all we're almost family.

Within seconds he returns. 'Molly, she'd like to see you.'

Florence's face is the strange green of an unripe tomato but the blood has been mopped up and a plaster stretched across the bump on her forehead and her eyes are open.

I look questioningly at the medical officer. 'Is she OK?'

'I am an idiot,' she mutters.

'No you're not, you just fainted. I'm surprised you were the only one – it was unbelievably hot in there, even I felt terrible. I think we should complain about your working conditions – they're worse than a sweat shop in Taiwan.'

'It was the cigarette as well – I'm not used to it. You know the strange thing?' She's still very breathless.

'Shh, Florence, I think you should rest. Don't try to talk.'

She lies back, her head resting on the pillow. 'The smell of the burning match when they lit the cigarette reminded me of my childhood: we used to have oil lamps and my mother would light them in the evenings.'

There's a knock on the door and Gabriel enters, an injection of nervous energy. 'How is she?'

'OK.'

He walks over to Florence and kneels down. 'Don't worry, we've got the shots we need. You were right, it looks better with you sitting down. You rest up now, but do you think you'll be OK for next week?'

I'm about to protest when Florence says, 'All I've got to do is lie there and how hard is that?'

'Well, we'll check with the doctor – they're sending one over right away to give you a thorough going over.'

'That'll be nice but there's no need,' says Florence.

'You just rest and we'll get a car to take you home. Hope the head doesn't hurt too much. Well done, Florence.'

She smiles weakly, lapping up the praise. As he turns to go I have to ask, 'The close-ups – was the glass in shot?'

'No, it was fine. Why do you ask?' he says, not knowing who I am.

'Oh, nothing. I just wondered,' I reply, determined to keep my guilty secret to myself.

As he leaves I turn back to Florence. 'Shall I call Bill? I thought he'd be here.'

'No, he's gone back.'

Her words take a few seconds to register.

'Back? Back where?'

'Home to Canada.'

'So soon?'

'He'd been here for two weeks – he needed to go home.'

'Oh Florence, I'm sorry.'

'Don't be.' But as she turns her head I notice a tear roll down the side of her face. I'm surprised how deflated I feel, like a child

216

dressed up for a party who's been told it's been cancelled. I take Florence's hand and squeeze it.

'Thanks for the lift,' Jo says, looking at her face in the small mirror above the passenger seat and wiping away the eye-liner that has smudged. 'I hope Florence will be OK. I'm not surprised she fainted. It always gets so hot and stuffy on sets, I often feel like keeling over.'

She puts on a deep russet-red jumper and turns to show it to me. 'Do you like it? Finn bought it for me for Christmas – my heart sank when he gave it to me as you know how terrible his taste is but I think it's OK. He must have got someone to help him buy it.'

'It's a good colour on you.'

She puts her parka on over the top and then typically changes the subject. 'I like Florence and she's obviously fond of you.' Jo has a butterfly brain.

'Do you think so?' I ask, amazed at the thought.

'Oh yes, she's always watching you.'

'She can be very difficult.'

'That doesn't surprise me – she's quite a toughie – but she's all there. I just hope I'm like that at eighty-three.'

I'm not saying much, debating whether to mention Florence's suspicions about Jo's relationship with Gabriel. I decide on an oblique approach.

'Gabriel's . . . interesting,' I say, giving Jo a sideways look.

'Mmm,' she says non-committally.

'Have you worked with him before?' I ask.

'Yes, he did the advert – that anti-ageing cream ad that I did before Christmas. I suppose that's how I got the job.' She sounds almost bored.

'He must have thought you were good,' I probe.

'I suppose so.'

She's not revealing anything.

'Do you like him?'

'How do you mean?' she says, absentmindedly staring out of the car window.

'Well, is he . . . good to work with?' I say, not wanting to really speak my mind.

'He's OK.'

I look at her again and she's staring straight ahead at the road, her face betraying no emotion. I think Florence must be wrong and I feel pleased that I haven't been crass and suggested that there could be anything going on between them. I suppress a chuckle to myself and think how fanciful Florence is.

'He's good in bed.' Jo interrupts my thoughts.

'Sorry?' I say, wondering if I misheard her.

'We're having an affair.'

We look at each other and then I remember I'm supposed to be driving.

She laughs. 'I've never said that before. It sounds dramatic. But it is fantastic – the best sex I've had in years, in fact ever, and I feel great.' She grins as if she's talking about a visit to a health spa or an excellent holiday resort. 'I wasn't going to tell you but you were being so bloody obvious.'

'What about Finn?'

'What about him? This doesn't change anything except to make it better. Oh Molly, don't look like that – it's just sex and that's the beauty of it – both of us are married with children and neither of us wants it to be anything more than something physical. Sex, sex and more sex – it's fantastic.'

'But why? I don't understand.'

'Don't you? Is your sex life with Aidan so great that the idea of an attractive man who actually wants to have sex with you holds no appeal?'

My sex life with Aidan at the moment is non-existent. 'Well, of course there are times when you think about it, but there's a big difference between thinking about it and doing anything about it.' The thought of Bill flashes through my mind, but what happened with us was innocent in comparison.

Jo continues, 'If anything I think it's helped Finn's and my relationship – I feel I can cope better with him now that I've got this separate part of my life.'

'And the children?'

'They need never know.'

'Yes, but what if they did find out, how would you feel then?'

'They won't find out.' She looks at my sceptical face. 'Look, Molly, men have been doing this for years, it was almost expected of them – wife at home and mistresses all over the place – well, the world has changed now. We can be equal, in fact we can be better, and I don't see what harm this can do. The way I see it, everyone benefits. I tell you, I'm far nicer to my children at the moment because I feel better about myself.'

The conversation is unsettling me, and although I understand what she's saying I feel implicitly that she's wrong, but my arguments seem prudish and dated.

'Well, be careful, that's all I can say.'

'I will be – don't worry.' She looks so confident and glowing that I try to overcome my misgivings and smile at her.

The only good thing about Florence's collapse means that I'm home early. So by five o'clock I find myself walking into an eerily empty house. Usually the five to seven slot is busy time, the domestic equivalent of rush hour, with jams in the kitchen, on the stairs and in the bathroom culminating in a fit of mother rage just before lights out.

I check my mobile but there are no messages and then I hear the unmistakable sound of someone at the front door. The silhouette behind the glass in the door appears to be swaying slightly, pointing and jabbing a key in the general direction of the lock, without much success. I open the door to see a dishevelled Aidan and even over a gap of five yards the aroma of beer and cigarette smoke wafts through into the house. I have never seen him like this.

'Sorry,' he mutters, and staggers past me before collapsing on the stairs.

'Aidan, is this happy drunk or desperate drunk?'

'Depends,' he slurs at me.

'Depends on what?'

'Your point of view.'

'I'll make you a cup of coffee. Do you want to have a shower? It'll make you feel better.'

As I turn to go back to the kitchen Aidan grabs my arm and pulls me to him.

'Aidan,' I say, exasperated, 'stop it.' He tries to kiss me and I turn my head away.

'Why?' he says sadly, and then with supreme effort to get the words out coherently he says, 'Molly, stop. Look at me.'

I do as he asks, registering his olive skin, the slight bristle on his chin, the lines around his eyes, the thin red veins in the whites of his eyes, the blue iris dulled through the years that I've known him . . . my husband.

'They hated it,' he says, his voice full of disappointment.

'I'm sure they didn't,' I say, my heart sinking, but thinking, 'I knew it, how could they not?'

'Did they say anything encouraging?'

'Nope . . . well, they gave me the name of another company which they thought I could take it to.'

'Well, that's something.' I try to sound encouraging. I can hear someone walking up the path to the front door and I hope it's the children, but it's just another flyer being pushed through the letter box advertising gut-rotting pizzas.

'Come on, I'll run you a bath – let's talk about it later,' I say, my efficient manner similar to Eleanor, the home administrator's. As I turn on the taps I feel faintly reassured that at least someone is having a bath at 6.30, even if it's not one of my children.

Once I've helped Aidan into the bath I hear the front door open and the unmistakable sound of my children arguing. My mother looks exhausted.

'What's been happening? Are you all right?' I ask her.

She sighs, 'I need a cup of tea,' and then she sees my expression and says reassuringly, 'We're all fine. I was worried about Evie; she's got a verruca which won't heal and I thought we should check it out. I didn't want to disturb you and so I rang the doctor's and they gave us a cancellation. We had to wait hours – you know what it's like.'

I feel terrible that I didn't even know that Evie had a verruca. I give her a kiss and say, 'Does it hurt?'

'No, not much, but it keeps bleeding because I'm picking it.'

My mother winces at her frankness and while I make her a cup of tea I tell the children to go upstairs and get changed for bed.

'How have they been?' I ask my mother.

'Oh, fine. At the doctor's Max wouldn't keep still. He kept fidgeting, and once we got inside the consulting room he walked over to the window and started banging his Action Man's head against the pane. Just as we were leaving he said to the doctor, "Action Man isn't very well, he's got a headache."'

I laugh. 'That sounds like Max.'

My mother continues, 'And the doctor stared at Max without a hint of a smile and said coldly, "I wonder why?" Molly, why is everyone so grumpy these days? Do you remember Dr Stanley? Such a nice man, and nothing was too much for him. He'd think nothing of coming out in the middle of the night and you felt as if you had a proper relationship with him. He knew the family, saw us all through our ailments. Everything is so different now, people are too busy or too overworked these days. It's a ridiculous way to live.'

She sips her tea and I don't know what to say – her complaints are the constant lament of the old who struggle to make sense of the world they still have to live in. She looks at her watch and puts the tea down on the table. 'I must dash if I'm going to make it home in time for *Emmerdale*. See you tomorrow, Molly.'

The children shout out their goodbyes down the stairs and I go in to see Evie in her bedroom.

'How was first day back at school?'

Evie is fiddling with her spy glasses. She puts them on and ignoring my question she says, 'How much longer are you going to work?'

I put my arms round her and kiss her cheek. Her skin is warm

221

and smooth and it feels as if it's been a long time since we spent any quiet time together.

'I miss you,' she says.

I feel the tears starting to well up in my eyes. 'I know, I miss you too.'

'So when will you stop working?'

'I don't know, Evie, but not for a while.'

She shrugs, silent yet resigned. I tuck her in and she scratches her head again. Is it my imagination or is a small bald patch beginning to develop just above her ear where she's been scratching so much?

'Can I have a story?'

'No, it's too late. Go to sleep.'

I walk into Max's room but he's already fast asleep, snuggling his muslin, his new holster peeking out from under the pillow. I stroke his hair and give him a kiss. I miss them both. I feel distanced from them, I don't understand their everyday concerns, and my thoughts, my emotional commitment are elsewhere. They've turned into inconvenient responsibilities who need looking after – a continual nagging which stops me from concentrating on work. I peer at my watch through the dim light in Max's bedroom and then I remember Aidan.

He's still in the bath, fast asleep, his mouth open, a little trickle of dribble seeping down the side of his chin. I put my hand into the bath to feel the tepid water. His skin has turned white and his fingers are puckered and wrinkled. 'Aidan,' I call as softly as possible, 'Aidan, you've got to wake up.'

He jolts awake, looking surprised by his waterbed. I hold out a towel and help him out of the bath. He's moving slowly like an old man and mumbling,

'I'm so sorry. I'm such a nuisance. Sorry,' he repeats over and over again. Once in bed he turns on to his side, ready to fall back into sleep, and then very clearly he says, 'Molly, will you read my script and tell me honestly what you think?'

'Shh,' I say, desperate to change the subject and hoping he's too drunk to know what he's saying. 'You get some sleep.'

I slip quietly out of the room and pray that in the morning he won't remember a thing.

Eighteen

The coffee cups jump as Aidan slams the script on to the kitchen table. Evie and Max look up at their father's dishevelled face, not sure whether he's cross with them or with me.

'I want you to read it and give me an honest opinion,' he grunts as he opens the fridge door to find some orange juice. I don't know what to say so I concentrate on unloading the dishwasher, hoping that the gleaming plates and bowls may give me inspiration as to how to find a way out of this.

'Molly?' Aidan looks at me, despair in his eyes.

'I don't know if I should,' I say nervously as I put the white mugs into what I call the 'Conran' cupboard.

'Why not?'

'Well, what if I don't like it? It doesn't mean it's not good – it's just that it might not be the sort of thing that I like,' I say lamely.

'But you know the story and you've always been so encouraging about it. Why are you being so negative now?'

'I'm not being negative. Listen, I've got to go or I'll be late for filming.'

'For God's sake, Molly.' Aidan is raising his voice. 'Stay just for a minute.'

I'm getting my jacket and searching for my programme notes.

'Molly, for Chrissake . . .' The tone in his voice stops me in my tracks. 'I'm fed up with this. We never see each other, we don't talk, we don't have . . .' He stops and looks at the children who are staring at us both like spectators in a tennis match. They turn to look at me to see how I'm going to react but I'm speechless, so they turn back to Aidan as he continues, 'All we do is bark orders at each other. This isn't a marriage, it's crisis management.'

'Aidan,' I plead, 'not now, let's do this later.'

'But we never do – you just avoid me – there never is a "later". We used to talk things through, not any more. You just think that if you wait long enough things will sort themselves out. God, you're such an ostrich, Molly. What are you so bloody frightened of? I . . . I . . . oh, I give up.' And with that he storms out of the kitchen and back up the stairs.

'What's an oddridge?' Max asks Evie.

'It's a funny bird with long legs,' Evie says informatively and hardly drawing breath goes on, 'Mum, we're doing body parts at school and they look disgusting. Yesterday Miss Watling showed us pictures of the liver and Scarlet just covered her eyes and went "Eugh". Miss Watling had a model, one side looked normal, but on the other side you could see the bones and all the stuff inside. She put her hand in and pulled out the heart.' Max is staring at Evie open-mouthed.

'It isn't real, Max,' I say, trying to follow Aidan up the stairs while continuing the conversation.

'But it is real,' Evie protests.

'Well yes, it is real in that you have a liver and a heart, but Miss Watling wasn't holding a real heart, was she?'

Evie pretends to look sceptical for Max's benefit, then scratches her head above her ears. I stare at her, aware that she's doing it again, and I wonder if it is a nervous tic and whether seeing Aidan and I argue is making it worse. I shout up the stairs after Aidan, 'Look, I'm sorry,' but he doesn't reply.

'Aidan, I'm sorry,' I repeat, but still no response.

'I've got to go. I'm not being an ostrich, I just can't do this now. I'll call you later,' and feeling a coward I kiss the children on their heads and run out of the front door feeling as if someone has somehow managed to reach through my ribcage and is squeezing my heart.

'I can't do it,' Matt says, looking embarrassed at this admission.

'But why not?' I ask him. 'After all, you say you love her.'

He's unpacking the crew car and takes out his camera and

puts it on the ground. His girlfriend Ann has at last given him a final ultimatum.

'I don't know – I just don't want the commitment.'

'Camera men, you're all the same. You're just hoping someone better will come along.'

He looks genuinely hurt. 'I'm not – honest I'm not – I know she's great but maybe I'm not ready for kids – I look at you and think I couldn't do it.'

'Do you mean you never want children?'

'No, I'm not sure I do. Is that a terrible thing to say? Do you think I should?'

'That's a big one. I can't say whether you should or shouldn't but I don't regret having them for a minute. Yes it's hard and it's a terrible responsibility but there's nothing like it – I can't begin to explain the feeling you have towards your children. I wouldn't have missed that for the world.'

He looks thoughtful as Gerry drags another box out of the car. 'I don't want to interrupt the counselling session but I wouldn't mind a little help here,' he says pointedly. I take the circular light reflector off the top of the heavy silver box he is holding.

'So, Matt, have you got to move out?'

He looks very sorry for himself and scratches his head. 'Yes – do you know anyone who's got a spare room?'

'I'll have a think about it.'

Florence looks distinctly uncomfortable sitting in silence at the table with Margery, Violet and Bernard. She pushes her plate away looking faintly disgusted by the unappetising sight of tough beef the colour of cheap leather, overcooked stringy beans and boiled potatoes covered with a thick gravy. She narrowly avoids knocking over the vase of fresh daffodils in the middle of the table and looks up at me.

'I'm sorry, I just can't stomach it today.'

The fall yesterday seems to have shaken her and I feel guilty that we're filming. Florence puts her hand up to her head, touching the plaster.

'Do you want to go back to your room, Florence?' I ask, concerned.

Wendy Wannabe is trying to help feed Bernard who stares angrily at us as we film, frustrated by his own helplessness. He picks up a fork and slams it down on the table, making the rest of the cutlery jump in attendance, and Wendy pushes her chair back to try to avoid getting splashed by droplets of gravy. She controls her irritation, aware that we're filming, and starts quietly mopping the front of her dress and pulls her chair back in.

'Would you like a hand?' says a timid voice, and we all turn to see Dora standing by the entrance.

'Dora dear,' says Florence, 'you're back, how lovely to see you.'

'Maybe for good this time,' says Dora, her face full of excitement. 'My daughter is getting married and I think I may have persuaded Eleanor to let me stay. How are you all?'

Bernard's face doesn't betray anything but as Dora sits down, taking Wendy's place, his shoulders droop and one side of his mouth turns up in an attempt to smile.

'We haven't seen Elspeth for a few days – she's had a chest infection and doesn't want to see anyone,' says Florence, and everyone looks uncomfortable.

'Do you think she would mind awfully if I took her aromatherapy appointment, because you know how difficult they are to get, and if she's not up to it it would be a pity to waste it?' Margery says timidly. No one says anything but they all seem to be deferring to Florence who eventually says, 'I'm sure she wouldn't mind – it's a shame for it to go to waste.' She looks miserable. 'I think I need a little siesta today – I'm going back to my room. Good to have you back, Dora.' Florence gets up slowly.

'Where are you going, Florence?' Wendy says sharply.

'I can't face it today I'm afraid. I'm going back to my room.'

'Can't you wait a few minutes?' Wendy asks her, looking anxiously around at the others in the canteen.

'Don't worry, I'll make sure she's all right,' I offer.

'If you're sure,' she says, shrugging her shoulders as if I don't know what I'm taking on.

Florence and I begin the slow walk back to her room, stopping to rest occasionally whenever her hip starts to ache. As we make our slow progress I think that today she's subdued as if she's sobering up after a good party. She carries on walking down the long corridor and I walk beside her, trying not to be over-attentive.

'I enjoyed meeting your friend.'

'You mean Jo?'

She nods, her head concentrating on walking along the corridor.

I sigh, 'Well, you were right, she is having a thing with Gabriel.'

Florence stops and almost looks triumphant. 'I thought so – years of experience – I can smell sex a mile off.'

Wendy Wannabe comes round the corner and Florence smiles at me. Wendy does a quick check to see if we're filming and then, realising that we're alone, smiles a terse hello and walks past. As we walk on I tell Florence everything that Jo said.

'Her excuse was that men have been doing it for years and there's no reason why she shouldn't. She's determined it's not going to change things except for the better. I don't know, maybe she's right and there's no harm in it.'

Florence stops and looks at me sadly. 'It's never that simple. I think there is harm in it as someone always gets hurt.'

She says it with such intensity that I know she's speaking from personal experience. I look at her questioningly and she carries on walking.

'Let's just say it wasn't always easy living with a touring musician. I learnt to deal with it but it doesn't mean to say it didn't hurt.'

'Did you ever talk to him about it?'

'No, it was one of those things we never spoke about. He tried to keep it from me and in a strange way I respected that. It was his other life and although it sounds odd he was always very good to me. You could say we had an "understanding", but to be honest I never really understood it and I found it very painful. I wouldn't recommend it.'

'Were you ever tempted to have an affair yourself?'

She chuckles and repeats the question. 'Was I ever tempted? Of course, but I never did although it would have been tempting just for my self-esteem as much as anything, and I knew that if I did that would be the end of the marriage and I never wanted that. Neither of us did. Maybe it can work for some people and perhaps your friend is one of them but I've never seen it work long-term.'

'What if you fall in love with someone else?'

'Well, that's something altogether different. I think women fool themselves they're in love to make an affair more acceptable but I don't think your friend is in love with Gabriel, do you?'

'No,' I reply, but I'm not thinking of Jo.

She carries on the long, slow, painful journey down the corridor and I walk slowly by her side.

'How is my favourite girl?'

For a minute I think she's asking about me and then I realise she means Evie.

'She's all right but I am a bit worried about her. I think she may be developing a nervous tic because she can't stop scratching. It started after she had a shock and I wonder if it's a form of post-traumatic stress syndrome.'

'What was the shock?' She's looking at me with an amused expression and I know she thinks I'm over-reacting.

'She saw some chickens after they were slaughtered by a fox. It was very gruesome – enough to give me nightmares, let alone Evie. She keeps on scratching, even this morning when Aidan and I had an argument. Maybe whenever she gets worried she starts to scratch.' I scratch my own head and Florence smiles.

'She's got me doing it now – I'm scratching in sympathy.'

Florence pats my hand. 'Maybe she's got nits.'

'Nits?' I say, horrified. 'She's never had nits in her life. No, I don't think it's nits.'

*

'There's one,' I hear Max shouting as I close the front door.

'Oh my God, I can't do this any more.' My mother sounds exhausted. 'It's a job for your mother.' I follow the sound of the screams, which are coming from the bathroom.

'Ow, that really hurts,' shrieks Evie melodramatically. She is cowering in the bath holding on to her head while my mother kneels beside her brandishing a small white plastic comb and looking exasperated. 'Please stop it, you're hurting me, that's enough,' pleads Evie.

Max is combing a Mer baby's purple locks with another small plastic comb.

'Mummee,' screams Evie as if to say, thank God you've arrived to save me from this terrible fate. My mother turns round and leaning against the bath slowly eases herself to full height.

'Thank God you're back – I'm too old for all of this,' she says, wincing as she straightens up. 'Evie's scratching.' She points at the white plastic comb in her hands. 'It's nits, nothing emotional, no trauma, just good old-fashioned nits.' She wrinkles her nose. 'You and Tim never had nits when you were young,' and I immediately feel guilty. It's yet another example of what a bad mother I've become.

'Shall I go and paint the red cross on the door now or wait until tomorrow morning?'

She has the grace to laugh. 'Miss Watling, her teacher, mentioned she thought we might have "little visitors" so we went to the chemist and bought something that smells like weed killer but I've never seen anything like it – they've been jumping off in their thousands. I can't believe we haven't noticed them before.'

'Obviously camouflaged nits – I'm so sorry.'

'Can I keep one as a pet?' asks Max.

'Not a great idea,' I say, smiling at him.

'Come and have a look and I'll show you the eggs but they're really difficult to see.' She shows me the tiny translucent eggs close to Evie's scalp behind her ear and at the nape of her neck. 'They're hard to see because they're practically the same colour as her hair.'

'You're very knowledgeable.'

'The chemist explained it all to me – don't bother to wash all the linen as they can only survive a short time away from the head, but they're clever little so and so's who can hold their breath when you wash the hair, so they're very hard to get out.'

'Shall I have a go with the comb?'

'I'm going to call it the Not comb,' says Evie bitterly.

'It's no good with the eggs – you have to do those with your fingernails – it's a bloody nightmare.'

Evie sucks in her breath, admonishing Granny for using a swear word, but her grandmother ignores her.

'The chemist told me we've got to use the comb every couple of days for the next few weeks if we want to get rid of them.'

As I listen to her I start to scratch my own head.

'We've all got to do it as it's very likely we've all got them by now.'

'What about Max?'

'I found a few on him but nothing like Evie's, and at least his hair is shorter so it doesn't take so long to comb through.'

Evie looks miserable and now the water is getting cold she's shivering. Max is intent on playing hairdressers with the Mer babies, honing his Nicky Clarke skills at an early age.

'Is Aidan upstairs?'

'No,' my mother replies, looking disgusted. 'He disappeared as soon as I mentioned bathtime and made some pathetic excuse about seeing his friend Terry. I shall miss *Emmerdale* again at this rate.'

'Mum, is it that good?'

'Not really but it's become a habit. I'll leave you to it. Have a good weekend and don't forget you've got a bridesmaid fitting with Helen and Tim tomorrow. Bye, girls and boys, and be good.' She waves at the children who shout back in chorus, 'Bye, Granny.'

Aidan looks relieved when I tell him that I'm taking the children off for bridesmaid dress fittings. It's the first time we've talked since our argument and we've managed to avoid each other up to now but the resentment between us lingers in the air like the smell of burnt toast. I've avoided mentioning his script but I notice he's left it on the dressing-table in the bedroom where it taunts me every time I brush my hair or put on my earrings. He's right about me being an ostrich. I can't face having to tell him what I really think about his precious script. It would be the end of our marriage. I've never criticised him professionally and I'm sure now is not the time to start. I sit staring out of the window, preoccupied with my thoughts, so that I hardly notice when Max comes into the kitchen until he tugs at my hand and says wistfully, 'Who's looking after me today?'

'Me,' I say, grabbing hold of him and pulling him on to my knee.

His face lights up. 'Really?'

I hug him, loving the softness of his skin and the boyish smell that is uniquely his. Aidan gets up and goes upstairs to the study, I assume to work. Children can be such a useful diversion, and Aidan and I could exist in this state for months, maybe years, never finishing a conversation, never confronting the real problems because of the continual interruptions. The children demand immediate attention, and to be honest right now I'm grateful for the distraction, using them like emotional human shields.

'What are we going to do?' says Max.

'Well, we've got to go and see Helen and Granny about the wedding – they've got some dresses for Evie to try on.'

He looks disgusted. 'That's boring.'

'There might be sweets and biscuits,' I say, thinking I never used to bribe my children before I went back to work.

We've never been invited to Helen's flat before and I am curious to see what it's like. It's in a 1920s mansion block, meticulously decorated in thirties style right down to the Art Deco lampshades. Next to a drab lamp, its shade made of multicoloured glass, is an ornate silver frame with a photo of Tim and Helen arm in arm. I pick it up and study it. They look totally at ease with each other, as if they've been married for years. I think about Aidan's and my wedding photo, which was contrived by Aidan to look contemporary, me in front of frame and him slightly out of focus in the background looking off into the distance. They seemed so original and romantic at the time but now, comparing it with the picture in front of me, I feel there is no warmth, no connection between the two of us.

Tim's voice echoes out from the kitchen. 'I'm just making some tea – I don't suppose any of you would like chocolate biscuits.'

Evie grins and follows the direction of the voice while Max practises drawing his guns on a tall, willowy woman who is sorting through some fabrics.

'It's a lovely flat, Helen,' I say, and she beams proudly.

'Thank you, we like it.'

I wince at 'we' as I'm sure this isn't Tim's taste.

'It's taken me three years on and off to do it up and now I think it's finished. Actually I've just indulged myself and splashed out on a new sofa.' She points to a hideous pale green thirties-style sofa which is covered with swatches of material. 'Molly, meet Phyllida – she's going to make Evie's dress and she's doing mine as well; she's very clever.'

'Nice to meet you.'

Phyllida shakes my hand. 'So lovely to meet you. And who's this little man?' she says to Max in a patronising voice.

He stares at her and then moves closer and says, 'I've got nits.' She instinctively takes a step back and laughs a little too loudly. I quickly say, 'He's called Max and he *had* nits but we've sorted it out.'

'Well, to business,' says Phyllida efficiently, moving away from Max and glancing nervously at his head. 'I've brought a few things along based on those measurements you gave to Helen.'

She perches on the pale green sofa, patting her hand on the flat cushion to indicate that Evie should sit down beside her, which Evie ignores.

'Oh, great,' I say, immediately worried about the accuracy of the measurements, as my skills with a tape measure are about as reliable as my ability to read a road map. Phyllida is wearing dark-rimmed glasses of the sort that made an appearance in B movies when the lab assistant would take off her glasses and the doctor would say, 'Why, Miss Jones, you're beautiful.' The only difference being that even the lack of glasses wouldn't transform Phyllida, whose features all seem just too big for her face. As if to compensate, she is dressed expensively in a very elegant pencil skirt and cashmere baby-pink cardigan and she's sitting with her long legs entwined. I used to try to sit like that at school but my thighs were always too fat and I'd struggle to wedge my toe under the calf, hoping to force my legs round.

Phyllida sorts through the materials and dresses she has laid out on the sofa. 'Shall we try on a few things?' She beckons Evie over.

'I was thinking of this one,' says Helen, holding up a piece of pink taffeta.

Evie screws up her face and before she can say 'Eugh' I say quickly, 'That's lovely, but she doesn't look great in such a bright pink – it seems to drain her.' Phyllida holds the piece of material up against Evie and says, 'Mmm, I see what you mean.'

Helen looks disappointed. Evie looks as if she's about to faint. 'Have you got anything purple?' she asks hopefully.

'Well, there is some lilac in the same taffeta as the pink.' Phyllida scrabbles around for the material. 'Here we are.'

'Oh, that's perfect,' enthuses Evie.

Helen looks uncomfortable. 'There's just one problem,' she says. 'I hate purple.'

'It's not puple, it's lilac,' reprimands Phyllida. 'The Duchess of Weymouth had it for her bridesmaids at her wedding – it's very stylish.' Helen doesn't look impressed.

'Well, seeing it's Helen's wedding I think she should choose a colour she likes,' I say, ignoring the furious looks Evie is throwing in my direction.

'Does it have to be a colour? What about this lovely Cath Kidston floral material? It's divine,' suggests Phyllida.

'Oh, that's fantastic,' I say.

Evie clutches the lilac material in the hope that we will all see the light very soon. Helen decides on a simple A-line shape in the Cath Kidston material and we all agree that Evie will look wonderful and that we'll be able to use the dress afterwards in the summer. Evie plugs in her Spy Kids' earphones and gloomily munches a chocolate biscuit. Max, who has been playing with Tim, joins her and between the two of them they hoover all the biscuits on the plate.

I go into the kitchen in search of a paper towel to wipe their fingers and find Tim doing some washing up. 'Nice shirt,' I say, indicating his pale blue shirt.

'Helen got it for me; she says it goes with my eyes. She's gradually sorting out my wardrobe.'

I wouldn't dream of telling Aidan what to wear – it's normally the other way round in our relationship.

'I didn't expect you to be here,' I say.

'Moral support,' he grins.

'Are we that scary?'

'Definitely, and I wanted to see the children – couldn't care less about you,' he jokes – at least I think it's a joke.

'Are you OK?' he asks me.

'Not really.'

'What's up?'

'Marriage. It's not easy.' I grin at him.

'Thanks for that, I'll bear it in mind.'

'Do you come here often?' I ask him, joking.

'Actually I more or less live here at the weekends; it's better being away from the college. It gives me perspective, and I've been writing a few articles for academic journals and I like Helen to read them and tell me when I'm becoming too obscure or pompous.'

Helen works in a secondhand bookshop near the university where Tim teaches – they met when she found him a book that he thought was long out of print. When he told me about her I knew it was serious and I was looking forward to meeting her. He talked about her in such glowing terms that I suppose it would have been hard for anyone to live up to that kind of build-up. He smiles at me fondly and I realise that I've forgotten why I've come into the kitchen.

'Do you want me to dry up?' I offer, pleased to have this time alone with him.

'I thought you'd never ask – the tea towel is hanging on the cooker handle over there.'

I start to dry up and for a few minutes we're both silent, concentrating on our individual tasks, until Tim suddenly stops washing up and says, 'I've been meaning to ask you – would you do the wedding video for us?'

'Oh God, are you sure about this?'

'We want it to be different from the normal ones people have done – you'd give it a personal angle.'

I suddenly remember our father's super 8 camera. 'I could use Dad's camera – it would make it look lovely and grainy. No sound though, but that could be an advantage as the wedding speeches can get a bit tedious.'

'No, I think I want something a bit more abstract to capture the essence of the day.'

'You're wasted at that university – you should be working in advertising.' I pause. 'I never had you down as a white wedding boy.'

'Helen was keen but I'm not averse to it. It appeals to the historian in me and I've got nothing against churches, particularly when they're empty.'

'So you're just not going to invite anyone to the wedding then?'

He makes a face at me. 'You know what I mean. Sometimes I go down to our local and just sit there and have some quiet time.'

'Do you go to the church as well?'

'I thank you,' he says, doing his best impersonation of an old music-hall comedian. 'I think your friend Florence is rubbing off on you.'

'Aidan says that too. Do you think more about religion since Dad . . .' I ask him carefully, aware that it's an area we don't usually discuss.

'Yes, I think it's inevitable, but I suppose the older I get the more I think that this is it, we only have one life so we need to make the most of it.'

'Is that why you decided to get married?'

'Yes, maybe, but it was more that I found someone I felt comfortable with.'

It's an interesting thought. I married Aidan because he was exciting. Comfort never came into it. In fact we used to despise people who said they felt comfortable, as if they weren't living life to the full.

Tim has finished the washing up and he's emptying the bowl of soapy water into the sink. I watch him dry his hands on a *Past Times* tea towel.

'You're very happy, aren't you?' I try not to sound accusatory.

'Yes, I am. And you?'

I realise I'm close to tears. 'I'm sorry, I think I need a hug.'

'What's up between you and Aidan?' he says quietly into my ear as he puts his arms round me.

'I don't really know – maybe I need some quiet time in your local to sort it out in my head.'

Helen runs into the kitchen. She can hardly speak she is so upset, and all she can do is point back towards the sitting room, mouthing to Tim, 'The sofa.'

We follow her back into the sitting room to see Max and Evie looking shamefaced and all over the brand-new sofa are the chocolate handprints of my two children. Phyllida is logging the effect into the design database embedded in her brain – no doubt thinking she could sell the idea to Linda Barker. Helen is furiously scrubbing the sofa with a cloth and one look at Tim's face tells me it's time to make our excuses and leave. I can see the look of relief on Helen's face, and as I close the door I wonder whether I should have a badge made up with the words 'I'm sorry' written large, which I could have pinned permanently on my chest. I seem to be upsetting so many people these days.

Nineteen

It's early in the morning and there are very few people in the street outside the big glass doors to the office. It's the end of another week's filming and I've arranged to meet Matt here so that he can collect some more video tapes and I can find some extra research notes I think I'm going to need. Matt is leaning against the wall, and as I approach, to my horror he scratches his head.

'Can't you get in?' I ask as I walk up to him.

'The stock hasn't arrived yet and Gerry's gone in search of a lens box so I thought I'd wait for you here.'

He keeps scratching while I stare at him. 'What?' he asks, seeing my expression.

I'm in a dilemma. Should I tell him about our nit problem or pretend it has nothing to do with me? When I ran the nit comb through my hair I discovered at least five little animals, some still wriggling, and I feel ashamed, as if the presence of nits in my children's hair confirms that I'm a neglectful mother. I say nothing, but Matt is looking at me strangely so I ask as casually as possible, 'Have you had your hair cut recently?'

He looks at me as if I'm clearly insane. 'When would I have had the time for that exactly? Come on, Gerry,' he says, more to himself than to me.

'I'll just go and pick up the research notes I need and I'll see you back here in five minutes.'

He scratches his head again and as I walk past I surreptitiously try to look at his scalp to see if I can detect any nits or little white translucent eggs. He backs away from me as if to say, 'Keep your hands off me, you madwoman,' and I smile at him and quickly disappear through the electric doors.

*

There are only a few people in the office and the desk I was using before I started filming is full of someone else's files. Stuck to the computer with a piece of old-fashioned Blu Tac is a picture of a young boy smiling coyly at the camera, his nose wrinkling and one hand over his eyes shielding them from the sun. He looks about two years old because he still has wonderful curls cascading on to his shoulders that remind me of Max at that age before he was shorn, like Samson, marking the transition from toddler to big boy. I loved Max's curls but he was so proud of his new short haircut, and I remember having to turn away so he wouldn't see how upset I was. The boy in the photograph holds up a red toy train, James from *Thomas the Tank Engine*, and suddenly I want to be at home with Max. Knowing that this is impossible and trying to be practical, I stop staring at the photograph and search the desk trying to find my files, wondering how people manage to work like this.

'Can I help you?'

I jump, startled by the voice, and turn to see a young girl in her late twenties.

'I'm looking for some files I left here.'

'Are you Molly?'

'Yes,' I say, feeling pleasantly surprised that she knows my name.

'They're all over here. I only started two weeks ago – I'm setting up the genealogy programme. I'm Lucy.'

She is so different from the others I've met at the office. I point at the photograph on the computer. 'Is he yours?'

'Yes, that's Jonah.' Her face softens as she looks at the photograph.

'He's lovely.'

'I think so, but he has his moments.'

'Don't they all?' I say, smiling.

I'm aware of someone standing behind us listening to our conversation and I turn expecting to see Matt, but it's Cassie and I've never seen her look so lost. Within seconds her expression has changed and she says breezily, 'Molly, what are you doing here? Aren't you filming today?'

'Happy New Year to you too, Cassie.' I go to give her a kiss but she is distant and unresponsive.

'I had a few things I needed to pick up before we go filming,' I explain.

She turns round and I follow her back into her office. 'I've been meaning to ring you to say thanks for all your help over New Year – Aidan said you were great with the kids.'

'My pleasure,' she says, sounding like she's forgotten the meaning of the word.

'Are you all right?' I ask and to my amazement she starts to cry. I've never seen her cry in all the years I've known her – angry, upset, unhappy, but never crying. I try to put my arms around her and she recoils as if I've burnt her.

'Don't.'

She makes no noise, and she's curiously unemotional and doesn't sob, but the tears pour down her face as if someone has turned on a tap. I sit down on the sofa and wait while she wipes her eyes, turning away from the glass that separates her from the rest of the office.

'This is ridiculous,' she says, frustrated with herself.

'Is it something to do with work?'

'God, no. When I'm at work I'm on automatic pilot and I never feel like this. I don't care about the work. It means nothing, it's pointless except when it comes to paying the bills. The longer I'm here the more meaningless it becomes.'

I say nothing. She looks at me and then starts to talk, the words pouring out of her. 'If you'd said to me in my twenties, when we first met, you'll never have children, I wouldn't have believed you. You would have been wrong – I did get pregnant when I was seventeen but I had a miscarriage around three months and do you know the terrible thing? I was so grateful. I knew I was too young, I wasn't even eighteen, and it wouldn't have been convenient.' She spits out the word.

'I never knew.'

'No, I haven't told anyone.' She stares at me. 'So you see, I never thought I would be in this position – I just assumed I would have children, lots of them, when I was settled, when the time was right. My career was going so well that time never came and because I knew that I could get pregnant I just thought I could have them when I wanted. I took it for granted and it never crossed my mind that anything might be wrong.'

She mops her eyes. 'I keep thinking to myself, if only I'd done something earlier and got myself checked out maybe I wouldn't be in this position. If Will had really pushed me about having children maybe it would have been different, but he wasn't sure, he was worried about the responsibility, the money, and by the time he'd decided he was ready it was too late.'

'It's not Will's fault,' I say gently.

'No, I know it's not his fault, it's mine,' she replies.

I get up and pour her a cup of water from the dispenser. As I hand it to her I say, trying to be helpful, 'It's no one's fault.'

'I know, it's a fact, and one that I've got to learn to live with.'

'You know, having children isn't everything,' I say.

She takes a sip of water. 'I know what you're trying to say but at the moment it feels like it. I've spent thirty-eight years just thinking about myself and I'm so bored of it. I'm going to become more and more selfish and end up a batty old lady living on my own with a houseful of cats.'

'You don't like cats,' I say, trying to change the tone.

'Well, dogs then,' she snaps.

'I know it sounds pathetic but the future scares me. Who's going to look after me?'

'I will, or Jo and all our children – an extended family. The geriatric commune, remember?'

She tries to smile. 'Like that's going to happen.'

'To be honest, I think my children like you much more than they do me. But Cassie, you can't think about the future like this. Who knows what will happen? I don't even know that the children will be around to look after me. Maybe they'll emigrate and find it impossible to come back or maybe they won't make it to my old age.'

'Don't say that,' she says quickly, 'even if you are trying to cheer me up.'

I touch an old wooden ruler she has on her desk. 'Listen, Cassie, I love my children but it's not all wonderful. There are huge problems that go hand in hand with bringing up children – you know that. The responsibility is overwhelming and the fear of something happening to them and losing them is terrifying.'

She looks at me almost mockingly. 'But that is what's important – it's the intimate relationships that matter.'

'But you can have that with other people, not just your children.'

'Yes, but that bond between you and Evie and Max is completely different to anything you might feel for someone else – you're their mother.'

The tears start to roll down her face again and I realise that I'm not helping her. So I change tactics and appeal to the practical side of her nature.

'OK, so let's be brutal about this. You can't change the fact that you've split up from Will and you won't be able to have children. So what are your options?' I can tell she's not really listening to me. 'You could meet someone else who already has children and become a stepmother, wicked or otherwise, or you could adopt – plenty of people do that these days or . . .'

'Or I could just stop,' she says, finishing my sentence.

'What do you mean?'

'Nothing,' she says flatly. 'You must go – you're going to be late.'

'It doesn't matter,' I say, worried about her.

'Yes it does,' she says.

Aware that nothing I say seems to make any difference, I get up and walk over to her. I put my arms round her, feeling her tense up, and I hold her tight, refusing to let her go.

I walk up the iron stairs in an attempt to keep out of everyone's way in the busy West London studio where Florence is due to start filming the second day on her comedy drama. As usual there is a buzz of activity and I see that Florence is already sitting inside, beside a large workbench. She is sipping a mug of tea and listening to Jo, who is already in costume and talking to her intently.

Florence looks up as I approach. 'Molly?' She seems unsure whether it's me.

'Florence – how are you feeling?'

'Oh, fine.' She's being very reticent. 'Your friend is here.' Florence looks unsettled as if she's searching for something. 'Oh, this is annoying, I used to be so good at this – I'm sorry, my dear, I've forgotten your name.'

'Jo,' says Jo, grinning at me.

After my conversation with Cassie I'm pleased to see her.

'They need me back to do some final shots and I'm not complaining.'

I'm finding it hard to concentrate and I want to tell Jo how worried I am about Cassie but it's not the right time. On the journey to the location I've thought about nothing else. However hard I try, I can't imagine how I would feel in her position and consequently I don't know how to make her feel better.

Wendy Wannabe is sitting the other side of Florence. 'Isn't this amazing?' she says, wide-eyed like Bambi when his mother showed him the big meadow for the first time. She's eagerly looking around at everyone setting up for the day's filming, practically shivering with excitement.

'Wendy was keen to see that I was going to be well looked after,' says Florence archly. We both know why Wendy is here and I smile.

'Are you sure you're up to all this?'

'Oh yes, I had an early night last night – got my beauty sleep,' Wendy Wannabe says, laughing loudly and attracting a lot of attention to herself. She then makes a fuss about being so loud, thereby attracting even more attention.

'I wasn't talking to you.'

Wendy fails to notice my tone of voice but remembering the reason she's here, turns her attention to Florence and starts pulling up the blanket that she's got draped over her knees.

'I don't want anyone to fuss. I'll be fine.' Florence shivers as she clutches her thick towelling dressing-gown close around her. She sees me looking at it. 'Not the delightful purple one today – this one isn't a costume – it belongs to Makeup.'

'Have you got your costume underneath?'

Florence smiles. 'I suppose you could say that.' She's watching me closely. 'What's up?'

'What do you mean?'

'You look upset.'

'Do I?' Her searching look breaks my reticence. 'I've just had a very upsetting talk with a good friend.'

Florence glances over at Jo who has gone to check with Vicks when she will be needed.

'Not Jo but another friend, Cassie – she helped me get your recording of "Lucky Star".'

'What's the problem?'

I look at Florence's face which is genuinely interested. 'I don't want to bother you with all of this – you've got a big scene today.'

'No, I want to know; to be honest I enjoy the distraction.'

I find myself telling her all about Cassie and our distressing conversation. 'I can't imagine what it must be like to be in her position – I'd be devastated if I couldn't have children, but then again lots of people don't and are still content with their lives. I feel I want to give her something to hold on to – a reason for it all.'

'Maybe that's too much to ask – you can't provide all the answers. Maybe she just needs someone to listen?'

'What do you think is the point of it all?' I look at her, hoping that she might be able to provide an answer.

Florence laughs. 'Who do you think I am? I haven't got the answers, Molly. I'm just like you, flailing around trying to make sense of it all.'

I feel disappointed, and she smiles at me. 'I can only talk personally but I suppose the point is this.' She looks around at the set.

'What, work?' I say, unconvinced.

'No, I don't mean that, I mean the moment, each new experience, the different people we meet and the connections you make. It is about love, about giving and receiving.'

She pauses.

'Does that sound pat?' she asks.

'Perhaps – but you're right.'

'Your friend is your age?'

'Yes – well, I'm a bit older by a couple of months, but nothing significant.'

'How does she know things won't change?'

'I think that's what she's worried about – that things might get worse.'

'But how does she know that they won't get better? The way I see it, we're all going to die so you've got to make the most of life while you still have it.' Her tone changes and she says, suddenly serious, 'That's what I'm doing.'

'I want to help her.'

Florence pats me on the leg. Wendy gives a loud yawn and stretches her arms above her head.

'Just keep listening to her and she'll work her way round this. I think you're a good friend.'

'I don't know about that, especially not at the moment,' I say, simultaneously embarrassed and pleased by the compliment. 'But I'd better get on with some work. I don't know what's happened to Matt and Gerry – don't let the others start filming without us.'

As I get up I see Gabriel the director talking with Jo and I stop for a minute to watch them to see if there are any signs of intimacy. She's engaging with him today, smiling a lot and being attentive, but Gabriel seems more interested in Wendy Wannabe who is now shamelessly stretching her remarkable legs out, perfectly aware that the crew are staring at her, watching her every move. Gabriel cuts Jo off in mid-sentence and makes his way over to Florence, his eyes on Wendy sitting beside her.

'How are you feeling this morning, my darling?' he says to Florence, half-heartedly looking at her for a brief moment.

'Oh, don't you start – I'm perfectly fine.'

'They're just about to put on the heaters – don't want you catching a chill,' Gabriel says, his attention wandering back to Wendy who is now sitting demurely on the other side of Florence. Even though it's January and pretty cold inside the studio, she's wearing a low-cut top which makes her look like an advert for a particularly powerful Wonderbra, and stretch jeans which are being stretched to their limit. As I leave the studio in search of the crew, I hear him say to her, 'An actress as well as a carer – what an interesting combination.'

Outside in the white winter sunshine Matt and Gerry are struggling across the courtyard towards the studio, loaded with gear.

'How kind of you to join us,' Matt says sarcastically. 'What have you been doing?'

'Keeping the talent happy.' I smile. 'Actually that's not strictly true – I've been picking her brains.'

'What about?' asks Gerry as he stops to put down his lighting equipment.

'The meaning of life.'

'Oh, so nothing important then.' Gerry scratches his head and I involuntarily scratch mine. Matt scratches behind his ears and I say quickly, 'They're going to start filming soon so we need to be ready.'

'What are they doing today?'

'I haven't a clue.'

'Good, glad to see that you're doing your research properly,' says Matt, teasing me.

'Florence wouldn't tell me and whenever I ask her she says enigmatically, "Let's just say there's not much acting required."'

We set up as close to the large workbench as possible, trying not to trip up over the piles of boxes, rusty old tools, a bent bicycle, paintings covered in dust and piles of rubbish to make it look like an authentic cellar. A man is laying cobwebs on to the bicycle with a special machine, which looks similar to Evie's candyfloss maker except that it's much kinder on teeth. A track has been laid round the table for the camera to move around and five enormous industrial heaters are blasting out hot air. Vicks, still in good voice, bellows, 'OK, everyone, if you could take your places please.'

The runners pull the powerful heaters to the back of the studio for the moment, keeping them turned on to combat the cold.

'Clear the set,' says Gabriel, looking pointedly at Jo. 'I don't want anyone here who isn't needed.'

Jo looks upset, but leaves the studio.

Wendy helps Florence stand up and when she gets to the table Gabriel says, 'Are you ready, Florence?'

She nods and without a moment's hesitation she takes off her dressing-gown and hands it to Wendy. I can't believe what I'm seeing – Florence is standing completely naked apart from a pair of sturdy support pants. My initial response is to look away quickly but then curiosity gets the better of me. I turn back to see the wardrobe girl standing in front of Florence holding up a simple white sheet, with which she subtly tries to cover her as she climbs on to the table and lies down on the bench, covering her breasts but leaving her head and neck exposed.

Florence shuffles down on the bench. 'I'd better watch out for splinters,' she mutters as she tries to get comfortable, and then looks over in my direction to gauge my reaction.

Matt turns to look at me, eyebrows raised, as if to say, 'What on earth?', and I shake my head in disbelief.

A woman clutching a script is standing nearby and I whisper to her, 'Can you tell me what scene you're doing?'

'Yeah, sure,' she says helpfully. 'It's the one when the gran has died and Ed's older brother comes home – he's a medical student and he thinks it would be a wonderful opportunity to familiarise himself with the human body – you know, take a look and have a bit of a prod around.'

She looks at my shocked face. 'It's not real, you know.'

'I thought it was a comedy drama?'

'Well, that's quite funny.'

'Oh, right,' I say, unconvinced.

'Nothing really happens because Ed comes in and finds the brother about to do his own autopsy and stops it in time – it's a turning point for Ed.'

'Ahh,' I say as if it all makes perfect sense.

Vicks goes up to Florence and I hear her say, 'We're going to rehearse the shot, Florence, so don't worry about flickering eyes or heavy breathing. The camera will track round and we'll end on a deep two shot when we eventually get parallel with your head in foreground with Tom behind you. OK? Tom, you've got your mark and whatever happens you mustn't move off it.'

Florence nods. I see that Gabriel has manoeuvred Wendy over to the monitor where everyone is huddled close together, looking at the opening position of the camera.

'OK, everyone, it's a rehearsal . . . and action.'

The camera starts to move very slowly round the bench. The actor playing Tom enters the room and walks to his mark. He looks at Florence and picks up the sheet to look underneath, then reaches for a scalpel which is lying near to Florence's left hand. The camera stops moving, Tom picks up the scalpel as the door opens behind him, and Vicks, after checking with Gabriel, shouts, 'Excellent, everyone.'

She walks over to the table and touches Florence's hand. 'Not too cold?'

'It's the first time I've had erect nipples in years,' Florence says, and it's the only time I've seen Vicks at a loss for words. She quickly recovers – 'OK, everyone, happy with that?' – and looks over towards the monitor to see if Gabriel wants any changes. He seems happy enough but that might have something to do with the fact that Wendy is so close she's almost perching on his knee, pretending to be fascinated by something technical.

'Switch off the heaters.'

It suddenly seems very quiet in the studio. No one says a word, the concentration palpable, everyone focused on his or her particular job.

'Going for a take, turnover, ready . . . and action.'

This time Florence has her eyes shut and is lying very still. She seems to know instinctively when the camera reaches her head and she stops breathing. I find it unsettling, seeing her lying so still, playing dead, and I wonder what on earth would make her want to do something like this. The actor playing Tom has picked up the sheet but the scalpel has been placed just out of his reach and he's having trouble stretching to pick it up without moving off his mark. Suddenly a hand picks up the scalpel and gives it to him and the hand belongs to Florence.

'Cut,' shouts Vicks and everyone starts laughing.

Florence tries to sit up, clutching her sheet modestly around her. 'I'm sorry but I thought I could help him out.'

'Florence,' says Vicks in an exasperated tone, 'you can't help anyone do anything; you're supposed to be dead, love. Let's go again.'

Next time the shot seems to work very smoothly but at the end Vicks shouts, 'We're just going to check that back.' One of the runners looks anxiously at Florence whose lips are turning a shade of blue.

'It's very good makeup, isn't it?' says the girl with the script who was explaining things to me earlier.

'I'm not sure that's makeup, it's bloody freezing in here.' I'm concerned about Florence.

'Can I turn the heaters back on?' the runner asks Vicks.

'What – oh yes, of course.' The heaters roar into action.

'We need to do it one more time. Florence, it was fine, but there was a bit of flicker on the old eyelids.'

'Not so much of the old if you don't mind,' says Florence frostily.

'Sorry, love, but you know what I mean – try to relax them a bit more if you can.'

They do the shot three more times, making sure she doesn't

breathe at the wrong moment and that her eyelids are stuck firmly to her sockets.

When it's all finished Florence sits up and swings her legs round so that she's sitting on the bench, clutching the sheet around her. She looks cold and exhausted. I walk over to her and see that she's having difficulty breathing and her chest sounds congested.

'Oh Florence, you shouldn't be doing this.'

She tries to speak but she's having difficulty catching her breath.

'Don't try to speak. Do you think you can walk?' She looks at me, panic in her eyes as she nods her head.

'I'll get you a wheelchair.'

The makeup girl wraps Florence in her thick white towelling dressing-gown as I run to find Wendy. I can hear her saying, 'I was down to the last five hundred in *Pop Idol*. I'm thinking of trying for *Fame Academy* next year – I think it's a bit classier, don't you?' I interrupt her: 'Florence is not well – she needs a wheelchair to get her back to the trailer.'

Wendy reluctantly drags herself away from Gabriel but when she sees Florence she hurries over. 'Don't worry, darling,' she says, looking worried herself. 'We'll soon have you back home.'

A wheelchair materialises as if it's powering itself and then I see that the rather short but eager runner is pushing it. Between us we ease Florence into it – one of her arms round the young runner and the other round me. I've never seen her like this before and a feeling of panic surges through me as she's wheeled away and I follow in her wake. Outside the studio Jo is waiting for me.

'What happened?'

'Florence is not well,' I say.

'She didn't faint again?' Jo asks, looking worried. 'But she seemed fine this morning.'

'I don't know what's happening but I think we'd better get her back to Russell Court as soon as possible. I'll see you soon, Jo.' I kiss her goodbye. 'Take care.'

'Oh, I will.' She gives me a big smile, all eyes and teeth and no heart.

I travel with the crew, sitting in the back seat, and after Gerry scratches his head for the fourth time I say, 'I've got something to tell you both.' Matt gives me a worried look and Gerry looks nervous.

'No, it's nothing too bad, it's just . . . well, you know you're both scratching a lot?'

'Are we?' Gerry asks Matt. 'I hadn't really noticed.'

'Well, I think you might have nits.'

'Nits!' Matt slams on the brake at a zebra crossing to let a woman with a child in a pushchair cross.

'I had those when I was a kid,' Gerry says. 'Now that was itchy.' They both scratch their heads again.

'I discovered that Evie had them last night and she's probably had them for weeks. I've got a few and I suspect that you've caught them off me.'

'Bloody kids,' Matt grumbles. 'I knew there was a good reason not to have them.' Then, feeling guilty, he glances across at me and adds, 'Don't worry, at least it's nothing too serious.'

Twenty

Florence is awake when I peer round the door. She's staring out of the window, lost in thought, and doesn't hear my knock at first. I've left the crew downstairs so that we can have some time alone and I can find out how she's feeling. She's still dressed and sitting in her comfortable chair and she looks up at me, much frailer than I've ever seen her before.

'Come in, Molly dear. You look all flustered.'

'I'm fine, Florence – more to the point, how are you feeling?'

She leans her head against the back of the chair and closes her eyes. 'Tired.' Then she opens one eye. 'But still game.' I can't help but smile.

'Where are the others then?' she asks, looking for Matt and Gerry.

'Don't you ever stop?' I ask, amazed by her stamina.

'No, I'm like you,' she says. 'I feel in the mood for charades.'

I groan. 'Florence, don't be silly – you're exhausted. I don't think we'll do any more filming today but we'll come back tom—'

'I want to have you all in here,' she growls at me, and I'm surprised by her vehemence. As an afterthought she adds, 'Please' through gritted teeth. Not wanting to upset her, I go downstairs and galvanise the crew, who are playing a game in the hall which involves rolling a small reel of masking tape into a paper cup from a vending machine. The inventiveness of crews never ceases to amaze me.

'Your go, Molly,' says Gerry.

'Florence wants to see us all.'

'Are we going to do any more filming?' asks Matt surprised.

'Oh God, I don't know – I would have thought she was exhausted after today's efforts but she wants us all in there and

I haven't got the energy to disagree. Come and give me some moral support.'

Matt puts his arm around me and gives me a friendly hug, then moves his head away. 'I suppose I shouldn't get too close – never know what else I might catch.'

'I'm really sorry, guys.'

'It's all right, I'll charge the nit comb to expenses,' Matt says.

'Do you need a hand carrying anything?' I ask, as if to compensate for giving them nits.

'Oh, don't you worry, my lady – we'll manage.' Gerry tugs at an imaginary forelock and then screams as if there are thousands of little animals running up his arm. He pretends to shake them off just as Eleanor the home manager walks past. When he sees her he stops immediately and smiles as if nothing has happened and she looks at him with the expression you would use to indulge an overactive child. Gerry and Matt somehow always manage to make me feel better, like a couple of brothers who tease me and stop me taking myself too seriously. We chatter together as we walk up the grand staircase, trying hard not to scrape the portraits and the playbills with the camera boxes as we pass them, and as we get closer to Florence's room we fall silent. She's waiting for us, still awake.

'Would you like a cup of tea, Florence?' I suggest.

'No, what I fancy is a game of charades. I'll start.'

Resigned, we all find places to sit – Matt on the edge of the bed, Gerry on an upturned camera box, and me on the arm of a chair, an unenthusiastic audience. Florence makes a circling motion with her arms to indicate 'the whole concept' and puts up two fingers to show us that it's two words and then three syllables.

'Wait a minute, is it a play, book, film or a TV programme?'

She puts her finger to her lips to indicate that we should be quiet. Very shakily she gets to her feet and pretends to lift up her imaginary skirts. She points her toes and makes a circling motion and then very slowly kicks one leg in the air and then the other.

'Dance,' Gerry suggests, and Florence nods encouragingly at him.

'Is it a type of dance?' I ask.

She nods her head and turns her back to us, then pretends to fling her skirts in the air and wiggles her bottom.

'Cancan?' says Matt, slightly bemused.

She turns quickly and points at him, then puts her hands together so that they're almost touching, as a sign that the word should be shorter. The effort is exhausting her and I wish she would sit down and rest – we can play games tomorrow – but now there's a strange and determined sense of urgency in her manner.

'Can,' says Matt, and Florence smiles her assent. She then stands to attention like a soldier and salutes an imaginary officer.

'Salute,' I suggest, and she shakes her head and repeats the action.

'Soldier,' says Gerry, and Florence nods her head from side to side as if to say we're on the right track.

'Sir,' I shout as she salutes again, and she claps her hands together as if applauding me.

'Can . . . sir,' I say, putting the two words together. Florence looks at me and very quickly she puts up two fingers to indicate she's on to the second word and she touches her ear to make the 'sounds like' sign. She then mimes a noose going round her neck and pulling tight, and her head drops.

'Hung,' says Matt quietly. He's quicker than I am at realising what Florence is doing.

'Lung,' I say slowly as Florence gently eases herself back into the chair. For a second she catches my eye to see if I've understood.

'Lung cancer,' I say slowly. My throat constricts as I say the words. I'm finding it hard to speak or breathe as the impact of what she's telling us hits me. Florence rests her head back on the chair and turns away from all of us. Matt looks at me, comprehending everything that's been said, but Gerry clearly hasn't understood a word. He looks anxiously from one to another of us like a child longing for an explanation. I don't know what to say – I'm winded by emotion and all I can do is look at the floor and watch the swirly pattern of the chocolate-brown carpet swim before my eyes as they swell with tears.

Twenty-one

There's something soothing about sitting in Eleanor's office. Maybe it's to do with the tidy desk, the ordered bookshelves and the gleaming clean surfaces and quiet, regular ticking of the clock on the mantelpiece. I understand and have always understood that Eleanor is in control and I'm hoping that she will be able to explain everything to me, to make things clear.

'How long have you known?'

'For the past four months. She was diagnosed at the beginning of October, a week before filming started.'

'With Robin?'

'Yes,' says Eleanor, tight-lipped with disapproval at the memory of the Boy Wonder.

'Why didn't you say anything?'

'Mrs Bird didn't want us to.'

'So that's why we couldn't film on Thursdays, because that was when she went to see the consultant?'

'Yes.'

She is not wasting any words on me, feeding information on a need-to-know basis.

'Can't they do anything – surgery, chemotherapy?'

'It wouldn't be worth it, and she made the decision to have some quality of life before she dies.'

'How long . . . ?' I can't finish my sentence, but Eleanor knows what I'm asking.

'I'm not sure. The figure six months was mentioned.'

'Could it be longer?'

'Maybe. Maybe less. You can never tell in these situations.'

'I never would have guessed she was that ill.'

'She didn't want you to.'

'Does she talk about it with you?' I ask, finding it hard to imagine Florence and Eleanor having intimate conversations about anything.

'No – I don't think she talks about it with anyone.'

'Is it definite? I mean, could there be some mistake?'

She shakes her head.

Suddenly I feel a wave of anger. How typical of Florence to break the news to us like this, and how dare she do this? For a minute a ridiculous thought crosses my mind and I think, I won't let her – I'm not going to let her die.

Eleanor is watching me and her expression softens. 'You've become close – you and Florence.'

'I suppose so,' I say, still feeling angry.

'It's OK – it's normal to feel like this.' I'm surprised by her sympathetic tone – this is a side to her I've never seen before.

'I'm not sure what I should do.' It's half question, half statement.

The sympathetic manner dissolves as quickly as it came. 'Well, that's for you to work out, but if you don't mind, I know that I've got a hundred and one things to do before the end of the day,' and I am dismissed efficiently from her office.

I stand for a few minutes outside her door, unsure what to do or where to go. I walk slowly down the corridor and as I pass one door I look in to see Elspeth lying in bed without her trademark turban, her long grey hair splayed out on the pillow. With her beautiful eyes closed, she looks unlike herself, ordinary. She's muttering, and as if aware of my presence she opens her eyes.

'Have you come to see me?' she asks with obvious delight, although she's speaking slowly, her voice frail.

'I was just passing.'

'Will you come and see me soon? I would so like it.' She points to a bowl on her dressing-table which I can see is full of sweets as if to tempt me. Prompted more by guilt than desire, I go into her room and stand beside the bed and she leans back, her head on the pillow.

'How are you feeling, Elspeth?'

'I've felt better – I just can't get rid of this chest infection, it's very debilitating.' She slowly enunciates every syllable. 'I've lost my "zing".' She's slurring slightly, and thinking I haven't heard her properly I ask, 'Your what?'

'My "zing", my spark, my zest for life. I just haven't got the energy any more.' Her long bony arm, the veins bulging, drops down beside the bed and she lets it hang there as if she can't muster the energy to pull it up again.

I look around, searching for something to say. 'You've got a lovely room.' My words sound hollow and my heart is still bursting with Florence's news.

'They move me around a bit,' she says slowly, as if she's surfacing from a drug-induced sleep.

'Is that upsetting?'

'No, I like it, it reminds me of touring. I never liked staying in the same place for too long, far too boring for me,' she says sleepily. Her eyelids droop and eventually close and from the sound of her deep rasping breaths I realise that she's fallen asleep, so I quietly leave her room, closing the door behind me.

I find myself walking along the corridor and out of the front door and instead of going to the car park I turn right, through a gate in the brick wall and into the gardens. I do up the buttons on my coat, tie my scarf round my neck and stride off towards a cluster of oak trees. It's the end of a dull grey January day and although it's cold it's a relief to be outside. The grounds are deserted and I feel like I'm the only person alive in this twilight world. I sit down on a bench under the trees, my back to Russell Court, and I put my hand out to touch one of the trees; the feel of the sturdy, rough bark is reassuringly solid, reliable. There's no colour in the gardens except for a sludgy green – even the sweeping lawns look grey, the stark trees stripped of leaves as the light fails.

The phone in my pocket rings, its trigger-happy tone crudely puncturing the silence. It sounds unnaturally loud out here under the trees.

'Hi, Molly?' I don't recognise the distant voice on the other end of the line and I pause, struggling to work out who it is. 'It's Bill.'

'Oh,' I say disingenuously.

'How are you?'

'Not great, and you?'

'Not great either. I guess you know?'

'Yes, I know.'

'Eleanor just rang me and said that you'd been told.'

Silence, but I can hear him moving, breathing far away, the other side of the world.

'I wish you'd told me.'

'Molly, I couldn't. I promised her I wouldn't.' He sounds very close. 'Now do you see why I was so upset about the filming? I couldn't believe she'd agreed to it.'

'I thought it was me you had a problem with.'

There's another pause the other end of the line. 'Now that's just being paranoid.' He pauses again. 'Look, I'm sorry I haven't called before, I just thought you'd prefer it if I didn't.'

'Yes, you're probably right.'

'I had to come back home anyway – I thought about ringing to say goodbye but I felt too awkward about the whole thing. I didn't know what to say. I still don't.' He goes quiet.

'How's everything back there?' I say, making polite conversation.

'Difficult, and to be honest I'm all over the place.'

I suddenly feel a wave of sympathy for him. 'Are you coming back?'

'Yes, but it's so difficult to get the timing right. She's very insistent that life should go on as usual. I want to be there but I'm having to travel a lot for work at the moment.'

'They're long trips too,' I add.

'Some of them.' Then he pauses.

'How many days does it take to get to the moon?' He can hear the smile in my voice.

'Sorry?'

'It must be very tricky for you astronauts.'

I hear him chuckle. 'Oh yeah, right. Molly?' I love the way he says my name – there's something appealing about his slight Canadian accent. 'Do you want to know what I really do?'

'No, I don't think I do.'

'OK,' he says slowly. 'I don't know when I'm coming back but I speak to Florence nearly every day and Eleanor gives me updates, which are a little more revealing than my mother's.'

'Does Florence talk about it to you?'

'It?'

'You know what I mean.'

'Nope, we've never discussed it.'

'Never? Not even when she told you?'

'She didn't tell me, Eleanor did. It's what my mother wanted.'

'God, that must be so difficult for you – aren't there things you want to discuss, things you need to say?'

'I think she knows all the important stuff.' He doesn't sound sure. 'Are you going to carry on with the film?'

'I don't know – I can't imagine Florence will want to now,' I say.

'I don't know about that – nothing has changed for her, so why would she want to stop filming?'

'But . . . oh, I see,' I say, realising for the first time that of course Florence has known all along, so nothing has changed for her except that now we all know. 'What do you think she'll want us to do?'

'Carry on.'

'What . . . see it through?'

'Yes.'

'Why? I don't understand why she would want that.' My heart is pounding and I feel sick at the thought of watching Florence every step of the way, getting thinner and weaker, losing her spirit and eventually fading away.

'I'm not sure – I keep asking myself the same thing and the only thing I can think of is that it's got something to do with putting it all off. The reason that she wanted to do the film, even after the initial upset with the Boy Wonder, was that it was her way of delaying the inevitable. Maybe she thought that if she was being filmed the worst couldn't happen.'

'It sounds almost superstitious.'

'Well, no – I think it's plain and simple denial. She knows that she's very ill but she can't really believe it – she just can't accept it. I can understand that.'

'So is it a good thing for us to continue filming?'

'I can't answer that. You need to talk with my mother.'

'I'm looking forward to that conversation.'

Bill laughs and then says seriously, 'I can't do it, I've tried but she doesn't want to know. It's between you and her.'

'And potentially millions of viewers.'

It's getting hard to see and I realise how cold I feel. I look at my watch. 'I'm sorry, I've got to go.'

'Of course,' he says, resigned. 'It was good to talk to you. And Molly?'

'Yes?'

'Will you call me as things change?'

'Yes, I will.'

'I'm glad we've talked.'

'Me too.'

Neither of us wants to say goodbye.

'I must go.'

'Yes, you said.'

'OK then. Bye.'

'Bye, Molly.'

I put my phone into my pocket and turn to walk back to my car. In the fading light the outline of Russell Court looms ominously before me, some of the windows illuminated. I look up, trying to work out which one is Florence's room. I know she's on a corner about four floors up and just as I've found it the light switches off. I rearrange my scarf, check the car keys in my pocket and walk back to the car park.

It was my father who told me that you should make a wish if you were lucky enough to be under a bridge when a train was passing over. When I was little, every day on my way home from school we had to walk through a small tunnel under a railway bridge. It was dank and dark and I was very scared of the noise the train made and would hold my hands over my ears until I was sure that it was long gone. My father probably made the whole thing up to make me feel better, but it worked, especially when my wishes began to come true. It was when Susan O'Connell got chickenpox and I was made captain of the rounders team that I knew that he must be right. Eventually I began to linger under the bridge waiting for the trains, storing up my wishes.

I'm nearly home, and looking over the tops of the cars driving sedately in front of me I can hear the familiar rumble that announces the imminent arrival of a train. I put my foot on the accelerator so I'm nearly nudging the bumper of the car in front. I see the driver looking anxiously into his mirror as I edge closer, and I wonder what I'm going to wish for. I run through the options – that the children are healthy, that Cassie feels better, that Aidan's script isn't as bad as I think it is, that this film is a big success or that Florence doesn't . . . ? I can't bring myself to think it, let alone say it. I can see the front of the train beginning to cross the bridge. I accelerate, but the train doesn't check its speed as it twists and turns, rattling on its way, and with a flick of its tail the last carriage disappears into the distance. I drive under the bridge, silent now, the train long gone, the desire for a wish replaced by an even deeper longing to see my father again.

Although it's late I can guarantee that Rod will still be at work. He doesn't have a personal life or if he does, it's a limited one and usually connected to someone with whom he's been filming. He has been married three times and London is littered with his children. When I ring him on my mobile he is typically curt.

'Yup.'

'Rod, I need to see you.'

'When?'

'Now.'

'OK – bye.' He puts the phone down before I can explain.

Now, as I sit in his office waiting for him to get off the phone, he's being equally abrupt while rolling his eyes at me to indicate that the person on the other end of the line is an idiot. I make a mental note never to talk long enough on the phone to give him the chance to make a mockery of me in this way.

Then Rod surprises me by suddenly slamming the phone down. 'God, why can't people make their own decisions and stop bothering me all the time?'

'Problems in an edit?' I say, trying to be sympathetic.

'No, my brother trying to decide whether to put my mother in a home because she's gone gaga,' he says without an ounce of compassion, and I wonder whether it was such a good idea to come and consult him after all.

'So what did you want to see me about?' He turns his freckled face to me, his eyes glinting, the eyelashes so pale that they're almost invisible. There's something predatory about Rod; he reminds me of the foxy gentleman in *The Tale of Jemima Puddleduck.*

'I've got a bit of a problem and I needed to ask your opinion.'

'Oh, not another one – can't you sort it out by yourself?' he says, exasperated.

'Well, I can, but I think that in your capacity as executive producer you need to be involved in this decision.'

'Well, go on, what is it?' and just as I start to tell him he interrupts me. 'It's nothing personal, is it? Only I don't want to know about childcare issues or marital problems – I'm not that sort of boss,' he says with disgust. No, I'm wrong, at least the foxy gentleman pretended to be interested in Jemima's problems before he lured her into his den.

'No, don't worry – it's nothing like that.' I hesitate and then dive in. 'But it's bad news. I'm afraid that Florence has just told me she's got lung cancer.'

'Oh, I see,' he says. I watch him digest the information. 'And who's Florence?'

'Florence – you know, Florence Bird – the old actress I'm filming with at the moment,' I say, irritated by his callous approach.

'Oh yes, of course ... OH, I see,' he says, understanding at last why I'm telling him. 'How long has she got?'

'Well, she was given six months but that was four months ago.'

'Mmm, good, OK.'

I can't believe what I'm hearing. 'Good' – what is he talking about?

'Why is that good?' I ask, thinking that perhaps he hasn't understood what I'm saying.

He doesn't answer the question but checks his palm organiser as if he's finding the right place to write in the due date. I feel exasperated.

'And the problem is ... ?' he asks me blankly.

'My problem is this.' I'm having to fight very hard not to shout at him. 'What should I do? Should I carry on filming or should we stop?'

Rod looks like I've squeezed his bollocks. 'Stop?' he says incredulously, 'Are you mad? God, this is perfect, it's exactly what we need. I hoped something like this would happen. A death would be great for the ratings,' he says, and I can see he's planning the programme billing already, honing his BAFTA acceptance speech. I knew he was ambitious but I'm shocked by his callousness. He's pacing up and down, full of enthusiasm. 'No, this is good – really good. I'll just have to juggle the budgets to get some more money for you to extend your filming period but it's worth it for this. It's what the programme needs, Molly – it's not going to be boring now.'

He looks at me, his face shining with excitement. 'We need to see death on television – proper death, I mean, none of this EastEnders nonsense or hospital dramas with all that tomato ketchup rubbish – I mean plain, honest death – the sort that happens to most of us.'

'Do we?' I ask, my stomach sinking at the thought that I might have to be the person to do this. 'Why?'

'Why?' he says, looking surprised I should even ask the question. 'Because everyone is so fucking scared of it – but isn't it the most natural thing in the world? We all run screaming from the room rather than talk about it. It's the final taboo – we're happy enough to talk about sex and money but death is a "no no" – the big unmentionable. It's as if we think if we don't talk about it we can put it off and pretend it doesn't really happen. We're living in a ridiculous age, Molly, where people will take desperate measures to try and keep young and beautiful – just look at Lesley Ash's lips. We need to remind people how to grow old gracefully, to accept the inevitable and not to fight it, and it's up to us to bring death out of the closet. Only a hundred years ago it would have been considered normal to lose at least a couple of siblings, and the chances of all your children surviving were minimal. In those days everyone learnt to live with it, death was part of life, but nowadays it's all hidden away and we're protected from it, which only serves to make it much more frightening.' He pauses, but before I get a chance to say anything he continues his speech. 'I mean, it would be different if she was a young woman but she's not – she's had a good life and it's coming to a natural end. She has to make room for the next generation. It is an entirely natural process and you, you lucky thing, can capture every minute of it on film right up to her dying breath.'

I want to cry but I'm not going to give him the satisfaction. Instead, I sit stunned into silence, not only by what he's saying but also by the enthusiasm with which he's saying it. I was so desperate to make this film but, unbelievably, I never thought of the possible outcome. Obviously there was always the likelihood that something might happen to Florence – after all, she is eighty-three years old – but she has always been such a splendid life force that I can't imagine that stopping.

'Dying peacefully in your sleep – I mean, how often does that happen? I want to know what a normal death is really like, if there is such a thing. Is it one big agonising struggle or can it be a welcome release? Don't you see, if we know what to expect it will be less frightening. This could be public service broadcasting at its best.'

Rod continues to talk excitedly, his mouth opening and closing, none of it reaching my ears. 'Molly.' He is standing inches away from me. 'Are you listening to me?'

I look up into his face and say slowly, 'Has anyone close to you ever died?'

He looks at me blankly, then thinks for a minute and shakes his head.

I get up, put on my jacket and say very calmly, 'I don't think I can do this.'

At last I've silenced him and he stares at me, speechless, his mouth open, his eyes unable to comprehend what I've just said. I don't stay to hear his response but walk briskly out of his office, down the corridor and into the lift before anyone can stop me.

There are no bridges on the way home and even if there were I'm not sure I'd notice them. I don't see the road ahead, only a pair of hands clawing at the air as if trying to stop it from escaping, to keep it secure, holding on to life. I know the hands belong to my father and I'm shaking, aware that my own palms are sweaty as they slip on the steering wheel. I don't want to have to think about this. I've put it out of my mind for seven years, suppressing the images when they surface, pushing them down, drowning the memory.

By the time I get back the children are fast asleep and Aidan is on the phone ordering a Chinese takeaway and I'm not even sure it's for both of us. He doesn't look up when I shut the front door so I go straight upstairs to Evie's room and rearrange her purple duvet, which is about to slip off the bed on to the floor. She mutters in her sleep and turns over, pulling the duvet back to exactly the same position it was in when I went into the room. I stroke her head and tuck a stray strand of blonde hair behind her ear, and even though she's sleeping she still manages to look cross that I'm fiddling with her hair.

*

Max in the bedroom next to ours is flat on his back, free-falling through his dreams. When I go in he opens his eyes and stares right through me, registering nothing. 'No, Evie – it's mine,' he says, and then turns over and goes straight back to sleep.

I run myself a bath and half expect Aidan to come up and say hello but he doesn't. I turn out the lights because I don't want to see myself. I quickly get into the bath – the water is almost too hot to bear but I step in, punishing myself, lying back and submerging my head as if washing away the disturbing thoughts of my father.

After my bath I feel too tired to go downstairs but I know I ought to eat something and I need to face Aidan. Again he doesn't look at me but says grudgingly, 'There's some Chinese in the oven.'

'Thanks.' I can hardly speak I'm so exhausted, but trying to make the effort I say, 'Listen, I want to read your script.'

'Oh, don't bother – you're right, it's crap.'

'No it's not – I mean I'm sure it's not,' I say, correcting myself. I take the plastic dishes out of the oven that have been warped by the heat and start helping myself to crispy fried beef and noodles.

'I've had a terrible day,' say Aidan.

'Well, that makes two of us.'

'My laptop crashed for no reason – I've lost at least two scenes and I can't find a hard copy of the script. They've all disappeared.'

I haven't the energy to be sympathetic. It all seems so insignificant.

'I've had some bad news.'

We're like children playing paper, scissors, stone.

'Florence has got lung cancer.'

My voice breaks as I say the words and I push my plate away, feeling sick at the thought of food. For the first time that evening Aidan looks at me. 'Oh God.'

We say very little to each other for the rest of the short evening we have left, but later in bed he reaches over to me and pulls me close to him so I can feel the contours of his body. He kisses the back of my neck and I feel nothing but weary reluctance, but as he starts to trace his finger up and down my back I'm surprised that I begin to feel desire and I turn to face him. He moves to kiss me but I turn my head to one side, and then for the first time in months we make love.

Twenty-two

Portobello Road is quieter than usual and my mother looks glum sitting behind her stall wearing a Russian hat and thick grey scarf. Her face lights up as I approach.

'Molly, I didn't expect to see you today, how lovely – come and sit down.' She pats the stool beside her. Even though she's been looking after the children full-time she hasn't missed a single Saturday at the market and I'm impressed by her dedication. I squeeze round the table, careful not to knock into any of her stock. I feel exhausted, and although Aidan seemed happy enough this morning, humming to himself as he shaved, last night did nothing to alleviate my mood.

'How's business?' I ask my mother.

'Terrible – it's been bad for months now.'

'Is that because you haven't been able to concentrate on it?' I say, feeling guilty.

'No, everyone says the same. The Americans have stopped coming over and the bottom has fallen out of the market. It's getting very hard to find any new stock. I've only bought one new thing in the last two months. If it carries on like this I think I'm going to have to give it up.' She looks deflated at the thought.

'That's so sad,' I say, sitting down beside her.

She shrugs. 'I just can't afford to do it any more – I'll miss it dreadfully.'

I've learnt in the past that the way to cheer her up is to talk about the stock – she loves it with such a passion.

'What's the new thing you've bought?'

Her face lights up as she bends under her table and takes a small rectangular shape wrapped in newspaper out of a brown crate. Very gingerly she unwraps the newspaper to reveal proudly a small brass box with fine filigree engraving of flowers on the top. In the centre is a small oval lid, which she dusts off with a cloth, carefully turning it to clean all the surfaces. A chunky brass key is sellotaped to the bottom of the box and she pulls it off and places it in the hole in the side to wind it up, before putting it back down on the table. Nothing happens. We both stare at it. She lifts it and bangs it on the table but still nothing happens.

'Oh, bugger it. It must need a polish or something. It was working perfectly yesterday.'

'Mum, I haven't got long – I just wanted to see you.'

'You're not ill, are you?' she says anxiously.

'No, nothing like that. I'm fine.' I wonder why I've come. 'Look, I've just been told that Florence has got lung cancer and only has a few months left.'

'Oh, I'm sorry – that's awful – poor thing.' She looks visibly relieved that it's nothing to do with the children or me.

'What's worrying me is whether I should carry on making the film.'

'I see.'

'My boss is determined I should, in fact he's positively delighted – he thinks it will be good for the ratings.'

'I don't want to watch that sort of thing on television.'

'Don't you?' I ask, genuinely interested.

'Absolutely not.'

'Why not?'

'I want to be entertained.'

'Yes, I understand that, but isn't there a place for illuminating documentaries which can help us understand our lives a little better?'

'Our lives?'

'Well, all right, and our deaths – I mean it's part of life, isn't it? Rod thinks that if we show it and talk about it it will take away some of the fear. He might have a point.'

My mother starts polishing an inkwell and I can tell she's uncomfortable talking like this. 'Maybe it's a little too close to home,' she says.

'The thing is, I don't think Florence will talk to me about it, and if I'm going to carry on filming she is going to have to open up – after all, that's the point of the film, according to my boss. You don't like talking about these sort of things so what I wanted to ask you is why not? Why do you think she doesn't want to talk about it?' I turn to my mother, as always hoping she'll be able to help.

'Talk – what is there to say? Why is everyone so obsessed with talking about things?'

'Maybe it is a generational thing. Surely sometimes it could be a good thing?'

'Perhaps, but it's gone mad. All this counselling rubbish – I think it makes it worse. Didn't I read something the other day about some study they've done that's discovered that counselling after a national disaster like Zeebrugge compounds the problem, and makes it harder for people to move on with their lives? What do you want her to say, Molly?'

'Well, I suppose I'd like to know how she feels.'

'Oh God,' she laughs, in fact it sounds more like a derisory snort.

'Do you think it's something to do with your generation? A legacy from the war years when everyone had lived under the constant threat of death so that the only way to carry on was not to acknowledge it and to be grateful for what they had. Stiff upper lip and all that?'

'Maybe,' she says, pursing her lips.

'Don't you think it might help some people to hear someone talking about what it's like when you've only got a few months left to live? It is an undeniable truth that we are all going to die, so this might help prepare us and make it less terrifying.' I'm thinking out loud now and surprising myself.

'Sometimes there just aren't the words, and if there's nothing you can do about it what good does it do to talk about the inevitable?'

'Well, like Dad – we never talk about that.'

'What is there to say?' She looks down and I can see her hands are shaking.

'I'm sorry, Mum, I don't want to upset you.' Being wedged next to her on this tiny stool there isn't enough room to turn and look at her properly. 'And because we never talk about him it's as if he never existed. He is well and truly gone.'

'There are some things you just can't talk about, they're too personal.'

'Perhaps I need to talk about it.' I look at her closed face. 'I suppose I just want some advice,' I say hopelessly.

She picks up the box, starts polishing the brass engravings and changes the subject without looking at me. 'How's Aidan?'

'Oh, OK,' I reply.

Now she's looking at me and she leans towards me and says, 'Sometimes it's more important to know when to speak and when to stay silent. I hate to make generalisations, but you know the trouble with your generation is that you all talk too much and give up too easily.'

The box in front of her bursts into life: the lid flies open and a tiny bird with bright blue and green feathers flaps its wings and sings. It's not a tune but the sound of real birdsong, and for at least ten seconds it twists and turns, singing its heart out, until the lid slams shut and we're left in silence. My mother gives my knee a reassuring pat and I detect a smile in the corner of her lips as she puts the box back into its position on the shelf.

I'm sitting at Cassie's kitchen table watching her fill her kettle and thinking that this may possibly be the first time we've been alone together for a very long time. After last night Aidan is being very sensitive, and when I came back from seeing my mother, still no wiser about what I should do, it was he who suggested I should ring Cassie.

'I think Rod has a point. People are terrified of death but it is a natural process.' Cassie plugs in the kettle and turns to face me. 'There have been a couple of films about death but I think they concentrated on the physical aspects, what exactly happens when you die. This would be more emotional.'

I'm amazed by the ease with which she talks about it. 'So you think I should film Florence right up to the end until she pops her clogs?' I'm trying to make light of it despite the fact that I feel faint just talking about it.

'Yes – if she wants you to film, which I expect she does.'

'I don't think I can do it.'

'Well, that's your decision. What is it exactly that bothers you about it?'

'Everything – I don't want to think about it.'

'I've been thinking a lot about it recently,' Cassie says without any emotion in her voice. 'Particularly about choosing when you die.'

'Most people don't have a choice.'

'But they do – we all have the choice. Under the right circumstances I think it's understandable.'

'What would be the right circumstances?' I ask, worried by the direction this conversation is taking.

'I don't understand why people get so upset about it. Speaking entirely rationally, if I choose to end it all and make sure it's not too upsetting for anyone discovering me, then isn't that my choice? It's not as if I've got any dependants, my parents are dead, there's no one close.'

Steam shoots out of the spout of the kettle and the lid rattles. 'It's broken,' says Cassie, 'it can't switch itself off.' I watch her take two mugs out of the cupboard.

'When you say no one close, what about us, your friends?' I say, surprised and appalled that we're having such a normal conversation about something so terrible.

'I know you'd be upset but you'd get over it.' Her practical tone distresses me. 'Cup of tea?' she asks, holding out the box of tea bags.

'How can you say that?'

'I thought you might be thirsty.'

'No, I don't mean that. Is this just a joke? You're not really serious, are you?' I can feel the anger starting to rise.

'Yes I am – deadly serious.' She smiles at the unintentional joke. 'I'm not religious and I don't think life is sacrosanct – my death is not going to make much difference to the way things are. I don't see the problem and it strikes me there's almost something empowering about choosing when you're going to die.'

'Cassie, I know that you're having a difficult time at the moment but it will change. Things always change. I don't understand why you're talking like this.'

'I'm not talking about topping myself tomorrow, it's an academic exercise. Don't get so worked up – all I'm saying is that in principle I don't see why I can't stop, if I want to. I'm thinking of joining EXIT.'

'I used to have this thing that when I was ecstatically happy I'd think to myself, "OK, I could die now – this is as good as it gets,"' I say, thinking that it has been a long time since I have felt like that.

'So you see my point?' She hands me a mug of tea.

'No, it's completely different. I'd never think about doing something like that; I think it's a cop-out.'

'Why is taking your own life a cop-out? It's incredibly brave if you think about it.'

I can't seem to get through to her and I'm struggling to communicate what I know to be crucially important. I want to make her understand but my frustration is making me inarticulate.

'I think there's something implicitly wrong with us sitting here drinking tea talking about this when Florence is . . . well, you know . . . she'd love to have more time and here you are being cavalier with it.' I take a sip of the tea and burn my lip because it's too hot.

'I'm not the one being emotional about this. All I'm saying is that it wouldn't be the end of the world if I decided to die.'

'That's exactly what it would be, you daft cow. I think you should go and see someone – maybe you've got a chemical imbalance or something. I can't believe we're even having this conversation.'

My mobile phone rings, making me jump. 'Hello?' I say angrily.

'Molly, Rod here.'

My heart sinks.

'Just want to know what's happening.'

'I'm going to see Florence tomorrow to discuss it and then I'll let you know.'

'OK, but Molly, remember – to be a really good documentary film-maker you have to be able to detach yourself emotionally.'

'Yes, Rod, but what does that make you as a person?' I say, thinking that he should talk to my children about my ability to detach emotionally, as I feel very distant from them at the moment. I glance across at Cassie and wonder whether the emotional detachment she has learnt from being a successful documentary producer is the reason she can talk so calmly and rationally about the possibility of her own death.

Rod doesn't react to my comment but says instead, 'If you can't deal with this then I'm going to take you off the project.'

I want to say, 'Yeah, and how easy is that going to be? I've gained Florence's trust – it's me she wants,' but as if reading my thoughts he says, 'No one is indispensable – I'll do it myself if I have to.'

'I'll call you when I've seen her.'

We both put the phone down, neither of us saying goodbye. I look at my dear friend sitting opposite me stirring her tea as if she's just told me she's thinking about taking a holiday. She looks up and holds my gaze.

'Don't worry. Go and see Florence, talk to her, maybe you'll feel differently.'

'And you, will you feel differently?'

'Don't worry about me, I'm fine.'

But I don't believe her.

Twenty-three

As soon as I walk into Russell Court, I can sense the change in atmosphere, like tapping an emotional barometer. I meet Comfort pushing an empty wheelchair through the grand hall.

'I think you've lost something,' I try and joke, indicating the empty chair, but for once Comfort doesn't smile.

'Are you all right, Comfort?' I ask, concerned.

'I'm afraid Elspeth passed away this morning,' she says in a baritone voice that could lull a teething baby to sleep in seconds.

'Oh, I'm so sorry.' I feel awkward, inarticulate, and I stand back for her to pass. As I walk along the corridor I come to Elspeth's room where I last saw her alive. The door is closed and I wonder if she's still lying there. Heart pounding, I walk faster, willing my feet to take me towards Florence's room, although I'd give anything just to leave Russell Court and never come back.

I'm quite anxious about seeing Florence. It's the first time we've spoken since she broke the news and I don't know how to behave. I bought some white roses on the way here and now I'm regretting my decision as I've never bought flowers for her before and it will only draw attention to the way things have changed. I knock on her door, feeling sick to my stomach.

'Who is it?'

'Me, Molly,' I say, clearing my throat.

'About bloody time.' She sounds more amused than annoyed.

I push open the door, unsure what to expect, but I'm surprised to see Florence sitting in her chair smiling.

'Molly, my dear, I thought you'd deserted me.' And without pausing to let me answer her she says, 'Did you see this?'

She takes off her glasses and hands me a letter with neat childish handwriting, which to my surprise I recognise to be Evie's. 'Such a lovely letter. Has she started using the camera yet?'

'She's taken some photos of the beanie toys in her bedroom and some of Max. She did ask me the other day if it would be possible to take a photo of her liver.'

Florence looks surprised.

'They're learning about the human body at school,' I explain. 'This week it's the heart and last week was the liver. She got very cross with me when I said that it might be a bit difficult to take a picture of her own liver. She just pointed out that she'd seen lots of photos of livers and I was just being mean not letting her take a picture of hers. But I have to say she's thrilled with the camera, it was very kind of you.'

I've been gabbling because I am nervous, but Florence is listening and nodding. 'Maybe she'd take one of you – I'd like that.'

'I'll have a word with her, but I'm not sure she'd think that I'm a very interesting subject.'

There's an uncomfortable pause.

'Oh, I bought you these,' I say, remembering the flowers.

'You didn't need to do that.'

We're both being very polite with each other.

'Shall I find a vase for them?'

'There's one in the bathroom.'

I put the flowers down on the chest of drawers and as I'm in the bathroom searching in the cupboards Florence says, 'Have you heard about Elspeth?'

She's changed the subject and caught me off guard. I'm glad she can't see my face.

'Yes, Comfort just told me. I'm very sorry.' I feel terrible – I just don't have the vocabulary and all I can do is keep repeating the same inadequate phrase.

'It's very unsettling,' Florence says, sounding distracted. 'I went and saw her last night and she didn't look marvellous but I didn't think she was that bad.'

'No, I didn't realise she was so ill,' I say, as if making casual conversation.

'It was pneumonia – it gets a lot of us in here.'

But not you, I think to myself.

'You know,' Florence continues, 'there's a kind of unwritten rule that when you get ill you keep to your room. You don't rub people's noses in it, don't remind them of what may happen. If you haven't got the energy for a good final performance then you have to hide away out of courtesy.'

'She was a good friend of yours, wasn't she?' I say, still in the bathroom. I've found the vase and I fill it up with water from the tap and walk through to start arranging the roses.

'She made me laugh. Elspeth was one of my regulars – I could always rely on her and she added a bit of colour to the place.'

Florence fumbles for her glasses and I notice that her hands are shakier than usual. 'You should go and have a look at the photographs in her room before they clear it out. They all wanted to photograph her – Norman Parkinson, Angus McBean, Cecil Beaton.' She pauses. 'It's so hard to imagine that she's no longer here,' she says, sounding bemused.

I know that I have to seize the moment, be brave and say something. 'Florence, we need to talk.'

'Of course.'

I feel relieved that she's not going to make it difficult for me.

'Now, what do you want to talk about?' she says, looking at me innocently.

'Florence, please.' I sit down on the side of the bed and look at her face. I know all her wrinkles, the way her mouth can curl up at the side when she's amused, and I've studied her eyes, the colour of sea on a stormy day. 'What you told us the other day . . . well, we're all shocked by the news.' I'm stammering and still finding it impossible to find the right phrases. 'I still can't believe it, especially when I see you looking . . . well . . . looking so well. But you must understand that now everything has changed there are things we need to discuss.'

'Like what?' She's looking at me and doing that thing with

her eyes again when she doesn't blink, which is very disconcerting.

'Like, do you want us to continue filming?'

She looks at me, amazed. 'But of course.'

'Are you sure? Because if we do we can't just pretend nothing is wrong. If we continue I've got to ask you about being ill, and they want us to film everything, and I mean everything.' I emphasise the word. 'Have you really thought it through?'

She sighs. 'What is there to talk about?'

'There's lots to talk about – how you feel about it for a start.'

She raises an eyebrow, '"It", Molly? I think this bothers you as much as it does me.'

'Maybe, but I'm not the one being filmed. Do you really want the whole world to see everything?'

'I know you're a good film-maker but even you don't get such good ratings, Molly.' Sensing my frustration and before I can say anything she says, 'What, so you're pulling out – you want to stop?'

'Yes, I mean no, I think we should carry on and do some in-depth interviews when you can talk more about your life and what you've learnt and speak frankly of what it's like to . . . be in this position.'

'And then you stop?'

'Yes, then we stop.' I know that Rod will be furious but I don't think I can do anything else.

'Over my dead body,' she says angrily.

'Well, isn't that the point, Florence?' I say, feeling the anger surge in me. 'What do you want? Why on earth do you want to do this? I can't believe that you want to put yourself through this.'

Suddenly she seems exhausted and confused. She twists the large topaz ring on her index finger. 'I don't know . . .' she says wearily, and trying to keep her composure she goes on very slowly, 'I suppose I thought I could put it off – that in some way I'd be protected. You know, nothing bad could really happen to me if you were filming. And you know, with you, Molly – I thought I could do it with you.'

At last she's being serious and I feel my eyes fill with tears, which I know is unprofessional.

'I don't want to film you . . .' I still can't bring myself to say it.

'But I . . .' she pauses, finding it hard to breathe now, '. . . don't want you to go.'

I look at the white roses standing straight in the vase and try to pull myself together. 'So will you talk . . . openly?'

'Yes, I'll try.' She smiles bravely. 'And you, will you stay with me till the end?'

I feel sick to my stomach but when I look into her eyes and see her fear I say quietly, 'Yes, I'll try,' and she reaches out her hand to seal our pact.

Nobody answers the phone and this is the second time I've tried to speak to Cassie. The phone switches on to answer-machine.

'Hi, Cassie, just wondering how the suicidal tendencies are going today and thinking how nice it would be to meet up and go for a drink or a bite to eat.' My voice tails off as I know it's a poor joke, and I wonder what I can say now to make amends. The machine beeps at me and switches off, leaving me feeling foolish.

I ring her again. 'Me again – sorry about the last message – I hope you're OK. I'm worried about you, please call me.'

Twenty-four

I could drive down these narrow lanes to Russell Court with my eyes closed, I know the route so well. The landscape has changed, and although it's late February I can see yellow dots in the woods which must be the early primroses beginning to push through the undergrowth. Over the past few weeks I have concentrated entirely on Florence and I can feel my world narrowing, focusing on the elderly woman living out her final days in her modest room. My mother and Aidan are looking after the children between them and I feel like I've handed over all responsibility. Aidan and I seemed to have reached a silent agreement but I'm not sure either of us knows or fully understands what it is. I can't allow myself to think about it; all my energies are saved for Florence.

My mobile phone rings and as I reach over to pick it up I wonder how people survived before they were invented.

'Molly – it's me.'

I usually feel a little irritated when people say that, as if I'll automatically know who is calling – it seems so arrogant – but in this case I know who 'me' is because of the Canadian accent and I love hearing his voice.

'Hi, Bill, how are you?'

'Fine, how about you?'

'I'm OK and I'm on my way to see your mother now.'

'Feeling nervous, huh?'

'Yes, how is it that you always can tell?'

'It's in the voice. You sound brusque and efficient when you're worried. When I talked to you the morning you started filming after you heard the news you sounded like this, but in the evening after a day's filming your tone changes completely,' he says, and I wonder how he has got to know me so well.

'So suddenly you're the voice expert?' I tease him and it pleases me to hear him laugh.

'I know it's silly – you'd think I'd get used to this – but every day I walk up those steps into Russell Court I still feel sick with fear and I have to brace myself because I'm worried about what I might see, or what might happen.'

'I don't think that's silly at all, it's perfectly understandable.' He pauses. 'Has she changed much?' he asks, and I have to be careful because I don't want to upset him. I don't want to tell him how her face turns white with pain, how she struggles to conceal it from me, and how even when she's sleeping the pain makes her surface until Jane, her new specially appointed care nurse, gives her something to make her feel more comfortable.

'Yes, you'd notice a difference, she's much thinner, but in herself she's amazingly buoyant.'

He chuckles. 'She's got a new mission in life, or death, to enlighten the great British public. I think she views this as the greatest role in her career,' he says.

'Well, I don't have to worry about her opening up – my problem is getting her to stop – but it's all fascinating. I just worry that we might be exhausting her – there are times when she finds it difficult just to breathe – but she always battles on. She's unbelievably determined and she wants to discuss everything.'

'Well, that can only be good for you,' he says, his sadness palpable.

'And you – she's talking about things you might never have known about, and even when she's gone you'll have the film as a record. It's going to be a powerful testimony of a remarkable woman in the last stages of her life.'

'Sounds like you've written the billing already,' he teases me. 'So I imagine your boss, the Rottweiler, must be happy.'

'I'm not sure Rod is ever happy, but he keeps ringing to find out how it's all going.'

I don't tell him that the real reason I expect Rod keeps ringing is to see how close Florence is to the end.

'And home – how's everything there?'

We don't often talk about really personal things. I don't even know if he's got a girlfriend.

'Home is on hold – I'm concentrating on Florence at the moment.'

I hear him sigh. 'Be careful, Molly.'

'I'll be fine – they understand – it's always like this when you're making a film.'

As I say this I feel worried that he might think that I don't care about Florence and that she's just another subject so I add, 'Of course, this is different – I've never made such an . . .' I'm searching for the right word '. . . such an intense film in my life.' Bill is quiet the other end of the phone.

'Are you all right, Bill?'

'I just wish I could be there.'

'When are you coming back?' It feels like a loaded question and I'm aware it's not just Florence I'm thinking about.

'I can't come at the moment because of work, Nick is having problems at school, and I need to sort out a few things this end.'

'How is Charlie doing?'

'Got picked for the team last week, tell that to his grandma.'

Nick and Charlie are his two boys. I know so much more about his life because of these phone calls, and it's as if we've got to the pillow-talk stage without any of the usual sexual intimacy that precedes it.

'I will, but Bill, don't leave it too long,' I warn him.

'No, I know, but you'll keep me posted, right?'

'Of course, but remember I'm not exactly an expert – I don't know how long she's got.'

'I understand. I keep in regular touch with Eleanor.'

I flick my indicator to turn right through the gates and along the winding drive which leads to Russell Court.

'I must go, Bill.'

'Molly?'

'Yes?'

'I'm glad it's you.'

'I'll call you,' I say as I park the car next to the crew's van.

*

When I reach Florence's room Jane, the community palliative care nurse, is listening to Florence's lungs with a stethoscope. She's an impressive woman in her mid-forties who manages to be both practical and warm, creating a calm and loving atmosphere. When we first met I asked her a few questions about her job.

'I'm here to make it easy for Florence,' she told me. 'I don't want her to have any unnecessary pain and when the time comes my job is to ease the way.'

'To help her have a good de . . . ath.' I said the word hesitatingly because I always find it hard not to wince when we talk about it but I knew I had to because of the film.

Jane is very matter of fact without being insensitive. She sighed. 'This notion of a "good death" is very difficult. How can it ever be good when you lose someone you love? To be honest, it can be a messy business, so my job is to keep things neat and painless and to make sure she doesn't feel alone.'

I wished she wasn't so honest – she was giving me more information than I wanted. She continued, 'I sometimes think it sets up false expectations. We've all got this image of the tranquil deathbed scene, and it can be like that but sometimes it's not, so people think we're doing something wrong and get more distressed. It's often a struggle. Sometimes there does come a point right at the end when there is a moment of calm but it's hard to generalise.'

I was beginning to feel sick. 'Do you ever get used to it?' I asked her.

'Well, it is my job.' She looked at me. 'But I never take it for granted and I don't think it's anything to be frightened of. It's something we're all going to have to go through – it's part of life, a natural process, and I feel privileged just to be here at this time. Being with people at this stage can be wonderful and very rewarding. I've learnt a lot over the years.'

When I broached the subject of including her in the film she said kindly but firmly, 'I don't think so,' and I replied, 'Of course, it's insensitive of me, you don't want to cheapen your role at this difficult time.'

'No, it's not that – it's just that I look awful on camera.'

Gerry comes over with a takeaway cappuccino.

'For you – we stopped at Starbucks.'

'Luxury.'

He smiles at me and I think that if Matt, Gerry and I were a strong team before, now we're bound together by something even more important than making a film.

When Bill and I speak I don't tell him quite how much Florence has noticeably deteriorated. She can still move independently when she has the energy and she still manages to perform for the camera. Initially I worried that our filming and the in-depth interviews would be devastating, rubbing in the hopelessness of her position, but they seem to have the opposite effect. Jane jokes that it's better than any injection she could give her.

'You're making my job easier,' she says. 'When someone is dying they often feel the need to give shape to their life, to try and make sense of it all. They can do that by talking about it but sometimes it's hard for me to give them the time and attention they deserve. But you're doing that for her with all your questions. It's wonderful, and it means that when she's ready she'll find it easier to let go.'

There are moments when Florence exudes panic, but today when she looks at me I can see by her expression that she's eager to get started while she still has the energy.

'It's a beautiful day; shall we do some filming outside? Do you feel up to being wheeled around and me asking more impertinent questions?'

'Goody,' she says, like a child who's been offered a treat.

'Is that all right?' I ask Jane anxiously.

'Of course, just wrap up warm, take these blankets, and don't be out too long.' They're the sort of instructions I would give to someone looking after my children.

Florence is still very aware of her appearance. She's much thinner, so many of her trousers don't fit, but she still manages to look elegant in a fine woollen skirt and roll-neck jumper. I ease her arms into her jacket and between us we help her into the wheelchair and out into the corridor to the lifts. It's difficult for all of us to fit into the lift as well as the equipment and I can't help thinking what a strange team we make. We travel down in silence, all of us wanting to conserve our energies for the important moments when everything can be recorded. We just stare from one to the other until Florence looks pointedly at Gerry.

'Gerry,' she says, straight-faced, 'was that you?'

Gerry's face flushes red as he says, 'What?' Matt and I giggle like schoolchildren.

Wendy Wannabe is waiting for us by the ramp that leads from the wide door to the left of the entrance. When I rang down to ask for someone to help push Florence's wheelchair while we film, I knew exactly who would offer her services. I imagine her quick response to the call and think of what she's left behind: Bernard stranded on a commode, Maurice sitting in his chair, his bedclothes left sprawled all over the floor, the clean sheets waiting neatly laundered and folded on the side of the bed, or a spoon hanging in mid-air and Phyllis's mouth wide open like a baby bird waiting to be fed. Luckily for us Wendy never keeps us waiting and she appears breathless, putting on her coat, her scarf dangling round her neck. She takes over behind the wheelchair and I slip beside Matt, so close I could almost put my arm round his waist. Once outside, Florence puts her head back and closes her eyes, letting the fresh, cool air wash over her face.

'You just carry on and we'll follow you and I'll ask questions. Is that all right, Florence?'

She nods, her eyes still closed.

'Are you ready, Matt?'

'I'm rolling,' he says, and I nod at Gerry who is wearing head-phones and carrying his boom. We head off along the path around the side of the house, through a narrow gate towards a walled garden.

'Autumn used to be my favourite time of the year but now I'm not so sure,' says Florence as she takes in the early blossom trees.

'Do things look different to you, Florence?'

'Yes, even the air tastes good and little things look impossibly beautiful.' She studies the leaves on the birch tree as she's wheeled past. 'All those years I took it for granted and the problem now is when you're not feeling well it's not so easy to appreciate it. I hate feeling ill.' She pauses because she has no breath and she holds up her hand like a schoolgirl in a classroom.

'Shall we stop for a minute?' I ask, and she nods her head. I wonder if I've been too ambitious bringing her out here. Wendy pushes her chair alongside a simple wooden bench. On the back of the bench is a plaque: 'In memory of Rodney Calvert who looked at every exit as being an entrance somewhere else.'

Florence glances at it and raises her eyebrows as if to say, 'Please.'

'Elspeth told me she has left some money in her will for Russell Court to buy a peacock,' she chuckles, 'to remind everyone of her.' She looks up at me. 'I expect the gardens are packed full of rosemary bushes. Over the years there have been a few memorable Ophelias staying at Russell Court, even since I've been here.' She smiles at me. 'What should I do to remind everyone of me?'

'What were you thinking of?'

'I don't want a bloody bench – someone sitting on me – no thank you. Something prickly would be suitable.' She smiles again.

'A cactus plant,' I suggest.

'Not the right soil,' she says knowledgeably. 'I remember going for a walk with Tommy on a bitterly cold winter's afternoon. The footpath went past a very pretty Norman church and we'd often stroll through the graveyard, fascinated by the names and simple stories that you could fathom from the inscriptions on the gravestones. On this particular day there had obviously been a funeral the day before and on one new gravestone there was a bunch of red roses covered in frost, like they'd just been taken out of a freezer. They looked so beautiful, preserved in ice. That's what I'd like, frosted roses, but I'll make it a condition in my will that they keep them frosted all the year round, even in the height of summer – that sure as hell would make them remember me.'

'Have you left strict instructions so that people know what to do after you've . . .'

'Do you mean have I set my affairs in order?'

I nod my head.

'Did that years ago but I never could decide whether to be cremated or buried.'

She grins at me and a cough starts deep in her chest and I wonder whether we should go back inside. Wendy passes her a tissue and she coughs into it. Once recovered, she continues, 'Decisions, decisions, decisions, it never stops, even when you're dying.' She pauses, watching Wendy trying to catch the stray tendrils of her hair and wedge them back up into her hair-clip. 'What do you think about a cardboard coffin?'

'Interesting idea.'

'I like the idea that people could write on it.'

'What sort of things?'

'Memories, good wishes. Everyone could be involved and it would make it less formal.'

'An interactive funeral,' I say, and she laughs.

'One of the disadvantages of dying old is there won't be so many people at the funeral, maybe no one would write anything.'

'I don't think that will be a problem for you,' I say gently.

'Of course it might look a terrible mess – I'd need an art director. You could do that, couldn't you?' she says, looking at me. 'It's a very modern idea – it would be biodegradable and so I'd be doing my bit for the environment.'

'Do you want a religious ceremony?' I ask, trying to keep her focused.

'I don't know . . . I like ceremony and a good singalong, but as for God . . .' She tails off.

'Is He invited?' I ask.

'If He's around He's very welcome to come but I'm not sure He is and that's the problem really, I'm not sure about anything, except for what's gone before, and even that can get a bit hazy sometimes. I wish I knew what came next.' She shuffles in her chair, trying to get comfortable. 'You know, what irritates me is all this rubbish about "You're born alone and you die alone", well, it's nonsense. Before you're born you spend at least nine months cocooned inside your mother, listening to every word she speaks, absorbing her thoughts and emotions, all experience of the world muffled by her. Then you're pushed out and a team of midwives and doctors, a doting father and your mother greet you – there's nothing solitary about that. But now, at the end of your life, well . . . now there's no one.'

She looks at me. 'Well, there's Bill of course, and Jane and Wendy.' We both look at Wendy who is studying another stray strand of hair that has escaped from her hair-clip. 'And you,' Florence says, glancing up at me. 'But you can't come all the way with me, can you?'

I shake my head. Her eyes turn a darker shade of green, or maybe it's just that a cloud has passed overhead. 'What really frightens me is being alone when I die. It would be hard to go through death without someone who cares, someone who knows what my life has been – I don't want to be an anonymous patient – some old woman croaking it.'

'That's not going to happen.'

'No, because even if Bill doesn't make it, you'll be there.' She looks straight at me and then adds lightly, 'You know what they should do, they should start ante-death classes, like ante-natal classes, to help you prepare for it. They could help you choose your position, the different types of pain relief, and how to get your breathing right.' She wheezes as she laughs. 'When I was having Bill the midwife kept going on about the breathing. I felt so cross because she'd forgotten I was an actress and if there's one thing I know all about, it's breathing.' She pauses again, searching for the breath. 'I've always tried to do things well and this should be no different.'

'Have you much experience of death?'

'Well, you can't grow up in a vicarage and not have some

experience of it. You could say I've lived with death – we used to have boxes of unclaimed ashes on the mantelpiece and I thought it was fascinating that after it was all over we could fit into those little boxes. The first person close to me to die was my mother, who died when I was on tour, and although it was upsetting in a strange way it was a relief because she'd never approved of me. I felt oddly liberated, free to do what I had always wanted – isn't that terrible?'

'What did she die of?'

'Cancer, but nobody liked to mention it because in those days it was a dirty word, as though it was your fault if you got it, somehow it was shameful. Not like that nowadays – everyone's always going on about their bloody cancer stories; they wear it like a badge.'

She leans back and I can see that we haven't got much longer this morning, as she looks exhausted.

'And your husband, Tommy?'

Tears start to pour down her cheeks. I've never seen her cry before.

'I'm sorry – shall we stop?'

'No, I don't mind if you don't.' She dabs at her cheeks with her sleeve. In my pocket I feel a tissue which Max must have used months ago but it's all I've got so I hand it to her.

'I was with him when he died in hospital. It was quite quick. He'd been having dizzy spells and they discovered a tumour in his brain, but it was secondary and they never managed to find the primary. They fought so hard to save him, he had months of chemotherapy which didn't seem to make much difference, and by the end I think he just wanted to go, but they wouldn't let him and I was stuck in the middle. I don't want to go like that and that's why I refused the ghastly treatment and why I don't want to be in hospital. I mean, what's the point at my age of giving me a few extra months during which I'll feel dreadful, even worse than I do at the moment? And if I lost my hair – where's the dignity in that?'

She looks at me and I know she can smell my fear.

'The strangest thing was that the moment he died he put his head back and roared – I'd never heard a sound like it, and from a man who never shouted or raised his voice in his whole life, it was very peculiar. The nurse who was with us later told us it wasn't so unusual – just the body releasing everything.'

Matt looks up from the eye-piece of the camera.

'Sorry, we need to change tapes.' He looks at me encouragingly and I follow him over to his camera bag where the tapes are stored.

'It's interesting – keep going,' he says.

'I'm glad you're enjoying it,' I remark drily. 'I'm worried it's exhausting her,' I say, concerned.

'She'll stop when she wants to.'

We walk back and I bend down so that I'm level with Florence. 'Are you all right to continue?'

'For a bit,' she replies. 'Sorry about the tears.'

'Don't be silly,' I reply.

'We're at speed,' says Matt

'Tell me about you and Tommy. How did you meet?'

I can see Matt look at me with exasperation as I've moved on to safer territory but I've had enough detail about Tommy's death for the time being.

'We met through Evelyn.'

'Your friend in the picture?'

'Yes. We were at school together and we both became actresses – she was the pretty one and I was the funny one. We toured together for a while – she sang and I did jokes. We were terrible. She met Tommy when he was in the Jack Payne orchestra. She thought he was lovely. He certainly was a classy trumpet player.'

'So what happened?'

'I don't want to talk about it.'

I say nothing but think how interesting it is that she's happy to talk about the intimate moments of her husband's death but not to discuss the details of how they met. The sound of two birds fighting over a food dispenser hanging from a lilac tree fills the silence. One thing I remember from making my earlier documentaries is that during an interview if you wait long enough people tend to fill in the gaps and it can be very revealing. Florence doesn't disappoint me.

'Oh, all right, I might as well tell you. During the war they both signed up – she went into the FANYs and he into the Navy. I was in ENSA and my leave always coincided with Tommy's.' She shrugs her shoulders. 'I suppose it was inevitable really but I'm not proud of it.' I can't tell whether it's the chilly wind or the emotion making her eyes water again.

'There's no easy way to tell someone something like that. At first she didn't believe me and then she was just angry. She never spoke to me again and then two days after I told her about Tommy and me she was killed. It must have been one of the last raids in London and I feel as if I personally dropped that bomb. Maybe she would have got over it. I know she probably would have met someone else, but I don't know if she would have ever forgiven me. I certainly haven't.'

She looks at me as if appealing to me for forgiveness, and all I can do is smile at her sympathetically as she struggles to make sense of the past.

'There's nothing I can do about it now but I think about it more and more,' Florence says sadly.

The sun disappears behind a cloud and we're all stamping our feet with the cold.

'Let's go back,' I say to Wendy. Matt and Gerry run ahead to set up the tripod to do some wide static shots of Florence being wheeled in the garden, while I keep out of sight.

Back in Florence's room, the crew have broken for lunch, Florence is sleeping and I'm staring at the picture of Evelyn looking impossibly glamorous in her uniform. A hint of a smile hovers around her eyes and cheekbones. It's a dated look, so very different from the cheesy grins that smile out at us from most photographs today. I'm not hungry, so I sit down in the chair next to Florence's bed and watch her chest rise and fall.

Wendy Wannabe, now without her coat, puts her head round the door. 'Molly,' she calls to me in a throaty voice full of smoke and sex, 'would you give these to Florence? She promised me that she would send them on to Bill.'

Perhaps it's something in the familiar way she says his name but there's no denying I feel a strange tightening sensation in my stomach. Perhaps I am hungry after all. She hands me the envelope and I smile politely and say, 'Yes, of course.' Then with an embarrassed giggle Wendy does her model cat-walk flounce out of the room. The only reassuring thing about her is that she's indiscriminate in her quest to be admired, so both men and women get the full blast of her well-rehearsed repertoire of enticing moves.

She leaves me alone to listen to the steady sound of Florence's heavy breathing. So why does Wendy want to send Bill a big brown envelope filled with God knows what? The awful thought slowly dawns on me that perhaps Wendy got to know Bill as well as I did or even better. I look at the brown A4-sized envelope which has emblazoned across it 'Photographs – Do Not Bend.' Of course it's possible, probable even. Now I feel stupid that I didn't notice anything and even more foolish for thinking that he could possible have had any feelings for me. It must have been an impossible decision trying to choose between a young, gorgeous, flirtatious, available blonde with everything in its perfect place and a married woman on the brink of middle age who tries to pass off her wrinkles as laughter lines and has an attitude problem. The envelope taunts me from the table and I wonder what sort of photographs are inside the innocent brown packaging. I look at the seal. It doesn't look very secure – sometimes they just peel open, practically by themselves. I would be doing Wendy a favour if I opened it and then stuck it back down more securely so it wouldn't get damaged in the post. I'm sure no one would notice. I pick it up, Florence stirs in time with my conscience, and I immediately put the envelope back down again. What am I thinking of? It really is none of my business.

*

293

Florence is in a deep sleep and I move the envelope to the side table, near the photograph of Evelyn, and fill up her water jug. Nowadays she becomes very thirsty, which Jane says is due to the morphine patch she has on her chest. I have to confess to being frightened by any physical contact with Florence; it seems so intimate and I'm worried that I might do something wrong and make her feel worse than she does already. The health visitor has installed a hospital bed to make it easier to care for her, anticipating the final stages. The sound of her breath is hypnotic. I begin to feel drowsy and have to fight an overwhelming urge to lie down beside her. Her eyes open but it seems to take a while for her to focus.

'Are you thirsty?' I ask her.

She nods and as I hold the glass of water to her lips, she coughs. The movement makes me spill the water on to her covers.

'Oh, I'm sorry – I'll get a towel.'

When I get back to the bed and start mopping up she says, 'I have such vivid dreams.'

'What about?'

'I just dreamt I was diving down through water and when I looked to my right Tommy was beside me.' She looks at me and smiles. 'Don't worry, he wasn't standing at the foot of my bed beckoning me to come to a better place.'

She half laughs and half coughs. 'In my dreams I'm always young – it's as if I haven't caught up with my life.'

'I have that too. What else happened in the dream?' I ask her gently.

'Despite the fact we were under water Tommy was playing the trumpet. It was frustrating because the sound was muffled and I couldn't hear him properly. I loved the way he played. He had a lightness of touch but he always knew how to pack a punch as well; it could be heart-rending.'

'Is that what attracted you?' I ask her, intrigued because until today she's never gone into details about their relationship.

'Yes . . . I think you saw the real Tommy when he played his trumpet. He wasn't a talker, but he didn't need to be with me around.' She smiles thinking about him. 'I must have driven him mad. I hope he didn't have any regrets – I wonder if he ever thought about it, about what it would have been like if I'd been the one killed in the raid. We never spoke of it. Maybe that's why he fooled around a bit. I know that's why I accepted it: I felt it was my punishment.'

She lies back and looks at me. 'What about you and your Aidan – how did you meet?'

I'm surprised by the question because I've got used to our roles and the attention is usually focused on Florence, but as I'm alone and the crew aren't listening I answer her.

'We met when I'd just started directing and I was working on a women's magazine programme. I had to interview him as he'd been put in charge of the latest campaign for underarm deodorant.' Florence makes a face. 'I know it sounds terrible but it was a revolutionary advert and he was considered to be a pioneering force in advertising. He was very impressive, always thinking of ideas – he looked at life in a totally different way from anyone else I'd ever met. He was one of those people who didn't predict trends, he created them, and I suppose I was flattered that he should be interested in me.'

'Style isn't really your thing,' Florence says, looking at my ubiquitous jeans.

'No, I think at first he found it refreshing – the fact that I've never owned a pair of Manolo Blahnik shoes or a Lulu Guinness handbag. I wasn't like most of the women he'd been out with.'

'What about now?'

'Well, now we're married, things have changed, and of course there's the children.'

'How is it different?'

'I don't know.'

'Do you still love him?'

'That's a hell of a question.'

'That's ripe coming from you who never stops asking intimate questions.' She's grinning and I wonder if it's her or the morphine talking.

'Yes, yes, of course I love him,' I say, choosing my words cautiously, 'but I think of what he was like before and how he is now and I'm not sure when it changed and whose fault it is.'

'What do you mean?' Florence urges me on.

'Have I changed or is it him? Before, I thought he needed to be nurtured, so I protected him from the mundane domestic details, but now it's different and I can't do that any more and I don't want to. I want him to share the responsibility and he's trying as best he can, but it's not in his nature and all he wants to do is lock himself away to write his script and live a creative life.'

I'm feeling my way through an emotional maze. 'I think . . .' I pause, not sure what it is that I think, but the words come of their own accord, 'I've lost faith in him, especially since I read his script – I'm not sure he is a genius any more and even if he is I've realised that it's not easy living with a genius. Before, I would tolerate his idiosyncrasies but now they irritate me.'

I've never articulated these thoughts to anyone, let alone myself.

'What was it like before he lost his job? Were you happy then?'

I think back through the years to when Evie was born and try to think about my life with Aidan, but the moments that are most vivid are the time spent with the children and he doesn't really feature. It's like looking through a photo album and seeing family groups with one person missing who you assume is taking the photograph, and then remembering that they were in fact always taken by a passing stranger because Aidan was too busy being creative to spend much time with us.

Florence senses I'm struggling and throws what she hopes will be a lifeline. 'Did you make each other laugh?'

'Not that I remember – I mean, there were funny moments with Evie and Max . . .' I tail off, 'but Aidan was always interesting, so laughing didn't seem so important,' I say, trying to defend him.

'Sense of humour is what kept Tommy and me together all those years – more than the sex.' Florence sighs. 'Sometimes I wonder if I married Tommy because of Evelyn. Because of what happened I knew I had to make it work. That doesn't mean I wasn't happy with him – despite everything I was. It's a complicated business. Do you want to make it work?'

I don't answer her but I'm aware she's watching me as I busy myself clearing up the spilt water. I have to lean near her face to plump up her pillows but I'm careful not to get too close to her, and she says so quietly it's almost a whisper, 'Molly, what are you so frightened of?' and as I look into her eyes she puts her hand to my face and strokes my cheek. 'After all, I'm the one that's dying.'

Twenty-five

Looking at the road sign ahead, I'm shocked at how far I've come and how little I remember of the journey. I've been mulling over all the things Florence and I have been talking about – Tommy's death, Wendy's photographs and the things I said about Aidan, which now articulated have become sealed in cement, real, solid. A sign flashes at me 'Slow down'. I look at the queue of cars ahead and wonder what is the likelihood, being so close to London during the rush hour, that I'd be able to drive faster than ten miles an hour anyway? To my left I'm approaching a sign and I read every detail because I'm driving so slowly it's a welcome break in the relentlessness of the motorway. It takes me a few seconds before I realise that it's the turn-off to where Cassie lives. I've left a number of messages on her answerphone, none of which she's returned. I look at the clock – it's 6.30 p.m. and suddenly, rather than sit in a traffic jam, I make the decision to go and visit her.

When I push her bell there's no welcoming voice on the intercom so I ring again and wait, feeling worried. After a few minutes I walk around the side of the flats to see if I can see anything through her window. The uneasy feeling in the pit of my stomach grows when I see that her curtains are drawn, and as I peer through the chink where the curtains don't quite meet I see a bottle of pills on the floor. I feel sick and my mind races, desperately trying to recall everything she said during our last conversation. Scenes from our friendship flash through my head, that first meeting in the queue of researchers, Cassie helping me with interviews, our adventurous holidays – the camel safari in India, the morning of my wedding when she and Jo came and dressed with me. She's been an integral part of my life for so many years. Why didn't I come to see her earlier?

A low voice behind me makes me jump and I swing round to see Matt.

'Do you make a habit of snooping round people's flats and peering into windows?' he asks.

'No, you don't understand – this is a friend of mine's flat and I'm just worried about her as I think she might have . . .' I don't want to finish the sentence but instead I take hold of his arm and step aside so he can look in through the window.

'What do you think this looks like?'

'Like someone left their flat in a hurry this morning.'

'But the pills on the floor?'

'Well, maybe they knocked over the bottle as they were leaving. It's not as if they're spilling out all over the carpet.' He looks at me. 'Are you suggesting that your friend in her attempt to commit suicide would calmly take the pills and then screw the top back on?'

'She might have done.'

'There's one problem – the bottle is still full of pills.'

I look again at the bottle and realise that he's right. The pounding in my heart alleviates and I slowly come to my senses.

'What are you doing here anyway?' I ask him.

'I've come to see a flat – 1a Digby Mansions – there was a notice up at work about a room for rent.'

'But that's Cassie's flat.' I grab his arm.

'Cassie Harwood – that's right, I spoke to her this morning and we arranged to meet here . . .' He looks at his watch. 'Five minutes ago.'

I laugh with relief. 'She's always late.'

'I'm not,' says an indignant voice. 'Sorry – usual delays on the Tube.'

She looks brown, rested and much happier than the last time I saw her and I feel relieved to see her and give her an affectionate hug. She steps back, overwhelmed by my reaction.

'Steady on.'

'I've been worried about you.'

'That makes a change.'

'What do you mean?'

The relief at seeing her safe and well is now being slowly replaced by anger, like when Max ran across the road without looking and a car screeched to a halt, missing him by millimetres. I didn't know whether to laugh or shout, so I did both, much to Max's confusion.

'I've been thinking about you a lot, especially after our last conversation – I've rung at least three times. Why haven't you called me back?'

I'm aware that Matt has turned away out of embarrassment and before Cassie gets a chance to reply I continue, 'It's selfish – there are people who care about you, you know?'

'Selfish? I don't think I'm the one that's selfish, Molly – I've been working so bloody hard for you. Who was the one who introduced you to Rod, who encouraged him to see you, who helped you with all that research and who spent hours trying to get that fucking tape for you at Christmas and who spent New Year mopping up when you left Aidan and the children? Christ, you haven't even had time to have a single evening with me on our own since Will and I broke up. Selfish – that's what I call selfish. I've even tried not to go on about how low I've been feeling and kept out of your way because I know you're close to melt-down. But I've had enough, so you can just piss off and stop coming over all sanctimonious with me.'

Matt has tactfully walked round to the front of the block of flats and I hope he's out of earshot, but before I can say anything Cassie continues, 'Anyway, I did bloody call and I spoke to Florence.'

'Florence?' I say, amazed at how involved she seems to be getting with my personal life. 'But she didn't mention anything.'

'I called you on your mobile but you were off somewhere and she answered it for you. I was surprised how much she seemed to know about me.'

She looks at me accusingly and I feel shocked by her vehemence.

'It was her suggestion that I take a holiday and she was dead right. I've made a few decisions, sorted things out in my head, and I felt a lot better, well, I did until now.'

As if she can't bear to be anywhere near me and not waiting to hear what I might have to say, she turns and walks back along the path that leads to the front of the mansion block where Matt is waiting by the front door. I follow her, stopping only when the irritating sound of a mobile phone has us all reaching into pockets and bags.

'Hello?'

'Hello?'

'Hello?'

'Molly, it's me,' – another 'me' who is arrogant enough to assume I will immediately know who it is, but this time there's no Canadian lilt and to my annoyance I do recognise Rod's clipped voice. He's the last person I want to talk to at the moment as I'm still reeling from Cassie's accusations.

'How's she doing?' he asks with little genuine concern and it takes me a moment to realise he's talking about Florence, not Cassie. He's desperate for her to get a move on and die, I can hear it in his voice.

'She's OK considering,' I say impatiently.

'How long do you think she's got?' He makes it sound as if he's asking me the time of the next train.

'I don't know – I'm no expert.'

He sighs with impatience. 'But you must have some fucking idea?'

'When she was diagnosed they said anything up to six months and that was in October. We're now coming up to March and they say it could still be weeks, maybe longer.'

'Weeks!' he screams down the phone and I take it away from my ear.

'We took her outside this morning.'

'What, to speed things up?'

'For God's sake, Rod, what do you think I am? No, she just felt up to it. She has a morphine patch but they haven't started the drip yet . . .'

He interrupts me. 'Molly, look, we've got a few problems this end. We're running out of money and they've gone way over budget on the whining schoolboy film; all the attention has gone to his head and he was caught shagging his teacher in the stationery cupboard, and now there's an embargo on all our footage before the court case . . . and what with the initial problems with your film . . .'

'Which were nothing to do with me,' I remind him.

'Yes, as you say.' I can almost hear the sound of his footsteps as he paces the floor of his office.

'I think we're going to have to stop filming.'

The feeling of immense relief is soon tempered by confusion. Now it seems likely that I won't have to film Florence to the bitter end but at the same time I made a promise to be with her and I don't want to let her down.

'How much time have we got?' It's my turn to ask him.

'I can give you a week, maybe I can squeeze you two weeks, but just see what you can do.'

'You don't mean that, do you?'

'What?' he says innocently.

'Well, for a minute I thought perhaps you were suggesting I should do something, but I obviously misunderstood you.'

'Obviously,' he says drily. 'But try taking her out for a few more walks . . .' He tails off as he can hear that I've gone silent the other end of the phone.

'I hope, for your sake, that no one's been taping this call,' I say.

'Oh God, you don't think they would, do you?' he says, paranoid as ever.

'Well you never know.' I'm enjoying hearing his panic. 'Goodbye, Rod.'

Walking back towards the others I hear Cassie and Matt talking, and looking at Cassie you'd never imagine we'd just had a distressing conversation.

'So you're Matt – I've heard a lot about you. In fact I tried to get you to work on the police project I did recently.'

'Was that the series that went out a few months ago? I thought it was very good. I seem to remember the dates didn't work out because I was filming abroad.'

'It was a shame – I've heard good things about you.'

'I pay people lots of money to say nice things,' he laughs.

'So I suppose you'd better come in and see the flat – I'm sorry it's a bit of a mess at the moment.'

'Oh, don't worry,' he says, smiling at her.

When I reach them I say, 'I'd better be going.'

Cassie ignores me as she fumbles in her bag for her keys but Matt looks embarrassed by the situation.

'See you tomorrow,' he mumbles.

'OK, bye.'

Cassie finds her keys and without looking at me begins to unlock the door. I walk back to the car and as I drive off I see her opening the front door, Matt beside her, and they're both talking animatedly until they disappear inside together.

'I've found some great tights but I wanted to check whether she'd wear something lacy.'

Cassie's words are still reverberating in my head and I've thought about nothing else for the rest of the journey home. What is so difficult is that she's got a point, I have neglected everyone, but what else could I do? It seems so unfair because it's not my fault.

'I'm sorry, Mum, what were you saying?'

I'm watching Aidan as he gets himself a beer out of the fridge and pours it into his favourite white frosted-glass tumbler. He sits down at the table and opens his leather-bound notebook and starts writing. Everything about him is so calculated, from his antique 1930s Mont Blanc fountain pen to his writing – small, perfect and precise.

'Molly, what do you think? I haven't got long because Tim and Helen are coming over for supper tonight.' She sounds impatient.

'Sorry Mum?'

'The tights, will she find them too scratchy?'

'Too scratchy for what?'

'For the wedding – bridesmaid tights – I just need to know her size.'

'Seven to eight.' My voice sounds distant, as if it belongs to someone else.

As my mother collects her things getting ready to leave she asks, 'How's the filming going?'

'Fine, but I think we're going to have to stop soon as we've run out of money.'

Aidan doesn't react; he's not listening to my conversation.

'Oh, I'm sorry, do you mind?' says my mother, looking concerned.

'I feel relieved in some way – the whole idea of filming her all the way through always bothered me, but I don't know how to break the news to Florence.'

'I suppose the good thing is that you'll definitely be around for the wedding.'

'I was always going to be at the wedding, Mum,' I say, feeling irritated. Why is everyone having a go at me today?

'See you tomorrow then.' My mother kisses me on the cheek. 'Bye, Aidan.'

'What?' says Aidan distractedly, and my mother gives an exasperated shrug of the shoulders as if she despairs of ever getting any sense out of any of us.

Evie walks into the kitchen in her pyjamas that came from the Boden catalogue two years ago and are now far too small for her.

'Mum, I'm not going to do my homework.'

'I'm afraid you've got to.'

'I can't, I hate maths, it's just stupid – why do I need to do it anyway when I can use a calculator?'

'Evie, let's talk about it in the morning, we're all tired now.'

'I'm not.'

'Well I am,' I snap back. I go to give Max a hug but he wriggles free and grabs my mother by the hand and says, 'I want Granny to tuck me up.'

'Well, Granny needs to go home now,' I say, trying to keep calm.

'I could stay for a few minutes if you like?' she says, not sure what would be the best thing. I look at Max's sullen face and have to remind myself that I'm the adult around here. The problem with dealing with a four-year-old is how little time it takes for them to reduce you to their level, and I struggle not to stamp my foot and throw a tantrum.

'I'll take Evie to bed and she can do her reading and I'll come into your room in a minute.'

'Oh,' says Evie disappointedly, feeling she's drawn the short straw, and before I know it both children run to my mother, giggling and flinging their arms around her waist so that she can hardly move. I feel inadequate and rejected as I watch her try to disentangle herself from the children.

'Evie, Max, don't be silly.' I try not to overreact. 'Come on, guys – it's late and it's school tomorrow – Max, come on, it's bedtime.' My voice is becoming insistent.

'I'm not sleepy. I'm not going.'

I feel the anger burn inside me. 'Oh yes you are.'

I pick him up, and he screams and wriggles until I can't hold him any more. Before I know it I'm shouting at him, 'For God's sake, Max, do what you're told and go upstairs. NOW.'

He looks at me and starts to smile. Again the anger wells up inside and washes through me. I feel like I'm going to slap him but instead I grab his wrists. I'm holding him tightly, the anger coursing through me. He stops smiling and shouts, 'Ow – stop it, you're hurting me.'

'I don't care,' I say grimly as I start to drag him towards the stairs. Evie looks worried and immediately runs up the stairs into her bedroom. Max is still resisting.

'I hate you, you're a horrid mummy.'

'You think this is horrid?' I say, surprised by the vehemence I feel.

'Molly,' my mother gently admonishes me, and Max bursts into tears. I let go of him and he runs to my mother.

'Come on, Maximilian, I'll chase you upstairs.' She gives me a warning look and as if a light has been switched on Max smiles and runs upstairs screaming excitedly, leaving me feeling wretched and guilty.

I follow them up slowly, wondering what is happening to me, and go into Evie's bedroom. I sit down on her bed where she's writing in her Harry Potter diary.

'How are things, Evie – is everything all right at school?'

'As if you cared.'

I'm shocked by the tone of her voice. 'Of course I care,' I say, hurt.

'Well, you don't seem to.'

'What's wrong?'

'Maths – I hate maths.'

'So did I – maybe I can help you with it?' I'm trying to be conciliatory.

'You never have time,' she says.

'I'll get up early tomorrow morning and I'll make time.'

She looks at me sceptically but puts away the diary, pulls the purple duvet up to her shoulders and scratches her head.

'How are the nits?'

'Fine,' she says quickly, and I can see that she's worried I might drag her into the bathroom and start greasing copious amounts of conditioner into her hair, pulling at it with the dreaded nit comb. She lies back and I lean forward and start picking at her hair, checking to see if there are any black specks or little translucent eggs. It becomes obsessive, like popping bubble wrap.

'Sorry about this,' I say.

'No, it's nice, I like you being here,' and that goes some way to alleviate the guilt I feel about how I treated Max.

My mother comes into Evie's room and strokes my head. 'His Lordship would like to see you now.'

I give Evie a hug and kiss her smooth cheek and my mother and I walk on to the landing together.

'You are working too hard; this is not like you. I'm worried about you.'

I feel the tears starting to well up again.

'I'm a mess. I've just had a terrible argument with Cassie and I feel so involved with Florence and so removed from home.'

'This can't go on – you can't go on living like this – for your sake and the children's.'

'I know, but I can't think about it until I finish the film.'

She looks at me, her worry clearly visible. 'Are you all right if I go?'

'Yes, of course – thank you – what would I do without you?'

'That's one thing you don't have to worry about at the moment.'

Max is sitting up in bed looking sleepy, our terrible moment apparently forgotten. I perch on the side of his bed.

'Max, I'm sorry about what happened downstairs. It's the end of the day and everyone is tired, but if I ask you to do something you must do what I tell you.'

He's staring at me, his brown eyes wide with tiredness. 'I had a nasty dream last night. There was this huge black tank with big big guns pointing at me. It made a terrible noise like it was growling and I was really scared. It was rolling towards me and I couldn't get out of the way and then the top opened up and when I looked inside there was this tiny, tiny bunny and it was so sweet.'

I'll never understand the male psyche. I hand him his muslin, which he holds close to his nose, finding comfort in the familiar smell and softness, which helps him sleep. I feel that we have some unfinished business so I continue, 'I hate rows.'

'Oh, I love them,' he says enthusiastically.

I look at him in amazement. 'Well, you picked the wrong mother then because I don't like them and I don't think we should have any more.'

'If you say so,' he says, snuggling down under the bedclothes. I kiss his soft cheek and breathe in the wonderful smell of him, which is distinctively Max.

''Night, lovely boy.'

''Night.'

I get to the door and turn out the light.

'Mama,' says a little voice from the bed, 'what are rows?'

Downstairs Aidan is pouring two glasses of champagne but I couldn't feel less like celebrating.

'I think I've finished the script,' he says with pride.

'Don't you think this might be a bit premature?' I say, looking at the bubbles rising in the long-stemmed glass. I don't feel like drinking champagne.

'What do you mean?'

'Well, you haven't sold it yet – that's when we should bring out the champagne.'

He picks up his glass and looking at me defiantly, drinks it down in one. 'You might be wrong there, my darling. Someone is interested in buying my script, and not just anyone.'

I'm finding it hard to drum up the enthusiasm. 'What are you talking about?'

'Dreamworks – Spielberg no less – they've requested a meeting. It was all because of Terry. He sent it to them and they were on the phone the next day. I'm a bloody genius.'

'Oh Aidan, that's just amazing.'

I'm stunned by the news and part of me wonders whether he's making it up.

'It doesn't mean they're going to buy it but at least they're interested. I'm going to do some rewrites that Terry has suggested before meeting with them, but it's the break I need.'

I drag myself out of the uncomfortable sofa and put my arms around him. He gives me a brief kiss and then he moves away, restless and excited. 'Listen, I've been thinking we should go away, all of us, when you've finished this bloody film.'

I immediately feel defensive about my film. 'Don't say that.'

'You know what I mean.'

He pours himself another glass of champagne. 'Terry says we can use his cottage in Dorset whenever we want, so shall we go?

That is, if I don't have to go to America to meet with the man himself.'

He can't stop grinning and I feel so tired. I take a sip of champagne and it tastes sharp and leaves my mouth feeling dry.

'Yes, that's a good idea, but we have to be back for Tim and Helen's wedding in March.'

'Naturally,' he says, slurring.

'Have you had any supper?'

'I'm not hungry.'

'He's pouring himself another glass of champagne. I force a smile and aware that I'm watching him, he holds out the bottle and says, 'Are you sure you don't want a top-up?'

'No thanks, I'm going to have a shower.'

'Oh, and Molly,' he calls as I reach the stairs, 'you'll have to read it now.'

'Of course. I can't wait.'

I go upstairs, my legs feeling heavy. What's wrong with me? I should be feeling happy for Aidan, for all of us, but I don't. In the bathroom I get undressed and shiver as I step into the shower. The hot water pummels my back. I feel my eyes prick with emotion and for a moment I fight it but within seconds tears are streaming down my face. I turn to face the wall and sob silently so as not to wake the children.

Twenty-six

'How long?' asks Matt.

'A week, maybe a few more days, depending . . .' I hate the look in his eyes.

'You can't do this to her.'

'What, it'll kill her?' I say.

'That's not funny.'

'I know, I'm sorry.'

'I don't think you are – you never wanted to film her right through to the end, did you?'

'Don't do this, Matt, this has nothing to do with what I wanted, but we have no more money and Rod won't let us continue. He's as upset as the rest of us, if not more so.'

'How are you going to finish the film?'

'I don't know yet until I've seen all the rushes but it won't be hard, I've got a lot to work with. Maybe we could use the shots of her in the drama with voice-over, or Christmas when she's listening to her recording. I know I'll be able to work something out.'

He looks genuinely distressed and I understand that he feels compromised. Matt has never been afraid of anything in his life except emotional commitment. He can deal with any situation and almost relishes the danger – his boundless curiosity makes him a good cameraman. He's intrigued to see what will happen and he wants to be there to film it.

'How are you going to tell her?' He can barely hide his anger with me.

'I don't know, but soon, probably today so that she's prepared.'

He runs his fingers through his hair and Gerry walks into the hall carrying a large silver box full of sound equipment. We both watch him and he grins at us when he sees us and says genially, 'What have I done now?'

Matt walks over to him and breaks the news to him. They both turn to look at me.

'But you can't pull out now?'

'I have no choice, Gerry.'

'Can't you ring up network centre or something and get someone to give us more money – even if it's just a few more weeks?'

'But it might be longer than a few weeks – she's doing so well, better than they expected.'

Wendy walks past and for a minute both men are distracted.

'Morning, boys and girls,' she rasps. 'See you later.' As she walks upstairs in the direction of Florence's room, all the eyes in the portraits lining the walls seem to follow her.

'We'd better get started – come on, Florence is expecting us.'

I pick up one of the boxes and Matt says gruffly, 'Don't worry, we can manage.' He tries to take hold of the handle but I hold on.

'Please don't be like this, Matt, it's hard enough as it is at the moment.'

He lets go of the box and picks up the camera. 'Come on,' he says, walking up the stairs, disappointment dripping from his shoulders.

As soon as I walk into Florence's room I can see that she knows. She's sitting in her comfortable armchair, a wooden stick to the left, her glasses perched on the top of her head, while Wendy, looking a little pink in the cheeks, is straightening the sheets that Florence insists on having as she's never got used to duvets.

'I'll be off then,' she says to no one in particular and she leaves the room quickly.

Matt looks at me and says under his breath, 'Do you want us to go?'

'No, stay.'

'Good morning, everyone,' Florence says bravely, not allowing her disappointment to affect her manners.

'Morning,' I say, and I sit on the bed beside the chair.

'Would you pass me my earrings?' she says, and I lean over to the other side of the bed where her chunky pearl earrings are resting on the side table. Our hands touch as I give her them and she looks at me.

'What did Wendy say?' I ask her directly,

'She said, "Isn't it a shame that they can't carry on filming?" and then one look at my face stopped her in her tracks. I suppose it's true?'

'Yes.'

'Why?'

'It's nothing to do with you – you're being brilliant – it's just we've run out of money. We're all devastated by the news. No one wants to stop.' I look over at Matt and Gerry who are staring intently at the floor, embarrassed.

'No one?' she asks me, and then more quietly she says, 'You promised.'

'I said I'd try and I have. I'll still come and see you even though we won't be filming. I'm not going to abandon you.'

She smiles coolly, making me feel guilty.

'I give you my word,' I insist.

'Well, we haven't got much time left so we'd better make the most of it,' she says. 'I've still got so much I need to tell you,' she wheezes.

'OK,' I say, turning and looking at the crew. 'Let's get cracking.'

'How are you?' It's the first question of the day with the camera running.

'Good today,' she says. 'Well, I was until I heard the news.' She pauses, her breath wheezing. I feel the blood rush to my cheeks but Florence continues, 'I have good days and bad days. The nights are another thing.'

'Do you sleep well?'

'No, I can't remember the last time I slept through a whole night, even though I take the pills. I have to get up at least three times a night. I try to get back to sleep by imagining I'm walking through all the houses I've lived in. Last night I was in the house where I grew up. I make myself walk through the front door and I see everything vividly, as if I'm actually there – the stairs in front of me, the kitchen out the back, and our front room to the right. When I walk into the room I see the fireplace, the brass coal scuttle, my father's old chair, the small table beside it and the ashtray, always there as if stuck with glue. I can even remember the china dog that lived on the mantelpiece.' She smiles. 'At least it stops my brain chattering.'

'What does it chatter about?'

'Oh, you can imagine, about what's going to happen or how it's going to happen.'

'Does that frighten you?'

'Yes,' she says in a small voice, but she struggles to explain. 'Then I do feel sorry for myself and wish that I could have died in my sleep or had a nice quick heart attack. I suppose it still could happen.' She pauses and I say nothing but try to look encouraging. She says slowly, 'I am frightened about how I'm going to die. I've heard that your lungs can fill up and you drown . . .' She takes a deep breath as if to reassure herself. 'But they tell me there are things they can do to help and I suppose I have to trust them.'

She strokes the arm of her chair as if it were a cat. 'There are some advantages with it happening like this – I get the chance to say goodbye and I can still make some of my own decisions. I want to die here, not in some anonymous hospital, and they seem to think that will be possible.'

'Do you think you become more resigned to it?' I ask her gently.

'I'm not sure you can. It still seems unbelievable, like I'm acting a part – maybe I'm still playing that old granny in the drama and this isn't really happening to me. I wonder if it's nature's way of coping, of making the whole thing more accept-able. That first day when they told me I had inoperable lung cancer I couldn't believe it – I knew I hadn't been well, but lung cancer? It seemed ridiculous. It's the strangest thing because of course we all know we're going to die but we don't believe it. Even now it's difficult to really comprehend and some days it's all right and other days it's not.'

'What do you feel when you know it's OK?'

'I suppose I feel detached and start thinking, "OK, this is different – I haven't done this before and it's a new experience."'

'To die would be an awfully big adventure,' I say.

'No, not that, but it's going to happen and on good days I feel reconciled. It's about how you view your life – if you feel you've lived well then it makes it a little easier. I can't complain – it wasn't a bad old life. There have been some disappointments . . .'

'Like what?'

'I wasn't a household name, a star, but there are advantages to that. I don't regret the work I did; through it I caught glimpses of worlds I would never have experienced if I'd lived the life my mother planned for me. I met some extraordinary people and it was never dull, always changing, and I found that exciting.'

'What about your personal life?'

'I would have liked a daughter. I'm lucky to have Bill, I know that, but I would have loved to have had another child, a girl.'

'Do you ever think that having Bill affected your career?'

She smiles, the skin round her eyes creasing like a child's paper fan folding. 'I don't know and I don't care – I would have found it hard not to have had a child. It's hard to explain, but it's taught me to love and bond in the deepest way, though there's a price to pay. It's painful because you can't protect them, they have to leave you, and now I'm going to leave him.' The tears well up in her eyes.

'Is that the hardest thing?'

'Yes. That and the feeling that you're just going to stop, but maybe that's just my ego. You see, always a notice box.' She dabs at her eyes with a tissue. 'I'm off again. Do you mind?'

'Not at all,' I say. I'm finding it hard sitting beside Matt, holding back and not being able to comfort her; it feels inhumane.

Florence leans forward as though telling us a secret. 'I'm not ashamed to cry.'

'I remember when I had my first child I cried at everything, even the adverts,' I say, hoping to make her laugh, which she does until she starts to cough.

'When I was pregnant with Bill I remember walking down Hammersmith High Street and passing a stream of people. As each one passed me I thought, "He was born, she was born and so was he." It seemed ordinary and extraordinary at the same time – a commonplace miracle. I suppose it's the same now, everyone is going to die, but when it happens to you it feels special. Yet you have to accept that it's part of the natural order of things, a natural process. In some ways my little personal tragedy is the triumph of ongoing life; we die so others may live – to make room for the next generation.' She has to pause to recover.

'Don't for God's sake feel sorry for me because in some ways it's been one of the most extraordinary times of my life. Everything becomes so intense – the little things and the big things and it's all important.'

She leans back, exhausted by the effort but determined to continue. 'I've always enjoyed my browse through *Hello!* and just because I'm dying doesn't make me enjoy it any less – I need to know whether Liz Hurley is going to get married before I die – don't we all?' She grips the chair.

'I have to make the most of every little minute left to me.' She turns to me. 'And so must you, all of you.'

'Is it hard to do that?'

'Because my life is more or less limited to this room?'

I nod my head.

'You know, there's something liberating about handing over all responsibility to other people. It is like a second childhood and I'm lucky that people are looking after me well. I'm allowed to be myself although my body is deteriorating.'

She shivers and her face is very pale. 'Could you pass me that blanket? I'm very cold.'

I pass her the thick blanket on the end of the bed even though I'm tempted to take off my jumper, the room is so hot.

'Shall we have a break?' I ask Florence gently and her face floods with relief.

Matt stands up stretching his legs, stiff from crouching beside the camera. 'I'm just going to get some air. Coming, Gerry?'

Florence watches them as they saunter towards the door and I wonder if she feels envious that they can come and go as they please. The sound of a phone ringing interrupts my thoughts.

'Molly,' Matt calls to me from the door, 'your phone is ringing.'

'It can't be – I'm sure I turned it off,' I say, surprised.

'Well, it's either that or your lipstick is playing a tune.'

I look apologetically at Florence and she waves at me, giving her permission for me to take the call. I walk out into the corridor and sit down at the top of the stairs. I hear someone shouting and as I look down through the banisters I see Bernard in a wheelchair, being pushed by the long-suffering Dora, his face contorted in anger as he tries to pick up a book that has slipped from his lap. Dora picks it up for him and after she places it in his lap she bends down and kisses him softly on the cheek. He reaches up and touches her face with his hand in such an intimate way I feel I shouldn't be watching. They stay like that for a minute before Dora smiles and pushes him towards the bar. The voice on the phone pulls me back.

'Hi, it's me.' Despite everything I feel a tightening in my stomach and my heart beats faster. It's been a few days since I spoke with Bill.

'You've been quiet – I was getting worried.'

'Sorry,' I say, trying to sound nonchalant. 'It's been busy.' There's a pause.

'Did you get the photographs?'

'What?'

The connection is not very good.

'The photographs that Wendy sent you?' I try to keep a disapproving tone out of my voice.

'Yeah – they arrived. Did you see them?'

'No, of course not – do you think I'm the sort of person that goes round reading other people's mail?' I say indignantly, wondering if he remembers that that was what he said to me the day we first met.

'No, I just wondered whether she'd shown them to you.' He can tell something is wrong by my frosty tone of voice. Then to my irritation he chuckles. 'Molly, do you know what the photographs were?'

'No, but it's none of my business – I really don't care.'

'Molly, you . . . realise . . . reason . . . she sent . . . to me . . .' The line is breaking up and I'm struggling to hear what he's saying while trying to pretend not to be interested, '. . . because I'm . . .' The line goes dead and I'm left wondering what he was trying to say.

Walking back towards Florence's room I hear voices, and I wonder who has come to visit her and think that maybe it's one of the other residents or the television that she sometimes has on as background noise. As I reach the corridor outside her room I realise that it's not talking but Florence singing to herself, her soft voice reaching for the breath to finish each note, like a runner close to the end of a marathon. It's heart-breaking hearing her struggle and I don't know whether to interrupt her or to let her finish. After a few seconds of silence I decide to go into the room. She's sitting in her chair as before with her eyes closed and a smile on her face but as I approach she opens them.

'Sorry, I must have dozed off. What was I saying?'

'You were singing.'

'Oh yes. What is it about singing that makes you feel better? I'd better watch it, I'm beginning to sound like a regular Julie Andrews.'

I sit down beside her.

'Who was that on the phone?' she asks as if she already knows the answer.

'It was Bill but he went out of range.' I don't know if she knows that we've been speaking regularly.

Florence says nothing but her gaze is disconcerting, so I try and change the subject. 'I'd better just go and find Matt and Gerry.'

'Must you?' says Florence, her eyes not moving from my face.

I get as far as the door, just level with her chest of drawers with all her framed photographs balanced on the top. I look at the pictures, Bill with a mortar board on his head on his graduation day, Florence and Tommy on their wedding day, Florence bending down and giving a bouquet to a little bridesmaid, everyone beaming. Beside that, jumping generations, Bill's two freckly boys grinning happily and another one of Bill, which I hadn't noticed before, dressed in a dinner suit at a big occasion. I peer more closely at it.

'That's when he got his award,' says Florence from her chair.

'Award for what?'

'His first film.'

'I'm sorry?' I turn round amazed.

'I thought you knew – he's a film producer in Toronto. It's not Hollywood but he doesn't do too badly most of the time – there's quite a thriving industry out there.'

She pauses. 'Funny, I would have thought you two would have talked about it – interests in common. I wonder what you do talk about then.' She smiles mischievously at me.

It takes a moment for the news to register in my overstressed brain and to make the necessary connections. Wendy must have been sending her spotlight photos to Bill. Of course I should have realised that she never does anything that won't further her career. It's none of my business whether he's having a relationship with someone or not, but I feel pleased at the news and for the rest of the day when I think about it I find it hard to suppress a smile. Matt and Gerry, however, have been quiet and distant throughout the day, cross at the way I've acquiesced to Rod's demands. I try to make amends and as Matt is packing up his lights I ask, 'How did it work out with Cassie and the room?'

'Good – I've moved in.'

'Already?' I'm surprised.

'There wasn't any reason to wait,' he says without looking at me, then as if he can't resist it he asks, 'She's interesting – who was living there before?'

'She's just come out of a long relationship; it hasn't been an easy time.'

'Mmm,' he says thoughtfully, and then as if he remembers that he's supposed to be cross with me he says accusingly, 'You should go and see her.'

'I don't think she wants to see me at the moment.' I wonder if she has said anything to him about our disagreement. Not wanting to talk about my friendship with Cassie, I try to appeal to him. 'Matt, I'm sorry about the filming but I can't do anything about it.'

'You could at least put up more of a fight.' He looks at me impatiently.

'It wouldn't have done any good.' I feel exasperated.

'How do you know until you try? I'll see you tomorrow, Molly.'

He picks up his camera and walks down the corridor, leaving me feeling alone, stranded outside Florence's room.

Twenty-seven

I can tell Aidan is nervous from the way he keeps tapping his off-white coffee mug with his teaspoon.

'You'll be fine – what time is the meeting?'

He glances at his watch. 'In three hours twenty minutes and ten seconds, not that I'm counting.' He jumps up and starts pacing around the kitchen, slamming cupboard doors shut and wiping down surfaces.

'Good luck and I want to know everything,' I say, finding it difficult to kiss him goodbye because he's constantly on the move. 'Mum should be here in a minute.'

I go to the bottom of the stairs and shout up, 'Bye, Evie.' Silence. 'Bye, Max.'

Max comes running downstairs and I notice he's got blue eye shadow and lipstick on.

'What on earth are you wearing?'

'I think it looks nice – Evie did it.'

'Evie,' I shout up the stairs, 'why have you put makeup on Max?'

'He wanted it,' she shouts back. Max sits down to eat his breakfast which has gone soggy, it's been sitting so long at the table.

'You'll need to wash it off,' I say to Aidan.

'What?' he says, oblivious to anything other than his thoughts about the impending meeting.

'The makeup on Max's face. See you later.'

It's very different when I shut the front door these days and I feel relief rather than guilt. Despite what Rod thinks, I've learnt to cut off as soon as the door is closed and to concentrate on the world outside my family. As I try to remember where I left my car last night I notice my mother's little dark blue Citroën parked along the road. She's still sitting inside, her head leaning back on the head rest. I tap on the window and she jumps.

'Are you all right, Mum?' I'm worried because she looks half asleep.

She opens the door. 'I'm fine, just a little tired that's all. I found it very hard getting out of bed this morning. I think I'm fighting something off.'

She struggles to get out of the car and I put out a hand to help steady her.

'Will you be all right?'

'Of course – once the children are at school I'll put my feet up – I've got a while before I have to pick up Max. Don't fret.'

Her eyes are slightly puffy, her face a chalky white, but she manages to smile at me. 'Off you go and don't start worrying about me – you've got enough on your plate.'

'Are you sure?'

She's steadier now and I'm no longer afraid to let go of her arm.

'Absolutely – see you later.'

I walk to the corner of the road where I've parked my car and when I turn back she's already by the front door and she gives me a wave. I wonder how much longer she will be able to look after the children as it's obvious that I've been asking too much of her these past few months. Thank God it's coming to an end, and if Aidan's script is sold then maybe we can go back to the way things were. Is it possible for it to be that simple?

Today we've been doing a lot of establishing shots which will be useful for editing purposes. Wide shots of Russell Court, close-ups of the magnolia trees beginning to flower, their upturned flowers like 'fairy boats' as Evie describes them. There are a number of red camellia bushes in the gardens that are past their best, their petals spilling on to the lawn looking like the blood-spattered remains of an accident. Matt and Gerry are still cross with me and the atmosphere between us is restrained. When we break I decide to say something.

'I know how you're feeling but please, we mustn't let it ruin the last few days of filming. You've been so supportive and I couldn't have made the film without you. But try and understand my position. If not for me, think of Florence. She doesn't need any bad feeling around her at this point in her life.'

Gerry nods his head. 'I'm just disappointed but you're right – it's been an extraordinary experience. I don't want to ruin it. I don't think I've ever worked on a film like this.' He smiles at me. 'Thanks for asking me.'

Matt is more reserved but he agrees with us and I feel pleased that I've cleared the air. The three of us make our way inside along the corridor towards Florence's room. Comfort passes us, wheeling an oxygen cylinder, and as we stop to let her pass Matt says to me, 'Molly, while we're being straight with each other, I know it's none of my business but I really think you should go and see Cassie or ring her.'

'Is she all right?'

'I just think you should call her.'

'I will, when I get a minute of course I will, if you're sure she'll talk to me.' The memory of our last meeting is still painful because everything she said was true and the guilt of it is weighing heavily on me. I'm filing it away in my emotional 'To Do' pile which every day seems to be getting bigger.

At lunchtime I call Aidan to find out how the meeting went.

'Good,' he says elliptically.

'Can you talk?'

'Oh yes, the meeting finished about ten minutes ago.'

'So what did they say?'

'They're very keen to do it – they want to buy it and Spielberg himself is keen to direct it.'

'Aidan, that's fantastic.' I can hardly contain my excitement. So much can change in just one morning, but then I remember what I thought of Aidan's script when I read it. There must be something seriously wrong with my judgement as I can't imagine Spielberg or anyone wanting to direct the script that I read.

'You don't sound very happy about it, Aidan?'

'You know, I'm not sure about it.'

'About what?'

'I'm not sure that he's the right person to do it.'

I can't believe what he is saying.

'I'd prefer it to be a bit more radical. I think it could be more interesting getting someone like Ang Lee or Almodovar to put a different spin on it. With Spielberg it's going to be Americanised, sanitised.'

'But it is an American story,'

'Well, it's based in America but a lot of the guys are Mexican or Puerto Rican.'

'So what did you say to them?'

'I said I'd think about it and that I'd like to speak to Spielberg and hear how he plans to shoot it.'

I gasp, 'You didn't?'

'Yeah, I did.'

'So what's happening?'

'I don't know, they're going to think about it.'

'Aidan, are you mad?'

'No. It's got to be right, Molly.'

Matt is waiting to speak to me about the next set-up.

'We can talk about it later.'

'If you like, but I know I'm right.'

As I put the phone down I want to scream with frustration. I can't believe the arrogance of the man. This is the first script he's written and he seems determined to jeopardise this opportunity. There are writers all over the world who would sell their souls just to have a meeting with Dreamworks, but not Aidan. He's decided to play hard ball and thrown their offer back in their faces. But a small part of me admires his confidence, and on the phone he sounded like the Aidan I used to know and not the man he's become.

We spend the final hour of the day with Florence. I'm aware of the oxygen cylinder standing guard in the corner of the room, her 'nasal specs', as she calls the plastic tubes that fit into her nose and around her head, sitting on the bedside table. They enable her to breathe with the cylinder when she needs the extra oxygen. I can't stop the fear cramping my heart and at the end of the day as the crew have finished packing up Florence calls to me, 'Do you have to rush off? I've hardly seen you today. Stay and talk to me for a bit.' She smiles encouragingly at me and sees me glancing at the oxygen cylinder.

'It bothers you, doesn't it?'

I don't know if I should admit it and show my weakness.

'I hate to see you in a state. It's such a waste,' she says, her voice cracking. She leans forward and takes a sip of water. I thought I was hiding everything so well. I sit down beside her and I think of my mother's expression this morning and how tired she looked. Suddenly I feel overwhelmed with exhaustion. I look at Florence now lying back on the pillows, her thin face open, receptive, her big eyes still curious, and I long to confide in her.

'But it's not professional,' I say, torn between wanting to confess everything and fear of beginning to speak and then never being able to stop.

'Bugger being professional,' she says in her inimitable way. 'I'm worried about you.'

I pour us both a glass of water.

'You know, I used to be scared of things,' she says.

'I can't imagine that.'

'I had a terrible fear of heights. Sweaty palms, palpitations, the lot. One of my first jobs in revue was doing a comedy sketch of Romeo and Juliet with Jimmy Edwards. Do you remember him – handlebar moustache, big stomach – no? Before your time. Anyway in those days he was doing well and it was a good opportunity for me to appear alongside him. We rehearsed on stage and that was fine but they built an enormous platform, which was supposed to be the balcony. It seemed to go on for miles, higher than Big Ben, bigger than the Statue of Liberty. I was petrified and I just knew I wouldn't be able to go up it. First few times I managed to bluff my way out of going up it. Once I managed to climb halfway up the ladder and then I had to make some pathetic excuse and come down quickly.' She chuckles at the memory.

'The next rehearsal I turned up with my arm in a sling and pretended I'd sprained my wrist but the stage manager rumbled me. He didn't say anything until the following day when he came up to me as I was in the wings watching the previous act. They were circus performers, all brothers, who could build a human pyramid. Just watching them made me feel sick, but the stage manager, Eddie his name was – funny how it comes back – pointed to a man sitting in the back of the auditorium and said, "Flo – see him? – he's a talent scout from the West End – you do this rehearsal right and you'll be made, lassie."

'I couldn't get up that ladder fast enough, did the scene and never looked back. It was the thought of it that was much worse – I just tried not to look down and it was fine. It was a great lesson—'

'Is that how you got to the West End?'

'No – turned out he was just the cleaner on his break; it was dark and I hadn't looked very closely. Eddie had made the whole thing up, canny bastard.'

She smiles at me. 'A life lived in fear is a life half lived, Molly.'

'Is that what you're doing now with us and the documentary – facing your fear?'

'Yes, I suppose it is, it gives me a way to approach it with a degree of objectivity – I can almost pretend it's research for a part. I don't know if that's healthy or not but it helps me deal with it. It's also the idea that I'm doing something useful – helping to explain something that's going to happen to all of us. I don't think I could have done it without you, not in this way, but I don't think you're what I'd call a willing partner.'

'How can you tell?'

She gives a wheezy laugh and I smile at her.

'Just because you're on your last legs doesn't mean you lose

325

all your faculties and maybe some become sharper, like a blind man whose hearing becomes more acute. My body is giving up on me but my instinct is stronger than ever. I'm glad something is.'

She looks at me sympathetically, her eyes large in her thin face. 'Would it help to talk?'

I say nothing.

'You've helped me so much just by letting me witter on. Go on, you try while you've still got time to do something about it all,' she says, encouraging me.

'I don't want to bother you with my personal problems.'

'Hasn't stopped you before. Listen, it would help me take my mind off everything, and maybe I can help and that would make me feel better, honestly. It's the least I can do – probably one of the worst things about getting older is that life is all take and no give. I'd love to be able to help even just by listening. You'd be doing me a favour.'

I take a deep breath. 'You know I told you I stopped working after I had Evie?'

'Yes,' she says encouraging me.

'I didn't stop because of Evie, I stopped because of my father.'

She doesn't say anything, letting me continue in my own time.

'I was working, filming in Scotland with Matt, making my first drama, and it was a big opportunity for me. We'd been having difficulties – the weather had been unpredictable, so we'd been delayed and were falling behind; money was tight and tempers high but I was coping. Then I got the phone call from my brother telling me that Dad had had a stroke. I couldn't take it in. He was only sixty-six and he'd never had any problems before, so although I knew it was serious I just didn't believe it.'

I struggle to restrain my tears.

'There was a lot to do, the weather took a turn for the better, so I carried on filming. I was in a world I could control and I knew what I was doing, at least I thought I did, so I stayed, I didn't go home.'

I pause, letting the words settle. 'It was the biggest mistake of my life. My brother rang again the next day but by the time I got there it was too late.'

Florence is watching me and says sympathetically, 'I'm sorry.'

We're both quiet for a minute while she digests what I've been telling her and I try to regain my composure.

'Would it have made any difference if you had been there?'

'I don't know – Tim says he wouldn't have known, but I'm sure he's being kind to me. It would have made a difference to me. He was always there for me – every important event in my life, my father never missed it, and even for the unimportant ones he'd always make the effort. He watched every programme I ever made and was always so encouraging and supportive, and I couldn't even be there when he died. But I was scared, Florence, I didn't want to see him like that, and now I'm tortured by the images of what it must have been like. In my imagination I see him dying and it's terrible.'

The tears escape and pour down my cheek. I wipe them away, furious at the emotion.

'Have you talked to anyone about how he died?' Florence asks tentatively.

'No, I can't.'

'Maybe it wasn't so bad.'

I look at her, disbelieving, and then I feel guilty, worried that this talk of terrifying death might unsettle her, but she looks calm as she prompts me to continue my story.

'So what happened after he died?'

'I finished the film and it was fine. It got a few good reviews and I had some nice letters and a few pats on the back from work colleagues and then it was forgotten. It wasn't worth it, Florence, nothing was worth it.'

'But you didn't do it deliberately – he might have lived for another day or longer – you're not a doctor, how were you to know? You were just unlucky.'

'When Evie was born I never wanted anything like that to happen again and I thought if I'd learnt anything it was that my family should take priority. So I handed in my notice, much to

Aidan's surprise, but luckily he was doing well and we could cope financially, that is until now.'

'Has it been so terrible coming back to work?'

'It's confusing. When I'm working I feel like myself again, how I used to be, and I have enjoyed being with you making the film, thinking creatively, but it's been so stressful because of the situation at home that I can't help feeling I've made the same mistake again. Since I've come back to work I've neglected my friends, I never see the children except at night to pick out their nits, I'm making my mother ill because of all the extra work I'm making her do. It's as if I've learnt nothing.'

Florence coughs from deep in her chest and when she recovers she asks, 'Was it the right decision all those years ago to give up?'

'Yes, but I made it too late and I don't think my mother has ever forgiven me.'

'Has she said that?'

'No, we can't talk about it – it's just become one of those things we don't mention. She can't talk about him at all.'

Florence leans forward and pats my hand. 'Why don't you try?'

'I have and she can't do it.'

'Keep trying – it's important.'

I mop my eyes with a tissue from the box beside her bed.

'Thank you for telling me – it helps me to understand.' She leans back on her pillows, exhausted by the emotion.

By the time I reach home I too feel exhausted, not only because of the filming but because of the conversation I've had with Florence which has brought back so many memories I'd rather forget. The house is dark, except for the night light shining in Max's bedroom. I open the door quietly, not wanting to wake the children, and I walk into the kitchen, which is in semi-darkness, partially illuminated by the reflection of the lights in the surrounding houses shining through the windows. I'm surprised to see my mother sitting very still at the table and beside her is my father's camera.

'Mum, are you all right?' I ask, my voice puncturing the quietness.

She doesn't reply but after a few seconds she says so quietly that I have to lean forward to hear what she's saying, 'I still can't believe he's gone. I go into his study at home sometimes to tell him something and it's only when I see his empty desk that I remember. Some days I make two cups of coffee and then I have to pour one away and wonder what was I thinking of. I still haven't done anything about his clothes hanging in the wardrobe although what I'm waiting for I don't know – I just can't bring myself to look at them, let alone touch them, so I avoid that cupboard. Sometimes his very absence is too hard to bear. I'm sorry, I'm being silly.'

'No you're not.' I'm so relieved that she's talking about him. 'I'm so sorry, Mum,' I say, sitting down beside her.

'What are you sorry for?'

'For not being there when he died.'

'Oh my dear girl – it wasn't your fault.'

'But it was – I should have left the filming earlier – I should have come immediately.'

'But you couldn't – they needed you.'

'They could have coped – this was so much more important – but the thing is, the reason I wasn't there . . .'

'Shh – you don't have to do this,' she says, reassuring me.

'I do, I have to tell you,' I say urgently, not wanting to let the opportunity slip away. 'I didn't come because I couldn't face it – I was so terrified of what I might see, of seeing him struggle and then watching him die, so I tried to pretend it wasn't happening. I'm sorry that I let you and Dad down.' Tears are pouring down my face. 'I never said goodbye.'

'Oh, my poor dear girl.'

My mother turns in her chair and takes me in her arms and rocks me like a child.

Twenty-eight

I surface out of my sleep and immediately my heart pounds as I fumble in the darkness trying to find the phone that is rudely ringing so early in the morning. I check the clock and at this time of the morning it can only be bad news and I immediately think of Florence.

'Molly, I'm sorry to do this to you but I feel dreadful – I think it must be flu. I can't come today.'

It isn't Florence's deep voice but my mother's, sounding frail and croaky. I sit up in bed.

'You poor thing, of course I understand. Can I do anything for you?' I hate to think of her alone in the cottage.

'No, don't worry, I'll be fine. I'm going to dose myself up with Lemsip and stay in bed. I'm so sorry, Molly, to let you down when you've only got a few more days' filming.'

There's been a cautious tenderness between us since our cathartic conversation a few days ago and although I still feel stretched to my limits I'm aware something has shifted and loosened, and consequently I've been sleeping heavily. I look to see if Aidan is awake but his side of the bed is empty although it has definitely been slept in. I didn't hear him come back last night and I suspect he's upstairs in the study worrying at the script. There's still no word from Spielberg but undeterred, Aidan has retreated into a creative frenzy, as if spurred on by the interest they initially expressed. I creep upstairs, careful not to wake the children, to find Aidan huddled over his laptop.

'How are you getting on?'

'Good. I had an idea for another script last night so I was just writing it down before I forget.'

'Are you around today?'

He's very distracted and I can tell he's finding it hard to tear himself away from the words on the screen.

'Molly,' he groans, 'I've got to work, don't you see? I think I can do this and I've got a great idea, and I have to write it up now and I want to take it over to Terry and run it past him.'

'Why Terry?' I say, feeling infuriated with Aidan for not being more cooperative.

'Because he seems to be the only person close to me interested enough to want to read my work,' he says, looking at me accusingly.

'I do want to read it but I've been very busy – I don't have enough time to read with the children, let alone read your script. I will read it.'

'When?'

'Soon, when we go away, but today I've got a problem because Mum's not well.'

'Couldn't you take them with you?' He's gone back to staring at the screen.

'Well, they've got school and it's too difficult now. It's not the same as it was at Christmas, Florence is fragile, it will be too much of an imposition and the children might find it distressing. Please, Aidan, just for today.'

'But it won't be, will it? I can't work like this, Molly.'

'Neither can I,' I say, wanting to punch him with frustration. 'OK, leave it to me and I'll try and sort it out. Thank you for being so bloody helpful.'

Furious, I go back downstairs and get back into bed, punching the pillows in my frustration. I ring Jenny, Sandra and even Jo in my desperation, but none of them can help me today. Feeling despondent, I snuggle down the bed, pulling the duvet up around my ears, blocking out the rest of the world. By the time the children wander into our bedroom, yawning, the sleepy dust fresh in their eyes, I haven't found anyone to take them. They both clamber into bed, arguing over who is going to go which side, and we lie together, arms entwined, and I'm tempted to stay here in bed all day. I don't even bother to answer the phone when it rings again but I hear Aidan take it upstairs. He shouts down, 'Molly, it's for you.'

When I lean over Max to pick up the phone he tries to tickle me under my arms.

'Molly, it's Helen here, I wanted to check with you about Evie's bridesmaid shoes. I've got them here but I thought that she should try them on before the day just to check that they fit.'

'Oh, Helen, yes of course, um, how shall we do this?'

'Well, I've taken time off work for the run-up to the wedding. I could pop them in today if you like?'

I pause and then I have an idea.

'Helen, I know this is a lot to ask, but Mum's got flu and both Aidan and I have to work today. There isn't any way you could pick the children up from school and sort of stay with them until one of us gets back, is there?'

I cross my fingers and look at Evie who, realising that I'm talking to Helen, shakes her head and mouths, 'No way' at me. Max frowns; neither of them has recovered from the sofa incident, and from the silence the other end of the phone I can tell they're not the only ones.

'I know it's a lot to ask but you'd be doing me such a favour.'

I swear I hear her gulp.

'OK.'

'Really?' I'm amazed.

'Yes, anything I can do to help. I've got a few things to do over your way, so I'll come over now and you can show me where everything is.'

'Helen – I can't thank you enough.'

She laughs nervously, but any reservations I may have had about her are beginning to evaporate.

I fling open the door the moment that Helen lifts the door-knocker, and to her surprise I rush out and give her a hug. She looks shocked, embarrassed and a little pleased by my effusive welcome.

'I'll show you where everything is, and Aidan's upstairs for the morning if there's anything you need to know.' I pause. 'On second thoughts, it's probably better to ring me on my mobile.'

Helen puts down her bag and a Sainsbury's plastic bag she's brought with her and takes off her jacket.

'I spoke to Elizabeth; she sounds very poorly. Do you mind if I make her some soup while I'm here, and when you get back I can drive down and take her some provisions? I've bought the ingredients.'

'Of course.' For a minute, prompted by guilt, I think St bloody Helen, and then I check myself, considering I'm on the receiving end of her saintliness. I show her round the house.

'It's very modern, isn't it?'

I think of her Art Deco flat, which Aidan would hate. 'Yes, but don't be put off, it may be white but it's pretty hardy. It's had to be to cope with the children. Food is in the fridge and please try and make sure Evie does her homework when she comes back, but if you've got any problems, just put on a video. I'll try and make it back as soon as I can. Thank you, Helen.'

To my surprise I make it to Russell Court before the crew, and as I walk up the stone steps I hear the crunch of gravel and the arrival of another car. I turn, expecting to see the crew car, but it's Cassie's unmistakable red Mini Cooper. She bought her first Mini after seeing *The Italian Job*, out of a strange loyalty to Michael Caine. In the car I see Gerry wedged between boxes of equipment and Matt balancing his camera on his knees. Cassie looks straight through me as she parks the car in front of the house and Matt opens his door and eases his way out, stretching his legs as if he's just been on a long-haul economy flight to Australia.

'Bloody murder.' Seeing the curious look on my face, he explains, 'Couldn't get the car started this morning, so Cassie gave us a lift.'

He walks round to the driver's door and leans in and to my surprise gives Cassie a kiss goodbye.

'See you later, and thanks, Cass.'

Gerry walks past carrying his boom and a box, his headphones already round his neck. 'Morning, boss,' he says, whistling.

Matt turns and as he passes by he nudges me. 'Go on, talk to her.'

I shake my head. 'If she wanted to talk to me she would.'

Cassie glances in the rear-view mirror and switches on the engine.

Matt explodes. 'God, women! You two are as bad as each other and so pig-headed. Give me strength. I give up, I bloody give up,' and he stomps up the steps into Russell Court.

Cassie starts to reverse, and I look at Matt's retreating back and think of all we've talked about over the past few days with Florence, and suddenly it all seems ridiculous. I shout, 'Cassie,' but she doesn't hear as she straightens up the car.

'Cassie,' I shout again as I hear her change into first gear, and as she begins to move off down the drive, I run after her shouting and waving my arms. She's beginning to pick up speed but I accelerate, trying to overtake until I'm running beside the car. I lean over and bang on the roof, and Cassie turns and sees me, and with a look of total surprise she slams on the brakes and I find myself running alone, the car having stopped. I try and catch my breath as I walk back. Cassie winds down the window and her expression is stony.

'I'm . . . I'm . . . so . . . sorry.' I manage to get the words out despite feeling as if my lungs will burst. 'I've been a useless friend. Will you forgive me?'

She looks up at me and eventually she smiles. 'I might do.'

I collapse on the side of the driveway, still fighting for breath. Cassie opens the car door and comes and sits beside me. It's a beautiful spring morning but the grass is damp.

'I didn't mean to be so harsh but I was a bit fed up with you.'

'I can see why,' I pant.

'I've been doing a lot of thinking – it was one of the reasons I went away.'

'What were you thinking about?'

'Everything – Will, you, me, the job and the way we live our lives. Anyway, I've made a decision.'

'Oh God, you're not going to top yourself, are you?'

She smiles. 'No, I've decided to retrain and become a teacher.'

'What, you're going to resign, leave television?'

I'm shocked, as it's the last thing I expected of her. For years she has been defined by the job and it seemed to be the one constant in her life, and now she's prepared to give it all up.

'Yes.' She looks the happiest I've seen her for a long time. 'I figure if I can't have my own children, I'll have everyone else's. I've been thinking about it for a while because at first I worried it was one of those holiday decisions that you live to regret later on.'

'You mean like bringing back Ouzo from a Greek island and expecting it to taste the same in Tooting?'

'Exactly,' she laughs.

'By the way, where did you go on holiday? Thailand, or a spiritual retreat in India?'

'Ibiza.'

We laugh, and Cassie puts her arm over my shoulder.

'The more I think about this decision the happier I am with it. Television is exciting but it burns you out; you know what it's like. I can see it happening to you now. It's time to stop.'

'I've only just started again,' I say, feeling a wave of despair wash over me.

The sound of a horn hooting makes us both look up. Cassie's car is blocking the entrance to the house and a driver in a white van winds down his window, shouting at us, 'Come on, move your bloody car, I've been stuck on the motorway for hours.'

We both get up. Cassie kisses me and waves at the driver. She jumps into the car and backs up very fast to where the drive widens in front of Russell Court. Once the van has passed by she drives back down until she's parallel and leans out of the window.

'You'd better get to work or you'll be late. Let's have an evening soon.'

'Definitely,' and as she starts to pull away I say, 'Cassie?'

'Yes?'

'Were you just snogging my cameraman?'

'I'm not sure he's yours any longer.' She grins and puts her foot down on the accelerator and speeds off down the drive and out through the gates.

Even before I open the front door I can hear Evie's shrill voice singing along with her S Club CD. 'Reach, climb every mountain.'

Her voice is distorted because it's too close to the microphone and as I walk through to the kitchen I see her doing an interesting dance move while Helen and Max sit on the sofa, a captive audience.

'Look at this, Mum,' says Evie excitedly, and she drags Helen up from the sofa and they do a short dance routine together, which ends with Evie falling backwards into Helen's arms who then pushes her forwards. Max runs to kiss me and all seems happy in the Taylor household.

'Has it been all right?' I ask anxiously.

'It's been brilliant,' Evie says, flushed from dancing.

Max runs to show me a row of paper planes, lined up in formation on the central island unit. 'Helen made them.'

'It's the only thing I could remember how to do,' she says as if apologising. 'I didn't do much, they entertained me. Do you need me to come tomorrow? I don't think your mother is up to it.'

I watch her making me a cup of tea. Her calmness is soothing and now I completely understand why my brother wants to marry her; even I would like to marry her at the moment. I love this woman. She hands me the tea.

'That would be fantastic.'

'There were some messages – Jenny apologising for not being able to help out and are you all right? Elizabeth – well, that was for me really, and Steven Spielberg.'

I sit upright. 'Who?'

'Steven Spielberg,' she says without changing her tone.

'Oh my God, did you tell Aidan?'

'He's not here. It's not the real Steven Spielberg?' She looks shocked. 'I just assumed it was someone playing a joke, a friend mucking about.'

She sits down beside me, stunned, and then she gets up and gathers her things together. 'I've got to go – I can't wait to tell Tim. I've left some soup on the side for you and the rest I'm going to take up to your mother's tomorrow after I've finished here. Bye, kids, bye, Molly, and thank you.'

'No, Helen, thank *you*.' But she's out of the door and it slams behind her.

I look at the long list that is covered with yellow Post-it notes which I add on every time I think of something else that we need to take away with us: Wellington boots, Max's muslin, macs, audio tapes for car journey, brilliant *I'm Bored* book for ideas on how to keep children occupied on long journeys, buckets and spades (perhaps a little bit optimistic), swimming costumes (positively optimistic), goggles, rushes (I need to view them while I'm away to start working on an edit list), programme notes, CDs for car journey, Calpol, nit comb.

At the very bottom of the list in Evie's small joined-up writing it says simply, 'Buy Evie more sweets.'

I've left a message for Aidan but he's not answering his mobile, so I start packing my favourite sweater, a couple of T-shirts, two pairs of jeans and some warm socks, throwing them into an enormous black holdall. Aidan does his own packing as he has a special way of folding his shirts, which apparently I haven't begun to master. He always travels with his turn-of-the-century Edwardian leather suitcase, which I can't lift even when it's empty. Apart from that he travels light, which I'm incapable of doing. I like to have my things around me. I wonder what I'll be like if I ever have to move into a home and what I would take with me.

There's a loud knocking at the door and I run downstairs quickly, glancing at my watch. It's ten o'clock, and I can't begin to imagine who would be coming round at this hour unless it's an emergency. I put on the chain before I open the door and as I peer into the dark street I see a familiar flash of streaked blonde hair.

'Open up, darling, it's me.'

'Jo – what are you doing here?'

'I happened to be passing,' she grins at me.

'Yeah, right.'

'Actually you sounded in such a state this morning I just wanted to check you were all right. What are you doing?' she asks.

'Packing.'

For a minute she looks shocked. 'You're not leaving, are you?'

'No, we're going to Dorset tomorrow to stay in a cottage. We're going straight down after my last day of filming with Florence. Fancy a cup of tea or something stronger?'

'Glass of red wine would be lovely.'

She takes off her coat and wanders around picking up photos, looking at everything as if she's refamiliarising herself with our home. I find the corkscrew and open a bottle of cheap Rioja I bought a few weeks ago as a gesture of defiance. It's rare to find a bottle of red wine in our house, as Aidan prefers white wine. It's the carpets he worries about.

'Do you mind bringing it upstairs and we can talk as I pack – otherwise I'll never get it done.'

'Fine. Lead on, Macduff.'

'Remind me. What do you do?'

'You wouldn't believe it but I'm an actress.'

'No, really?' I say in mock surprise.

We slip back into the usual routines and suddenly I'm glad she's here. She slips off her shoes, swings her legs up and lies back on the bed.

'God, this is a firm mattress – not a lot of bounce on this bed.'

'Aidan likes it – took me years to persuade him to get rid of the futon and this was our compromise.'

I open the bottom drawer of the chest of drawers where I keep my jumpers and try to decide which one to take.

'Is Aidan here?' Jo asks, looking around as if expecting him to appear at any moment.

'No, I don't know where he is, but you'll never guess who rang today.'

Jo looks at me blankly. 'No?'

'Steven Spielberg.'

'You're kidding,' she says, raising her eyebrows. 'What did he say?'

'I don't know, I didn't speak to him – Helen was here.'

'Helen?'

'Yes, amazingly she came and looked after the children. Needless to say I've reviewed my opinion of her.'

I walk into Max's room and without waking him try to open the chest of drawers to get out some trousers and jeans. There's only one pair of combat trousers: I check all the drawers and the wardrobe and find nothing. Swearing under my breath, I go and search the dirty linen basket, to find it heaving with soiled and smelly clothes. I go through them, gingerly picking up knickers and socks, sometimes smelling them to see how dirty they are. I only hope there's a washing machine in the cottage.

When I walk back into our bedroom Jo is flicking through a book which she's taken from the enormous pile on my side of the bed. She looks up.

'So is Spielberg interested in Aidan's script?'

'I don't know. He had a meeting but Aidan is not sure Spielberg's the right director.'

Jo, in the middle of taking a sip of wine, splutters. 'God, isn't he infuriating?'

'I suppose he's got integrity,' I say, choosing my words carefully. 'At least he's not just grabbing at the first offer. It's an admirable trait.'

'But what about you? Here you are working like this with no help except for your poor old mum and he's being dilettante with your future. You're always so supportive of him.'

I sigh. 'Isn't that a good thing?'

'Sometimes, but come on, Molly, he just walks all over you and you run around trying to make life easier for him. I bet he had nothing on today – he's just too bloody selfish to think about anyone else.'

'We've always disagreed about Aidan. Let's not talk about this now – I'm too tired.' I push the clothes down in the holdall hoping that they'll fit in.

'How long are you going for?'

'Three or four days, we're not sure yet. It depends . . .'

'Yes?' She looks up questioningly. I can't avoid her gaze.

'You do the same thing as Florence with your eyes – never blink.'

'It's effective, isn't it? But it works better on camera.'

'Jo, will you promise me one thing?'

She goes very serious. 'Yes, of course, whatever you want.'

'Turn away when I pack my knickers – it's very embarrassing but they've turned a delicate shade of grey and I haven't had a chance to buy any new ones for months.'

She watches me as I open the drawer, and I'm trying not to think about what she has just said about Aidan.

'Don't look,' I say emphatically, and she turns away, her head facing towards the door.

As I pick out a bra Jo turns back. 'Your lucky one?' she asks, looking at the ordinary black bra in my hand.

'No, still wearing that one.'

'So last day filming tomorrow – that's going to be emotional?'

'I can't bear to think about it.'

'Remind me, why are you stopping?'

'There isn't enough money to carry on filming but also, I don't think I can do it. I can't sit there and watch her struggle. I just can't.'

'How is she?'

'She's . . . well, she's dying.'

I pull out an old jumper from the bottom drawer and hold it close. 'I told her about Dad.'

'Did you?' she says, amazed.

'Talking about it was a sort of release – I think it's helped. I feel all sorts of things are changing.'

I pause and sit down on the bed beside Jo. 'I talked to Mum about it.'

'And was that all right?' she asks.

'Yes, I think it was.'

I feel the tears threatening to flow again. I fling the jumper into the bag and try to change the subject. 'But you didn't come over for me to get all tired and emotional – I'm sorry, Jo, I feel so raw at the moment.'

'Don't be silly – I'm glad I came now.'

'Why did you come?'

'Well, I was worried about you and I just thought . . .'

'What?'

'Well, I wondered . . . what are you going to wear for the wedding?'

'You came all the way over here at ten o'clock at night just because you wanted to know what I was going to wear for Tim's wedding?'

She looks flustered and I think she needs to work on her technique as she's giving a poor performance.

'All right,' she gives in gracefully, 'I wanted to see you.'

'Is everything OK with Gabriel, Finn or whoever?'

'Gabriel, history,' she says unemotionally.

'And that's OK?' I ask.

'Absolutely fine – well, I miss the sex and the excitement of it all, but that's all it was – I told you that.'

'Well, if you're sure.'

'At the time it was a positive thing for our marriage but . . .'

'Yes?'

'Well, I think Finn is seeing someone.'

Part of me wants to laugh but when I see Jo's face I feel only sympathy.

'I haven't got a leg to stand on, have I?' she says hopelessly. 'The terrible thing is that I think I'd do it again. It's like I need to – for the excitement and the thrill of it. The idea that the only person I'll ever sleep with again is Finn is too depressing, but at the same time I don't want to lose him and I don't want to be on my own.' She looks at me despairingly. As an afterthought she says, 'It's not even that the sex with Finn is bad, it's just . . . well, normal.'

I sit down on the side of the hard bed and Jo takes a big sip of wine.

'Is it the same with you and Aidan? Haven't you ever been tempted?'

'Yes, I have.'

'Why didn't you tell me?' she asks, sounding amazed and hurt at the same time.

'I'm still trying to work it all out.'

I tell her about Bill, what happened on New Year's Eve, and more importantly about the way the relationship has developed through our intimate phone calls. 'I feel very close to him but I don't know whether it's because of the film and my relationship with Florence.'

'This film has had a big effect on you, hasn't it?' says Jo seriously.

'It's not so much the film as Florence. Being with her at the moment is physically and emotionally overwhelming, like looking after a newborn baby. I know it sounds strange but I feel like she's become part of me. I come home and I can smell her on my skin, and I catch myself copying some of her mannerisms, like the way she rests her finger on her top lip and how she twists her big ring. In a way it's like falling in love. What if these intense feelings for Bill are because of Florence? I don't know if I can trust them.'

She's listening intently to every word I say. 'I know what you mean – it's like intense acting jobs, where you become so involved with each other and it's hard to work out what is real. It's why so many actors have affairs, I suppose.'

'But this isn't theatre.'

Neither of us says anything, lost in our own thoughts.

'Anyway it's probably ridiculous – we only had a kiss and it's hardly grounds for divorce. I've got to stop thinking about him.'

'Why?'

'Because of the children and Aidan.'

'Interesting that it's that way round.' Jo takes another big gulp of wine.

'Did you drive here?' I ask.

'Bugger it – I can't even get pissed these days.' Reluctantly she puts the glass down.

'The way I see it, you have two options, Jo. One: you carry on and have your affairs and he has his and you enjoy the excitement but realise there's a risk that the marriage could collapse; two: you could stop it all now. Tell him what you've done, say that you know that he's seeing someone else but that you want to make the marriage work, a clean slate.'

'That's a scary thought.'

'But it's the brave way.'

It's so much easier telling other people how to sort out their lives. I think of Florence's advice to me.

'But can I trust myself?'

'Well, that's for you to work out.'

The sound of the front door shutting downstairs surprises us both.

'And you?' she says quickly. 'What are you going to do?'

'I don't know. Not think about it until after tomorrow.'

Jo puts her arms around me and we sit together on the side of the bed, undisturbed until Aidan walks into the room.

'Sorry to interrupt,' he says, looking surprised to see Jo, but I can see he's excited.

'Did you get your messages?'

'Yes, and I've spoken to him. He rang me on my mobile and we talked for about half an hour.'

'What was it like?' Jo and I chorus, eager to hear details.

'Good.'

'And?' I prompt him.

'He wants me to go over to the States and work on it with

him. He's talking about getting me over there for six months or so.'

'Oh,' I say, the repercussions sinking in.

Jo gets up. 'I'd better leave you two. Good luck tomorrow, Molly, and have a good break.' She gives me a kiss and turns to Aidan. 'Make sure she relaxes or you'll have a sick wife on your hands. Well done, Aidan, it's fantastic news. See you both at the wedding.'

The door slams, leaving us alone together. I start folding up the dirty laundry and putting it into the holdall.

'I think that's dirty,' says Aidan, watching me rolling one of Max's T-shirts and shoving it down the side of the bag.

'That might be because no one has done any washing for weeks,' I say tersely.

'I suppose that's my fault,' he says, sitting down on the edge of the bed. He puts his arms above his head and falls backwards, sinking into the bed, and I can't blame him for not thinking about the washing when he's being wooed by one of the most successful directors in the world.

'I feel pissed,' he says, smiling at me, 'but I haven't had a drink,' and seeing that I'm not over-enthusiastic he checks himself and half sits up, leaning on his arm. 'They want me there next week,' he says, and without checking my response he continues, 'It might be longer than six months, especially if they can get it into production quickly.'

I walk out into Max's bedroom to find his trainers. As I come back into our bedroom I realise I've forgotten to get his spare fleece and turn back, my brain straining like a camera when the batteries start to run down, my feet as heavy as my thoughts.

'Can this wait until Dorset? I'm so tired, I need to pack, and I need to try and keep my head clear for our last day filming. I'm really excited for you and I don't want to put a dampener on it now – sorry.'

I leave him staring at the ceiling and go into the bathroom to get ready for bed. I turn on the taps and stand in front of the mirror, not really looking at my face but focusing on the individual bits I'm cleaning as I do every night. The eye makeup remover stings my eyes as I wipe away the remaining traces of mascara, the white cotton wool soiled by dark grey streaks. I smear cream on to my face and rinse it with water and when I glance up I feel a strange fascination as if I'm looking at myself for the first time in years. My face is older, more lined, the skin less pliant. It gives away nothing of the thoughts churning in my head and I feel curiously detached. The steam from the hot water slowly passes across the mirror and obscures me from view.

Twenty-nine

Florence's feet are smoother than I imagine, and when I look up I can see that she's enjoying watching me rubbing the cream into her toes and the soles of her feet, massaging them, just as Jane, the care nurse, has taught me.

'Look what I've reduced you to,' Florence chuckles.

'I don't mind if it helps.'

'It does.'

Florence's room has changed in small, subtle ways during our last few visits. Now there is the oxygen tank in the corner of the room, which hisses and sighs into life when it's needed. When we arrived she asked for water, so I went to get it from the fridge in the bathroom and as I opened the door I saw the pre-measured hypodermic syringes of morphine in the door. As I massage her feet I catch a glimpse of the canula strapped to her thigh, a permanent fixture.

Lying in her bed she looks shrunken, as if she's imploding, like a helium balloon the day after a party. Her arms are bony and the rings she loved to wear sit in attendance on the bedside table, the topaz taking pride of place. Her face is hollow, the skin draped over her bones like a cover over a lamp, her eyes huge, still glowing with spirit. She's wearing no makeup today. It's the first time she's appeared on camera without lipstick, bedridden. As if reading my mind she says, 'I can't make the effort any more – do you mind?'

'No, not at all,' I say, but I know that she's signalling the end.

On a tray over her bed alongside the vitamin E cream there is a log book recording her medication doses, and on top of that a copy of *Hello*! magazine. As if following my thoughts she says, 'I've even lost interest in Liz Hurley – that can't be good.'

'Oh, I don't know, some might say that's quite healthy.'

She smiles. 'Do you believe in fate?' she asks, struggling to get her breath.

'I don't know – do you?'

'Sometimes I think things happen for a reason.'

'Like what?'

'Like meeting you, sometimes you find people when you need them.'

I look at her feet, the remnants of red nail polish still visible at the end of her knobbly toes. I try to compose myself.

'This morning I was thinking about a man I met once in a restaurant. He was there with two women and having a wonderful fuss made of him. He looked like he was thoroughly enjoying himself, so I leant over and said, "Are you celebrating anything special?" and he replied, "Just being alive – I do it every Wednesday."'

I smile at her and put down her swollen right foot, carefully placing the left one in my lap. I start massaging it gently, hoping that it's giving her some comfort and taking her mind off the pain.

'Think about it – are you doing all you need to do with your life, Molly?' I feel embarrassed as we're filming but Matt and Gerry are keeping silent, their concentration almost palpable. She doesn't wait for an answer and begins to ramble, her thoughts often not connected, I suspect because of the drugs. She groans and shifts in the bed as if trying to fight the pain. She's struggling as if she's in labour, and I glance anxiously at the door and wonder whether I should get Jane. I hate seeing her in pain.

She sees my expression and very slowly, struggling to get the words out, says, 'My father had this phrase that he'd use if he was really enjoying something, and I've always remembered it. He often used it at Sunday lunch when he'd take his first mouthful of roast beef and Yorkshire pudding, which he loved, and he always said it with a glint in his eye: "I'll be glad when I've had enough."'

She shifts uncomfortably in the bed, the pain and discomfort written all over her features. She says hoarsely, 'I think I've had enough.'

Matt and Gerry silently pack away their equipment and Florence is clearly uncomfortable, her sighs quiet but audible. The door opens and closes as first Comfort looks in to check that Florence has everything she needs and then Jane, who quietly takes out the morphine from the fridge door and taps the syringe expertly to clear the bubbles before she administers the injection.

I feel useless. 'Can I do anything?' I ask Jane.

She smiles at me.

'Just sit with her until she sleeps – it won't be long.'

The last silver equipment box packed away, Gerry waits awkwardly at the door, looking embarrassed by the emotion he feels. Matt comes over beside the bed. 'We'll be seeing you, Florence,' he says quietly.

Florence puts out her hand and says, 'So good of you to come,' like a hostess at a drinks party who has drunk too many bellinis, her voice slurring.

Matt takes her hand and in an uncharacteristic gesture he kisses it. 'A pleasure, Florence, it's been a real pleasure.' He places her hand gently back on the bed covers and squeezes my shoulder. 'Will you be OK to get home?' he asks, concerned.

'I'll be fine. I'll call you so you can come and see the edit.'

'I'd like that. See you then.'

I watch him leave and when I turn back to Florence her eyelids are drooping. I collect my bag from the other side of the bed and look around the room that has become my world over the past few weeks.

'I think Bill should come soon,' she says slowly.

'I'll tell him.'

'No, not yet, but soon.' Her voice is dreamy. 'Will you look after him?'

Without thinking I say, 'Of course I will.'

'That's good,' she says sleepily.

I sit down again.

'Come back, my lovely girl,' she whispers. I watch her eyelids close and hear her easy breaths occasionally punctuated by air-hungry sighs. I lean forward and kiss her forehead, the skin soft and dry.

'I will,' I say under my breath.

The hall is deserted but the sound of voices takes me into the library. I feel like I want to say goodbye before I leave although I know it won't be long before I'll be back to visit. I find Bernard sitting in the library, Dora reading the newspaper out loud to him.

'What did you say – you're muttering – can't you speak more clearly?'

Already they're like a married couple. Dora looks up when I enter and smiles nervously at me.

'I just wanted to say goodbye.'

'Who is it?' asks Bernard, looking blankly in my direction.

'It's me, Molly, the director.'

'Television director,' he corrects me, as if that doesn't really qualify me to be classified as a proper director.

'How long have you got to edit?' he says gruffly, determined to show me that just because his eyesight is failing and his body deteriorating, his mind is still functioning well.

'Four weeks, but I'm having a break before I start. I'll see if I can organise a screening here for all of you if you like.'

'No good to me,' he says, but as if to make amends for his gruffness he adds, 'Good luck with it.'

Dora pats his hand and he smiles in her direction and then she looks up at me. 'How is Florence?'

'Sleeping at the moment.'

'I thought I'd take her up some lavender from the garden – it smells so lovely and she appreciates it so much.' Tears well up in her eyes. 'She's going to miss having you around. We all will.'

'I'm going to miss you all as well but I'll be back after my brother's wedding next weekend. I'll come and find you.'

As I turn to go Bernard shouts out, 'I hope you did enough

wide shots – people need to know where they are – biggest lesson of my career.'

'Thanks, Bernard, I'll remember that.'

As I reach the door I hear my name being called and I turn to see Eleanor, marching along the corridor towards me.

'Goodbye, Molly.' She stretches out her hand. I take it and say, 'Goodbye, and thanks for letting us film. Sorry about fusing the lights but I hope that we weren't too much of a disruption.'

'Well, we coped.' She smiles at me. 'It's going to be a bit quieter once you've gone. Florence wants you to have this.' She hands me Florence's topaz ring. I take it in the palm of my hand and turn it over, seeing the light reflected in the splendid stone. I give it back to Eleanor.

'No, tell her she can give it to me herself, next time I come to see her.'

The sound of his voice in my ear is comforting, and if a day goes by when we don't speak I have to admit I miss it. I ring him today for the first time – up to now it's always been Bill who has rung me, as I didn't want to make the first move or appear to be too keen. The delight in his voice when he hears mine makes me feel better.

'How are things?'

'Fine. Have you spoken to her?' I ask.

'Yes, but it's getting harder to understand what she's saying. Do you think I should come now?'

'I don't know, Bill, she says she wants you to come soon but not quite yet.'

'I want to be there, I hate being so far away. I've booked a flight for next Saturday and Eleanor said she'd call me if I need to bring it forward. I've got my bag packed already; it's sitting here in the hall.'

It reminds me of waiting to go into labour with Evie. I had my hospital bag packed at least a week before she deigned to make an appearance. It was full of nappies, muslins, feeding bras, unsightly string pants, huge absorbent pads, calendula cream for cracked nipples, books on how to breastfeed, a fresh nightie and clothes for an unknown baby, all things to help ease the aftermath of labour. There is nothing Bill can bring that will help Florence, except himself.

'How are the boys?' I try to take his mind off the future.

'We hired a campervan last weekend and took to the mountains. It was fantastic. I made sure I could ring in to Russell Court every day to check on Florence but for three days we hardly saw a soul. We lit camp fires, went for long walks, counted stars, did boys' stuff – you know what I mean.'

No, I don't know what he means. The idea of Aidan taking the children off for a holiday is unthinkable. He's never spent any time alone with them apart from the few snatched hours after school before I come back from work and neither the children nor Aidan would say they'd enjoyed it.

'You've gone quiet.'

'I think I'm just very tired.'

'Molly, when I come over could we . . .' His voice tails off and then he tries again. 'Do you think we could spend some time together?' And then, before he's hardly finished saying the words, I can tell he's regretting them, worrying that he's put pressure on me and made a fool of himself. 'Sorry, I don't know what I was thinking of. You make me say and do these things. I can't help myself.'

'Don't be sorry. I understand, it's an emotional time for you.'

'Don't do that.'

'Do what?'

'Don't push me away pretending this is all about Florence. It's not – this is between you and me.' His tone is urgent, emphatic.

'How do you know that?' His words are fighting their way through the jungle of muddled thoughts in my brain.

'I know.' He sounds so sure.

I long to be so sure. I want to collapse, take to my bed and sleep for days and forget all about the terrible muddle which is my life.

Thirty

The pages flap wildly and I sit hunched, trying to protect the script from being battered by the wind. I read the final line and look around for a stone large enough to weigh down the script so that it won't blow away. I stretch out my legs and watch Aidan hard at work building a huge skyscraper of a sandcastle. Beside him is a pile of detritus gathered from the beach – bits of driftwood, seaweed and a mound of interestingly shaped pebbles which he collected earlier. He is meticulous in the way he is constructing the walls, building small bricks of sand and placing them one on top of each other like a proper bricklayer and then smoothing them down. Evie has abandoned him and is writing her name in the sand with her toe. Max, easily bored, starts to dig a tunnel in the middle of Aidan's construction.

'Not there, Max – that's the wrong place. You can dig a moat round here,' Aidan shouts at him.

'I don't want to dig a moat, I want to make a dungeon,' Max says crossly.

Aidan's pained expression is echoed by the cry of a seagull. He glances across at me, suddenly aware that I'm watching him. 'Have you finished it yet?' he shouts across the noise of the sea. I nod my head and he abandons the skyscraper and walks towards me. He stands over me, his back to the bright sun, and I shield my eyes, staring up at him.

'Well?'

'It's very good,' I say, meaning it.

'But?' he says, bracing himself.

'No buts.'

'Really? So it's not as bad as you thought it would be?'

'Not at all – I think it's fantastic.'

He looks pleased and allows himself a smile. The script that I've just finished bears no relation to the one I read at New Year. It's the same subject but handled in a very different way. I must have stumbled across an early discarded draft, which will teach me to read things behind people's backs in the future.

'Did it make you laugh and cry?' he asks hopefully.

'Both. I can see why Spielberg is so keen.'

Delighted, he sits down beside me and puts his arm around me, squeezing my shoulders and kissing my cold cheek. 'That's very good.'

I turn to look at him, watching the wind tugging at his hair. 'When do you go?'

'As soon as possible. They've got an apartment I can stay in. They're also keen to have first refusal on any other ideas I might have and I've been thinking about what I'd like to do next.' He's talking quickly, the words tumbling over themselves in his enthusiasm. 'This is the greatest feeling, thinking that everything that I've ever done in my life, all the emotions I've felt are now useful material. Suddenly there's a purpose to it all.'

How ironic, I think to myself, that just as Aidan starts to make sense of everything, I feel my world is unravelling. I can see he's not given me or the children a moment's thought. He looks at me and I can see skeins of silver in his grey hair like thread in a fine cloth.

'Aidan, what are we supposed to be doing while you're in America?'

He looks surprised by the question. 'Same as usual – you don't have to carry on working if you don't want to because they're going to pay me a big development fee. You could come over if you want, bring the children.' He doesn't sound very keen.

'Is the apartment big enough?'

'I don't know, but you could stay in a hotel or something. Don't be like this, Molly – think of it as an adventure.'

'I don't feel very adventurous. What if it's more than six months?'

'It probably will be, but does that make a difference?' he says, irritated by my lack of enthusiasm. 'I have to go, Molly.'

'Aidan, do you ever think of anyone other than yourself?'

The shock on his face makes me hesitate and an objective part of my brain is saying, 'Are you sure you want to do this?' I could carry on as before, indulging him, letting him live his life without thinking about us, his family.

'That's a bit unfair – I've been scrabbling around the last few months trying to look after the children, squeezing in the writing while you spend all your time with that woman.'

'That woman? Aidan, I've been working because of you, and if it wasn't for "that woman" as you call her, we'd all be starving.'

'Now you're just being melodramatic.'

'Well, it's about time I was allowed to be something rather than pandering to your needs all the time.'

'Oh God, you've been reading those women's self-help books again.'

'Aidan, listen to you. I'm fed up. I don't think this is how it should be . . . how I want it to be.' I drop my voice as Evie glances up and looks in our direction.

'All your life you've been spoilt, first by your mother and then by me – you're a useless father and a frustrating husband.'

I dig my toes into the sand. 'I'm sorry,' I say, feeling immediately guilty.

'You're just tired, that's all,' he says, trying to reassure himself.

'No it's not just that – I don't want to continue like this. Something has got to change. Maybe you going to America is the natural break we need.'

'I never realised you were so unhappy,' he says, hurt.

'It's not just me but you too – you can't do all of this,' I say, sweeping my arm around indicating the beach, but he knows what I mean. He follows my arms and sees Max brandishing his small model jet airplane and crashing it into the top of the skyscraper sandcastle.

'Stop that at once, Max,' he yells.

'Aidan, you've written this script and you'll write another and another and I'm sure you'll be really successful but we'll be hanging around at home waiting for you to spend some of your precious time with us. That's not the sort of family life I want. It's not fair on any of us.'

Now Aidan is distracted by Evie who is ruining the smooth walls of the sandcastle that are still intact by sticking in stones to give a pebbledash effect.

'Evie, don't do that,' he shouts, and then turns back to me. 'What are you saying? That we should part?' His expression is incredulous,

'I don't know. Are you happy?'

He falters, and for the first time he looks away and doesn't answer me.

'Think about it, Aidan.'

I've said it – it's out there. My heart aches.

'Stop . . .' His voice trails off as if he can't bear to contemplate what I'm saying. Neither of us says anything; the long silence stretches away like the empty beach until Max interrupts us, running over, dragging the big spade. 'Can I bury you?' he asks me eagerly.

I lie back, my head spinning with the immensity of what I've done, and Max starts covering my feet with sand. Aidan gets up and walks away down the beach, the light shining on his silver hair making it glimmer in the sun. I close my eyes while Max works hard digging, scraping and patting. I can't move because of the weight of the sand, which is surprisingly heavy, and rather than struggle I relax, feeling like I'm being absorbed into the ground, and as I lie smothered by solid sand the surrounding sounds become more acute. Max's panting as he works, the spade digging, the seagulls crying, a dog barking, the sound of the sea washing over the shingle and the relentlessness of the tide as the world breathes in and out.

At first I think I must be imagining it but I'm sure I can hear someone crying or rather sobbing in Rod Harman's office. I've dropped in on the way back from Dorset to collect some photographs of Florence for the edit, which starts on Monday, and the office is deserted. Rod's door is open and there are no lights on, so I have to screw up my eyes to see if there is anyone there. I can just make out a figure sitting hunched in the chair.

'Hello, are you all right – can I help?' I call out.

The figure moves, I hear scuffling, and the sobbing stops but there are still loud sniffs. Curiosity overwhelms me. I switch on the light and I'm amazed to see Rod, tears pouring down his face, a handkerchief stuffed in his mouth in an attempt to muffle the noise of his sobs.

'Oh, sorry,' I say, realising that I've interrupted an intensely private moment. He stares at me, unable to hide his misery, and slowly pulls the handkerchief away from his mouth and uses it to mop his eyes.

'Can I get you anything?' I ask him. 'Are you hurt?' And as he stares at me his face crumples and he starts to cry again. I don't know what to do. Rod is the last person I'd expect to see in tears; it's like discovering Saddam Hussein dressed in drag.

'God,' he says angrily to himself, 'this is ridiculous.'

I walk into the office. 'Can I get you a glass of water or something?'

He doesn't answer but carries on talking as if I'm not there. 'I don't think I can cope without her.'

I think back to the last conversation we had in the office late at night and remember that his mother was unwell and was going into a home.

'What's happened, Rod?' I ask, concerned.

'She's dead,' he says pitifully.

'I'm so sorry.'

Despite everything I do feel sorry for him, but a part of me can't help thinking that perhaps now he'll have a little more empathy.

'Of course she'd been ill for a while but I never really believed it was serious.' He wipes the tears from his cheek and turns his head away from me. 'I didn't do enough for her.'

'I'm sure you did,' I say, not sure at all but wanting to comfort him. I look at my watch, worried about the others waiting in the car downstairs, and Rod sees me doing it.

'Go on, go home to your family.' He spits out the word.

'It's just that they're waiting for me outside.'

'Yes, of course you must go.'

'Is there anyone you can be with tonight?'

He looks desolate. 'Don't worry about me.'

'Well, if you're sure.' I turn to go.

'Molly, before you go, would you like to see a picture of her?'

I turn back to see his eager face and there's no way I can refuse.

'Yes, of course.'

He gets up and goes over to the coat stand and feels in the pocket of his coat for his wallet. He pulls out a photograph, slightly battered and torn around the edges. He holds it out to me. I walk over and take it from him. The photograph is of a white West Highland terrier sitting on her back legs, her head cocked to one side as if listening, and a red ball beside her. For a minute I think I've misunderstood, and then I realise that he's been talking about the dog and not his mother.

'I had her sixteen years,' he says mournfully.

'You could always get another one?' I suggest practically, and he looks at me as if I've gone mad.

'I don't think so. You'd better get going.'

'Bye then. Hope you feel better.'

He sits back down in his chair and as I walk to the lifts I glance back to see him hugging the photograph to his chest and staring out into the night sky.

Thirty-one

As soon as I put my leg into my tights I see the hole.

'Shit,' I say, hoping that the children can't hear me. I never checked to see if I had a good pair of tights for the wedding and now it's too late. I rummage through the drawer, weeding out any black tights that still look intact. I lay them out on the bed next to my black Joseph suit (the only decent thing I have in my wardrobe), which I bought for my father's funeral. I think it's acceptable these days to wear black at a wedding. It suits my mood. I feel like I'm in mourning. I've got a white top to wear underneath to relieve the unrelenting blackness of the outfit.

The children, ready to go, are watching the *Spy Kids Two* film on television downstairs; Aidan is tidying up the kitchen after a hurried breakfast. Beside my suit lies my father's camera in its battered leather case, the strap thin and worn, having been carried through the years capturing hundreds of special moments. I'm not even sure that my childhood memories are genuine, not as I remember them, but all through my father's eyes, preserved for ever in our home movies. Why did he have such a passion to record everything? Was it just to remember, or to give his life some meaning?

As I pull on my black skirt I think about Florence like I do every day and I wonder how she is. I've arranged to go and see her tomorrow evening and I hope that Eleanor has made sure that she knows I'm coming. I switch on the light since it's a dark, damp day, and looking out of the window I check the puddles to see if it's still raining. I go into the bathroom to put on some makeup, and there I can hear the steady drizzle of the rain mingling with the muffled music and explosions from the television that filter up through the ceiling. I put on some eye-liner and mascara, trying hard not to get it on my hair which flops in front of my eyes, in desperate need of a cut.

The sounds from below stop as the film finishes and all I can hear is the relentless rain, but then very softly, as if it's coming from far away, I hear the sound of a voice. Not just any voice, but Florence's voice as a child, faintly reverberating around the small bathroom. I look in the mirror, half expecting to see Florence standing behind me, but there's nothing there apart from my own reflection. The young voice sings on: 'In my imagination I touched the starlit sky so bright'

I shiver and quickly apply my lipstick, but when I walk back into the bedroom the voice is still there.

'And then one day I found you.
How could I help but realise,
My lucky star was smiling, right there before my very eyes.'

I walk down the stairs, wondering if this is what it feels like to go mad.

'Aidan,' I shout,

'You are my lucky star . . .' the music and voice continue.

'What?' he says, preoccupied as usual.

'Can you hear it?' I ask, trying to keep the note of desperation out of my voice.

'Two lovely pair of eyes were beaming, gleaming, I was star struck,' the voice is still singing.

He walks to the bottom of the stairs holding a dishcloth, which looks incongruous against his dark Paul Smith suit. 'What are you talking about?'

'The singing.'

The voice sings on: 'You've opened heaven's portal here on earth for this poor mortal.'

He stares at me and then he realises what's bothering me and starts to laugh. 'For God's sake, did you think you were hearing voices? The children's film stopped and they switched on the video. You left the rushes in when you were viewing them last night.'

'You are my lucky star.'

The song finishes and I feel foolish. I find the children lying across each other on the sofa, watching Florence on the screen in the darkness surrounded by candles and the remains of Christmas lunch. I point the zapper and the image freezes on the screen.

'Come on, guys, we've got to go or we'll be late.'

'But I'm not dressed,' Evie whines.

'I told you, you're going to change at Helen's flat and they're going to do your hair – you'll look gorgeous.'

'I don't want to look gorgeous. I want to look cool.'

I sigh, and as I turn, the flickering image of Florence disappears from the screen to be replaced by grey and black dots and a hissing noise.

The film cartridge clicks into position into the compartment and I shut the door. When I hold the camera to my eye I feel protected from emotion; I can view everything dispassionately. I take a few shots of the pretty but unpretentious grey stone church. Helen has done all the flowers herself and there are two miniature white rose trees standing to attention at the entrance to the church, protected from the rain.

I find Tim inside the church nervously trying to attach a white rose to his button-hole. There are a few people milling around whom I don't recognise and as soon as he sees me his face relaxes.

'Want a hand with that?'

'I'm all fingers and thumbs – silly, I don't understand why.'

'Perhaps it's something to do with the fact that you're getting married today?'

'Ah, that would be it. You look good,' he says, smiling at me.

'Sorry about the black but I haven't got anything else smart enough.'

'It looks fine.'

'Here, hold this and I'll do your button-hole.' I hand him the camera.

'Is this Dad's?'

I nod my head. 'Don't you recognise it?' I ask as I push the stem of the rose through the hole in his lapel.

He puts the camera to his eye. 'I could never get the hang of it. Can you still get the right film for it?'

'Yes, if you know where to go.'

He hands it back to me and I look at him through the eye-piece close up, his nervous face preserved for ever, stamped on celluloid for future generations to see. This was your grandfather just before he got married. I film him as he walks up the aisle to the back of the church. Our mother is waiting in the entrance, wearing a cream suit with a matching hat, looking a little lost. She doesn't like formal occasions at the best of times and since Dad died she finds them particularly hard, missing the moral support.

If Aidan and I separate, will I feel the same? The only difference is I've grown accustomed to being on my own on important occasions, often making excuses for him if he decides not to come. I haven't mentioned our beach conversation to anyone and nothing has been resolved, but over the last few days in Dorset he became more thoughtful, absorbing everything I had said. Some days I feel a blind panic, especially when I watch him with the children, and then on other days a calmness settles when I think that for them their lives would change so little.

'Should I go and sit down?' my mother asks anxiously as I kiss her.

'Why not? Aidan and Max will come and join you, when they arrive – they've been making sure that Evie is OK – they dropped me off here.'

'I'll take you there,' says Tim. 'I probably ought to get into position.'

'I'd better go and get filming. See you later, and Tim . . .'

He turns, looking so nervous I want to hug him.

'Good luck.'

I decide to stay at the entrance of the church, protected from the rain which is beginning to pour down. Guests are arriving, umbrellas shielding the fine suits and hats, tights speckled with muddy water.

The church is beginning to fill up and I see one of the bridal cars arrive with Evie staring forlornly out of the window, Phyllida beside her trying to straighten her Accessorize diamanté tiara while Evie slaps her hand away. Aidan and Max run down the path, Max splashing into as many puddles as he can without Aidan noticing.

'What about Evie?' I ask as he reaches me and smooths back his wet hair. I try to brush as much of the rain off Max as possible. He needs wringing out but he looks content.

'They're going to keep her in the car until the bride arrives.'

'Everything OK?' I ask.

'Yes,' he says, smiling sadly at me, and he takes my hand. I stare at it as it rests in his, the engagement ring dull and lacklustre from not having been cleaned for years.

'Did you mean it?' he asks, his eyes full of questions.

I nod my head but a part of me wants to shout, 'No, I've made a terrible mistake, I've changed my mind,' but I don't, and another part of me is strangely curious to hear what he's going to say.

'I've been thinking a lot about this.'

'I know.' I nod my head.

'I don't know, Molly, it seems so sad but you might be right.' We stare at each other and I wonder if I ever should have said anything. Maybe we could have carried on for years as we were?

Aidan leans towards me and kisses me and then lets my hand go. He turns to walk into the church, putting his arm around Max, who glances back over his shoulder looking at me strangely as if he's aware something is happening between his parents. As I watch they seem to walk away in slow motion and everything around me evaporates. What have I done? Is that it then?

The sound of Jo squealing brings me back to the present.

'I'm soaking,' she laughs as she, Finn and the two boys spill out of a taxi dressed in their wedding best but wearing wellington boots. Jo is holding on to a beautiful old straw hat, the fresh flowers sewed into the brim beginning to droop, battered by the rain.

'Anywhere we can quickly change into our shoes?' she asks

me. 'Like the suit,' she adds as an afterthought. I help her struggle out of the boots and put them carefully to one side while she changes into her shoes. I find it hard to concentrate but I welcome the distraction.

'This is a bit efficient,' I say, nodding at the wellington boots.

'A new leaf,' she replies, grinning.

I look round to see Finn busy helping the boys with their shoes, blocking the entrance for everyone else trying to get into the church.

'Sorry, won't be a minute,' I hear him say.

'Have you said anything?'

'Not yet,' Jo replies, pulling a face, 'I'm working up to it.' She gives me a kiss and then, seeing everyone is ready, she straightens her hat and turns to go into the church. As she walks down the aisle she takes Finn's hand and he smiles at her, and I can't help feeling envious. Max spots the boys and fires his invisible gun at them, Jake collapses and pretends to die in the aisle while Jo hisses at him to behave.

I look at my watch. The church is nearly full but there is no sign of the bride. The windows of the car where Evie is being held captive have steamed up so that I can't tell what's going on inside. The sound of a mobile phone echoes through the church and I think how incongruous it sounds. Heads start to turn as they try to work out to whom the mobile belongs and with horror I realise that it's coming from my bag. I quickly put down the camera, and for a minute I wonder if it's Helen and there's a problem, or Phyllida ringing from the car asking for reinforcements to help her deal with Evie rebelling about the scratchy tights. All heads turn to look at me and I retreat into the porch of the church to answer the call.

'Molly, it's me.' Rod Harman's clipped consonants ring in my ears.

'Rod, I can't talk,' I whisper into the phone.

'I thought you should know. That woman from the old luvvie home just rang.'

'What, Florence?'

'No, the home manager, impossible woman. She says it's not going to be long and she wanted to let us know.'

'What do you mean?'

I hear him sigh. 'Do you need me to spell it out? The old woman – she's on her last legs, any minute now, and I thought you should know. The son has been notified but it's touch and go he'll get there in time. You should go and be there with her and take your camera with you. It's what she wants.'

'It's what *you* want.'

'I'm not going to deny it but you know that she wants you there. She's said as much. I know, I've seen the rushes.'

I feel a wave of despair seep through me.

'Rod, it's my brother's wedding. I'm standing in the church waiting for my future sister-in-law. I can't leave now.'

'Well, she's only going to die once,' he says brutally and hangs up. I look inside the church and see the back of my mother's head tilted to one side looking up towards the altar, and as if aware of my gaze she turns, searching for me. Tim catches my eye and walks down the aisle towards me.

'What's up?'

'I'm sure they'll be here in a minute.'

He turns to go back to his place. 'Tim,' I hiss, 'I've just had a call from my boss about Florence . . . she hasn't got long and she wants me there.'

He turns back and I can see the sadness in his eyes.

'I'm sorry, this is the last thing you should be thinking about when you're about to get married.'

'No, it's OK,' he says, as understanding as ever. 'What are you going to do?'

'What do you think?'

'It's up to you. Of course I want you here but if you decide to go . . . well, I understand.'

When I look at his disappointed face I make my decision. I made the wrong choice eight years ago – I'm not about to make the same mistake again.

'Don't worry. I'm not going. I want to be here with you.'

He kisses my cheek and holds both my hands. 'See you when it's all over,' he says and as he walks down the aisle he looks back and holds his crossed fingers up at me.

I feel confused, part of me relieved that I've made the decision to stay and the other part in shock that I may never see Florence again and aware that I'm letting her down after all I promised. I feel like I'm going to be sick and I force myself to take deep breaths.

I turn to see the wedding car draw up, white ribbons flapping along the bonnet like a pair of reins. The door to the bridesmaid car shoots open and Phyllida nearly falls over in her hurry to get away from the demon child. Evie, looking pink-faced and cross, clambers out inelegantly pulling up her tights and wiping her nose on her arm. Phyllida, holding an umbrella over both of them, looks away in disgust as I wave at Evie who waves back. Transformed in the classic cream dress with the Cath Kidston floral band, clutching the small simple bunch of pale pink and white roses, she looks angelic if you ignore the expression on her face.

Helen's father walks round the big white Bentley, carrying a huge golfing umbrella. I film it all as he opens the door and Helen steps out and for the first time I think she looks beautiful. Abandoning Evie, Phyllida sets about Helen, picking up the hem of her dress so that it doesn't trail in the puddles. Evie looks like she's going to make a run for it but Helen's father puts a firm hand on her shoulder and draws her under his umbrella, waiting for his daughter to be ready. I venture out into the rain and film Evie getting into position and she crosses her eyes when she realises I'm focusing on her. I walk backwards, filming Helen as she glides along the path towards me, her arm slipped through her father's. She smiles at me through the camera and I stop to let her pass.

'You look lovely.'

'Thank you,' she replies, beaming.

I walk beside her filming a close-up. The white of her veil makes her look ethereal, and then I stop letting her carry on and as the last piece of gauze from her veil leaves the frame I'm left focusing on a large gravestone. I stop filming and take the camera away from my eye. I look from the graveyard towards the church, at Helen standing in the porch, Pyllida still fussing, the congregation waiting inside. Florence fills my mind. I think of the moment she told us she was ill and how later, after we'd made our promises, we shook hands. I look past Helen and see Tim at the end of the aisle standing up and turning round expectantly. Through the camera I zoom in close and see his features that have aged so that now I can see our father in his face. I don't know what to do. Dad, what should I do? Helen is standing still while Phyllida smooths the seams of the dress and pulls out the train. Evie picks her nose and looks at me nervously when I stroke her head, expecting me to tell her off.

'Helen, I don't know how to say this.' I stop, unsure whether to continue.

'Molly, are you all right?' she says, concerned.

'Florence is dying. I promised I'd be there but it's your wedding . . .'

Helen glances at Tim and then at me, her calmness impressive. 'This day is important but you will be able to see us again. For us this is just the beginning but for Florence it's another matter.'

'I think I should go.' My words surprise me.

I look at my brother as he rubs his shoes on his trouser leg to wipe off the smudges left by the rain.

'I'll explain it to him,' says Helen, and I lean forward to kiss her cheek, careful not to smudge her makeup.

'Will you tell him how sorry I am and how much I'll be thinking of you both?'

She nods. 'Just come back as soon as you can.'

'Thank you, Helen.'

She smiles at me. 'Go on . . . go.'

Jo is sitting on the end of a pew on the right-hand side of the church, and when I drop down beside her she looks startled to see me.

'I've got to go,' I say, not wanting to draw attention to myself, trying not to compete with the organ voluntary.

'What?' Jo leans forward to hear what I'm saying and the people sitting in front turn to look at us.

'It's Florence. Can you take over the filming until I get back?'

Jo looks surprised. 'Well, if I have to – but I'll need a camera,' she says, looking at the camera in my hand.

'I'm going to need this.' I instinctively pull the camera close to me like a comfort blanket.

'So what am I going to film with?'

'Well, you're an actress, surely you can find another camera,' I say impatiently. The organ starts to play the opening music to announce the bride.

'I've got to go – thanks, Jo.'

The music changes to announce Helen's arrival.

'Tell Tim and Mum that I'm sorry and I'll be back as soon as I can.'

I run back up the aisle, standing aside to let Helen pass. She smiles reassuringly at me and I give a little wave to Evie who waves her bouquet at me as I walk quickly out of the back of the church.

Outside it is still raining and my feet are drenched. I realise that Aidan has the car keys but he's sitting right at the front of the church. I look at the two wedding cars waiting by the gate. I run to the bridesmaid car and tap on the driver's window. It winds down slowly and I resist the temptation to lean on it to make it move more quickly.

'There's an emergency,' I stutter. 'I need to be somewhere as soon as possible. It's about half an hour away. Can you drop me there and then come back here to pick up the others?'

He looks at my wet face, my hair sticking to my skin and tracks of mascara running down my cheeks, and sees the desperation in my face.

'OK, love, where to?'

Thirty-two

I pull the curtains, shutting out the damp world like a nurse pulling a screen around her patient. I'm trying to get the right level of light and I wish Matt were here to help. My hands feel clammy, the camera slipping and sliding in my grip until I wipe my palms on my skirt and take off my jacket, throwing it on to Florence's big armchair.

Florence is lying in bed and in one week there have been so many changes that I hardly recognise her. She seems to have shrunk since I last saw her and she doesn't respond when I talk to her. I keep my distance, wary of the stranger on the bed.

'Florence, I'm here and I'm going to stay with you now. Bill is on his way; he'll be here soon.' I hesitate but still she doesn't respond. I feel awkward, I don't know how to behave. I only know what I've seen in films or on television – the final deathbed scene. I feel like I'm acting a part and I have to resist the urge to laugh, thinking how much Florence would have appreciated this moment. She is breathing with difficulty and I feel relieved when the door opens and Jane, the care nurse, comes in.

'I heard you were here. That's good, she'll be pleased.' She straightens the blankets, smoothing the sheets and making sure that Florence is comfortable.

'Can she hear me?'

'It's hard to say but I think she's probably aware of you even if she doesn't respond. They say that hearing is the last sense to go.'

'Are you going to stay?' I ask, desperately hoping she will.

'I'll stay for a bit but there's not much we can do now.'

I busy myself filming the bottles of medicine and tubes of cream on the side table, the photographs on the chest of drawers, focusing on anything but Florence herself. I'm aware of Jane watching me.

'Just setting the scene; all these could be useful cutaways,' I say, to convince myself as much as Jane.

She says nothing and as I continue to film all I can hear is the whirring of the camera and the sound of Florence struggling to breathe. When I've finished a shot of Florence's coat hanging on the back of the door and her empty armchair, I put the camera back in its case. It's so light that I wonder if it really is recording anything. I check the bag to see how many more film cassettes I've got with me. There are three, all only five minutes long, so I have to be careful not to waste the film.

'How long do you think?' I ask Jane.

'Not long now.'

I worry about Bill not making it in time, and from nowhere I have an image of my father, his presence palpable. Tears well up in my eyes and I stroke the strap of the camera case, running my hands along the worn leather, touching the part that would have rested on his shoulder when he was alive. I become aware of Jane looking at me.

'Do you want a glass of water?' she asks me.

I try to force a smile. 'Don't worry about me, I'm not the patient.'

Ignoring me, she goes into the bathroom and brings me a glass of water poured from Florence's fridge. The icy water brings me back to the moment and after taking a sip I hold the glass to my cheek. I must concentrate on Florence.

'She's holding on. This is quite normal.'

'Waiting for Bill to come?'

'Maybe. You know, sometimes you have to give them permission to let go. She looks settled – I'll come back in a while,' says Jane, putting the palm of her hand on Florence's forehead while dabbing a small pink sponge on her lips and letting a few droplets of water fall into her half-open mouth. 'She gets very dehydrated and this helps,' she explains. 'Touch is very important at this stage, it's very reassuring and helps them feel less lonely.'

'Don't go,' I say, trying to keep the note of panic out of my voice.

'Don't worry, I'll be back in a while.'

'But what happens if she . . .'

'Just come and get one of us if you notice anything change. It's just a question of being there. This is a natural process, Molly, a special time.'

She closes the door, leaving Florence and me alone together. I look at my watch – the wedding ceremony should be over by now and I expect that they're taking photos by the church. I wonder if anyone has noticed that I'm not there. I walk over to the window and pull back the curtain to see if it's still raining, which it is. Florence moans and I let the curtain fall back and return to her side. I put another cartridge into the camera and it clicks loudly into place. Outside is silence, as if the rest of the world is holding its breath. I start filming again.

'My brother is getting married,' I say, wanting to break the spell. My voice sounds loud and incongruous but it is a relief to hear it. I'm pleased that there's no sound being recorded, even though Rod won't be happy as the viewer won't be getting the full experience, just an impressionistic sense of Florence's last few hours.

'Bill should be here soon,' I say again, reassuring myself as much as her. Florence's breath sounds more rasping now as if she's struggling for air. I never thought I'd miss her inscrutable stare but I long for her eyes to open, for her to swing her legs round as she did when she was filming, pretending to be dead, but now she isn't acting. She seems to be having trouble breathing, every breath pulling at the back of her throat and making a rasping noise. Now I begin to focus on Florence, on her thin face, her grey hair swept back and falling on to the pillow, her mouth slightly open as she struggles to find the breath. She stirs and I worry that she is in pain. Maybe I should go and find Jane, but what if something happens while I'm out of the room? My eye is locked to the viewfinder and I can't separate myself from the camera – it's my armour.

Out of the corner of my eye I notice Florence's hand move slightly, the fingers of one hand stretching out, the other slightly clenched in a small fist. The rhythm of her breathing is altering and I feel instinctively that something is changing. I refocus the camera, pressing the button so I can slowly zoom in on her face. I watch her struggle for the breath and as I wonder whether it will be her last I know that I can't go on like this. I put the camera down and reach for her hand. It's the first time I've touched her today and she responds by turning the hand that is clenched. Her fingers are slightly open and I can see a glint of topaz nestling in the palm, her gift to me. I lean forward – she smells of ointment – and I lay my head next to hers, hoping that the warmth from my cheek will give her some comfort. I whisper in her ear, 'It's all right, Florence. I'm here, if you want you can go now.'

I can't say the exact moment she died but I'm aware that she is no longer here even though she is still lying on the bed. I hold on to her hand and I never want to let go. I don't hear the door open and I don't know how long it is before I'm aware of him, sitting the other side of the bed watching his mother. Saying nothing, he reaches across the bed and we hold hands, our fingers linked together.

After a while I make myself get up and walk to the window and pull back the curtains. It has stopped raining and the sun is struggling to shine through thick cloud. The ground is still wet and the trees glisten, rain dripping from their leaves. I turn back to the room.

'I have to go – my brother's wedding,' I say simply, unable to form longer sentences.

Bill smiles. 'Of course.'

'I'll come back.'

'Molly,' Bill says as I gather my things together, 'well done.'

'I didn't do anything.'

'Yes you did – you did everything.'

*

371

I leave Florence, although she's gone before me. I walk slowly along the corridor trying to readjust to normality. Someone has been making toast and the smell makes me realise how hungry I am. I'm aware of each step I take on the blue carpet and I run my finger along the cream-coloured walls, feeling the lumps and bumps in the plaster. I walk down the stairs past the framed play-bills and the familiar portraits in the hall. I cross the hall and turn the large brass doorhandle, until the door opens and I'm outside. Everything is normal, it seems that nothing has changed, only I know how different it is.

I stop for a minute at the top of the steps to Russell Court, taking stock of how I feel, and although I'm sad and exhausted, I also feel strangely light-hearted, liberated. I take a deep breath and I'm aware of a strange desire to laugh or stamp my feet, anything to make a loud noise, like a child shouting in a tunnel, rejoicing in the echo. The shrill tones of my phone pierce the air and the name 'Rod' appears on the front. I stare at it, then very deliberately, with all my strength, I toss the phone high up, watching it twist and twirl in the air, as I walk down the solid stone steps, smiling.

Katie Pearson

Don't Try This At Home

When fate nudges Dot into a corner, she decides to give up her successful job and take on a new career as full-time mother. So what if her daughters can barely remember who she is – how hard can it be?

However, a thumb through *The Secrets of Happy Children* doesn't prepare Dot for the drama of children's parties, accident-prone hamsters and a nanny turned novelist. As if that weren't enough, an old flame makes a guest appearance and a serious illness is in danger of staging a comeback. All in all, it's a miracle Dot ever manages to get out of bed, let alone tackle the school run.

But amid the fears and flirtations, the gossip and the grubby hands, can Dot find a way to reach the gold at the end of the rainbow?

'Witty, honest and upbeat' *Family Circle*

CORONET BOOKS
Hodder & Stoughton